Welcome to the World, Baby Girl!

For Sam and Jo Vaughan, with love

Acknowledgments

I would like to thank the following, whose encouragement and support have been invaluable to me: Susie Glickman, Lois Scott, De-Thomas Bobo & Associates, Ulf Buchholz, Wendy Weil, Steve Warren, Sally Wilcox, Mrs. Ray Rogers, Evelyn Birkby, Colleen Zuck and staff, the State of Alabama, and especially all my friends and family, who are a joy to me every day.

"... Poor little old human beings—they're jerked into this world without having any idea where they came from or what it is they are supposed to do, or how long they have to do it in. Or where they are gonna wind up after that. But bless their hearts, most of them wake up every morning and keep on trying to make some sense out of it. Why, you can't help but love them, can you? I just wonder why more of them aren't as crazy as betsy bugs."

—Aunt Elner, 1978

Preface

Elmwood Springs, Missouri
1948

In the late forties Elmwood Springs, in southern Missouri, seems more or less like a thousand other small towns scattered across America.

Downtown is only a block long with a Rexall drugstore on one end and the Elmwood Springs Masonic Hall on the other. If you walk from the Masonic Hall to the Rexall, you will go by the Blue Ribbon cleaners, a Cat's Paw shoe repair shop with a pink neon shoe in the window, the Morgan Brothers department store, the bank, and a little alley with stairs on one side of a building leading up to the second floor, where the Dixie Cahill School of Tap and Twirl is located. If it is a Saturday morning you'll hear a lot of heavy tapping and dropping of batons upstairs by the Tappettes, a troop of blue-spangled Elmwood Springs beauties, or at least their parents think so. Past the alley is the Trolley Car diner, where you can get the world's best chili dog and an orange drink for 15 cents. Just beyond the diner is the New Empress movie theater, and on Saturday afternoons you will see a group of kids lined up outside waiting to go in and see a Western, some cartoons, and a chapter in the Buck Rogers weekly serial. Next is the barbershop and then the Rexall on the corner. Walk down on the other side of the street and you'll come to the First Methodist Church and then Nordstrom's Swedish bakery and luncheonette, with the gold star still in the window in honor of their son. Farther on is Miss Alma's Tea Room, Haygood's photographic studio, the Western Union, and the post office, the telephone company, and Victor's florist shop. A narrow set of stairs leads up to Dr. Orr's "painless" dentist's office. Warren and Son hardware is next. The son is eighteen-year-old Macky Warren, who is getting ready to marry his girlfriend, Norma, and is nervous about it. Then comes the A & P and the VFW Hall on the corner.

Elmwood Springs is mostly a neighborhood town, and almost everyone is on speaking terms with Bottle Top, the white cat with a black spot that sleeps in the window of the shoe repair shop. There is one town drunkard, James Whooten, whose long-suffering wife, Tot Whooten, has always been referred to as Poor Tot. Even though she has remarried a teetotaler and seems fairly happy for a change, most people still call her Poor Tot out of sheer habit.

There is plenty of fresh air and everybody does their own yard work. If you are sick, somebody's son or husband will come over and do it for you. The cemetery is neat, and on Memorial Day, flags are placed on all the veterans' graves by the VFW. There are three churches, Lutheran, Methodist, and Unity, and church suppers and bake sales are well attended. Most everybody in town goes to the high school graduation and to the yearly Dixie Cahill dance and twirl recital. It is basically a typical, middle-class town and in most living rooms you will find at least one or two pairs of bronzed baby shoes and a picture of some child on top of the same brown and white Indian pony as the kid next door. Nobody is rich but despite that fact, Elmwood Springs is a town that likes itself. You can see it in the fresh paint on the houses and in the clean, white curtains in the windows. The streetcar that goes out to Elmwood Lake has just been given a new coat of maroon and cream paint and the wooden seats shellacked to such a high polish they are hard not to slide out of. People are happy. You can see it in the sparkle in the cement in front of the movie theater, in the way the new stoplight blinks at you. Most people are content. You can tell by the well-fed cats and dogs that laze around on the sidewalks all over town and even if you are blind you can hear it in the laughter from the school yards and in the soft thud of the newspaper that hits the porches every afternoon.

But the best way to tell about a town, any town, is to listen deep in the night . . . long after midnight . . . after every screen door has been slammed shut for the last time, every light turned off, every child tucked in. If you listen you will hear how everyone, even the chickens, who are the most nervous creatures on earth, sleep safe and sound through the night.

Elmwood Springs, Missouri, is not perfect by any means but as far as little towns go it is about as near perfect as you can get without having to get downright sentimental about it or making up a bunch of lies.

The "Neighbor Dorothy" Show

Everyone in Elmwood Springs and thereabouts remembers the day they put the radio tower in Neighbor Dorothy's backyard, and how excited they were that night when they first saw the bright red bulb on top of the tower, glowing like a cherry-red Christmas light way up in the black Missouri sky. Because the land was flat, it could be seen for miles in every direction and over the years it came to be a familiar and comforting sight. It made people feel connected somehow.

Had you been there, between 9:30 and 10:00 A.M., unless somebody had knocked you out cold, most likely you would have been listening to the "Neighbor Dorothy" radio show just like everybody else except for old man Henderson, who still thought that radio was a silly invention for silly people. Both the high school and the elementary school scheduled study periods between 9:30 and 10:00 A.M. so the faculty could hear it in the teachers' lounge. Farm wives for miles around stopped whatever it was they were doing and sat down with a pad and pencil at the kitchen table to listen. By now Dorothy Smith was one of the most listened-to radio homemakers in the midwest, and if she gave out a recipe for maple swirl pound cake that day, most men would be eating it for dessert that night.

The show was broadcast live from her living room every day Monday through Friday and could be heard over station WDOT, 66 on your dial. Nobody dared miss the show. Not only did she give out household hints and announce upcoming events, you never knew who might show up. All sorts of people would drop by to talk on the radio or sing or tap dance or do whatever it was they had a mind to do for that matter. A Mrs. Mary Hurt even played the spoons once! Mother Smith played organ interludes. Other regulars you didn't want to miss were Ruby Robinson, the radio nurse; Beatrice Woods, the little blind songbird who played the zither and sang; Reverend Audrey Dunkin, the minister, who would often drop by for an inspirational talk or read an inspirational poem; as well as a handbell choir from the First Methodist church. Last year The Light Crust Doughboys came on and sang their hit "Tie Me to Your Apron Strings Again, Mother" and Neighbor Dorothy also had a visit from the Hawaiian Fruit Gum Orchestra, all the way from Yankton, South Dakota. This is not to mention two local gals, Ada and Bess Goodnight, who would sing at the drop of a hat, and the news, which was mostly good.

In 1948 Neighbor Dorothy was a plump, sweet-faced woman with the big, wide-open face of a young girl. Although in her fifties she still looked pretty much the same as she did in the first grade when her husband, Doc Smith, the pharmacist down at the Rexall, first met her. After high school Dorothy graduated from the Fannie Merit School of Home Economics in Boston and came home and married Doc and taught school for a while until she had her first child, Anna Lee. Anna Lee had a few health problems, nothing serious, just a little asthma, but enough so that Neighbor Dorothy thought it was best to stay home with her and Doc agreed. While she was home all day she wanted to keep busy so she began baking cakes—and more cakes. Tea cakes, lemon, banana, caramel, cherry, chocolate, maple, and jelly roll cakes. You name it, she baked it. But her specialty was theme cakes. You'd give her a theme and she'd make you the cake to go with the occasion. Not that she couldn't make a mean noodle ring or anything else you wanted but she was known for her cakes. There was not a child in Elmwood Springs or thereabouts who had not had a pink and white circus cake with the miniature toy carousel on top for her birthday party. Which is how she came to be at the Mayfair Auditorium over in Poplar Bluff on Home Demonstration Day giving out the recipe for her circus cake on the radio. She just happened to mention that she used Golden Flake Flour for all her cakes and the next day, when Golden Flake Flour sales doubled in four states, she was offered a show of her own. She told the Golden Flake Flour people thank you, but she could not leave home every day to drive the twenty-something miles to the station in Poplar Bluff and back, which is how the radio tower came to be put up in her backyard in the first place and how her youngest child, Bobby, happened to grow up on the radio. He was only two years old when Neighbor Dorothy first went on the air, but that was over ten years ago and he does not remember a time when there wasn't a radio show in the living room.

When she first asked Doc what he thought about the idea, he laughed and said, "Well, you might just as well talk on the radio, you talk on the phone all day anyhow." Which was not quite true, but true enough. Dorothy did love to chat.

Although radio station WDOT is only a 200-watt station, because the land is flat, on cold, still days when the skies are crystal clear, and it is really good radio weather, the signal from WDOT can tear a hole straight through the midwest all the way up into Canada and on one particularly cold day was picked up by several ships at sea. You can't say her show is clever or sophisticated or anything like that, but one thing you can say for sure is that over the years she's sold a heck of a lot of Golden Flake Flour and Pancake Mix and anything else she advertises.

Neighbor Dorothy's house is located on the left side of First Avenue North, and has the address written in big black letters on the curb so you can't miss it. It is the last house on the corner with a wraparound porch, a two-swing front porch, one swing on one end and one on the other. It has a green and white canvas awning all the way around to the side of the house.

If you were to walk up the porch stairs and look to your right you would see written in small gold and black letters on the window

WDOT RADIO STATION, NUMBER 66 ON YOUR DIAL. Other than that it looks just like everybody else's house, without the call letters on the window and the big radio tower in the backyard, of course. No matter what time of day you come to the front door you are going to find it open. No point in closing it. Too many people in and out all the time. The milkman, the bread man, the ice man, the gas man, her twelve-year-old son, Bobby, who goes in and out a hundred times a day, and of course all her many radio visitors, who often come by the busload and are always welcomed with a fresh batch of special radio cookies she makes every day for the purpose. As you walk in, to the right is a large room with a desk with a microphone on it that says WDOT. The desk sits in front of the window so she can always turn around and look out and report what the weather is doing firsthand. Mother Smith's organ is to the left, and about ten chairs are set up so people can come in and sit down if they want to. Neighbor Dorothy's house is on the corner where the Greyhound bus stops, so it makes it nice while people are waiting for the bus to go in and watch the show or sit on the front porch and wait, particularly if it's raining. The floors are dark wood and Neighbor Dorothy has some nice scatter rugs here and there. The curtains are green with a yellow and deep pink floral print with what looks like might be palm trees. She has recently put up brand-new venetian blinds, a Christmas present from Doc.

The dining room has a nice brass chandelier with four milk-glass shades with a little Dutch scene on them, and some lovely lace swag curtains on the bay window, and a pretty white tablecloth. The kitchen is still where everybody usually eats. It has a large white wooden table in the middle with a hanging lightbulb over it. The stove is a white enamel-and-chrome O'Keefe & Merritt with a clock and red and white plastic salt and pepper shakers to match. There is a large sink and drain board in a skirt of floral print plus a big Kelvinator icebox. The walls are beaded board painted a light green. Off the kitchen to the back is a large screened porch; Bobby sleeps there in the summer. On the other side is a group of miniature tables and chairs where all the children in town have their birthday parties and where Anna Lee and her friend run a nursery school in the summer to make extra money for clothes. The other two rooms on the left side of the house are Anna Lee's bedroom, a seventeen-year-old girl's room with a white canopy bed and a dresser with a mirror and a Kewpie doll with sparkle dust and a feather on its head sitting on top of a chest of drawers. There is a sunroom that Neighbor Dorothy and Mother Smith use as a sewing room and where Anna Lee keeps her scrapbooks on Dana Andrews, the movie star she is in love with this year. Three bedrooms are off the hall, Doc and Neighbor Dorothy's, Mother Smith's, and Bobby has the last room down at the end. Also living in the house is Princess Mary Margaret, who has free run of every room in the house and is famous in her own right. She is a ten-year-old cocker spaniel that Neighbor Dorothy got from Doc as a Christmas present the first year she was on the air. She was named through a name-the-puppy contest and when all her listeners sent in their choices, the name Princess Mary Margaret won first prize. A good name, because not only does England have a Princess Margaret, but Missouri has its own little princess, Margaret Truman, the daughter of Missouri-born president Harry S Truman and his wife, Bess. In 1948, Princess Mary Margaret is quite a celebrity. Not only does Neighbor Dorothy spoil her, so do her listeners. She has her own fan club known as the Princess Mary Margaret Club and all the dues money goes to the Humane Society. Princess Mary Margaret has received birthday cards from Lassie in Hollywood and many other famous people.

The other two residents of the house are Dumpling and Moe, the Smiths' yellow singing canary birds. Their white cage hangs in the living room and they can be heard chirping away all through the broadcast. Neighbor Dorothy's backyard is, as mentioned, like everybody else's except for the radio tower, with lots of open space all the way back to the railroad tracks and behind that are the cornfields. There are no fences so you might say that the whole town just has one big backyard and one leads into the other. The only difference between Neighbor Dorothy's house and the others is the clothesline that runs from her back door to her next-door neighbor's back door. Beatrice Woods, the little blind songbird, lives next door and that's how she gets back and forth to Neighbor Dorothy's house, by holding on to the clothesline. Apart from the fact that it has WDOT painted on the front window in gold and black letters, an organ in the living room, a radio tower in the backyard, and is a Greyhound bus stop and has a nursery school on the back porch and a dog living there that receives a personal Christmas card every year from the president of the United States, it is just an ordinary house.

And today is just another ordinary day. At exactly nine-thirty everybody hears what they have been hearing every weekday morning for the past ten years. A male announcer from the main station comes on and says, "And now ... Golden Flake Flour and Pancake Mix ... that always-light-as-a-feather flour in the red and white sack ... takes you to that little white house just around the corner from wherever you are, as we join ... your neighbor and mine, the lady with a smile in her voice, Neighbor Dorothy, with Mother Smith on the organ!"

The minute they get the on-air signal, Mother Smith hits the first strain of their theme song and starts the show off with a rousing rendition of "On the Sunny Side of the Street." In a moment, Neighbor Dorothy greets her radio listeners as she always does, with a pleasant "Good morning, everybody ... how are you today? Fine, I hope. It is a beautiful day over here in Elmwood Springs and I hope it's just as pretty where you are. We've got so many exciting things lined up for you today ... so just sit down, put your feet up, and have a cup of coffee with me, won't you? Ooh ... I wish all of you could see Mother Smith this morning ... she's all dressed up and looks so pretty. Where are you going today, Mother Smith? Oh, she says she's going downtown to Miss Alma's Tea Room for a retirement lunch. Well, that should be a lot of fun.... We all love Miss Alma, don't we? Yes, we do.

"We have so many letters to read to you today, and we've got those two recipes that you all have been asking for—one is Lady Baltimore cake and one for a baby Baltimore cake—so be sure and have your pencils and pads ready and later on in the program, Beatrice, our little blind songbird, is going to be singing for us.... What's your song, honey? Oh . . . she says she'll be singing 'When It's Lamp Lighting Time in the Valley.' That sounds like a good one.

"Also, we have a winner in our How Did You Meet Your Husband contest . . . but before I do anything else this morning I want to start with some good news for all the gals that went to Norma's bridal shower yesterday. They were all mighty worried when all the Lucky Dime cake had been eaten and nobody had gotten the piece with the dime in it, but Norma's mother, Ida, called this morning and said they found the dime in the kitchen—she had forgotten to put it in—so all you gals can rest easy . . . none of you will have to be x-rayed after all . . . so I know that's a relief. As you all know, Norma is our little June bride to be. She is marrying Macky Warren at twelve noon on June the twenty-eighth down at the Unity Church, so if you are in town, drop in at the reception at the VFW Hall afterwards. They say everybody is welcome. So all of you out there be sure to come on by and you don't have to bring a thing. Ida says it's all going to be catered by Nordstrom's bakery and luncheonette, so you know it will be good.

"Speaking of brides . . . June is such a busy month, so many events—weddings, graduations—and if you're wondering what to get the special lady, Bob Morgan of Morgan Brothers department store says wonder no more, because it's pearls, pearls, and more pearls . . . pearls for the graduate, pearls for the June bride, pearls for the mother of the bride, the attendants . . . pearls for everyone. Remember, pearls are right for any occasion. . . . Bob says come on in today . . . he'll be happy to see you.

"And let's see, what else do I have this morning . . . Oh, I know . . . I got a call from Poor Tot and her cat has kittens again and she says they are all ugly but one, so come on over, first come, first served . . . and in a minute I'm going to tell you how to clean your feather pillows, but first let's listen to Beatrice, our little blind songbird. . . ."

Twenty-five minutes later Neighbor Dorothy ends the show as she always does with "Well, I see by the old clock on the wall that it's time to go . . . it's always so pleasant to sit with you every morning and share a cup of coffee. You make our days so happy, so until we see you again, you'll be missed, so come back again tomorrow, won't you? This is Neighbor Dorothy and Mother Smith from our house to yours saying . . . have a good day. . . ."

❦   ❦   ❦

That evening, Neighbor Dorothy and her family were sitting on the porch all eating a bowl of homemade peach ice cream that Doc had made on the back porch earlier. Including Princess Mary Margaret, who had her own bowl with her name on it.

On summer nights almost every family in Elmwood Springs goes out to sit on their front porches after dinner, and wave to people as they walk on the sidewalk in front of the house, on their way to downtown to window-shop or coming home from the movies. All up and down the street you can hear people talking softly and see in the dark the little orange glow of cigarettes or the pipes being smoked by men.

Bobby, happy and sunburned, with the smell of chlorine still strong in his nostrils and his eyes all red from swimming underwater all day up at the pool, was so tired that he fell sound asleep in the swing while the grown-ups talked. Dorothy said to Doc, "You should have seen him when he finally came dragging in this afternoon; he'd been in the water so long he'd gone all pruney."

Doc laughed. Anna Lee said, "Mother, I don't think you should let him go up there anymore. He does nothing but swim around underwater all day pinching people." Mother Smith spoke up: "Oh, let the boy have his childhood; he'll grow up soon enough."

Just then Macky Warren and his fiancée, Norma, passed in front of the house. Norma had her little four-year-old cousin by the hand.

Dorothy called out to them and waved. "Hey, how're you tonight?"

They waved back. "Fine. We've just been up to the picture show."

"What did you see?"

Norma called out, "*The Egg and I* with Claudette Colbert and Fred MacMurray. It was a good one."

"How long is it playing?"

"One or two more days, be sure to see it."

"We will," Neighbor Dorothy said.

Macky called up to the porch, "How are you doing, Doc?"

"Just fine," he said. He nodded at the little blond girl and said to Macky, "I see she's got you baby-sitting tonight. Well, you might as well get used to it, you'll be having some of your own soon."

Macky smiled and nodded. "Yes, sir, good night."

"Good night."

After they had gone on, Dorothy sat back, looked over at Anna Lee, and sighed. "It seems like only yesterday when both my children were babies. Time . . . how fast it passes. . . . Next thing I know Anna Lee will be married."

"No, I won't," said Anna Lee.

"Yes, you will, then you'll be gone and Bobby will be a grown man before we know it."

They sat for a while and waved and spoke to a few more people walking by, and then Dorothy said, "Don't you wish you could just stop time? Keep it from moving forward, just stop it in its tracks?"

"Mother," Anna Lee asked, "if you could stop time, when would you stop it?"

Dorothy thought. "Oh, honey . . . I guess if I could, I'd stop it right now, while I have all my family around me, on this very night." She looked over at her husband. "What about you, Doc? When would you stop it?"

He took a puff of his pipe. "Now would be a good time. No wars. Everybody's healthy." He looked at Dorothy and smiled. "And before Momma loses her pretty figure."

Dorothy laughed. "It's too late for that, Doc. What about you, Anna Lee?"

Anna Lee sighed. A recent high school graduate, she had suddenly become very wise. "Oh, if I had only known then what I know now, I would have stopped it last year when I was still young."

Dorothy smiled at her daughter, then asked, "When would you stop time, Mother Smith?"

Mother Smith mused. "Well, I don't think I would. I think I'd just let it go on like it has been."

"You would?"

Mother Smith had been taken to the great World's Fair in St. Louis in 1904 when she was a small child and had looked forward to the future ever since. "Oh, yes. I'd hate to take a chance on missing something good that might be coming up, just around the corner, wouldn't you?"

"I guess you're right, Mother Smith," Dorothy said, "we just have no idea of what the future holds, do we?"

"No, we don't. Why, just imagine what life will be like twenty-five years from now."

Anna Lee made a face. "I'll be an old woman with gray hair."

Mother Smith laughed. "Maybe so, but I'll be long gone by then. At least you'll be around to see what's going on!"

BOOK ONE

* * *

The News

Elmwood Springs, Missouri
April 1, 1973

Norma Warren was a nervous wreck, waiting for Macky to come home and have his breakfast. She was about to burst with the news. He had only gone two blocks to take Aunt Elner a bag of birdseed. Aunt Elner had called at the crack of dawn and said her blue jays were practically knocking the house down because she had run out of seed. She loved poor old Aunt Elner; after all, she was deaf as a post. But why, of all mornings, did she have to pick this one to run out? Norma knew that Macky would get waylaid, stopping to yaya with everybody and their brother up and down the street. Usually she didn't mind but she did today. God knows where Macky could be at this point. Knowing him, he could be halfway across the county by now or up on somebody's roof or he could have gotten in a car with a perfect stranger, jabbering away about anything and everything. She sat there for a few more minutes and then gave up, put his breakfast in the stove to keep warm, and got the broom out and went onto the front porch and started sweeping, all the time looking for him and thinking how, later, she was going down to get one of those new beeper things and stick it on Macky.

After a few minutes she could not stand it any longer. She went in the kitchen and called. The phone rang and rang, until finally Aunt Elner picked up.

"Hello."

"Aunt Elner, are you all right?"

"I'm doing fine, honey," she said in a cheerful voice, "how are you?"

"I'm fine, I was just worried, you took so long to answer the phone."

"Oh, well, I was way out in the backyard and it took me a while to get back up to the house. Macky is helping me plant some sweet williams in the border of my vegetable garden."

Norma rolled her eyes but said sweetly, "Oh, I see. Well, no rush, but would you tell Macky when he gets through there to come straight on home and not to stop anywhere? His breakfast is getting cold. Could you do that?"

"All right, honey, I'll tell him. Oh, and Norma, are you still on the line?"

"Yes, Aunt Elner."

"My blue jays say thank you kindly. Well, 'bye-'bye."

" 'Bye, Aunt Elner."

Norma, a pretty brunette of forty-three, glanced at herself in the mirror over the sink and saw that her face was flushed with excitement.

About twenty minutes later, after she had almost swept the paint off the front porch and swept halfway up the block, she spotted Macky on the horizon, nonchalantly strolling toward home, waving and How-are-youing to everybody he passed by, including two dogs and a cat. She called out and motioned frantically. "Macky, come on, hurry up!"

Macky, a stocky, sandy-haired, friendly looking man, smiled happily and waved back. Norma ran back inside, took his plate out of the oven, put it down on the table, and got the coffeepot as the screen door slammed behind him.

"Macky, get in here and sit down before I have a stroke."

He sat down. "Hey, what's up, kiddo?"

She poured his coffee, was back in her chair staring at him before he could take the first bite of his scrambled eggs.

"Guess what?" she said.

"What?"

"You are *not* going to believe what happened."

"What?"

"You will never guess who called here in a million years."

"Who?"

"Not three minutes after you left, maybe not even that long—"

"Who?"

"Do you give up?"

"Yes, who called?"

"Are you ready?"

"Yes, honey, I've been ready. Who?"

Norma paused as a trumpet played a fanfare in her head and then, unable to contain herself any longer, she blurted out, "Baby Girl, that's who!"

Macky was sufficiently surprised and put his fork down.

"You're kidding?"

"No, I am not kidding, she called not three minutes after you left."

"Where was she?"

"New York City and guess what: she's coming home."

"She's coming here?"

"Yes!"

"Huh. Well, I'll be . . . Did she say why?"

"Well, she said she needed to get away from something or another. To tell you the truth, I was so excited I forgot what she said, but she said she had been under a lot of pressure at work and would it be all right for her to come visit."

"What did you say?"

"I said of course. I said, 'We've done nothing for years but tell you we want you to come home, would *love* to have you come. We've told you, this is your home, and whenever you want, don't stand on ceremony, just come on.' Haven't we said that I don't know how many times?"

"Absolutely."

Norma grabbed Macky's plate out from in front of him. "Here, let me heat up those eggs."

"No, they're fine."

"Are you sure . . . No, let me stick them in for a few minutes. . . ." She ran to the oven and put his plate in.

"What else did she say?"

Norma sat down and concentrated. "Well, she said hello, of course, how are you and all that, then she said she wanted to come for a little visit and would we be home. I said yes, of course, and she said for us not to go to any trouble or anything."

Macky frowned. "Do you think she's all right? Does she need for me to go up there and get her? I can be on a plane and be there tomorrow if she needs me to. Did you tell her that?"

"Yes, I told her you would be happy to come get her but she said no, she would make her arrangements, then let us know."

"I would have been happy to go up there and get her."

"Oh, I know you would but I didn't want to push at her. I was just so surprised she called at all—and when she said she wanted to visit, you could have knocked me over with a feather. You can imagine."

"You don't think she's sick or anything?"

Norma took his plate out again. "No, I don't think so. She sounded tired, maybe a little down—here, eat these now while they're hot—but she didn't sound sick."

Macky picked up his fork. "I told her she was working herself to a frazzle, I told her to slow down. I said that all along, didn't I?"

Norma nodded. "Yes, you did. You said she needed a vacation. You told her she was working too hard; when we were in New York you said it."

Norma saw that Macky was having a difficult time cutting into his scrambled eggs.

"Do you want me to fix you some more eggs?"

Macky, who would eat anything, said, "No, these are fine."

Norma reached for his plate. "It won't take me but a minute."

"Norma, these are fine. I *like* well-done eggs. What about her job? How's that going?"

"I don't know and I didn't ask. That's her business and it's up to her to tell us what she wants us to know. I'm not going to pick and pry at her. Oh, and the one thing she asked me not to do is let anybody know she is coming, particularly not the newspaper and all."

"Oh, good Lord, no, if that bunch finds out she's here they'll be crawling up through the pipes trying to get to her."

Norma agreed.

"Is Baby Girl still seeing that guy with the initials, what's his name?"

"I don't know and I didn't ask," Norma said, and added, "J.C."

"He didn't show me much."

"Well, she likes him and that's all that matters. All I know is that she's coming home and I intend to do everything in my power to make sure she feels like she has some family in this world that loves her. She doesn't have any other relatives besides me and Aunt Elner. She must feel all alone. It just breaks my heart all these years she's been living from pillar to post, jerked here and there, with nobody that really cares. What if she really did get sick, Macky? Who would she have?"

"She'd have us, honey, we told her that, and she must have believed it or she wouldn't have called."

Norma reached for a paper napkin from the red plastic holder and blew her nose. "Do you think so?"

"Of course I do. There's no use crying over it."

"Oh, I know, I guess I got excited and I'm just so happy it was us she called. She trusts us."

"Yes, I think she does. She give you any idea about when she was coming?"

"No, I guess it could be as soon as tomorrow or the next day. Want some more coffee?"

"Just a little."

Norma gasped. "Oh my God."

"What's the matter?" Macky looked concerned.

"I just realized I don't know whether she drinks coffee or tea. Or what she likes for breakfast. I need to have everything here she likes, so I can have it just in case. Do you think we should go up to the bakery and buy a cake or do you think I should make one?"

"Whatever, either way."

"Edna's cakes are wonderful. I mean they are homemade, really. . . . But I don't know, maybe it would hurt her feelings to think I bought a cake and didn't go to the trouble to make one for her."

"Honey, a cake is a cake. How would she know whether you made it or Edna Buntz made it?"

"She'd see the box."

"Take it out of the box and put it on a plate. They all taste the same to me."

"To you, maybe, but don't forget her grandparents owned the bakery before Edna; she could tell. No, you're right, I'll make a cake. Good Lord, it's the least I can do. I mean, really. What room should we give her? Should we give her ours? It's the nicest."

"No, honey. She wouldn't take it. Let's put her upstairs in Linda's old room. She'll have more privacy."

"Yes, that's the quietest. I'll go up there later and make sure everything's OK, check out the bedding and all. We need to get those curtains washed and the rug cleaned for her. Thank God I'm getting my hair fixed this afternoon." She squinted at Macky. "You need to go up to Ed's and get a haircut yourself."

"Now, Norma, she's not gonna care one way or another if I get a haircut or not."

"Well, I will. We don't want to embarrass her, showing up at the airport looking like a couple of Elmer Fudds."

Macky laughed.

"I'm not kidding, Macky, she's used to being around sophisticated New Yorkers."

"Well, I guess I do need to get the car washed. No joke."

Norma looked at Macky with a pained expression. "Why didn't you let me get the house painted like I wanted to?"

"Now, Norma, just calm down. She said not to make a fuss."

"Yes, but I just can't help myself. I still can't believe it. Just think after all these years, Baby Girl is coming home!"

Hangover

New York City
April 1, 1973

When Dena Nordstrom opened her eyes she had that three-to-four-second grace period before she remembered who she was and where she was. Before her body announced its condition. And, as always after a night like last night, it started with a blinding, pounding headache, followed by a wave of nausea, and soon the agonizing cold sweats.

Slowly, one by one, the events of the previous evening came back to her. The evening had started out the way it usually did when she agreed to have a drink with J.C. After cocktails they had gone on to the Copenhagen on Fifty-eighth for dinner, slugging down God knows how many glasses of ice-cold aquavit and beer before and with the smorgasbord. She vaguely remembered insulting some Frenchman and walking over to the Brasserie for Irish coffee. She did recall that the sun was up by the time she got home, but at least she was in her own bed alone—J.C. had gone home, thank God. Then it hit her. J.C. What had she said to him? For all she knew they might very well be engaged again. And she'd have to think up a way to get out of it again. Always the same thing. He would say, "But you didn't seem drunk. I asked you if you were drunk and you swore up and down that you were stone-cold sober and knew exactly what you were saying." That was the problem. She never thought she was drunk and believed every word when she was saying it. Two weeks ago at a network party she had invited twenty people to her apartment for brunch the next day and then had to pay the doorman to tell each one that she had been called out of town because her grandmother had died. Not only could she not boil an egg, both her grandmothers had died years ago.

Dena tried to get up but the pain throbbing in her temples was so intense she saw stars. She slowly eased out of bed sideways holding her head. The room was as dark as a tomb and as she opened the door the light she had left on in the hallway almost blinded her. She made it to the bathroom and held on to the sink to keep from spinning around. She turned on the cold water but could not bend over without her head killing her so she cupped her hands and splashed water upward, toward her face. Her hands were shaking as she took two Alka-Seltzers, three Bayer aspirins, and a Valium. All she needed now was an ice-cold Coca-Cola and she might live.

She walked down the hall to the kitchen and when she got to the living room she stopped. J.C. was sound asleep on the couch.

Dena tiptoed back down the hall to the bathroom and drank water from the tap. She took a cold washcloth for her head, went in and quietly locked her bedroom door, praying to a God she didn't believe in. *Please make him wake up and go home . . .* please. She got back in bed, turned her electric blanket up to high, and went back to sleep.

It was around 11:00 A.M. when Dena woke again and needed more aspirin. Now her stomach was hot and burning, screaming for carbohydrates. She quietly unlocked the bedroom door, tiptoed down the hall, and looked in the living room. She was delighted. J.C. had left. Hooray. She called the Carnegie Deli across the street and ordered two grilled cheese sandwiches, french fries, a chocolate shake, and two packs of Viceroys. While waiting, she walked out on the terrace. It was a cold, brown, dank day. The air was stale and humid. Traffic was snarled at Fifty-eighth and Sixth as usual and people were yelling at the top of their lungs and honking at one another. The loud clatter hurt her head so she went back inside, where the sound was muffled. Still, an occasional siren or a shrill horn would slip under the door and scream into her ears like a sharp knife, so she went into the kitchen to wait. A note J.C. had left was taped to her refrigerator. *See you at eight for dinner.*

She spoke to the note. "Oh, no, you won't."

❖   ❖   ❖

After she had devoured all the food in less than five minutes, she went back to her bedroom, stepped over the clothes on the floor, and fell into bed with relief. She smiled to herself and thanked her lucky stars that this was only Saturday and she would be able to sleep until Monday morning. She closed her eyes for seconds—and then they flew open.

She had just remembered: *the affiliates were in town for the NAB convention.* Today was the day she was supposed to be guest of honor at their luncheon.

She moaned. "Oh, God . . . no, please don't tell me I have to go to that luncheon, I'd rather be beaten to death with a baseball bat with nails on it. God, kill me in my bed, anything, please just let me lie here, don't make me have to go to that luncheon . . . don't make me have to get up and put my clothes on."

She lay there for ten more minutes, debating whether or not she should try calling with a sudden attack of appendicitis, thinking of a serious enough ailment that could hit you on Saturday and be gone by Monday. God, she wished she had a baby; nothing better than a sick child, they're good for all kinds of sudden ailments. As hard as she tried to convince herself that she had a right not to go, that the luncheon was just public relations for the network and not real work, she finally came to the conclusion that she had to go because if she didn't she would feel so guilty she wouldn't be able to sleep anyway. She always liked to be dependable. *Especially* when it could do her some good, too. The affiliates had come from all over the country and this luncheon was for many the highlight of their trip. Most of the men had brought their wives along just for this occasion, to meet Dena Nordstrom in person. Some had followed her career from that first big interview with ex-senator Bosley, and she had become known to more of them after she went network. She was popular with almost all the wives, who watched her morning show every day. So she crawled out of bed and went back in the bathroom to see if there was any hope of getting herself together. She looked in the mirror expecting the worst, but was pleasantly surprised at what she saw.

Through some lucky genetic quirk, Dena Nordstrom was a woman who happened to look especially wonderful when she had a hangover. Her blue eyes seemed to shine, there was a wholesome flush on her cheeks, and her lips looked sexy and slightly swollen (after smoking a thousand cigarettes). No matter how many times this had happened, she never ceased to be amazed.

At twelve-thirty in the Tavern on the Green, a roomful of excited wives and their affiliate husbands were trying to pretend they were not looking forward to this luncheon. They kept glancing at the door to see if she had arrived yet. At 12:57 all attempts at conversation stopped. Every eye was on the tall, stunning, blond woman standing at the door looking "fabulous," as more than one wife put it, dressed in a camel cashmere suit, black turtleneck sweater, a pair of perfectly sized gold earrings, and wearing almost no makeup, so the wives would report to envious friends at home. There she was, in person, Dena Nordstrom, looking just like herself with that fresh, wholesome, open midwestern face of hers flashing that million-dollar smile.

As the entire room in one great mass leaned toward her, she stood at the podium microphone and apologized to everyone. "I'm so sorry I'm so late. Here I've been looking forward to this luncheon all year and wouldn't you know it, just as I was walking out the door, the phone rang and it was my sister calling long distance all the way from Copenhagen to tell me she was in the emergency room with a broken ankle. It seems that last night she and her husband had gone to some party and had been served all these strong drinks she was not used to . . . anyhow, long story short, she had tripped over a pair of wooden shoes so I had to run and dig out all the insurance information and give it to her or they wouldn't release her and they have a plane to catch. So please forgive me . . ."

She stopped there, rather than run on further. Why did all of her excuses somehow involve family? It wasn't very original and besides, she didn't have any family. But had she announced that she had just slaughtered six nuns with an ax, this crowd would have forgiven her. Afterward they rushed toward her, happily chattering away about how much prettier she was in person and wondering if they might have just one picture with her. What seemed like a hundred Instamatic flash cameras began snapping at her from all directions until she saw nothing but little white dots floating before her eyes. But she kept on smiling.

Aunt Elner

Macky had flushed the toilet and turned on all the faucets to make sure they were working. Norma was wondering if they needed a new bedspread and called him out of the bathroom. Macky looked at it. "I don't think so and I'll tell you why. I think it's best if we just leave things the way they are, not do anything different. I'm sure after the places she's been she won't be impressed with a new bedspread. We can't begin to compete with all those fancy apartments. What we need to do is try and make her feel at home, you know, something she can't get everywhere."

"Yes, but Macky, a twenty-year-old, ratty-looking chenille bedspread might not look homey to her, it might just look old and ratty. Did you ever think of that?"

"Honey, it's perfectly fine. I promise you."

"Well, if you think so. But I can at least wash the quilt and the bedclothes. I can do that, can't I?"

"Of course."

They started to strip the bed as Norma said, "Still, Macky, there is such a thing as not doing enough. I don't want her to think we're not excited she's coming home." She pointed at the windows. "Can you get those curtains down? I might as well do them all at once."

Macky started to take the curtains down. "Norma," he said, "of course she'll know we're excited she's coming home. She'll be able to tell. I just think we should try and live the way we always do and not try to put on any airs or do anything different. Isn't that why she's coming, to get away from all the pressures? She probably needs to spend some time in a normal home, eat normal food, and slow down."

"I know that," said Norma, "but don't forget when we were up in New York she entertained us royally, threw out the red carpet, catered to our every need. I don't want her to think we are not willing to do the same."

Norma looked suspiciously at the little oval rug on the floor. "This rug needs to be shampooed; can you do that for me?"

"All right, whatever you say. I'll come up and do it later. Anything else?"

"Yes, grab the towels and washrags in the bathroom. I don't know how long they've been there. And, honey, check that shower curtain for mildew."

❧   ❧   ❧

As they were walking downstairs, Norma said, "Macky, what about Aunt Elner!"

"What about her?"

"Are we going to tell her? Baby Girl said for us not to tell anybody she was coming. Do you think she meant Aunt Elner, too?"

"Did she mention Aunt Elner?"

"No. She didn't say a word about her."

"There's your answer, then. If she had wanted us to tell Aunt Elner, she would have mentioned it."

"I know, but I cannot imagine she wouldn't want Aunt Elner to know."

"All I know is we have to go by what she said."

"But she hasn't seen Aunt Elner since she was four; why *wouldn't* she want to see her?"

"Honey, I'm sure she will see her. Why not let her decide when she wants to?"

Norma put the first load of washing in, added detergent, closed the lid, and sat down with him at the kitchen table. "Macky, what if she doesn't want to see Aunt Elner when she's here, and Aunt Elner finds out that she was in town after she's gone? Aunt Elner will be so hurt."

"Norma, there you go making a mountain out of a molehill again, over something that hasn't even happened yet. Everything will work out fine."

Norma got up and poured herself a cup of coffee. "OK, this is what we will do. After she's been here for a while and gotten settled in and all, I'll just bring it up naturally, you know, in conversation. I'll just casually say, Baby Girl, I'm sure you will want to see your Aunt Elner. She would be so disappointed not to see you. She's so proud of you and brags about you to everyone in town when she sees you on TV. She always says, 'That's my little niece.' "

"In other words, you're gonna blackmail the poor girl into going."

"Don't be silly. Then, when she decides, I'll call and say, Aunt Elner, guess what? Baby Girl has just flown into town as a surprise. That way Aunt Elner can be surprised."

Macky offered another suggestion. "Why don't you just take Baby Girl over there, knock on the door, and *really* surprise her?"

Norma looked at Macky in utter disbelief. "Macky, are you thinking with your elbow? You can't just go up and knock on a ninety-three-year-old woman's door and yell *surprise!* She could have a heart attack and drop dead right there in the doorway and wouldn't that be wonderful for Baby Girl to come home and kill her aunt, just like that, right off the bat. That would just be a wonderful vacation for her, wouldn't it? How would you like to have that on your conscience for the rest of your life?"

"Well, at least she'd be in town for the funeral. . . ."

Norma looked at Macky and shook her head. "You know, Macky, sometimes I worry about you, I really do."

I Did What?

New York City
April 1, 1973

The luncheon went well. Extremely well. There were times today when Dena was smiling and shaking hands that she really cared about what the other person was saying. Sometimes it seemed the worse she felt, the nicer she became. A twinge of guilt. What if these people had seen her a few hours ago, sloshed to the gills? They would have been horrified. But although she was standing there looking calm and relaxed, emotionally she was crawling on her hands and knees. She had been lucky because the luncheon had not ended one minute too soon. At about 2:45 all the aspirin, Alka-Seltzer, Valium, and the two Bloody Marys she had managed to drink had started to wear off and she could feel that big, dark, pounding headache looming in the background, ready to hit her like a herd of buffalo. Her stomach started to burn again and every muscle in her body felt as if she had been dropped from a ten-story building. Only in the last ten minutes had she begun to sweat ever so slightly and noticed a tic beginning in her left eye. But she made it through.

She got into a cab and said, "One thirty-four West Fifty-eighth, please." Smiled and waved good-bye. When the cab made a left turn out of the park and she was out of sight, she almost collapsed with relief. It was over. She could finally stop smiling. Now she could go home, take more aspirin, another Valium, drink an ice-cold beer, and get in bed and sleep. All she had to do was just hang on a little longer.

But hanging on was not made easy by this cab driver. He drove in short spurts, slamming on his brakes and whipping one way then another. She leaned forward.

"Sir, do you mind not jerking the car. I'm just getting over a hip operation."

The driver paid no attention except to give her a dirty look and mumble something in a foreign language. He continued to oversteer and to jerk and slam on his brakes. She could feel the herd again closing in on her head. She tried again, "Sir, would you please—"

She could tell he was ignoring her. She gave up, sat back, and tried to hold on as best she could. Jesus, was there a cab driver left in New York who spoke English? Not only did this guy not speak English, he was mean, surly, and obviously hated women. His body odor was strong enough to strip paint off walls. She got out on the corner of Fifty-eighth and Sixth because she didn't have the energy to try and explain to him how to go around the block. After she handed him a five-dollar bill for a $4.70 fare, he gave her another dirty look, grunted something, and held out his hand for a tip. She said, "Listen, buster, if you expect a tip you better learn to drive, to speak English, and learn some damn manners while you're at it!" The driver screamed at her in his native tongue, whatever it was, threw her change on the ground, and spit at her. As he squealed off, he yelled the one English word he did know: "Faggot!"

Dena gave him the finger and screamed back, "You jerk—why don't you go back where you came from, you creep!" Not only did screaming hurt her head, it caused people to stop and stare. As she looked around she thought, Oh, great, here I am standing on a street corner with a hangover and turning into the Ugly American right before my own eyes. She was probably recognized and would be quoted tomorrow in *The Daily News*.

The only consolation was that as she walked away, several people applauded.

❧ ❧ ❧

As she entered the apartment, she started to take her clothes off. She headed down the hall for the medicine chest and took three huge swallows from the bottle of Maalox Liquid to help put out the fire. When she was opening the aspirin bottle she noticed her hands shaking. That was something that had never happened to her before, and it frightened her. As a matter of fact, she had always had nerves of steel. But she soon dismissed the thought. *It's just because you're tired, you're not an alcoholic, for heaven's sake, you've just been pushing yourself lately. Well, lately for about fifteen years.* She usually was in control of her drinking but she had noticed recently, about once every two weeks or so, she would go out and, like last night, get drunk out of her mind. Then wake up with a hangover from hell and swear she would never do it again. *Guess it's almost like a teakettle. I have so much pressure, I need to let off a little steam.* But the hangovers were getting worse and worse, and she wondered why she kept doing it. Her career was going great, she was on the highest-rated morning show on TV. You couldn't get any better than that, except for prime time, and that might be in her future if things kept going as well as they had been. She had finally gotten over that guy from D.C. It had taken her almost five years, but she hardly ever thought about him anymore. Well, hardly. *It must be I'm not getting enough rest, that's all. I'm not unhappy.*

She ran a tub of hot water, hoping it would help soothe her aching body. Going to the kitchen for that beer, she remembered—she had to call J.C. before she went back to sleep, and think of some reason she could not go to dinner.

She got into the tub, began to relax, and to feel a little better. She sat there admiring the beauty of the light amber fluid in the clear bottle, the way the condensation on the Miller bottle ran down the black and gold label, like it was a fine piece of art. That was the problem with alcohol. It was so beautiful to look at, how could you resist it? And what kind of place could be more inviting and seductive than a truly elegant cocktail bar? She had felt that way the first time she had been taken to a nice place by a friend of her mother's when she was twelve. From the very beginning she had been mesmerized by the rows and rows of bottles sitting on glass shelves on the mirror behind the bar, the way the glass was lit, and how the emerald green of the crème de menthe and the bright red of the grenadine seemed to glow, and how happy everybody seemed. She even remembered the lushness of the rugs, the little pink lampshades that sat on the tables, and the muffled sounds of the cocktail piano playing over in the corner. It was, to her, homelike. That was also the first time she had ever seen an honest-to-God gin martini in person. It seemed at the time to be the most glamorous thing in the world, other than Radio City Music Hall and the Rockettes. It really did look as if someone had melted a handful of icy-blue diamonds and poured them right into that tall, chilled, slender, stemmed glass. Not only did she want to grab it and drink it, she wanted to eat the glass as well, chew the whole thing up. She had felt the same way later about scotch. Just the name alone was inviting enough but when they poured that thick, rich, caramel-colored liquid into that short, thick-bottomed glass, she knew it must taste exactly like liquid butterscotch. She couldn't wait until she grew up and would be able to order a real drink instead of the Shirley Temple her mother's friend had ordered for her that first time. When she finally was able to order a martini, the first sip nearly knocked her head off. It was so *strong*. And how surprised she was that scotch tasted more like iodine than butterscotch candy. Two of the great disappointments in her life.

So now when she did drink, she often ordered cocktails like grasshoppers, pink squirrels, and brandy alexanders, compounding the mistake. Last night was an exception. She only drank aquavit with beer chasers because J.C. loved it and it was fun for the waiters to bring the frozen bottles to the table and pour. Poor old J.C. He believed anything she told him. He was such a good egg, really, he was fun, made the perfect escort, and he was so much in love with her that she could do pretty much what she wanted to on a date. And there were times when she was actually glad to see him. But most of all he kept other guys away. There was one other reason she wanted him around. She did not love him, and that was just fine with her.

She had no interest in love. Love had taken her in the back room and beaten her up pretty badly. Falling head over heels for a slick, handsome, fast-talking Washington lobbyist had done nothing but break her heart and keep her upset. She had been completely obsessed with him and spent years waiting for him to call, waiting for him to come back to town, catching him in lies. She vowed never to see him anymore but took him back each time. Whether it had been love or obsession, now that it was finally over, she wanted no part of it. It had been too painful.

Now she was perfectly happy being the one who was loved, and she was going to keep it that way. Sex, maybe, friendship, yes, but love, *no.* If she ever felt love coming toward her, she would cross the street to the other side. Besides, she was determined not to let anything or anyone stand in the way of her work ever again.

❦   ❦   ❦

After the bath she got into bed and called J.C. and was pleased he was not home. He had probably gone over to the sports bar to watch football, so she was able to leave a message with his answering service. It wasn't until she put the phone back on the table and took the receiver off the hook that she noticed her address book lying wide open—to the letter *W.* A wave of hangover anxiety came over her when she saw the names *Norma and Macky Warren, Elmwood Springs, Missouri.* She began to have a recollection of calling someone at six o'clock that morning when she had been out of her mind. She tried to remember. *Oh, please don't tell me I called them, tell me I didn't, surely I couldn't have done something that stupid.* But deep down she knew very well that she might have. She had called people before and not remembered. She didn't want to think about it so she put on her electric blanket, pulled the covers over her head, and went to sleep.

❦   ❦   ❦

Dena awakened at 4:00 A.M. on Monday morning, rested, but still a little guilty. She had slept all Saturday and Sunday. She showered, dressed, and was ready when the car picked her up at five and took her to the studio. She liked the city that time of morning. The streets were quiet and almost empty, only a few early risers and several stragglers going home after a long night. The aloneness was familiar. She saw one couple trying to hail a cab, the woman still dressed in a sequined cocktail dress and the man in a tux without a tie. At this time of morning Sixth Avenue looked as long and as wide as a football field but would soon be so packed with cars and people that by the time she left work, the buildings on both sides would look like they had each taken twenty giant steps into the middle of the street. She went into the building at the studio entrance. After four years she still had a hard time believing she actually worked at Rockefeller Plaza and no matter how many times she went in, the minute she entered she always had the feeling she had stepped inside an Ayn Rand novel, from the murals on the walls to the way her high heels cracked like gun shots on the marble as she walked down the empty halls to those smooth, brass elevators that shot her up twenty-six floors in five seconds. The only side effect of her lost weekend was that her eyes were puffy from so much sleep but Magda, the Yugoslavian makeup woman, would fix that as she always did, making her sit for ten minutes with tea bags on her eyes.

Her interview with Helen Gurley Brown went very well. It was supposed to have been a fluff piece on the *Cosmopolitan* editor but it turned out to be sharp, funny, and just spicy enough, so Dena was in a good mood when she got to her office and found a beautiful bouquet of flowers and a huge fruit basket from Julian Amsley, the president of the network, that said, *Heard you wowed them at the luncheon. Thanks from your network family.* She had almost forgotten the last, long evening until she started going through her messages and saw one that had come in while she was on the air:

Baby Girl, we are thrilled you are coming home! Please don't forget to call and let us know what flight you will be on so we can pick you up at the airport.

Your Elmwood Springs family,
Norma, Macky, and Aunt Elner

The people standing outside her door at the water fountain heard a loud "Oh, God." Dena leaned over her desk with her head in her hands wondering what in the world had possessed her to call and tell them she was coming to Missouri, of all places! Elmwood Springs was nothing more than the name of a town she had lived in for a short time as a child. Her father and grandparents were buried there, but other than that it was nothing more to her than some vague memory. She didn't even know where it was. And why Norma and Macky? Not only did she not know them well, she had not even *thought* of them in years. She couldn't even remember how they were related. She knew that Norma was her third or fourth cousin, or something. But they might as well be perfect strangers. Sure, they always sent her birthday cards, Easter cards, and some kind of preserves at Christmas, and for years, no matter where she moved, they always found her and sent her a subscription to a religious magazine, some *Daily Word* thing that she promptly discarded along with the weird brown preserves. Norma and Macky were sweet people but she hadn't even seen them but once and that was years before when they had come to New York for a few days. As nice as they were, it had been a strain. They had stayed at the Hilton and J.C., as a favor, had taken them to see the Statue of Liberty and the Empire State Building. All she did was get them tickets to Radio City and the *Tonight Show* and go to dinner with them and all they had talked about was meeting Wayne Newton, who had been a guest that night on the *Tonight Show,* and how really friendly he was. A friend of hers had arranged for them to go backstage after the show and meet him and get an autographed picture.

Dena was baffled. Why, of *all* the people in her address book, had she picked them to call? Maybe it was because she had been having that dream about her mother and that house again; maybe it had been the aquavit. Whatever the reason, she wondered how she was going to get out of this one.

This is not *my fault,* she thought. *I'm going to kill J.C. He's the one who ordered all those drinks in the first place.*

Going to Siberia

Elmwood Springs, Missouri
April 3, 1973

For dinner, Norma had tested several recipes out of *The Neighbor Dorothy Cookbook*. She had told Macky that she just felt like trying something new for a change, no big deal, but he knew she was trying out dishes to fix when Baby Girl came home. She knew he knew but they both played along. He had been served: Minnie Dell Crower's "Meatloaf Delight," Leota Kling's "Lima Bean and Cheese Casserole," Virginia Mae's "Scalloped Turnips," John and Susan Tate's "Light as a Feather Potato Puffs," Lucille's "Fly off the Plate Rolls," Gertrude's "Bing Cherry Salad," topped off with "Chocolate Peanut Butter Bunt Cake" from Vernelia Pew.

Everything passed muster with the exception of the turnips. Whoever Virginia Mae was, she was destined not to go to good-recipe heaven. After that, Macky could hardly move and was stretched out in the living room watching television. Norma was in the kitchen listening to the last of the turnips being ripped to shreds in her new garbage disposal when the phone rang and she picked it up.

❖   ❖   ❖

Five minutes later she came in the living room with a dejected look on her face, sat down, and looked at Macky. "She's not coming."

"Why?"

"She was so disappointed. . . . You should have heard her."

"What happened?"

"Well, she said she had planned on coming in tomorrow but decided to come tonight instead. She had made all the arrangements to come on the late flight to Kansas City and was going to call us from the New York airport, so we would be sure and know exactly what time she would be in. She was packed, had her ticket, had already called a taxi, and was headed out the door, was actually in the hall, when the phone rang. And she said she could just kill herself for even going back in and picking it up. Because wouldn't you know it, it was her boss and he was frantic because there was this very important interview already set up out of the country and the reporter that was supposed to go had a sudden attack of malaria, right at the last minute, and couldn't go."

"Malaria?"

"Yes, he got it when he was doing a story in some jungle—and you know that's recurring—so anyway, she didn't have a choice because the plane was waiting at the airport at that very moment. Bless her heart, it's a wonder she had time to call us at all with them jerking her all the way to Siberia. It's a good thing she did call, though; I reminded her to take a coat. You never know, she could have gotten over there and frozen to death in a snowstorm."

"Siberia? Who is she going to interview in Siberia, I wonder."

"She doesn't know; she said that it was so important and evidently so secret that they didn't even tell her. Really, though, as bad as it is, it was a blessing she was already packed and ready to go, but she probably just packed her light clothes thinking she was coming here. Well, at least I made her take a heavy coat."

Macky went over and started pulling down the big green *Colliers World Map and Atlas* book off the shelf. "Norma, are you sure she didn't say Sicily or Sardinia or something?"

"No, I'm sure she said Siberia. Why do you think I told her to take a coat? I wouldn't tell her to take a heavy winter coat to Sicily or Sardinia; I can tell the difference between Sardinia and Siberia." Norma suddenly looked alarmed. "I just thought of something. Aren't you supposed to get a vaccination when you travel out of the country?"

Macky's finger found Siberia on the map. "Yes, but I wouldn't worry. I don't think a germ stands a chance up that far."

"What about her passport, do you think she forgot it, being in such a hurry?"

Macky shook his head. "No, honey, with the way they have to go at a moment's notice, they probably have four or five of those things. She probably keeps one in her purse."

He was studying the map. "Whoever she's interviewing, you can bet your bottom dollar he's a Russian. Come here and look at this, it's perched right on the border."

Norma saw where Siberia was. "Oh my Lord! Isn't that behind the iron curtain? Do you think she'll be safe? You don't think they would kidnap her or shoot her or anything?"

Macky shook his head. "No, listen, if anything were to happen to her, everybody in America would know it. They don't want to fool with a famous television star, believe me. She's probably safer than anyone in the world. Did she say she might be able to come after she gets back from this trip?"

"No, she can't, she said this was the only time that she could have taken off."

"Well, it's a damn shame the way they work her like they do. She hasn't had a vacation since she started working there. That girl works too hard."

❀ ❀ ❀

A half hour later, when Macky was in the kitchen fixing the percolator for their morning coffee, Norma said, sighing, "Well, I guess I better call Aunt Elner and let her know she's not coming."

"She never knew she was coming in the first place, Norma."

But she was not listening and had already dialed. "Aunt Elner, are you still up? It's Norma." She said, louder, "It's Norma, go get your hearing aid, dear."

She waited. "Well, now the tale can be told because it's not going to happen. You will never guess who was coming home for a visit. *And* was going to come over to your house and surprise you. Guess . . . Well, I know you don't know . . . but guess. No, even better than Wayne Newton."

Macky laughed.

"Baby Girl, that's who. No, she's not coming now. I know it would have been wonderful, but just at the last minute when she was headed out the door, her boss called her and she had to go and interview somebody and fly all the way to Siberia to do it. Siberia." She spelled it out. "*S-I-B-E-R-I-A;* yes, that's the one. Macky thinks she's going to interview some big Russian mucky-muck. I feel so sorry for her I could just cry. They just send her hither and yon but the news waits for no man, as they say. Oh, yes, she was; disappointed is not the word. Heartbroken is more like it. She was trying to be brave but I could tell by her voice that she was on the verge of tears. I mean, we are all terribly disappointed but just imagine how horrible she must have felt. Here she had her bags all packed and ready to walk out the door headed for Missouri and winding up in Siberia instead."

Souvenir

Elmwood Springs, Missouri
November 1968

When Norma and Macky returned home after visiting Dena in New York, the first thing they did was to go over to Aunt Elner's house and give her the souvenirs they had brought for her knickknack shelf. One was a little bronze Statue of Liberty and another an Empire State Building paperweight with fake snow inside. Two hours later she called Norma with the paperweight in her hand.

"Norma?"

"Yes, honey?"

"You might have to come over here and take this paperweight away from me."

"Why?"

"I can't stop myself from shaking it up; it's just like a little winter in there, isn't it?"

"Well, I'm glad you like it. We didn't know what to get you."

"Oh, I'm just getting the biggest kick out of it, you have no idea."

"Good."

"And Baby Girl really seemed like she was getting along all right?"

"Oh, yes, but we didn't get to spend nearly enough time with her. They have her working morning, noon, and night."

"Is she still too skinny?"

"No, she's filled out and has quite a nice shape."

"Did she like her fig preserves?"

"Oh, yes, she was tickled pink to get them. She probably never gets anything homemade; they all eat in restaurants up there day and night."

"Well, bless her heart. Do you reckon she might like some hickory nuts? I've got a barrel full out on the porch. My tree just went crazy on me this year. Maybe I'll make her one of my hickory nut cakes with the caramel icing; do you reckon she'd like that?"

"I'm sure she would."

"It's still hard to believe Baby Girl is a grown-up woman! Last time I saw her she wasn't no bigger than a minute; what was she, four?"

"Four or five."

Then Aunt Elner asked the same question she did every time they discussed Dena.

"Did she mention anything about her mother?"

"Not a word."

"Well, what would you say if she did?"

"I'll just answer whatever questions she has as truthfully as I can, that's all I can do. As it is, she doesn't say anything and neither do I. I will have to follow her lead on it."

There was a pause. "That's got to be a hard thing for her to come to terms with, don't you think?" said Aunt Elner. "You know it must prey on her mind."

"I don't know, Aunt Elner, but I imagine it's hurtful for her to even think about so I just don't bring it up."

"Yes, that's probably best. Well, honey, thank you again for my present. I sure am enjoying it . . . and tell Macky to run over here for a minute, will you? My back door's stuck again."

"OK, I'll tell him."

Aunt Elner hung up and turned the glass paperweight upside down one more time and watched the tiny pieces of fake snow swirl and settle around the miniature Empire State Building and said out loud to herself, "Look at that . . . it's like it says, a winter wonderland."

❀   ❀   ❀

A day later Norma sat down and wrote a letter.

Mr. Wayne Newton
c/o the *Tonight Show,* NBC
New York City

Dear Mr. Newton,

Just a note to say hello again. As you know my husband and I and our Aunt Elner have always been your biggest fans. We always watch you when you are on television and have all your albums, and four years ago were lucky enough to see you when you performed at the Missouri State Fair.

So you can imagine how grateful we are to our cousin Dena Nordstrom for giving us an opportunity to actually meet you in person and get an autographed picture. It was the highlight of our trip.

You were so sweet to us and we were happy to find out that you are such a nice, down-to-earth person. I know that you travel a lot and probably don't get a chance to get to church so I'm sending you a subscription to the *Daily Word* and some fig preserves from our Aunt Elner. Mr. Newton, if you ever get anywhere near Elmwood Springs, Missouri, please know you have a place to stay and I can promise you some good home cooking. I am sure you must get tired of hotel food and we would love to have you as our guest.

                                Best wishes,
                                Mrs. Norma Warren

P.S. You are now on our "Wall of Fame" in a prominent place next to our cousin.

How She Got There

Sacred Heart Academy
Silver Spring, Maryland
1959

Fame is a funny thing. It knows who it wants and starts stalking people at an early age. Dena was only fifteen when it went after her. A photographer from *Seventeen* magazine came to her school and she was one of ten girls chosen to be photographed that day. She had never considered herself to be pretty, and she was getting to be too tall, but they had requested several blondes and she was one of the few in her class that year. Albert Boutwell, the makeup man, had been putting makeup on giggling teenage girls all over the country and when the slim, lanky kid walked in she was just another one in an assembly line of faces he was to make up that day. She sat down and he put a smock on her. He noted that she was particularly pale so he used a slightly darker base and a little more eyeliner to bring out her eyes. When he had finished, he glanced up in the mirror for a last-minute check. What he saw was astonishing. Looking back at him was what had become, at a touch, one of the most beautiful faces he had ever seen. Dena, who had never had on makeup before, was as shocked as he was. He asked her what her name was. "Well, Miss Dena Nordstrom," he said, "look at yourself. You are a knockout!" The next girl came in and took Dena's place.

A month later, back in New York looking at proofs, the photographer came to the Nordstrom girl's picture, viewing it through a magnifier, and he recalled the moment. "You're right. Look at this kid. Hell, you can't get a bad shot of her! This kid has a goddamn golden, million-dollar face." He turned to his assistant. "Find out who she is and how we can get in touch with her."

"I told you," Albert said. "When she walked in she was nothing. I slapped a little makeup on, did a little shading, and whammo."

The photographer was still studying the picture. "Damn, I just put her in a plain black turtleneck sweater and started shooting and look— *look* at that bone structure. What is she, Swedish or something?"

"I don't know."

His assistant came back in with a list. "Name is Dena Nordstrom."

"I knew it," the photographer said, "we got us a baby Garbo here or another Ingrid Bergman. How old is this girl?"

"Fifteen."

The photographer was disappointed. "Oh, well, I can dream, can't I."

Albert, who knew him well, reminded him, "Yeah, that's all you can do if you don't want another irate mother—or the law—after you."

The photographer sighed elaborately. He said to his assistant, "Call Hattie over at the agency and tell her we are sending over some pictures . . . but tell her we get to use her first."

Two days later, after a phone call was made to Dena's school and Dena's mother was finally located at work, Hattie Smith explained that she handled only the top teenage models and that she wanted to sign Dena to a five-year contract and start her to work right away. "You have quite an exceptional daughter. We think with the right representation she has a tremendous future ahead of her."

Hattie sat back and waited to hear what she always heard from mothers, how excited they were that their little girls were going to be models. This one said only two words: "Absolutely not."

Dena's mother was alarmed. She had not known that Dena had been photographed.

Hattie sat up. "Excuse me?"

"Mrs. Smith, I appreciate your interest but we will have to decline your offer."

"But we think she can be a big star. As a matter of fact, we were considering perhaps using both of you in a mother and daughter spread they are doing next month for *Family Circle,* so if you could send us a recent photograph of yourself—"

"Oh, I don't think you understand. I do not want my daughter's picture or mine in any magazine. I'm afraid I don't approve. I'm sorry."

Hattie was frustrated. "But I don't think you understand. Your daughter is capable of making money—a *lot* of money—posing for magazines or doing commercials. You don't disapprove of money, do you?"

There was a silence. "I work very hard for my money, Mrs. Smith, and I intend to have my daughter receive an education before we consider anything else for her future."

Hattie was not giving up. "We have no intention of interfering with her education, all of our girls continue their education; we can schedule her shoots around school hours. We already have a shoot lined up for her at *Seventeen* magazine, possibly a cover."

"Mrs. Smith, as I said before, I do not want my daughter photographed. I am trying to be as tactful as I possibly can, but thank you, no." And she hung up.

Hattie said, "Damn!"

In three years, when Dena was on her own, they called back and her first professional photo shoot put her on the cover of *Seventeen* magazine. After which she was offered a college scholarship to study drama at Southern Methodist University in Dallas. Dena was pleased, but she did not stay. After her sophomore year she quit to take a job as a weather girl at a television station in Ft. Worth. She had to support herself and as much as she loved the idea of studying theater, she quickly found out television was where the money was and she was good at it from the start.

After eleven months, she began to move from station to station, almost every time to a little larger market, and, in her mind at least, working closer and closer to New York. Dena didn't mind going from place to place; she was used to it. Her mother had moved all over the country from the time she was four. She was willing to get as much experience as possible, no matter how many places she had to go. When she hit the network, she wanted to be ready.

She worked in Arkansas; Billings, Montana; then Oklahoma; Kentucky; back to Billings; and on to Richmond, Virginia, where she started off as a weather girl again but eventually worked up to cohost of the local morning program, doing features about art shows, horse shows, dog shows, and occasionally interviewing celebrities coming through town. When the actress Arlene Francis came to Richmond, she liked the way Dena handled the interview and mentioned it to her agents. Sandy Cooper was a young talent agent who specialized in television and was on the lookout for bright new female talent. The women's movement was gaining momentum; he knew the networks had quietly started searching for more women to groom, because they knew it was only a matter of time before they would be obligated to hire one or two in the news departments. And Sandy wanted to get in on it from the start.

One weekend he and his wife drove to Richmond and stayed over to watch this Dena Nordstrom on the show Monday morning. He liked what he saw. Nordstrom's beauty was certainly distinctive, but she had characteristics he knew the networks were looking for. She was smart, she was quick, she had that nice-girl-next-door quality coupled with a smile that lit up the screen. She had all this going for her but most important, she passed the ultimate test for Sandy. His wife, Bea, who was short and stout and usually hated pretty women, liked Dena. All he had to find out now was if this girl was ambitious or not. That question was answered in less than five minutes after they met, and an hour later she was signed as a client of the William Morris Agency, one of the largest and most powerful agencies in the country. Three months later Sandy found out that a local New York station was looking for a girl to replace Nancy Lamb, and whoever got the position would be a candidate for an eventual move to network. He set up an interview for Dena with Ira Wallace, head of the station's news department.

Dena flew in from Richmond the next week. Sandy picked her up at the hotel. Sandy wanted to walk so he would have a little time to prepare her for Ira Wallace and warn her not to be put off by his personality. Even as far away as Richmond, Dena had already heard stories. The talent was terrified of him but she was not worried. She had rarely, if ever, met a man she could not charm. She was ready for this job, and she knew it. When they reached the right floor, Sandy gave the receptionist their names. They heard a loud, impatient voice bark back through the intercom.

"Yeah?"

"Mr. Cooper and Miss Nordstrom are here, Mr. Wallace."

"*Who?*"

The receptionist repeated, "Mr. Cooper and Miss Nordstrom. They have an appointment."

"I don't know who the hell that is." He clicked off.

The receptionist seemed unruffled and told them to have a seat.

Dena looked at Sandy. "Are you sure we have an appointment?" Sandy, as unconcerned as the receptionist, picked up a magazine. "Yes, he just does that to try and intimidate you."

Dena sat down. "Well, it's working."

"Don't let it bother you. He does it to everybody."

As they sat there they could hear Ira Wallace yelling obscenities at somebody or a group of somebodies. After thirty-five minutes, he buzzed the receptionist.

"Those two yahoos still there?"

"Yes, sir."

"Oh, Christ, all right. Send them in."

Dena stood up. "This is ridiculous. I'm not going in there. He doesn't even know we have an appointment."

The receptionist looked at Dena. "He knows you have an appointment. He's just an ass. Go on in."

Reluctantly, Dena followed Sandy down the hall. Sandy stood outside the office and knocked lightly. They could hear him on the phone, but he managed to yell, "Come on, I don't have all day."

Sandy motioned for Dena to go first. The room reeked of cigar smoke. She looked over and saw Wallace, a fat, bald man, who looked exactly like a big sea bass wearing a white shirt, black plastic glasses, and smoking a cigar, sitting behind a ten-foot-long desk. He did not get up. He glanced at her for a second and continued cursing into the receiver, leaving them standing. They waited while the little man with the shiny, sweaty head continued to berate whoever he was talking to. The longer Dena remained standing and ignored, the madder she got. She could feel her face getting flushed. If there was anything Dena had inherited from her mother, it was pride, and she was not going to let this little toad humiliate her, no matter how much she wanted the job.

The second he hung up the phone, she walked right up to Ira Wallace's desk, reached over, and forced him to shake hands. "How do you do, Mr. Wallace. I'm Dena Nordstrom. What a pleasure to meet you. No, don't bother to get up. We will have a seat, thank you."

Wallace looked at her as if she had just dropped in from Mars.

She sat down and smiled at him. "Now, Mr. Wallace—tell me a little about yourself. I like to really get to know people before I make any decision about accepting a job."

He looked at Sandy Cooper, who was clearly confused, too. Wallace took the cigar out of his mouth. "What . . . is she kidding?"

Sandy tried to recover. "Uh, Mr. Wallace, did you by any chance get to take a look at the tapes?"

Before Wallace could answer, Dena looked at her watch and said, "Oh, darn it all. I wish I could stay. I am *so* sorry, Mr. Wallace, but unfortunately, I'm already late for another appointment."

She stood up and walked over and shook his hand again. "It's always so nice to meet such a charming gentleman with such lovely manners."

She said to Sandy on the way out, "I'll call you later."

Both men, their mouths open, watched as she left.

As Dena waited for the elevator, she said, "That man is a pig."

The receptionist, without looking up, said, "Tell me something I don't know."

After the elevator door closed and Dena was alone, she burst into tears.

Back in the office, Wallace shouted at Sandy, "What is she, nuts? You waste my time with insane people? What's the matter with her?"

"I'm sorry, Mr. Wallace, I don't know what happened. I know she wanted the job; she flew in for the meeting."

"Are you sure she's not just some nut case?"

"Oh, no, she's very responsible. I don't know what to tell you . . . except maybe, maybe you might have hurt her feelings or something?"

"Hurt her feelings?"

"She's from the midwest. I think maybe she might be a little sensitive."

"Sensitive? Well, she'll have to get over that crap if she wants to come to work for me. I liked her tapes but I'm not putting up with any prima donna shit."

Sandy said, "You liked her tapes?"

Wallace shrugged. "She might have potential—if she don't go whacko on us."

"Oh, no, she's fine, I assure you."

"I don't know how smart she is—she could be just another dumb bimbo like the rest of them—but she's got the kinda look we want. That sappy, corn-fed, fresh-off-the-farm face and . . . well, some sort of class. So we might be willing to try her out."

Sandy changed gears in a hurry. "You're absolutely right about that, Ira. That's why I brought her to you before somebody snapped her up. Not only is she beautiful but she has a lot of experience—six local stations, but she was the most popular on-air personality in Richmond."

"I don't care if she was Miss America, she starts at the bottom here; she understand that?"

"Oh, yes," said Sandy.

"A lot of hard work. We'll give her fifty thousand a year, with a thirteen-week out clause. Ours, not hers."

Sandy said, "Great, great. And I can tell you she's not afraid of work. She does a great interview."

"All right, don't oversell."

Sandy started to back out of the office before Wallace had a chance to change his mind.

"And tell your princess-and-the-pea client, if she can find time in her busy schedule, to get her butt back in here tomorrow morning."

After the agent left, Wallace had to laugh to himself. The decision to hire her had been made a week before, based on her tapes. They had been head and shoulders above the rest. But he liked to see people cower. Of course, she hadn't, she had thrown it right back in his face. Quite a change from the usual sweaty-palmed types that crawled in and out of his office all day. She just might have what he was looking for. *If* she was smart enough to do what she was told.

✤ ✤ ✤

Sandy ran back to his office and called Dena at the hotel. She picked up.

"It's Sandy. Dena, are you sitting down?"

Dena started to apologize. "Sandy, I'm so sorry. I know that was a stupid thing to do. What can I say, I didn't mean to embarrass you."

"Dena."

"I know you are disappointed. I am, too, believe me. But I would rather be a hostess in a pancake house before I'd let someone treat me like I was a . . . a nothing."

"Dena, listen!"

"My mother may not have had much money, but she did not raise me to be insulted by some puffed-up little mutant. Who does he think he is?"

"Dena, are you finished?"

"Yes."

"You got the job."

"Oh, yes, I'm sure that I did. . . . The only thing I regret—and this is because I'm a lady—that I did not tell him what he could do with—"

"Dena, *listen* to me. I am not kidding. He liked your tapes. You got the job. He's starting you at a pretty low salary . . . but it means you're in."

"And I'll tell you something else, I wouldn't work with that man for a million dollars. How did he even get into television?"

"OK, Dena, so he is an obnoxious, disgusting pig. Just don't take it so personally. Believe me, he treats everybody like a piece of dirt. The point is, you got the job."

There was a pause. "Are you serious?"

"Yes, he wants you to go in tomorrow and talk to him—"

"You are kidding," she said.

"No, I'm telling you he liked your tapes. He thinks you have something."

"Really?"

"Yes."

"No joke."

"No."

"Oh. Well." There was another pause. "How much are they going to pay me?"

"Like I said, it's a little low to start . . . but—"

"How much?"

"Fifty thousand."

"I don't know, Sandy. I'll have to think it over. I'll call you back."

Sandy sat with the phone in his hand. He could *not* believe what he had just heard. He put the phone down and threw his hands up in the air and said to the ceiling, "She's offered the best shot in New York and she's got to think it over?"

Ten minutes later she called back. "Sandy, it's Dena."

He tried to sound calm. "Yes, have you thought about it?"

"Yes, I have. And Sandy, I would have taken fifty thousand and been glad to get it. But that man insulted me and now they're going to have to pay me twice as much."

Sandy groaned. "Oh, Dena, don't do this to me. I have a weak heart. Please . . . please . . . my nerves. Fifty thousand is not a terrible offer."

"It's not the money, it's the principle of the thing."

"Dena, you can't afford principles now. Wait until you're a star. Then you can have all the principles you want. Trust me, now is not the time to make a stand. You don't have anything to stand on yet."

"Sandy, if I don't do it now, I never will. I can't let this man treat me like dirt and get away with it. Besides, I don't think I could live with myself if I took it for less than I'm worth."

"Dena . . . who's gonna know how much you are making—you and me and some accountant in a basement somewhere. Please."

"I'll know."

"Dena, listen to me. I'm the agent. I'm the one who should be convincing you to ask for more money, not the other way around, and I'm telling you, take the money."

Sandy talked to her for twenty more minutes, but she would not back down. Before she hung up she added, "And Sandy, I want you to *tell* him the reason I want more money."

Sandy said, "I thought you liked Bea."

"I do. Why?"

"Then why are you trying to make a widow out of her? Ira is going to kill me if I call him with this."

"Well, then, I'll call him if you want me to. I'm not scared of him."

"No, no, I'll call. I would rather be attacked by a pack of wild dogs, but I'll call."

❊   ❊   ❊

Sandy held his breath as he dialed Ira Wallace's office. He was put on hold for five minutes and then heard Wallace's welcoming voice.

"Yeah?"

"Uh, Mr. Wallace. This is Sandy Cooper."

"What do you want?"

"Well, we have a small problem . . . on the salary."

"What the hell are you talking about?"

"On the Dena Nordstrom situation."

"Yeah, come on, cut to the chase. What?"

"That is, she feels she needs a little more, being that New York is so expensive and all."

"Are you telling me that your goddamn crazy client wants a raise before she even starts? Have you lost your mind? How much more does she want, for Christ sakes?"

Sandy took a deep breath. "She wants a hundred a year."

Wallace yelled, "Good-bye, buster!" and slammed the phone down in his ear.

Sandy sat by the phone all day, hoping against hope that Wallace would call him back.

Wallace waited for Sandy to call him back.

At four-thirty that afternoon Sandy called Dena again and begged her to reconsider but she would not.

At 6:05 Sandy answered the phone. Wallace was on the other end. "OK, you little putz, seventy-five, take it or leave it. You have five minutes!"

Sandy called Dena immediately and started talking fast. "Dena, it's me. Before you say anything, listen to me. I want you to think about what you are doing. Don't think local . . . think about where it can *lead*. Remember, you do well and one day you've got a shot at network, OK?"

"OK," said Dena, "I'm listening."

"I can't believe it but he called back with another offer. But promise me your—"

"How much did he come up with?"

"Seventy-five, take it or leave it . . . but think about your—"

"I'll take it."

"What?"

"I said fine, I'll take it."

"You'll take it? Just like that? Oh, my nerves. You put me through a heart attack which I haven't had time to have yet. I'll call you right back."

Sandy called and didn't bother to say hello. "Dena, it's OK. Do you know how nervous I've been all day?"

"You think you were nervous? I've been throwing up since noon."

"Do you know how close we came to losing this deal? I have to be honest with you—I never thought he would call back."

Dena laughed. "Neither did I."

"You lucked out this time. But promise me not to play any more Russian roulette with your career, OK?"

Dena giggled again. "OK, I promise."

"Hold on. I'm calling Bea on the other line. She's been lighting candles all day."

Dena waited until he came back on the phone. "Bea says congratulations. And she also informed me that I'm taking you two out to dinner. Where do you want to go? You pick."

"Twenty-One," Dena said.

"The Twenty-One Club?"

"Yes, let's go there."

"I doubt we can get in. It's like a private club or something. Anyway, we can't get reservations this late. What about Sardi's?"

"We already have reservations at Twenty-One."

Sandy was taken aback. "How did you manage that?"

"Oh, I have a friend here. I told him it was a celebration dinner."

"How did you know we would have something to celebrate?"

Dena laughed. "I didn't. Either way, I always wanted to go to Twenty-One for dinner."

"You're in New York for twenty-four hours and you already have a friend?"

"Well, actually it's a new friend I met yesterday on the airplane. He said if I ever needed a favor to call, so I did."

When Sandy hung up he was still amazed. Here he had lived in Manhattan all his life, and on her first night in town Dena was taking him places he'd never been before. Still, he couldn't help but wonder how a nice person like her would fare in New York. She might do just fine. He hoped so. But he also knew that New York was a tough town, full of ruthless types waiting to rip you to shreds if they could. Success here could be brutal. He glanced over at the headline on the front page of the local news rag his secretary had put on his desk earlier. These days being nice or even distinguished was no protection anymore. One slip and your reputation is ruined forever. Look what had just happened to Arthur Rosemond. Poor guy.

A Nice Person

Arthur Rosemond was born in Norway and at seventeen had become one of the leaders of the underground movement during WWII. Arrested in 1942, he was sent to a German war camp but managed to escape two years later. After the war, he came to America and received a master's in political science from Georgetown University and by age thirty-nine, he had written three books, served four years as special adviser to the secretary of state, and was only forty-two years old when appointed to his post at the United Nations, where he had been the spearhead in major peace negotiations for the past eleven years, traveling widely. Two years before he had shared the Nobel peace prize for his efforts.

In his personal life, Rosemond was considered somewhat unusual, because although happily married, he had as many women friends as he did men. He genuinely liked the company of women and he found their particular insights and observations about people helpful. One such friend was Pamela Lathrope. They had been good friends while she had been married and remained so after her divorce. Rosemond believed she had one of the keenest minds he had ever come across and he always asked for her advice whenever a particularly difficult negotiation was going on. They would often have dinner together to discuss it, sometimes with his wife or friends or sometimes just the two of them. Tonight was just such an occasion. He was having a hard time with the new man from France. He needed his support on several upcoming issues and was getting nowhere. He had enjoyed a wonderful working and social relationship with the previous French ambassador but this new man was a bird of a different feather.

Arthur needed to get together with him in the right social situation without dozens of people around so he could get a handle on what this guy was about, and he had called Pamela to help him out. Pamela was famous for her dinner parties and most people did not turn down an invitation. Like most, the French diplomat did not say no. It was to be just Arthur and his wife, Beverly; the ambassador and his wife; and Pamela. Arthur was anxious for Pamela to spend a little time observing up close. She was always able to see a person clearly and size him up much more precisely than he ever could. Three hours before the party, Arthur's wife called Pamela on the phone.

"Pam, it's me, Beverly. Listen, would you take a gun and shoot me if I didn't come tonight?"

"Of course not."

"I hate to call this late, but I am just walking on my knees, I am so tired. I've been out in the yard working with the gardeners since seven o'clock this morning. Wouldn't you know that this would be the day they would show up with all the new plantings; anyway, I'm filthy dirty, and by the time I take a bath, dress, and come all the way in, I'll be late anyway. So ... do you think Arthur will be very upset?"

"No, of course not. Don't worry, I'll tell Arthur; you just get in a hot tub and relax."

"You are an angel from heaven. I'll make this up to you, I swear I will."

Pamela, in fact, did not mind. She knew that Beverly, who was sixteen years younger than Arthur, adored him, but hated all the endless socializing. She would much rather stay home with her children and read a good book. Pamela couldn't much blame her for not wanting to come tonight. From what Arthur had said, the French ambassador and his wife were not what you would call Paris's fun couple, and he had been correct.

Nevertheless the dinner went well, and while Pamela was busy being a gracious hostess, she was also making mental notes about the small man with the stocky wife. After the evening was over, she closed the door and went into the living room, where Arthur was waiting.

"Well . . ." she said, "I see what you mean."

"I told you, I can't get a straight answer one way or the other. I never can pin him down."

Pamela lit a cigarette. "Well, first of all, you are never going to get any serious answer from him. He's not the man making the decisions."

Arthur nodded. "That's exactly what I thought, I just needed to get your read on it."

"Absolutely, that man never had an original thought in his life."

Arthur smiled, and suddenly winced in pain.

Pamela looked at him. "What's the matter?"

"I don't know, must be indigestion." He started trying to loosen his tie and seemed to be short of breath.

Pamela saw that he had broken out into a sweat.

"What's the—are you ill?"

"I . . . feel sick to my stomach."

Then another sharp pain hit him and he fell over toward the floor.

Pamela jumped up and tried to catch him but was not able to. She ran to the kitchen and buzzed downstairs to the doorman and screamed for help. Running back to the living room, she found him unconscious. She picked up the phone, called 911, went back to him, and took his tie off.

By the time the doorman came running in, she was frantic. She could not feel a pulse.

Trust Me

New York City
1968

Sidney Capello was born nervous. Tonight he paced up and down in his fleabag hotel room at Forty-eighth and Third, worried even more than usual. Something was off. Sidney had made a name for himself in certain circles as a freelance reporter who specialized in obtaining private information about public people. He had paid informants stashed in many nooks, crannies, and dark corners who covered New York like a giant spiderweb. There were not many moves that the rich or famous could make without Sidney finding out about them one way or another. But lately Sidney's people had been letting him down. His stable of snitches had been strangely silent. The gossip and rumor mill that sometimes spewed out profitable dirt twenty-four hours a day had suddenly ground down to a halt. Either people had been behaving themselves lately, or else they were beginning to be very careful. Or sneaky. Tonight Sidney hated all of them. They prevented him from making a living, with all the money they had. Greedy little ingrates each and every one. Although he himself was on an under-the-table retainer from one of the New York dailies, and two top gossip columnists, nothing made him more irritable than having to pay out money for nothing. It was making Sidney sweat. He had not had a big, fat, red-hot scandal in over two months, not even a really juicy tidbit. He was restless and couldn't sleep. He was just itching for a little something, anything he could grab by the throat and choke a story out of. At about twelve-fifty when the call came, he was ready.

It was Mary at the Midtown Ambulance Service. She had just dispatched a unit to Beekman Towers, Room 107. He was out the door and on the street in less time than it took a fireman to slide down a pole.

Sidney had never been a Boy Scout but he was always prepared. He kept about two thousand dollars in cash, a small silver German camera with a great lens, and preprinted release forms in his pocket at all times. He could not afford to waste a second with all the new boys in town trying to rip him off. Sidney was excited. The Beekman Towers was an exclusive eastside residential hotel near the UN and just about anyone there might be a story. Adrenaline set in and in five minutes he hit the building running, right on the heels of the ambulance, and was able to slip past any security and was soon outside 107 watching the paramedics work on a man lying unconscious in the hall. He had perfected the art of slipping in anywhere unnoticed. The three years he had spent as a private detective, working mostly on divorce raids, had been good training. Sidney was at his best working fast among people distracted by tragedy; and while the paramedics labored, trying to save the man's life, Sidney had taken at least ten pictures quietly before anyone knew what was happening, found out who the man was and whose apartment he had been visiting. It was all Sidney could do not to laugh out loud. There was a God after all. Jackpot! This could be a yelling and screaming headline and he could smell it, a real score, a bull's-eye, a home run a hundred feet over the wall. Arthur Rosemond had just done Sidney a huge personal favor by dropping dead of a heart attack in the apartment of a woman who was not his wife.

Mrs. Pamela Lathrope III was a socialite and ex-wife of multimillionaire Stanley Lathrope III, who had recently been elected governor of the State of New York. He had always heard vague rumors about Mrs. Lathrope and the ambassador, but he had never been able to get anything on them. Until tonight. He almost danced a jig. Man, it felt good to be back in the game. Soon, he had more names and pictures. He had a shot of the apartment, a picture of the doorman, but most important he had gotten the money shot, a great snap of the dead man's face as the stretcher went by. The only picture he had not been able to get was one of Mrs. Lathrope, but they could pull one at the paper. They kept photographs of every famous person on file, in case of sudden death or sudden infamy, whichever came first.

Tonight Sidney was king, on top of the world. He had been thrown a piece of raw meat and he had grabbed it right from under the noses of the other poor schmucks and was moving with it. And before the ambulance had reached the hospital, Sidney was on the phone in the lobby haggling in a low voice with an editor over how much money he could get for the story and the pictures. After he had held him up for as much as he could manage, the editor still wanted more than the facts. "Don't you have anything else I can use? I want intimate stuff, eyewitness accounts; can you get me that? Do you have anybody?"

Sidney thought fast. He noticed the doorman he had interviewed briefly earlier talking to a few residents. "The doorman says he was the first one in the apartment. He might give us something—for a price."

"All right. Just get it. Find out what the dame had on, were they dressed, did he find them in bed."

"He claims they were in the living room."

"Yeah, well, explain to him how much more the story is worth if he can suddenly remember he found them in the sack."

"How high can I go?"

"Up to fifteen—just get it."

Sidney, still looking at the doorman, said, "I'll get it. Don't worry. Don't I always?"

"And Sidney . . . get him to sign. I need it to cover my ass. I won't use it unless he *signs*."

"Yeah, right."

Sidney opened his pad and went over to the doorman.

"Mr. O'Connell, could I talk to you in private? It's pretty important."

"Yes, sir."

The doorman came over and Sidney flashed him a phony press ID from *The New York Times*. "Mr. O'Connell, my boss is on the phone waiting and I need to recheck a few facts, make sure I got everything right. Your name is Michael O'Connell and you were the first person to arrive at the scene, is that right?"

The doorman, large, uniformed, redheaded, was still shaken. "Yes, sir, that's right. I was in the lobby when Mrs. Lathrope buzzed, very excited like, and she was yelling for help."

"And then what happened?"

"Well, sir, I got up there as fast as I could, ran down the hall to her apartment. And when I got there the door was open so I ran in."

Sidney held up his hand. "Wait. Let me get this straight. When you got there, the door was open and you ran into the bedroom."

"No, sir, it was the living room, and then I saw Mr. Rosemond slumped over on the sofa."

Sidney looked up in surprise. "In the living room? You said bedroom before. Are you sure they were not still in the bedroom?"

The doorman looked hard at him. "No, sir, I never said bedroom. So, I helped Mrs. Lathrope lay him down on the floor."

"Wait." Sidney checked over his notes. "Yes, here it is. You said the bedroom door was wide open and you ran in."

"Well, I don't remember saying that . . . but they were definitely—"

"I see, but the bedroom door was open, wasn't it?"

"Well, I didn't notice. Might have been but I don't recall, sir."

Sidney smiled sympathetically. "Of course, you can't remember every little detail; who could, for Christ sakes? I imagine Mrs. Lathrope was pretty upset."

"Oh, yes, sir, she was!"

"What did she say?"

"She just kept saying, 'Oh, my God' . . . things like that."

"I see, yeah, when people are upset, they get confused. How in the hell could people expect you to remember every little detail, for Christ sakes, right? Let me ask you this. Is there the slightest possibility that he was in the bedroom and the open door you remember was the *bedroom* door? Couldn't that be possible, that in the excitement you forgot? It would certainly be a reasonable mistake."

"Why are you back on that? I wouldn't lie about a thing like that. Mrs. Lathrope and I lifted him off the couch and put him on the floor and she loosened his tie—I remember that. If you don't believe me, you can ask Mrs. Lathrope."

Sidney backed off. "Oh, no, we wouldn't want to bother her now. She was probably so upset she's not going to remember if he was in the bedroom, in the living room, or where the hell he was. You might not even remember that you ran into the bedroom; people get mixed up all the time. I cover these things and—"

He had pushed too far. O'Connell stiffened. "Look, I don't know what you're trying to pull, but he was in the living room and that's that."

"Hey, OK, OK. Have it your way. Whatever you say."

Then he sighed, shook his head, and slowly closed his notebook. "That's too bad . . . you can't remember, you being the first one on the scene. But, hey, look, it don't matter to me. It's just that my boss was willing to hand out a big hunk of change for a firsthand, eyewitness account. You got kids?"

The doorman said, "Kids? Yes, sir, I got six."

"I thought so. I just hate like hell to see them lose out on this deal. A thousand dollars is a lot of money. I just hate to see you lose it, that's all."

The doorman frowned. "What are you talking about?"

Sidney looked around and lowered his voice. "I'm talking about a thousand dollars. Tax-free. I've got it right here in my pocket . . . yours if you want it."

The doorman looked confused.

Sidney quickly glanced around the lobby and said, "Come over here with me for a minute," and took the doorman around the corner. He turned his back and pulled out ten brand-new hundred-dollar bills, as if they were dirty postcards. "Here, take it. You found him in the bedroom, so what? What the hell difference does it make now? The guy's dead, for Christ sakes, he don't care."

The doorman looked at the money. Then he said, "But he was a nice man. And he was in the living room."

Sidney was getting frustrated. "Look, my boss might even go up to twelve hundred."

Then Sidney saw what he had been looking for, working for: little beads of perspiration began to pop out on the doorman's forehead.

"Oh, hell . . . as a matter of fact, I know he'll go as high as fifteen hundred. You're in the catbird seat, man, the only eyewitness, you have him by the balls. That's a lot of money; you can't afford not to take it. Come on, don't be a chump. Can't you use the money?"

"It's not that I can't use the money." The doorman took his handkerchief out, took his hat off, and wiped his brow. "It's just, I don't think I can lie like that."

"Hell, it's not really lying. For all you know, it probably did happen that way, you just don't remember. Besides, you're not hurting anybody. Who's to hurt?"

"No, I don't think I could. I couldn't take the money for something—"

"Well, that's a damn shame. I bust my balls trying to do you a favor and you're too dumb to appreciate it. Don't say I didn't try."

Sidney put the money back in his pocket, slowly, and walked away from the doorman. Then he stopped for a moment and came back. "Look, I don't know why I'm doing this, goddamn it, but I'm going to tell you something that could cost me my job, you understand?"

He glanced around and spoke as if in confidence. "Listen, the truth is, my boss don't even need you. He's gonna write it the way he wants it and what you say or don't say don't make a shitload of difference one way or the other. See, it ain't no skin off my teeth if he wants to give away his money, I just hate to see you turn down a chance of a lifetime . . . if not for you, for your kids. Don't be a chump. He's got plenty, he won't even miss it. Come on . . . take it . . ."

The doorman swallowed hard. "What would I have to do?"

"Nothing, that's the beauty part—nothing. Just sign a simple paper saying you are giving us the exclusive rights to your story—there's no record of the money, and it's tax-free. This way none of the other newspapers . . . will be bothering you. This is for your protection as well as ours."

Sidney reached in his pocket and brought the money back out. "Oh, hell, make it two thousand. I'll tell him I had to bid. What he don't know won't hurt, right?"

The doorman looked as if he was about to take the money but again he hesitated. He backed away, shaking his head.

"No, I just can't. I'd never be able to face Mrs. Lathrope again; she's a lovely person."

Sidney did not miss a beat. "I can understand that. And why should you? Face her, I mean. My boss can set you up in any building in town; hell, he owns about twenty of them himself. I'll explain the situation. He'll put you on at the same salary, a little higher, even. He's a compassionate man; like I said, he's a generous guy. He don't have to pay you a dime, remember that."

Sweat was now pouring off the doorman's face.

"I'll make it easier for you. We won't even use your name. I'll just say 'an unidentified witness,' OK? Will that make it easier for you?"

"You won't use my name?"

"Give you my word on it."

Sidney looked at his watch. "Look, pal, I'm not trying to rush you but I'm on deadline. I gotta run. Yes or no?"

The doorman made no move.

He pushed the money at him. "Here, take it! I'm not gonna let you blow this chance." He slammed the money into the doorman's hand. "Put it in your pocket, sign right here, I'm gone, you're rich, nobody's hurt."

The doorman took the pen in a daze. "If you're not gonna use my name, why do I have to sign?"

"It's nothing, don't worry about it, just an in-house deal. It's filed for legal reasons. Nobody ever sees it. You don't have a thing to worry about. Trust me—I wouldn't steer you wrong."

As the doorman was signing, Sidney kept talking. "You're gonna thank me for this. Believe me, working guys got to stick together, right? Right?"

As soon as the last *l* in O'Connell was written, Sidney grabbed the paper and ran. He called over his shoulder, "Thanks, pal, you won't regret this."

The doorman called, "Are you sure you won't—"

But Sidney was out the door. When he reached the editor's office, he handed over the signed paper.

"Here it is. But it wasn't easy. That greedy mick held us up for twenty-five."

The editor opened a drawer, and pulled out the cash. "If I find out there isn't a doorman named O'Connell, you are dead meat, Sidney."

Sidney looked indignant. "What, don't you trust me? I could have held you up for three with a story like this. You think I would try and skim off you? You're like a father to me."

The editor waved him away. "Yeah, yeah, get out of here, you creep."

Sidney laughed and walked out the door. He was too high to go to bed so he hit a bar or two and the sun was coming up just as he reached the hotel. The world looked swell to him today. He even noticed the flowers in the window boxes. Were they always there? By the time he reached his room he was tired and could finally get some real sleep.

Not more than three minutes after Capello had drifted off, fat stacks of newspapers were being tossed off the backs of trucks all over town. You could almost hear the front page shout up from the sidewalk. To a few readers, the families and friends of the two parties involved, the headline and photographs would seem as brutal and heartless as a man exposing himself to children on a playground. To others, strangers hurrying by on their way to work, it was just another of the morning's entertainments, a slight jolt, an eye-opener, a sudden rush like a cup of good, strong coffee to help get the day started.

ROSEMOND DIES IN LOVE NEST!

Nobel peace prize–winner and United States ambassador Arthur Rosemond died suddenly last evening in the bed of his longtime mistress, Mrs. Pamela Lathrope, socialite ex-wife of Governor Stanley Lathrope.

Michael J. O'Connell, doorman at the swank East

Side Beekman Towers hotel, told this reporter in an exclusive interview that last evening at about 10:40 he received an urgent call from Mrs. Lathrope's apartment. When he reached the apartment, the door was open and he ran into the bedroom, where he found the scantily clad Mrs. Lathrope, hysterical with grief, leaning over the stricken Rosemond, O'Connell said.

O'Connell confirmed that Rosemond had been a frequent visitor to the Lathrope suite. O'Connell, still visibly upset from witnessing the night's tragedy, shook his head in sorrow. "He was a nice man but I guess he went out the way most men would want to."

Mrs. Arthur Rosemond was reached at the couple's home in Pound Ridge, New York, and informed of her husband's death.

Moving Up

New York City
1973

After Dena took the job at the local station in New York, she worked for three long years, smiling and nodding at the male cohost of the morning show with the bad wig, and interviewing authors of books about child rearing, interior decorating, and cooking, three subjects in which she had absolutely no interest. Finally, she landed what she wanted, and became cohostess of the network's morning show. It had been an easy transition. Still, although it was network, she found herself sitting, smiling and nodding at another male cohost with another bad hairpiece and doing more or less the same sort of interviews as before.

It was the best job most women could expect at the time and most would have been satisfied. But she had her eye on the new, hourlong prime-time evening news show that her old boss, Ira Wallace, had created and was now producing. Just as Sandy had predicted, there was pressure on the network to use a woman. Soon Sandy talked the network into letting her do several interviews on the evening show. Although they were fluff pieces used in between hard news, she was good at it and she was meeting some interesting and important people.

And yet, after a year, she continued to be thought of as

nothing more than a pretty girl who could fill in and handle a few lightweight interviews. Wallace or any other producer was not ready to assign serious, hard-hitting, news-making interviews to any woman. She knew if she was going to ever get one, she would have to go out and get it herself.

She spent weeks searching, and then one day found her man. Everybody suspected that when Senator Orville Bosley switched political parties and became a Democrat, he was positioning himself for something big, maybe the vice presidency. The press were curious. Reporters had tried in vain to get to him, but he was, uncharacteristically, very discreet and not granting interviews. Ever since Woodward and Bernstein and the Watergate investigations had started, politicians were suddenly leery of reporters and started to turn down many interviews. Luckily for Dena, Bosley thought he was God's gift to women. Dena thought him a complete and pompous ass, and right up her alley.

She found out he would be at a reception for newly elected Democratic senators and congressmen at the Shoreham Hotel in Washington. That afternoon, she took the train to Washington and that night Dena timed her entrance for about an hour after it had started. She arrived alone, wearing a long black dress with a slit up the side. She knew her legs and her hair were her best features. The only jewelry she wore was a gold choker around her neck. She did not want to look like a senator's wife and she didn't.

Bosley was over in the corner of the room surrounded, as usual, by a group of men who all had on the same suit and tie. He looked to be puffed up with his usual macho self-importance and was holding forth on trade policy when he glanced up.

She stood in the doorway, long enough to stop conversation, then walked straight through the crowd toward Bosley. People stepped aside like the parting of the Red Sea and she did not stop until she was standing in front of him. Her hair was parted on one side and when she turned her head slightly as she spoke, it fell forward, enough to intrigue him. She looked him directly in the eyes, smiled, and said, "So, Senator, I hear you and I smoke the same brand of cigar."

Three weeks later he was sitting across from her in the studio with a microphone around his neck, preparing to give his first major interview since switching parties. Ira Wallace was impressed. The regular male anchors were furious Dena had been the one to rope him in and hoped she would fall flat on her Scandinavian face. But the viewing audience at home did not see all the eyes behind the scenes or know that up in the booth they were focused on her as if she were about to jump off a tall building. All the audience saw was this nice-looking young woman in a simple, neat red and black wool suit, with huge, clear blue eyes and a peaches-and-cream complexion, who seemed, when they began, as calm and composed as if she were in her own living room chatting with an old friend. She smiled at her guest and appeared to hang on every word he was saying. She looked sympathetic when he told her about growing up in the Depression and having to eat pancakes for an entire year. She read a quote from one of his grammar school teachers, saying, "Orville was always a leader, even as a boy. I knew he would do well." They laughed over a photograph they flashed on the screen of little Orville in tattered overalls. After he was completely relaxed, she said with a smile, "Senator, people have said that even though you are a Democrat, your voting record is . . . actually, more like a conservative Republican's. Don't you feel it would be fair to inform your Democratic constituency that, while your party has changed, your position has remained the same?"

Bosley was caught off guard. He thought he would go on talking about his poor childhood and how he had worked his way through college picking cotton and digging ditches and he began to stutter.

"Well, uh . . . I think that charge is completely unfounded. Everybody who knows me and knows my voting record . . ."

Dena knew his record cold and she sat back and drew out his position, issue by issue. She was ready for him, carefully prepped by Ira's team of researchers. When he had finished one, she proceeded to cite his every vote on that and eventually every issue he mentioned, chapter and verse, with the efficiency of a machine gun. The male interviewers' hopes for her demise slowly faded. His voting record contradicted everything he had just said. She had busted him big time and she had done it in prime time on network television.

It had been a tightrope to walk. She had to look good, be

charming, have her facts ready, and yet make it seem as if they were almost a surprise to her as well. And she had done so in less than ten minutes.

After the director had called, "Off the air," Dena had the feeling she had just scored a touchdown at the last minute.

As she was being escorted off the studio floor, being congratulated by a pleased Ira Wallace, and by Sandy, she glanced back at Bosley. It was only a second, but long enough to see his face. He sat there, completely devastated by what had just happened to him.

A week later when she read that after the interview Bosley probably would not get enough votes to be reelected, let alone make a vice-presidential candidate, a wave of guilt flooded over her. She realized what she had done and understood even more now just how powerful the medium she worked in was. But it was too late. She could not look back, not now; she had to keep moving forward. Ira had hinted that if she played her cards right, in a year or so she might be the first female to be offered a permanent spot on the show.

She was definitely on the way up. Yet there had been a price to pay for Bosley—and for her. His career was wrecked and she started to wake up in the middle of the night with terrible stomachaches.

A Question for Macky

Aunt Elner was a roly-poly farm woman, soft as a pillow, with the sweet smile of a child. Her hair was gray but her eyes and her smile were still young. And she always smelled like a wedding cake, an effect caused by the Cashmere Bouquet dusting powder and the Dorothy Gray hot-weather cologne she wore, even in the winter, and her whole house smelled sweet. She had never had children of her own but she loved them and they loved her. Every Easter she would cut a pattern of a big pair of bunny feet out of a piece of cardboard and make bunny prints out of her talcum powder as if the Easter Bunny had hopped through her front door all the way through the house and on out the back door. Children would come from all over the neighborhood and find the little Easter baskets she said that the Bunny had left for them.

It was 11:00 A.M. and Norma was just thinking about what to fix for lunch when Aunt Elner called. "Is Macky there?"

"Yes. He's out in the yard."

"Tell him to come to the phone, will you, honey?"

"Do you want him to call you?"

"No, yell out there and tell him to come to the phone. I'll hold on. I've got something important I need to ask him."

"OK."

Norma went to the back door and called to Macky, who was digging in the red-worm bed. "Macky, you have a phone call."

"Who is it?"

"Aunt Elner."

"Tell her I'll call her in just a minute."

"She wants you to come to the phone right now."

"Find out what she wants."

"Aunt Elner, he says to ask you what you need."

"Well . . . I need to talk to him about something."

"All right. Hold on. Macky, she needs to talk to you right now."

"OK." Macky got up and brushed the dirt off his hands. He came into the kitchen and headed for the phone. Norma stopped him before he reached it. "Macky, wash your hands. I don't want worm germs on my phone!" He went to the kitchen sink.

"What does she want, do you know?"

"No, I don't. But it sounds urgent." Norma pulled a paper towel off her rack and handed it to him. "Here, use this." He dried his hands and picked up the phone. "Hi, what's up?"

Aunt Elner said, "Is Norma standing there?"

"Yes."

"Well, don't let on something is wrong, but I need you to come over here and look at what somebody put in my door and tell me what you think."

"All right."

"And look and see if there's anything stuck in your front door and if there is, get it and don't let Norma see it, she's nervous enough as it is."

"Okeydokey."

Aunt Elner was standing on her front porch waiting for him when he came walking up. "Was there anything in your door?"

Macky shook his head. "Nope, not a thing." And stepped over her cat, Sonny, who was lying on the sidewalk.

"Well, would you look what somebody put in mine? Take a look at this and tell me what you think about it." She handed him a bright, strawberry-colored piece of paper with bold black print:

BEWARE—ARMAGEDDON IS AT HAND. THE END OF THE WORLD IS IMMINENT! REVEREND CLAY STILES HAS HAD

A REVELATION FROM GOD REGARDING THE END OF THE WORLD. THIS INFORMATION IS BASED UPON IN-SIGHTS. INSIGHTS INTO THE FINAL EVENTS THAT HE RECEIVED FROM GOD THIS PAST APRIL AND HAS THE EXACT DATE. FOR FURTHER INFORMATION CALL 555-2312 FOR FREE BOOKLET.

Aunt Elner said, "What do you think, should I give him a call?"

"No, Aunt Elner, he's just some quack trying to get money."

"Do you think so? It says 'free.' "

"They just want you on their mailing list, to ask for donations."

"So I shouldn't worry that he knows what he's talking about?"

"He's just some idiot. Throw it out. It's just a scam."

"Oh, well, it's a good thing I called you first because I sure don't want to get on another person's mailing list, even if he is a preacher. I get enough junk mail as it is."

"That's right."

"Now that you're here, sit on the porch with me for a little while. I'll make some tea."

He walked up the stairs. "All right, I'll have some tea with you."

Macky sat in the yellow-and-white-polka-dotted glider and pushed himself back and forth, waiting. Aunt Elner came back and handed him his glass. "Let me ask you this, Macky."

"What?"

Aunt Elner sat down. "Would you want to know when the end of the world was coming? I don't know if I'd want to know; I think I'd just as soon wait and be surprised, wouldn't you?"

"I guess so."

"Is that sweet enough?"

"Fine."

"What would you do if you knew for sure the end of the world was coming next Tuesday?"

Macky thought a moment. "Oh, I don't know. Nothing, I guess. What could you do, really? What would you do?"

"I wouldn't clean house for a week, I'll tell you that."

"Maybe I'd go to Florida," Macky said. "Or something."

"I think it's better that none of us know when it's coming, or if it's coming in our lifetime. That way life's more of a gamble, don't you think?"

"Oh, yeah."

"People like to gamble, don't they? I like to play bingo. Not knowing when it's coming keeps us on our toes, keeps us guessing."

Macky agreed.

After a while, Aunt Elner said, "Do you think it's gonna rain?"

Macky leaned out and looked up. "God, I hope not. I want to go out on the lake this afternoon."

"What would make you want to go to Florida?"

"What?"

"If you knew the end of the world was coming."

"Oh, I don't know. Guess I'd like to get in some good fishing before I go."

"But, Macky, you don't want to be around a bunch of strangers in Florida when the end comes, do you?"

"Well . . ."

"I think it would be better not to travel at a time like that. Best to be in your own home, don't you think?"

"I guess so."

"You'd want Norma and Linda to be there, in your family group, wouldn't you? You know Norma would not go to Florida, you know her; she'd want to get the house spick and span. They say that will be Judgment Day. You want to be where you're supposed to be, so He wouldn't have to come looking for you. I think we better stay right where we are."

"I suppose you're right, Aunt Elner." He stood up. "Well, I guess I'd better head on back home, I've got some more stuff Norma wants me to take care of."

"OK, honey. I appreciate your coming over."

He went down the steps and Aunt Elner called after him. "Don't tell Norma what we were talking about. The end of the world and all that!"

"I won't," he said as he waved good-bye over his shoulder, and stepped over Sonny, who never moved.

A Dilemma for Dena

Dena had met the Reverend Charles Hamilton at several charity fund-raisers and had been surprised. Every year Reverend Hamilton was named as one of the ten most admired men in America. His church in New York was not the largest but he had become well known nationally because of his books. Although he and his wife, Peggy, had both come from humble beginnings, a small town in rural Kentucky, over the years he had become known as the man who swayed and inspired millions and counseled presidents. Still, apart from his popular public appearances, he tried to keep a low profile in his personal life. Dena had no special interest in preachers, but found the Hamiltons to be exactly what they seemed to be, two extremely nice and genuinely kind people.

At first glance Peggy Hamilton would not strike you as being beautiful, but she was one of those women who, after you spent some time with her, became more and more attractive and then, suddenly, became beautiful. When she talked she made you feel like you were the most important person in the room. Although she usually had only men friends Dena genuinely liked Mrs. Hamilton.

For years now everyone had sought a personal interview with the Hamiltons and they had declined; but, for a reason dear to their hearts, they agreed to give Dena an interview in their home. Years ago, Peggy had quietly founded Children, Inc., an organization that had escalated into a worldwide operation and fed and clothed children. But contributions had slowed and Dena promised to devote half the interview, which would be aired on the network, to promoting Children, Inc., and the other talking about their family life, their marriage, and the secret of its success. Dena was excited. She knew they had picked her to do it because they liked her and it couldn't have come at a better time. She knew Ira Wallace was getting closer and closer to a decision about possibly adding her to the major news show, and this would be another important interview she had brought in on her own.

Four days before the taping, Wallace called Dena into his office. When she walked in, she saw three men, two of whom she recognized as staff researchers. The third person, a ferret-faced man, was a stranger. For once, Wallace, who never bothered with introductions, said, "Dena Nordstrom, say hello to Sidney Capello; he just made you a star, kid!"

Dena glanced at the man, who managed some sort of half smile in her direction. She nodded. "How do you do."

Dena sat down. Ira looked like a wolf licking his chops after a serving of Little Red Riding Hood. He was pleased over something.

"I didn't tell you this because I didn't want to worry you but I've had my best people on this for weeks . . . and they kept coming up with zero, zilch, nothing. That son of a bitch was as clean as a baby's ass."

Dena was confused. "Who . . . are you talking about?"

"Who? Your reverend friend, Mr. White Bread. For the piece, whattaya think, we couldn't find a thing, not even a parking ticket, for Christ sakes. But I didn't give up. I knew this was probably the only chance we'd get to nail him and we're gonna blow that dumb redneck right out of the water and we got him—thanks to Sidney here. I knew there had to be some crack we could get into and Sidney found it. Not Hamilton but the next best thing—better, if it's handled right. The little wife, and we've got it, one hundred percent, on paper, sworn witness."

Dena felt a knot in her stomach, anticipating what might be coming next.

"Sidney went down to Kentucky to nose around and he scored big. Before Little Miss Holier Than Thou married Hamilton, she went and got herself knocked up. Not only that, she gave the kid away and hasn't seen it since."

"Oh, no, Ira, I can't believe that," Dena said, stunned. "Where did this come from?"

Wallace picked up a paper. "Straight from the horse's mouth, straight from the hayseed who knocked her up. I can't wait. You'll schmooze them along, get them going on that happy marriage routine, and then you slip it in. 'So, Mrs. Hamilton, how long has it been since you've seen your first child?' She'll be confused, she'll say whatever the name of her first kid is with Hamilton, and you'll give her that innocent look of yours and say, 'No, I was speaking of your daughter that, according to our records, was born in 1952, and you gave up for adoption.' Then all we do is sit back and watch them sweat and wiggle like worms on a hook. Oh, I love it."

Dena took a deep breath and sat back in her chair, feeling ill. "Does Charles Hamilton know about this?"

"Who knows, who cares? If not, more the better . . . we can see the great phony-baloney Christian marriage blow up right on TV. Biggest scoop of the year and you got it, thrown right in your lap; do I take care of you or what?"

Wallace was waiting for Dena to thank him for the scoop but she was not responding the way he thought she would.

"Ira, I know these people personally. They gave me this interview as a favor. They're going to think I set them up just to trap them."

Wallace looked at the others. "And what bait, right?"

They laughed. Wallace looked at Capello. "And don't let that innocent, corn-fed mug of hers fool you, Sid. She has the instincts of a killer. She sits there, smiling, batting those baby blues at them, they start to relax, and then, *wham*—straight for the jugular. They'll never know what hit them."

"Thanks, Ira, just what I always wanted to be, a killer," Dena said. "Could I talk to you alone, please?"

Wallace was getting concerned now. "Yeah, sure. Boys, take a hike."

The three men got up and left the room. Wallace looked at her.

"What's the matter with you? Do you know how lucky we were to get this thing? Capello could have taken it and run with it and sold it for a fortune. I had to promise the dago bastard to make him an associate producer but I got the story for you. You should be grateful."

"I am. It's not that, it's just that . . ."

Wallace was impatient. "What, just what?"

Dena leaned forward and looked him in the eye. "Why do it?"

"Hire him? I had to, he could have sold it right out from under us."

"No, why do the story?"

"What?"

"I said: Why do it?"

"Are you kidding me? It's news."

"Is it? I'm not sure. It seems so . . . I don't know, so unnecessary. I mean, shouldn't we at least let her know it's coming, and not just ambush her on the air?"

"Listen, we are handing these jerks millions of dollars of free advertising for Christ sakes and you're gonna let them control the interview? Hell, no. We ask them what we damn well want to, and when we want to; this is a free country."

"I know, but—"

"What's with you? All of a sudden you're Mary Tyler Moore? You've asked the hard questions before. Look how you nailed Bosley and the others. They're all still screaming, for Christ sakes, not to mention the ratings."

"Yes, but Ira, they were crooks and frauds, cheating the government. They deserved to be exposed. But Peggy Hamilton is a sweet lady who never hurt anybody. There's a big difference here. Besides, what's the point?"

"What's the point, what's the *point*? The point is people have a right to know what phonies they are. Now, come on, be happy. You got you the biggest story of the season, maybe the year, thrown right in your lap."

"Ira, do you have any idea what kind of position you are putting me in? And if I do ask the question, people will hate me for doing it."

"Oh, please, what, are you kidding? People are gonna love you. It makes them feel better about their own crappy little lives. You're gonna be a hero . . . the boys upstairs are gonna love you. Your fans are gonna love you for exposing the truth about these two. Don't feel sorry for them, they've got plenty of money. Grow up, they're not the poor, innocent people you think they are."

"What makes you so sure?"

"I know, believe me, they're no different than any other schlemiels out there grabbing. All this fund-raising for kids— fund-raising for the Hamiltons, probably."

"Ira, don't make me do this. They have children. Think how this is going to affect them. And whether or not you believe it, they have done an awful lot of good for people, people respect him."

"For Christ sakes, don't tell me you fall for all that religious hype; the man's a hypocrite."

"It's his wife you're talking about. What if she did make a mistake? She's human. Haven't you ever made a mistake?"

"Sure, but I'm not passing myself off on the public as some kind of saint. Let me tell you something. You want to be a do-gooder? This is your chance. That's what's wrong with this country . . . people need to know the truth about these bums. That's your job. You want to live in a dream world, go to Disneyland."

"I don't think they're bums."

"Well, whatever, just ask the questions. I know what I'm doing; you're gonna thank me. Now, get out of here."

Wallace waved a hand to dismiss her, picked up a rundown of the next show, and started working on it. Dena sat for a moment, went to the door, and turned back. "Why do you hate Charles Hamilton so much?"

Wallace looked up at her, genuinely surprised. "Hate him? I don't hate him. Hell, I don't even know him."

❖ ❖ ❖

Dena went to lunch but she couldn't eat. Ira had taught her well, and she knew it was not the answer Peggy Hamilton would give that could hurt her, it was the question. Once asked, it would open a floodgate of inquiries. And if she refused to ask it, she could destroy her chances of getting the network job. Nobody crossed Ira Wallace—if you did, you were out. She had worked all these years to get to this point, and now this. Ira had been right about one thing. She was certainly not a saint. She had smiled and charmed people into interviews before and suddenly surprised them on camera with a fact that Wallace's people had given her. She had been coached to get around her toughest interview of the year by smiling and saying, "I know our producers signed an agreement not to discuss on camera the assault and battery charges your first wife filed against you in 1964, and I respect that, but how do you feel about violence in general?" She knew the tricks and she was good at them. Too good. Ira knew she could do this kind of interview without batting an eye, but something was wrong. This was different. Maybe if they had uncovered something criminal or scandalous about Charles Hamilton, she might feel differently, but this was his wife they were going after. She also knew that Ira had started doing some pretty low stuff to get ratings, but this was a new low, even for him. In less than a year Ira Wallace had brought their news department from third place up to second, and now he seemed obsessed with beating out the first-place network no matter what he had to do.

Dena had been back from lunch a few minutes when Sidney Capello, without knocking, walked in her office and went over and flopped down as if he belonged there. Dena looked at him with the same revulsion as if a snake had suddenly crawled into her office and curled up on her red leather couch.

Capello did not bother to look at her. "Ira wants you to run your questions by me, make sure you get it right." His eyes darted around the room as if he were looking for flying insects. "You know, the knocked-up preacher's wife. He wants us to work together."

Dena stood up. "Oh, no. You and I are not working together on anything, you creep."

Capello's eyes darted in her direction. "Hey, I don't have to take any lip off any bimbo. You don't want to work with me, that's your problem, sister."

Dena did not hear the last sentence; she was storming down the hall. She barged into Wallace's office. "Did you tell that slimebag he could work with me?"

Wallace was, as usual, on the phone and looked at her. He put his hand up and motioned for her to sit down. Dena sat down and waited. She was so mad her stomach started to hurt again. She took some deep breaths, trying to cool off. Wallace put the phone down. "Now, which slimebag are you talking about?"

"Sidney Capello." Dena tried to remain calm. "Did you tell him he could work with me?"

Wallace seemed puzzled that there was a problem. "Yeah, so? I told you—I had to make him associate producer."

"Ira, you may be able to be in the same room with him but I can't. It's bad enough I have to work with those other two cretins you call researchers but this guy is disgusting."

"All right, whatever. I thought he could help you out, that's all. You two have a personality problem, OK, no big deal. We can work it out, problem solved. Anything else?"

"How can you trust him, Ira? He may be lying about the Hamilton piece. He could have made it up."

"He ain't lying. We double checked. He may be a slimebag, but he's an expert slimebag. You may not like what he comes up with but he's the best. Trust him? Please, he'd sell his grandmother for fish bait if he thought he could make a dime, but that don't mean he ain't good."

"How can you work with somebody you don't trust? I don't understand."

"Hey! What's trust got to do with work? This ain't no popularity contest we're in; you don't have to trust someone to do business."

"Well, maybe you don't, but I do, and I just don't feel right about asking that question."

"Not that again. You know, kid, you disappoint me, as hard as I worked for this. And you, angling for a permanent network shot."

"I know, Ira, but I know Peggy Hamilton and she trusts me, and her husband does, too. That's how I got the interview in the first place."

"Let me ask you something. She knows what kind of business you're in, right?"

"Yes, but . . ."

"So business is business. They know that. Why are they doing the interview in the first place? To hustle money, right? They know the score. You're just doing your job, they use you, you use them, business. Come on, you know better than this. You start thinking like a sap, you're gonna have your hat handed to you and be on the first bus back to Hicksville Springs."

Dena flinched. Wallace checked his watch and leaned back in his chair. "Let me tell you a little story. My grandfather came to this country, didn't have a dime. He had to hustle on the streets all his life. He sold buttons from door to door; he worked eighteen, nineteen hours a day. But when he died he had saved fifteen thousand dollars and he paid my way through NYU. Do you know how many buttons he had to sell? One day I was four years old, he took me in the kitchen and stood me up on a chair. He held out his arms to me and said, 'Jump.' I was scared. He said, 'Come on, jump. I'll catch you.' I still didn't jump. He says, 'What's the matter, don't you trust me? I'm your grandfather.' So I jumped—and *wham,* I hit the floor, flat on my kisser. He looks down at me and he says, 'That's your first lesson in business, boy. Don't ever trust nobody. Not even me, don't ever forget it.'" Wallace almost had tears in his eyes. "God, I loved that man and I'll tell you something else. I never forgot it."

"That's the difference between you and me, Ira," Dena said. "When I was little my grandfather did the same thing to me—only he caught me."

Wallace said, "Yeah, well, don't kid yourself. He didn't do you no favor."

Taking a Chance

New York City
1973

Dena sat in her living room at four-thirty Saturday morning eating a plate of Stouffer's frozen macaroni and cheese. She had been up all night struggling with herself about the Hamilton piece, going back and forth trying to figure out what to do. Making a decision about her career had never been hard for her. In the past she had always been crystal clear about her goal and had kept her eye on it even if it had meant leaving people in the dust. She had quit jobs overnight to take a better one and never looked back. But this was different. There was something about this interview that made her deeply uneasy, scared her, even. It didn't have anything to do with religion or because she thought the Hamiltons would hate her; she could always lie and say that her producers had told her that everyone knew about the first child. It was something else she could not put her finger on. Was she afraid that if she crossed the Hamiltons she would never be able to get an interview or be accepted by the right people again? Or was it simply because Peggy Hamilton was a woman and seemed so vulnerable, so defenseless? Was it because she had loathed Sidney Capello on sight? Why did she feel so threatened? She went into the bathroom and turned on the light and glanced up at herself in the mirror and was startled at what she saw. For a split second it could have been her mother's face looking back at her.

At eight she picked up the phone. The Hamiltons' youngest son answered and went to get his mother. Peggy Hamilton came to the phone right away with a cheerful, warm "Hello."

"Mrs. Hamilton, it's Dena Nordstrom."

"Well, hello again."

"Mrs. Hamilton, listen, about the interview. Would it be possible for us to meet, just you and I? It's really important. I need to talk to you."

"Of course. Come on over anytime. Or should I come to your office on Monday?"

"No, it would be better if we met somewhere else before then."

Dena had suggested Laurent on Fifty-sixth because it was a lovely, old-world place and she was positive Ira or anyone Ira knew would not be there. That afternoon, she showed up at the restaurant ten minutes early and asked for a table in the back. Dena had on a scarf and sunglasses, feeling as if she were in a bad Joan Crawford movie. At ten minutes after four, she was a nervous wreck, had already smoked half a pack of cigarettes, and had put away two screwdrivers, when Peggy Hamilton came in. She smiled.

"Oh, there you are. I almost didn't recognize you in those sunglasses. Sorry I'm late. Will you forgive me?"

"Of course, I just got here myself. Would you like a drink . . . or tea or coffee? I'm having a drink."

"I guess I'll just have a cup of tea."

Dena called the waiter over and ordered the tea and another drink for herself. Her hands were shaking as she tried to light another cigarette.

"Are you all right? Is there something bothering you? You sounded a little upset on the phone."

Dena had just lit the filter end of her cigarette.

"Well, yes, there is. I think I really don't know how to ask you this, it's sort of personal. Well, actually, it's very personal but . . ."

Peggy Hamilton waited, but Dena, who had rehearsed the speech twenty times, suddenly got cold feet.

"I know we don't know each other well, but . . . I felt that, oh God, I don't know if I can . . ."

The older woman reached over and took her hand. "Dena, whatever is bothering you, it is always good if you just talk to someone, and you know anything you say will be confidential. You know you can trust me, don't you?"

After the waiter had gone, Dena was still debating whether or not to go through with it.

"If I can help you with something, I'll be happy to try. You know Charles and I think the world of you."

Dena said, "That's the trouble. Oh, Jesus—excuse me—but this is harder than I thought it was going to be." She stopped. "Uh . . . well, the thing is . . . it's not about me, it's about you."

"Me?"

"Yes. But first of all, I want you to know that I didn't know about this until yesterday. But . . . when we do an interview, sometimes the people on staff do some research to help with questions and all, and . . . I don't trust this guy that my boss hired, so I need to know if it is true or not, or, if there is some sort of mistake, well, I need to know."

"What is it?"

"My boss wants me to ask you about the fact that you . . . or at least they think you might have . . . had a baby before you married."

One look at the fear in Peggy Hamilton's eyes and Dena knew the answer. The color drained out of her face.

"Oh, God, Peggy, I was hoping they were wrong. I am so sorry, if you only knew, I wasn't even supposed to ask you about this until we got on the air. But I just couldn't."

"How did you find out?"

"It wasn't me, Peggy, I promise you. Some lowlife that does this kind of thing went to your hometown in Kentucky, started asking questions, trying to find some dirt on you two, and found this guy who claims to be the father and was willing to swear to it."

Peggy Hamilton was devastated. "Why, why would he tell anybody that now, why after all these years?"

"Maybe he thought he could get something out of it. Maybe it's his one chance at fame, maybe he was promised he could get on television. People do this kind of thing."

"I see."

"Does Charles *know* about this?"

"Yes. It's my daughter who doesn't know." She looked at Dena. "I don't understand. Why would they want to ask me about this?"

"Oh, Peggy, I don't know." Dena shook her head. "It's part of the business, I guess, to try and come up with something that might shock people. It's not just you. It's . . . oh, hell, it's because they want ratings. It's as simple as that. I feel just like a low-down, dirty dog, but all I can do is warn you, and if I don't ask you about it, it probably will come out one way or another. Once it's out they use it."

"You know, it's funny. I was always terrified that one day it would come out. I worried about it for years and now that it has, I just feel numb. I never dreamed it would happen like this. I think I will have that drink, if you don't mind."

Dena said, "Oh, please, me too, I need another." She motioned for the waiter to bring two more and pushed her drink over to Peggy Hamilton, who sipped it. Now it was her hands that were shaking.

"Peggy, I am so sorry, believe me, I tried my best to talk them out of it but I couldn't. I'm just supposed to ask the questions. I could kill Ira. It wasn't even supposed to be about you. They tried to find some scandal about Charles, but this is what they came up with."

"I see. Well, I wonder where we go from here."

"Tell me, what happened, what were the circumstances? How did you manage to keep it quiet for this long?"

"I was barely fifteen, and he was twenty-three. I was so stupid. I didn't know anything about sex. I was one of eight children and I guess I was flattered by the attention he gave me. Probably I was starved for affection. He was my uncle. He told me he loved me and that I was special, and the next thing I knew . . . It only happened once, but about a month later, I started to get sick and I had no idea what was the matter with me. The doctor came and told my father I was pregnant. I know it's hard to believe now, but we were a pretty religious family and we never talked about things like that." Her voice trailed off. "What makes this so strange is he always denied it, he said it had not been him, that I was lying. And they believed him and sent me to live with my mother's sister. I had the baby, and the next day she was gone, and there hasn't been a day since that I haven't wondered about her, wondered if she was all right. If she was happy. But I signed a paper, I gave up my rights. You don't know how hard it has been not to try and find her, but I couldn't do that to her, expose her. And now this."

She looked into the distance. "If he hurts my daughter, I don't know how I will ever be able to forgive him."

Dena was suddenly upset again. "Forgive him? I don't think you understand. This is serious. Your whole life could blow up. All the great work you and Charles have done. You should be furious!"

"Oh, believe me," Peggy said, "I am furious and I am scared to death, but I don't know what I can do about it."

Dena announced, in a voice laced with vodka and false courage, "Well, I can do something about it, by God. I'll quit, that's all. I'll tell them if they pursue this, I'll quit. I'll probably get fired anyway if they find out I told you. So I'll just walk in there Monday morning and quit."

"No, you can't do that, Dena. You said it would come out sooner or later anyway."

"Well, not by me. And if it does, deny it. Say he's lying. People will believe you and Charles over this dirtbag."

"I can't do that."

"Think about it. This is going to ruin your lives. People put you two up on a pedestal. They are not going to care who you are trying to protect. All they are going to care about is that you had a baby when you weren't married and hid it. You think people are going to forgive you? You can't let your life be ruined over one mistake that happened over twenty years ago."

Dena touched her arm. "Listen to me, Peggy: cancel the damn interview. Say you're sick, say your mother is dying, say you're dying . . . anything, just don't do it. Hire a hit man, I don't care, but do something. It's nobody's business anyway. They're not playing fair. Why should you? Peggy, don't be an idiot, you don't have to be honest with these people. Jesus Christ himself would lie over something like this!"

"I have to talk to Charles. I don't know what to do."

"I'm telling you what to do. Lie."

"But it's the truth."

"Then say you were raped."

"But I wasn't, I mean . . . I started to let him kiss me. I think it might have been my fault and I didn't say no until he—"

"What do you mean it was your fault? You were only fifteen years old. How old was this guy again?"

"Twenty-three."

Dena's eyes lit up. "That's it, Peggy, threaten him; a twenty-three-year-old man and a fifteen-year-old girl. You were a minor. That son of a bitch could go to jail for statutory rape."

"Rape?"

"Yes!"

"No. I couldn't do that."

Dena glanced over at the couple who had been shown to the next table and realized that the restaurant was beginning to seat early dinner customers. "Look, I think we better get out of here. Go home and talk to Charles."

"Dena . . . I don't know how to thank you for warning me. I'm not sure what we can do at this point but pray about it."

"Well, you can pray if you want to, but in the meantime, I'd threaten to have him arrested."

"Dena"—now Peggy Hamilton took her arm—"no matter what happens, promise me you won't quit over this. I couldn't live with that on my conscience, too."

Dena nodded. "All right, I promise."

She squeezed Dena's hand. "Thank you."

Dena waited a few minutes so no one would see them leave together. When she got up and walked through the restaurant, she found that her knees were weak and realized she was not as brave as she thought she was.

The Power Play

For the next few days at work Dena waited like an inmate sitting on death row. Would Ira call? As the time for the interview grew closer she began to get terrified, and had trouble breathing. This morning she was just about to take a Valium when the buzzer almost made her jump out of her skin.

She answered. "Yes?"

Wallace barked, "Come in here!"

As she walked down the hall her heart was pounding. This last mile could be the end of her career. She knocked lightly.

"Come in."

Wallace got up and went over and closed the door. "Sit down."

He scowled at her across the desk.

"I know this ain't gonna break your heart, but we are going to have to pull the goddamn question about the goddamn Hamilton kid."

"Why?"

"Julian Amsley won't let us go with it. He's afraid of a lawsuit."

"Why?"

Wallace slammed his fist down and yelled, "Because the goddamned corncob Capello dug up is now claiming he lied about it and it never happened. And he had the goddamned nerve to deny the goddamned story, so we have to scrap it."

Wallace continued, "Can you believe the bastard is denying it? That son of a bitch reneged on a deal. But that's what you're dealing with now, liars, cheats, bums, no-good bums. People don't have any goddamned ethics anymore."

Dena had no idea how the Hamiltons had managed to talk him into denying it, but she quickly pulled herself together and put on an act that would have made her college drama teacher proud. She looked at him with the same face she would have shown if Ira Wallace had said he had decided to become a priest.

"Are you telling me, Ira, that after all you put me through on this piece, that now I can't use it? I can't believe it . . . I just *cannot* believe it!" She stood up and started to pace the office. "Well, I don't care if Julian Amsley is the president of the network, I'm going to ask the question anyhow. It's news, for God's sake. He can't interfere with the news!"

Wallace panicked. "Do you want to get us all fired?"

"I don't care, it's the principle of the thing."

"Well, I care. It's the principle of keeping my goddamned job."

"What the hell am I supposed to do, Ira? I had planned the whole interview around it. Now I'm left with some softball piece that I have to rewrite in less than twenty-four hours."

Wallace tried to calm her. "I know, I know, but what can I do? Tell me, what do you need? How can I help?"

"So Capello is the best! He didn't even check out his source and now look what I'm left with."

"OK, OK, it was stupid." Wallace raised his hands in surrender. "Shoot me."

Dena was enjoying herself now. "Well, I can't possibly be ready by tomorrow. You'll have to cancel the interview."

"No, no, we can't do that. It's already scheduled."

"Look, Ira, I'm the one who's going to look bad, not you. I ought to let you and Capello sit your butts on camera not prepared and see how you like it."

"All right, all right, you've made your point. How can I make it up to you? You want my firstborn, take him, he's yours. Just don't go nuts on me, all right? What do you want? Tell me."

The next thing Dena said surprised her, but once said, she knew she meant it. "I want you to fire Capello's ass."

"Yeah, I should. . . . But look, I'll have three assistants at your disposal, I'll send in dinner, breakfast, I'll even pay overtime. What else can I do?"

"I told you. I want you to fire Capello."

"I can't do that. I just hired him."

"I want him fired."

"You want him fired. Get serious."

"I am serious."

"Look, even if I wanted to, which I don't, I couldn't fire him. He has a contract. We're talking money here."

"Ira, don't tell me you didn't put a loophole in that contract. You always do."

It suddenly dawned on Ira. "Hey, wait a minute, you can't tell me who to fire. Who do you think you are? You ain't got the job yet."

She leaned on his desk. "Let me put it this way. If he's not out of here in the next hour, I'm going to be too upset to do the interview, and the Hamiltons won't do it without me. Like I told you before, they like me, they trust me. And you'll be left with twenty minutes of dead air."

"Oh, come on, now, you're kidding. Aren't you? You don't want to do this to Capello. The poor guy made one lousy mistake. Have a heart. The poor slob feels bad enough. You should have heard him. He hated letting you down like that. He was almost in tears. You should have seen him."

Wallace could see that she was unmoved. Dena had a determined look he had not seen before. They sat staring at each other. After a while, Wallace said, "All right, all right, but this is frigging blackmail. I'm telling you, you are making a mistake. Capello can do you a lot of good."

"One more thing." Dena stood up. "I want to be here when you do it."

Now Wallace could not believe what he was hearing. He looked at her with a hurt expression and slowly shook his head. "What's happened to you? You used to be such a nice, sweet kid."

She did not answer.

Forty-five minutes later Capello had come back from lunch and Dena was sitting across from Sidney Capello when Wallace fired him.

Capello immediately turned on Dena. "You bitch, I'll get you for this. You just wait, you—"

Wallace came around the desk and more or less pushed him toward the door. "Yeah, yeah, yeah, we all know how tough you are, Sidney; now get the hell out of here." He shoved him out the door and slammed it behind him.

Wallace went back to his desk. "Satisfied?"

Dena smiled. "Wouldn't have missed it for the world."

As she walked down the hall she felt a surge of something that made her feel strong. For the first time in her life she felt that heady rush of power and she suddenly understood why men fought for it. It felt good, and at that moment she was glad that she was not like Peggy Hamilton. She did not have to forgive Capello.

As Wallace leaned back in his chair and relit his cigar, he was also feeling a surge. Only it was admiration, for himself, for having pegged Dena Nordstrom. Damn, she was tough. She never flinched for a second while he was firing Sidney. She had not backed down an inch from him, either. He may have made some mistakes about people in the past, but he had always suspected that behind that innocent face was someone he could use to push all those sanctimonious types over at the other network—the types that looked down on him—right out of the business. Especially their lordly newscaster, Kingsley, who Wallace would love to knock off his pedestal. Howard Kingsley had once refused to work with him, costing him a big job at Howard's network, and he had not forgotten it. He reached over and buzzed Sidney Capello's new office. Capello picked up.

"It's me, Ira."

Capello started to curse him and to issue threats and Ira said,

"Hey, hey, hold on ... hold on. I know what I said but listen to me." He yelled. "Listen, for Christ sakes! You ain't gonna sue anybody. I called to tell you not to take this thing seriously. I just needed to clear up a little temperament problem so don't get excited. We can work your contract out, no big deal. So you just won't come into the office. What's so terrible? You stay home, you send your stuff in, you get paid. She don't know the difference. You're happy, I'm happy, she's happy. I know I promised to get you in the door here, but what can I do? She hates your guts. Look, you'll get paid and at the end of the year maybe a nice bonus, OK? It'll be better in the long run. Trust me."

Capello was bitterly disappointed. This was his chance, maybe his one chance to get into big-time television and he knew it. Wallace was the only one who would ever have hired him and now, thanks to that blond bimbo, he was right back where he started. Still nothing more than a paid informant working out of some seedy hotel room. There went the office, his producer title, everything, all because of some bitch who thought she was better than everybody else. Goddamn her.

As he packed up the office he had had for only a few days, he pacified himself somewhat by reading the plaque he kept on his desk. REVENGE IS A DISH BEST SERVED COLD. He smiled.

Life is a long time.

My Hero

Two weeks after the Hamilton piece ran, Dena and almost everyone else of any prominence in television, except Ira Wallace, attended the Heart Fund dinner at the Waldorf-Astoria. The Heart Fund man of the year was Howard Kingsley, the grand old man of news broadcasting and one of the last really great newsmen in the country. He was introduced as the man whose face and voice had become the one the country depended on in any crisis for the past thirty years, to calm us down, to reassure us that all was well, or to share our sorrow. That was certainly true for Dena; his face and voice were as familiar to her as if she had known him all her life.

Kingsley was now sixty-four years old and still a handsome man, distinguished for his thoughtfulness and balance, and beautifully spoken. His acceptance speech was gracious. He thanked his wife of forty years for sticking with him through thick and thin ("mostly thick") and said that without her he most likely would have wound up selling insurance in Des Moines, Iowa. That she and his daughter, Anne, had always been "his safe harbor on the rocky and stormy sea of broadcasting." After his short speech he received a five-minute standing ovation, and as professional and sophisticated as Dena thought she was, she was thrilled to be in the same room with him.

As dinner went on she tried to figure out what he had that was so different from most of the TV people she had met. Then it came to her: integrity, that's what it was. It wasn't really anything he did or said but you just had the feeling that he was a decent and honorable man who could always be trusted to tell you the truth. He wasn't really different than most men, but in the television news business, integrity was slowly becoming a rarity, more and more like a light in the dark. Dena looked over at his wife and daughter and felt that old feeling whenever she saw a father and a daughter, a sadness tinged with envy. All she had ever seen of her father was a photograph. She was even envious of Ira Wallace's little girl. He might be one of the most despicable human beings she had ever met but at least he did adore his daughter.

After the dinner, as they were walking out, J.C. said, "By the way, we have an invitation to the reception for Kingsley upstairs."

"What reception?"

"It's a small, private reception that Jeanette Rockefeller is having for a few friends." J.C. was a fund-raiser and knew a great many people. She did not want to go.

"Why not?"

"I won't know any of them. I'm not a friend of his; he might think I'm too pushy or something."

"Oh, come on, don't be silly. Jeanette is a friend of mine. Come on."

"You go and I'll wait for you."

But J.C. would not take no for an answer and five minutes later she found herself upstairs in a suite, at a party with the heads of all three networks, including Julian Amsley, the man who ran hers. She was horrified when he looked over and saw her. Oh, God, she thought, now he's going to think I'm some gate-crasher, but he nodded pleasantly at her. After about thirty minutes of trying to hide in a corner, Dena watched Jeanette Rockefeller approach and start to pull everyone over to meet the guest of honor. Now Dena stood in line with J.C. and wanted to drop right through the floor. She watched as Howard Kingsley came closer, shaking each person's hand and saying a few words, and at last when Dena was introduced, she had an almost uncontrollable desire to curtsy. But she managed to look calm and say, "Congratulations, sir, I enjoyed your speech." Howard looked at her with a slight little smile, and with a nod of his head said, "Thank you very much, young lady." As she started to move away he said, "Oh, by the way, Miss Nordstrom, I caught the Hamilton piece. Good work. Let's have lunch sometime."

Dena managed an "Oh, thank you," just as the hostess steered forward another guest.

Had she heard right? Had he actually said, "Good work, let's have lunch," or was she hallucinating? Maybe she misunderstood; he had really said, "Bad work, hated it a bunch." J.C. was still behind her and Dena grabbed him by the arm. "Did you hear him say, 'Let's have lunch'?"

"Yes."

"Are you sure?"

"Yes. I was standing right there."

"Oh, my God . . . what do you think he wants?"

J.C. laughed. "What do you think he wants? He wants to tell you, you are the most talented and brilliant woman in New York."

"Don't be silly. Did he really say, 'Good work'?"

"Yes."

"What do you think that means?"

"It means he thought you did good work."

"And he really said it?"

"Yes, Dena. Am I going to have to carry a tape recorder around to gather all these little kudos from now on?"

"No, it's just that you never figure that someone like him would be watching me. I mean, I'm a silly little fill-in interviewer."

When they got into the cab Dena said, "Oh, let's don't go home, I'm too excited to go home. Let's go to Sardi's."

All the way across town, Dena kept talking. "I still can't believe it. You know, J.C., I never told you but he's been sort of a hero of mine."

"You told me."

"I did? Well, it really would have been enough just to go to the dinner—but to actually meet him . . ."

J.C. chuckled. He enjoyed seeing her excitement.

"Don't laugh, J.C., it's true. Haven't you ever had someone you looked up to, wanted to be like?"

"Yes, Hugh Hefner."

"Oh, you're being silly. But really, aren't you surprised one little bit that he was so nice?"

"No."

"Why?"

"Because I already knew he wanted to meet you."

"How?"

"He had to approve the guest list. And he said he especially wanted you there."

Dena screamed, "J.C., I could just kill you. Why didn't you tell me? Why did you let me make a fool of myself? I could have rehearsed something to say, instead of 'Congratulations, I enjoyed your speech.' What a dork! Why didn't you warn me?"

"Because if I had told you, you would have been a nervous wreck and thrown up all over him."

"What did he say? Did he *say* he wanted to meet me?"

"No, he said, 'I'd enjoy meeting her.'"

"J.C., now this is serious. Tell me the exact words he used . . . don't guess."

"Dena, when he saw your name as a possible guest, he said to Jeanette, and I quote, 'Yes, I would enjoy meeting her.'"

Later at Sardi's bar, after she had four brandy alexanders, although actually less because she spilled two all over her dress, she looked at J.C. "I wonder what he meant by *enjoy*?"

When she got home she threw her dress down the garbage chute. It was expensive but she didn't care. She was still on cloud nine. She took a bath and crawled into bed and tried to go to sleep but couldn't. She wished she had someone to call, someone to tell. It was at times like these, when she was the happiest, that she missed her mother the most.

Let's Have Lunch

New York City
1973

Dena had managed to resist telling everyone at work what had happened when she met Howard Kingsley and now she was glad. It had been two weeks and she had not heard from him.

Maybe he had forgotten or maybe he said, "Let's have lunch" to everybody, and why not, she thought. I must tell ten people a day let's have lunch. And she rarely meant it unless she thought it could do her some good. What a fool she had been, what an egotistical fool, to think he would actually waste time with her. She was nothing but a no-talent jerk with no news experience trying to break into the big time. The phone rang.

"Miss Nordstrom?"

"Yes?"

"This is Howard Kingsley. I was calling to see if you might be free this Thursday for lunch."

"Oh, ah, um . . . Thursday. Let me check. . . ." She pretended to look at her date book and to flip through imaginary pages. "Let's see, Thursday, Thursday."

She suddenly stopped the charade. "Oh, who am I kidding, of course I'm free, Mr. Kingsley, and I would love to meet you for lunch."

Kingsley laughed. "Good. I usually like the Carlyle dining room. It's quiet and the food's good. Is that all right with you?"

"Oh, yes."

"Well, then, Thursday at, say, twelve-thirty?"

"Fine, I'll be there."

"Good, looking forward to it."

"Yes, sir."

She put down the phone and winced. Why had she said, "Yes, sir"? *He's going to think I'm an idiot. Remember, he's just a man, flesh and blood like anybody else.* She noticed her hands were a little wet as she took an aspirin. She didn't know why she was taking one except that she needed something to do. Then she thought she'd better check and see if she really was free. As if she would not have canceled anyone that day, including the queen of England, or Paul Newman. Well, she would have hated to cancel Paul Newman, but thank heavens she didn't have to make that choice. She was free.

Thursday finally rolled around eight years later, or so it seemed, and she was talking to herself all the way to the Carlyle. "You have been in this business almost seven years, you're not an amateur, you're a grown woman. You are not a child. He is not going to bite you. If you seem nervous you will make him nervous. You look wonderful. You have a peppermint Life Savers in your mouth to ensure wonderful breath, you have no pimples, no blemishes. Your nails are clean, you won't have a drink unless, of course, he does, then you can order a Bloody Mary . . . no, that gives you tomato breath. What would be good? Something light but not too wimpy." Just as she was deciding, the cab jerked to a stop. She was there. She overtipped the driver, finished chewing the last of her Life Savers, took a deep breath, and walked in. The maître d' saw her at once. "Ah, yes, Miss Nordstrom, Mr. Kingsley is expecting you. Right this way." He led her all the way to the back corner. The roomful of ladies-who-lunch and businessmen all glanced up and tried not to stare at the great-looking blonde with the great legs. All except a table of six Spanish businessmen, who made absolutely no attempt to be subtle and turned and looked. As she approached, Kingsley stood up and took her hand. "So glad you could make it. I know you must be a busy lady."

"Well, thank you," Dena said. "I'm flattered but believe me, I'm not as busy as you may think."

He smiled. "Enjoy it while you can; you will be soon enough. May I order you a drink?"

She looked to see if he had a drink. He did. She tried to sound casual. "Sure. I'll take a martini as well."

"Fine." He motioned the waiter over. "Jason, bring Miss Nordstrom one of the same." Then he turned back to her. "I can tell all these men are jealous and all the women whispering because I have such a lovely young lady at my table. It happens every time I take my daughter out, and I must say I enjoy it."

Dena relaxed as she realized she did not have to worry that he was on the make. He was a gentleman to let her know in such a nice way.

"Mr. Kingsley, I saw your daughter the other night at the dinner and she is a beautiful girl."

"Thank you. We're lucky she didn't take after me and got all her mother's good looks."

The waiter brought her martini and she took a big sip before she realized it was gin and not vodka. But she kept smiling pleasantly so that he wouldn't notice that her eyes were tearing. She had always been a little nearsighted but after one sip she could have read the small print on the menu across the room. He asked her how she had gotten started and where she had worked before. She gave him a short account of the long history of the years and the jobs she had had before New York. They ordered lunch and when they had finished, he ordered coffee for each of them. "I think I mentioned the Hamilton piece to you the other night."

"Yes, you did."

He looked straight ahead. Then he cleared his throat. "I understand you sort of went your own way on that piece . . . broke ranks with the network, so to speak."

Dena panicked. How did he know?

"Well, I, uh . . ."

"Charles and Peggy Hamilton are friends of mine."

"Oh, I see."

"You realize of course you could have lost your job pulling a stunt like that."

"I know."

"It was a foolhardy thing to do at the beginning of your career."

Dena's heart sank. She felt ten years old. "Yes, I guess it was."

"But, personally, I thought it was a damn decent thing to do."

"You did? I mean, you do?"

He smiled. "Yes. I do."

"Well, thank you. But to tell you the truth, I really don't know how decent it was. I think I was just trying to save my own skin without losing my job."

"You may have been trying to save your own skin, but give yourself credit; you went out of your way to save somebody else's as well. It was not an easy decision. I've been there myself. Whatever your reason, your instincts were correct. You took the high road and it worked."

"Just barely," Dena said. "My boss was pretty mad at me. I thought I might get fired there for a while. I can tell you that . . . he's pretty tough."

"Ira Wallace?"

"Yes. Do you know him?"

He nodded and said with a weary look on his face, "Oh, yes, I know him."

Kingsley sat back and seemed to be deciding something. "You know, Miss Nordstrom, I like you, I like what I see. You've got style, presence, and you've got class. You're just what they want—but, by God, I just hate to see those bastards get a hold of you." He grimaced. "But be that as it may, my advice for you is to get every red cent out of them you can because they are going to try and suck the very soul out of you. You gave my friends fair warning, so I'm giving you fair warning. You think you had trouble with the Hamilton piece? That's just the tip of the iceberg, child's play to what's coming. I can smell it, I can feel it, and it makes me sick." He looked directly at her. "Don't get me wrong, I believe in freedom of the press. That's what we're here for, to get the truth out there to the public. But as soon as someone like Wallace gets in the door, they start to pollute the entire industry and I see it happening more and more every day. They don't want news, they want audience, and to get it they want ratings and they don't care how they get them. But I'm sure you are aware of that."

"Yes," said Dena, "I am."

"I've covered three wars and have seen a lot of killing in my time. But this new bunch taking over are the coldest, meanest bastards I've seen and frankly, they scare the hell out of me. Mark my words, as soon as they can get rid of all of us old guys they're going to replace us with as many pretty young men and women, like yourself, to do their dirty work. To push their garbage and trash down everyone's throats while they hide behind their office doors making millions, laughing at us, while the whole damn country falls apart!"

People in the restaurant were looking over as Kingsley's voice got louder. When he realized what was happening, he was embarrassed and said softly, "I'm sorry, I don't know why I subjected you to all my rantings. Hell, I'm probably just a senile old fool thinking the worst."

"Mr. Kingsley, you mustn't say that. You're not old or a fool and you have a right to be upset."

He caught the waiter's eye and motioned for the check and laughed. "Call me Howard, please. You know, my wife says I should retire. Maybe I should, but I don't want to hand this medium or this network or this country over to those bastards, not yet anyway. Oh, they'll get it sooner or later, but until then, somebody has got to keep reminding people we aren't all the scum they are trying to turn us into."

"All the more reason why you can never retire. We need you. They sure won't listen to me."

He smiled while signing the check. "Miss Nordstrom, I guess what I was trying to say to you is—try not to let them use you too much. Fight back when you can." He paused. "And don't hesitate— call me if you need me."

"Oh, I will. And it's Dena, please."

As they walked out, she said, "You know, I really appreciate your talking to me. Truth is, I don't think I'm going to be offered a new contract. I think I might not have what it takes."

Howard opened the glass door leading to the street. "Oh, you are going to get offered a contract, all right. Julian Amsley's smart enough to know what he's got and he's not about to lose you."

Dena looked at him, dumbfounded.

He laughed. "No, I'm not a psychic. I play poker with Amsley every Friday and he likes to talk."

As he hailed a cab for her, he said, "By the way, you don't like to sail, by any chance, do you?"

"Sail? Oh, yes, I love to sail." She caught herself again. "Well, actually, I'd love to try it."

"Good, when the weather gets better, we'll give you a call. We have a little place in Sag Harbor, maybe we can get you out for a weekend." A cab stopped and he helped her in before he shut the door. "Oh, listen. On that contract thing. They've got two hundred thousand a year budgeted. Don't let your agent settle for less. They won't tell you but your popularity rating is through the roof. They'll offer one. Hold out for four and settle for three. Amsley loves it when he thinks he might lose something, and when he hears we had lunch together, that ought to scare him at least a hundred thousand."

He closed the door and handed the driver a ten-dollar bill. "Take this young lady where she wants to go for me, will you? And be careful, she's valuable property."

The driver beamed. "Yes, sir, Mr. Kingsley."

❊   ❊   ❊

As he drove off, he said, "Howard Kingsley, well, I'll be damned." He looked at her in the rearview mirror. "Last week I had Polly Bergen from *What's My Line?* back there."

"Really?"

He glanced at her in the mirror. "Yeah. And you look familiar; aren't you somebody?"

"No, I'm just a friend of Mr. Kingsley's."

The driver shook his head. "Pretty nice friend to have."

"You're right."

Dena sat back and thought about lunch. It was still hard for her to believe she had actually been with him and that he had talked to her and really cared. She was so glad that Howard had approved of what she had done. But there was a part of her deep down that wondered if she really would have quit if it had meant her job.

She could not be sure. She could never be sure of how she really felt about anything. All she knew was that she had been lucky this time.

A week later Sandy called, excited. "Guess what, you got the contract!"

"Wow, great, Sandy."

"I knew we could do it. And wait until you hear this—I had to work like the devil—but I finally got them up to two hundred a year and you should have heard what they started out with. Isn't that great news?"

"Sandy, tell them I won't do it for less than four hundred thousand."

There was a long pause. "You *are* trying to kill me, aren't you?"

Two weeks later, a battle-weary Sandy called. "All I could get them up to was three."

"Fine," Dena said. "I'll take it."

"Dena, I swear to God that if I die from heart failure, Bea and the kids are moving in with you."

Selma Calling

New York City

1973

Dena was in the editing room working on the interview with Bella Abzug when her secretary buzzed and told her that she had a long-distance call from a Mrs. Sarah Jane Poole.

"Who's that?"

"I don't know but she says it's urgent."

"Well, please find out what she wants. I'm in the middle of something."

Five seconds later her secretary buzzed again. "She says you know her, that she's a close, personal friend. Mrs. Sarah Jane Poole?"

"Oh, Christ . . . I have no idea who that is. Put her through."

An excited woman's voice was on the other end. "Dena?"

"Yes, this is Dena Nordstrom."

"It's me!"

"Who?"

"Don't tell me you've forgotten your old roomie, your college roommate, Sarah Jane Simmons Krackenberry from Selma, Alabama?"

"Sookie?"

"Yes!"

"Oh, for gosh sakes, why didn't you say it was you? How could I forget you, crazy thing. How are you?"

"Fine!"

"Are you still busy fighting the Civil War?"

Sookie screamed with laughter. "Of course, honey—you know me, never say die!"

"How is Earle?"

"He's fine. But I am mad at you."

"Me? Why?"

"Why? My mother-in-law read where you were coming to Atlanta to get some big award and you didn't even call and tell me you were coming."

Dena was confused momentarily. "Award? Oh, you mean the AWRT thing."

"Yes. Why didn't you let me know? I want to see you while you're here."

"I thought you still lived in Alabama."

"I do, silly, but I'm not going to let you get this close without getting a chance to see you."

"How far away are you?"

Sookie laughed. "Dena, I know you think I live way out in the boonies, but we do have superhighways down here. I'm only a couple of hours from Atlanta. I could run over there and pick you up and bring you here for a couple of days and we could catch up on old times. Earle and I would love to have you. We haven't seen each other in ages."

"Oh, Sookie, that would be great. But unfortunately I'm only going to be there for one night, just for the dinner."

"You can't stay even for one day?"

"No, I really can't. I've got to get back."

"Can't I see you at all? Maybe before the dinner or after?"

"I'm coming in and going straight to the dinner, and those things go on for hours. It could be one o'clock in the morning before I'd be free."

"Well, what about the next day, then?"

"The next day I get right back on a plane."

"What time?"

"Oh, I don't remember, nine or ten, something like that."

"Well, I'm coming anyway. I don't care if I see you just for five minutes. I know you, Dena Nordstrom; if I don't hog-tie you while you're down here, who knows when I'll ever see you. So, you're not going to escape. We can at least have breakfast or a cup of coffee together, if nothing else."

Dena was caught. "Well . . . I'll probably be exhausted and—"

Sookie interrupted. "Listen, you, it's not going to kill you to lose an hour's sleep for an old friend. You can sleep on the plane. We're both getting too long in the tooth not to see each other when we can."

Dena had to laugh.

"You know, all you rich and famous people have to put up with people who knew them when, so you're going to have to put up with me for life. That's your cross to bear, honey. That's what you get for being a star. Besides, can't you get a later plane?"

"I would love to but I can't. I have to tape some spots back here at five."

"Well, all right, but I'm still coming. I need to lay my eyeballs on you in person. Anyhow, don't you want to see me? I would think you would be pining away to see what I look like now that I'm old and feeble."

She had to give in. "Oh, all right. I can see you're not going to take no for an answer."

"That's right. Now, tell me where you are staying and I'll come to wherever you are and we can meet there, OK?"

"OK, but I'm not in my office and I don't know where they put me. I'll have to call you and let you know where and what time."

"Now, you better call me back because you're not getting off the hook. I'm going to keep up with you whether you like it or not, Dena Gene Nordstrom!"

"All right. And Sookie . . ."

"Yes?"

"You are still the silliest girl I ever met."

Sookie laughed. "Well, at least that's something."

When Dena hung up she had to smile. Of all the girls she had been in school with, Sookie had been her closest friend, so maybe it might not be so bad. It could even be fun.

Old Times

A week later, after Dena had given her speech, she did not get to sleep until 3:00 A.M. When her wake-up call came the next morning, she had to drag herself out of bed. What had sounded like fun a week ago now felt like sheer drudgery. What had possessed her to set up a breakfast date with Sookie? As she showered she thought the only consolation was that at least she would not have to do much of anything but listen because Sookie would do all the talking. She packed, threw her raincoat on over a pair of slacks and a sweater, and went downstairs.

Walking into the coffee shop, she immediately saw Sookie over in the corner, waving madly. Dena would have known her anywhere. She had on a neat cotton shirtwaist dress and still wore her short red hair in bangs, exactly as she had in college. She looked like she had dressed in a time warp. Sookie stood up and ran over and hugged her and jumped up and down, and squealed like a teenager. "Oh, Dena . . . I am *so* excited! I'm so glad to see you, oh, sit down and let me look at you. I'm so nervous, I'm about to have an epileptic fit. Here you are in person, and I hate to say it, but you still look the same, same gorgeous pale skin, absolutely glamorous!" They sat down.

"Take those dark glasses off," Sookie said, "and let me scrutinize you good."

As tired as she was, Dena found that she was glad to see Sookie, who still had the personality of a game show contestant and her enthusiasm was hard not to get caught up in. Dena removed her sunglasses. Sookie squinted at her and then sat back in mock disgust.

"Well, I just knew it! Not a stitch of makeup . . . and here I have to slap on enough makeup to paint a battleship just to look decent and there you sit, gorgeous and as young-looking as ever. I was hoping to see at least one or two crow's-feet, but no." She leaned in. "Look at me, honey, I'm getting new crow's-feet right in front of your eyes. Earle says they're laugh lines—of course he's blind as a bat. Marry a nearsighted man and you'll never look old."

"Sookie, you look great."

"I do? Well, I'm just an old married woman, with children now. My youth is a thing of the past, gone with the wind."

Dena laughed. "Oh, stop it. You don't look a day older than the last time I saw you. Now, tell me what's going on with you."

"Nothing, same old stuff, raising my kids, you know, nothing. But forget about me, you're the one with the exciting life. I still can't believe you're here. Do you know how long it's been?"

"No."

"Well, I'm not even going to tell you. But I want to hear about everything; tell me about the dinner last night. Weren't you just thrilled with your award? What an honor. Was dinner wonderful?"

Dena dismissed it. "It was all right as those things go."

"Didn't they give you some big award?"

"No, it was just a plaque."

"Oh," Sookie said, taken aback. "Well, I'd be thrilled if someone gave me an award and wanted me to speak."

"No, you wouldn't. Not after a while."

"Yes, I would, honey, I'd take any award they handed me and run like a thief!"

"I tell you what," Dena said, smiling, "next one I get I'm going to put a blond wig on you and send you. Come on, let's don't talk about me, you know what I've been up to; tell me about yourself."

"Me? Like I said, everything's the same. We moved out of Earle's mother's old house downtown and moved out to this cute little house in the suburbs and we love it, and I do some work in the community, you know, all that stuff."

The waitress came up to the table. Dena ordered coffee but Sookie told the waitress, "I don't want anything with caffeine, I'm so nervous now I'm about to faint. Dena, what time is it?"

Dena assured her that they still had some time before she had to leave. "OK," Sookie said, "bring me some Sanka, iced!"

"How many children do you have?"

"Honey, I've had two more since the last time I saw you. I'm like the old woman in the shoe—so many children I don't know what to do. I have three now, can you believe it, three little girls, Ce Ce, Dee Dee, and Le Le." Sookie whipped out a photograph of herself and three little miniature Sookies, bangs and all. "I wanted to bring all the albums to show you but Earle wouldn't let me."

"They are very pretty."

Sookie beamed. "I think so but I'm their mother. But Earle is beside himself; he thinks all three are going to grow up and become Miss Alabama. Of course, we're going to have to get their ears fixed before they start dating."

"What?"

"You can't see there, but unfortunately all three have the Poole ears. You remember how Earle's ears stick out. Daddy said at first that he looked like a taxicab with both back doors open. Anyway, thank heavens they're girls so I can just puff their little hair over them."

Dena looked at the photo again. "Sookie, are those mother-and-daughter dresses?"

"Yes, and don't you make fun. I know it's corny, but Earle's running for city council and he thought it was cute—for the poster and all."

"Oh, no, don't tell me Earle is going into politics."

"Oh, yes. He says it's good for business. Besides, he's very civic-minded. You can keep that picture, we have hundreds of them."

"Thanks. What about *you,* Sookie? Are you still busy trying to be Miss Popularity? You ran for every office on campus, I remember that."

"Now, you're not going to remind me of how silly I used to be. Honey, what did I know? When I hit SMU, I was straight out of Selma. Besides, that's not my fault. You remember Mother."

"Oh, yes, Lenore the Magnificent. How is she?"

Sookie rolled her eyes. "Unfortunately, fine, still terrorizing everybody within a hundred miles. Anyway, it was all her fault. She said I had to make all *A*'s or else be popular. She said if you can't be smart, be bubbly . . . and Lord knows I bubbled."

The waitress served them their coffee and a woman came up to the table behind her and spoke to Dena. "Excuse me, could I have your autograph, please? I'm one of your biggest fans."

Sookie was pleased and chatted happily with her while Dena had to dig through her purse looking for a pen and a piece of paper because the woman had neither. "Dena and I roomed together in college in the Kappa house."

"Is that right?" the woman said.

"Yes. I drove all the way over from Selma, Alabama, this morning just to visit with her for a few minutes. We haven't seen each other in years. But she looks just the same. I said to her, I said, 'Dena, here I am getting so old I'm falling in a heap and you look the same.' "

The woman smiled. "Well, isn't that nice that you girls could get together."

Dena finally found a pen and an old envelope and asked, "Is this for you? Or do you want me to sign it to somebody else?"

The woman said, "Oh, no, it's for me," and continued talking to Sookie. "I had a cousin who married a girl from Selma. Lettie Kathrine Wyndam."

"Oh, I know the Wyndams. They are a lovely family!"

"Well, Lettie was certainly a lovely girl."

Dena interrupted again. "Excuse me, I need to know how you want this made out."

"You can just make it out to me, honey."

Dena tried to be polite. "Could you tell me your name?"

The woman said, "Oh . . . I'm sorry . . . just make it out to Mary Lib Hawkins."

Sookie continued on. "I tried to get Dena to come over to Selma and visit for a few days but she's so busy, she has to fly back to New York to tape something this afternoon. Can you imagine that, making her work on Sunday? They must be heathens, if you ask me."

Mary Lib was sympathetic and looked at Dena. "Oh, you poor thing."

Dena handed her the envelope. "Here you go," she said, "and thank you."

"Thank you. And I hope you girls get in a nice visit."

Sookie answered for both of them. "Thank you, ma'am, we will."

After she left, Sookie turned to Dena, excited. "Wasn't she nice? I'll bet you get people coming up to you all the time. Doesn't that make you feel important? I feel important just sitting here with you. Don't you just love it?"

"No, not really."

"You do too love it, all that attention. Who wouldn't?"

Dena smiled. "It's all right. It's just ... sometimes I don't feel like being nice."

"Well, you better be nice to me, Dena Nordstrom, with all that I've had to put up with because of you."

"Because of me?"

"It wasn't easy being roommates with the best-looking girl on campus. It's a wonder it didn't warp me for life. I had to work for hours getting my hair to do right and get my makeup on. And you would just get out of bed and go and look better than all of us. Remember how you used to eat like a lumberjack while I had to practically starve myself? All I could have was one lettuce leaf for dinner, to keep my thighs from jiggling, and you still haven't put on a pound. I should just kill you in the name of all womanhood." Sookie laughed. "Oh, and Dena, do you remember that electrosizer machine I bought that was supposed to reduce your thighs? Right before the homecoming dance? I stayed hooked up to that thing for hours, made myself black and blue, and I still looked like a sack of grapefruit in that dress."

"Sookie, you were one of the most attractive girls on campus and you know it."

"Ha! Just when I'd get some boy interested, you'd walk by and he would leave me in the dust. The only reason I got Earle Poole was because he was nearsighted."

"Oh, don't be silly. Earle adored you."

Sookie said, "Well, don't forget Wayne Comer. When he saw you, he dropped me like a hot potato and started chasing after you. Broke my heart."

"For God's sake, Sookie, you never loved that geeky boy. He was an idiot!"

"Well, I know that now. Speaking of that, who're you dating? Anybody special?"

"Yes. I guess . . ."

Sookie's eyes lit up. "Oh, anybody I know?"

"No, I don't think so."

"Oh, pooh, I was hoping you were having a wild romance with some big movie star. Well, are you at least in love, then?"

"No, thank God."

Sookie was surprised. "Don't you want to be in love?"

"No, I tried that . . . and I hated it. Never again. It is better to be the one who is loved than the one who loves. Take it from me, that's my motto."

"Oh, Dena, remember in college when I was so in love with Tony Curtis and you were in love with that writer . . . Tennessee Williams? You had his picture over your bed."

"That's right, my gosh . . . how do you remember that? I had almost forgotten."

"How could I forget? Don't you remember, you dragged me all the way up to St. Louis, Missouri, on some sacred pilgrimage to see some dumb shoe factory where he had worked. And you cried like it was some sort of shrine!"

"My gosh, that's right. The International Shoe Company . . ."

"And then we took the streetcar out to some old ugly apartment building where he had lived."

"God, I had forgotten all about that."

Sookie sat back, pleased. "Now, see . . . aren't you enjoying your-self, remembering old times? Now, aren't you glad you came? I knew you were trying to wiggle out of it. I told Earle, I said she's going to try and wiggle out of it. Now, aren't you glad you didn't?"

"Yes."

"I always had to force you to be social. If it hadn't been for me pushing you, you wouldn't have ever been a Kappa. You wouldn't have known anybody except those weirdo theater majors if it hadn't been for me; now admit it, isn't that the truth?"

"Yes. I guess."

"Remember how shy you were? But I pushed you out into the world. As a matter of fact, I am completely responsible for your suc-cess today. At least that's what I tell everybody—so don't you dare tell anybody any different."

"OK."

"You know I'm kidding, but really, Dena, aren't you glad you got over your little theater and artsy phase?"

Dena was confused. "My artsy phase?"

"Oh, don't you remember how you used to go to that stupid movie house all the time, the one that showed all those weird pictures?"

"Do you mean the Lyric?"

"Yes. You made me go see some old stupid clown picture that wasn't even in English."

"*Children of Paradise?* It was French."

"Well, it was awful, whatever it was. You used to drag me to the craziest places, like I was a rag doll, and I let you. Mother said I had a weak mind and I guess she was right, but we had fun, didn't we? You used to do the craziest things, always acting like a fool. Remember how much trouble we would get into giggling all night? Remember Judy Horne, the one with the sinus problem? Used to bang on our wall trying to get us to shut up. Remember on Kappa alumni day when you pretended you were a transfer student from Sweden? You wore some funny outfit and had an accent; it was a scream."

"I did?"

"Yes, oh, and oh, my God—Greek week and that crazy song you wrote for the Kappa skit."

Dena looked puzzled.

"Oh, you know! You made us all put balloons in our sweaters and we all sang 'Thanks for the Mammaries.' We were silly and happy as clams, we'd laugh from morning till night."

"Really? I remember that you and I had fun but I don't remember being all that happy all the time."

"You were; nothing fazed you. You were always happy-go-lucky."

"I was?"

"Yes."

"Huh. Are you sure?"

"Of course, I was your roommate. I guess I know."

"That's funny. I remember being sort of unhappy at school."

"Oh, you were not! You were just a little moody, that's all. And I just chalked that up to dramatic temperament; you had all the leads in those awful plays. You used to spend hours over at that theater doing something, all night long, and I'd have to sneak down and leave the back door unlocked for you. You spent so much time over there, everybody thought you had a secret boyfriend and you just wouldn't tell us. And don't you remember the night Mitzy McGruder and I—by the way, she's married now . . . finally—snuck over to the theater and there you were at two o'clock in the morning prancing all over the stage all by yourself. You'd sing, then you'd laugh, and then you'd dance awhile; it was hysterical, you were a riot. What were you doing?"

Dena shook her head. "Lord knows. Acting, I guess, fooling with the lights. Who knows?"

"Well, whatever you were doing, it paid off. Here you are a big star. Now, tell me who all you've met."

"Like who?"

"Stars. Did you ever meet Tony Curtis?"

"No."

Sookie was visibly disappointed. "Oh, why don't you interview him sometime? I'll bet a lot of people would like to see that. You should listen to me, Dena, I'm the general public."

Then a heavyset waitress came over and stood staring at Dena and asked her what her name was.

Dena looked up. "Excuse me?"

"What's your name? Somebody said you were a celebrity or something."

Sookie was happy to tell her. "This is Dena Nordstrom; you've seen her on television."

The waitress, who had no idea who Dena was, said, "Can I have your autograph then?"

Sookie, an old pro by now, answered, "Sure, you can. Do you have a pencil and a piece of paper?"

The waitress handed Dena her check pad. "Here, put it on the back of this . . . make it to Billie."

Billie turned around and yelled, "Thelma, come over here and get her autograph and get Dwayne out of the kitchen!"

Then she asked Sookie, "Can Dwayne have one?"

Sookie said, "Dena, can you do one for Dwayne?" Then Sookie asked the waitress, "Who's Dwayne?"

"He's the cook."

"He's the cook, Dena; you don't mind, do you?"

Dena signed the other waitress's pad. "All right, but tell him to hurry up."

Billie handed her a piece of paper. "Here, just sign it. He's busy. I'll take it to him."

Dena signed, the waitress took it. "Thank you."

Sookie was beaming. "Oh, Dena, I feel just like a proud parent. I always knew you were going to be famous. I used to tell you that all the time, didn't I?"

"You did?"

"Yes, don't you remember anything?" Sookie looked at her wistfully. "Dena, don't you miss the good old days? I hate having to be a grown woman. Of course, I wouldn't take anything for Earle and my girls, but don't you wish we could go back and not have to worry about anything, just be silly and date? I still remember all my Kappa songs. Do you?"

Dena glanced at her watch and was surprised to see how late it was. "Oh, damn, Sookie, I've got to go."

Sookie wailed, "Oh, no. I feel like I didn't get all my visit in. We just got started good."

Dena said, "I know, but we'll do it again really soon. I promise."

Sookie suddenly panicked. "Wait! I almost forgot. I have to get a picture of us for the *Kappa Key*." She rummaged around in her purse and brought out a camera. "It won't take a second." She called Billie the waitress over and made her take a photograph of them.

Sookie walked with her out to the limo and hugged her good-bye. "Promise me . . . promise that if you ever get back south of the Mason-Dixon line, you'll call me and let me know. Because if you don't I'll find out and show up and embarrass you."

Dena, laughing, got in the car. "I promise."

"Oh, and listen, if you ever do meet Tony Curtis, tell him he has a big fan in Selma, Alabama."

"I will."

As she drove off Sookie waved and called, "Love you!"

On the plane, Dena ordered a Bloody Mary and sat there and thought about the girl Sookie had described. Could it possibly have been her? Could Sookie have been so wrong about her? The girl she thought she remembered had always been a sort of sad, dreamy kid who used to cry a lot, sit for hours staring at the leaves shining through the trees, longing for something so hard that it hurt. But what she had been longing for or where those feelings had gone, Dena did not know. The truth was she could barely remember that girl at all.

She ordered another Bloody Mary and slept all the way to New York.

City Lights

When Dena was seven her mother got a job at Bergdorf's in New York City and sent her to boarding school in Connecticut. She hated it—long, empty, dark halls and waiting to see her mother again. After about two months, the Mother Superior wrote a letter to her mother telling her that Dena was not mixing well with the other children. "We expect a certain amount of homesickness from our boarders, especially when the child is an only child, but I am afraid Dena is a hard case. It is clear that the child simply adores you and is terribly unhappy here. We usually encourage parents to allow their children time to get used to a new surrounding, but I am going to make an exception in our policy, and I wonder if she might have more weekends at home?"

Dena loved her mother's new apartment. It was off Gramercy Park on a pretty street lined with trees. She would sleep on the living room couch. The apartment was on the ground floor with the windows almost at street level. At night the light from the streetlamp on the corner would fill the room full of lacy black patterns on the wall as a breeze caused the leaves to ripple back and forth and dance in the light. Lying there late at night she could hear couples walking past the windows, the hard clunk of a man's foot and the sharp click of a woman's high heels hitting the sidewalk as they passed. She could hear their soft muffled voices, the deep voice of the man and the woman's laugh. Sometimes she would hear the music on a radio as a car swished by, shining its headlights through the ornate black bars on the windows and turning the small living room into a magical light-and-sound show. She was full of dreams and curiosity. She always wondered where the people were going and where they had been and dreamed of all the wonderful places she might be going someday. She longed to someday live in a white house like the one she often dreamed about. White against a green lawn, and her mother was always smiling. That Christmas her mother had let her come for a whole week. It had been a wonderful visit. Her mother had taken her to Horn & Hardart's for lunch, where they chose their food out of little glass windows, drank hot coffee, and ate pie. They walked all the way up Fifth Avenue, looking at hundreds of people, Santa Clauses on each corner, and windows full of miniature things swirling and moving to music, then on to Radio City to see the Christmas show, and she sat there with her mouth open, mesmerized by the spectacle of it all. She had never seen a live camel in her life and the Rockettes were dressed in red and gold uniforms and looked like live toy soldiers. She could hardly breathe watching all the lights, fascinated by the way they changed from one color to another, again almost like magic. While other children were watching the show, Dena had turned around in her seat to look at the spotlights that came beaming down all the way from the very back of the auditorium to form perfect circles of bright white light on stage and on the curtains. And if that wasn't enough, her mother astonished her when she told Dena that she knew one of the Rockettes and that they were going backstage to meet her.

When they got backstage, her mother's friend, a nice lady named Christine, gave them a complete tour from the huge mirrored rehearsal hall to the dressing rooms. Backstage was teaming with Rockettes, musicians, stagehands, and other costumed ladies but Dena wanted to know only one thing: Who made the lights way up in the curved ceiling of the auditorium change from one color to another and how did they do it? Christine had laughed at the question coming from such a small girl and introduced her to a man named Artie. He took her over and showed her the main control console, with its 4,305 colored handles that controlled the amber, green, red, and blue lights, and told her about the 206 spotlights. Dena stood listening, enthralled. Later they had dinner with Christine in the private Radio City Music Hall cafeteria, where all the dancers and the staff ate. That night Dena's head was still whirling. She had never been so excited in her entire life. She slept with her mother and held her hand all night and dreamed about the lights. Then, two months later, without warning, her mother suddenly quit her job and moved to the Altamont Towers apartments in an older section of Cleveland, Ohio, and Dena didn't see her at all until the summer. But she never forgot that night at Radio City and had been fascinated with lights ever since, any kind of light, sunlight, moonlight, lamplight, so much so that it was the lighting that first attracted her to the theater. She started working with the lights in college and was amazed at how she could change the mood of the stage set from a light and cheery room with pure white sunlight pouring through the windows to a dark, shadowy, scary room by just pulling a lever. She would sneak into the college theater in the middle of the night and play with the lights for hours. She learned how to create any mood she wanted. It was that year that she became totally obsessed with light, and eventually the light became obsessed with her. It was the first time she ever really felt in control of anything in her life. And the lights had pulled her all the way back to New York.

The SMU Kappa Newsletter

Selma, Alabama

1973

Hello, Kappas!

If you are wondering why I am in such high spirits, I can tell you that this year has been a fabulous year for finding and renewing old friendships and our new rush chair, Leslie Woolley, tells us that this year was the most successful rush of all. We have 34 NEW KAPPA KUTIES! I was on hand as each new pledge was given her special fleur-de-lis pin and was welcomed by all KAPPAS ON KAMPUS with lots of KAPPA KISSES and hugs. Each active named her special pledge with a KAPPA KNICKNAME to make her feel welcome. Then each senior stood and told what KAPPA has meant to her (that really got the tears going!). Then we walked all the rushes out and ended by singing the Porch Song.

And now for my most exciting news! I was able to catch up with one of our most famous KAPPAS in Atlanta last month. She was in town to receive an award from the American Women in Radio and Television and of course I am talking about none other than DENA NORDSTROM! She sends all the KAPPAS her best and we reminisced about the good old days when we were roomies! Back in the dark ages, HA HA. The picture below is out of focus but I am sending it anyway.

KAPPAS KONTINUE TO SET THE WORLD ON FIRE, so all you gals who have aspirations, maybe one day some of your KAPPA sisters will find you and say I REMEMBER YOU WHEN!

—Sookie Krackenberry Poole,
Class of '65

Ira's Pep Talk

New York City
1974

After her first lunch with Howard Kingsley, Dena tried her best to do something to stop the direction the show was going in but had little luck.

This was the fourth time she had asked Ira Wallace to program an interview with the blind woman who had just been named teacher of the year and for the fourth time he had turned her down. Wallace, who was having what was left of his hair cut by his personal barber, Nate Albetta, said, "Nobody wants to see that sickening candy-ass stuff, do they, Nate?"

Nate said, "Don't ask me, I couldn't tell you."

"Yes, they do, Ira," Dena said. "You don't know it but there are a lot of nice people out there. Everybody is not trying to rip everyone else off. You need to get out of New York and travel around this country and meet some of the people who are your audience."

Wallace said, "You're telling me I don't know my audience? Me? Have you seen the numbers this week?"

"No . . . but that's not the point."

"Let me tell you something, and this I learned from that great journalist, Walter Winchell: gossip is like dope; once you get people hooked, they need a little every day, and if you don't let them down, you have them for life."

Dena rolled her eyes. "Oh, great, Ira, why don't we put that on a bronze plaque and hang it on the wall?"

Dena looked at Nate with the straight razor in his hand. "While you're at it, why don't you cut his throat for me, will you?"

Nate laughed; he was used to their arguments.

"You know, kid, you're gonna have to get over this mistaken idea you have of human nature. This ain't nothing new. People can't wait to get the dirt on other people. That's what makes the world go round and pays your salary and you better hope they don't ever get over it. You've got some fantasy about brotherly love. It don't exist. You think people are some kind of pure, white feathered birds flying in the clouds. They're not. They're pigs and they love to wallow in the mud and dirt."

"A lovely sentiment, Ira. Gee, I'm glad you told me all this. I was starting to think that there might be one or two decent people out there. A good thing you caught me in time."

Nate laughed again while Wallace said, "Yeah, yeah"—he relit his cigar—"you may think it's funny but if you don't watch out, you're gonna get stomped on. You got some idealist idea about man being some noble creature ... and all this crap about how we can change human nature. You can't change it, you're beating your head against a brick wall. People have had a couple of million years to change and they ain't changed yet, have they?"

"Not much."

"No, and they ain't going to. Not in your lifetime. So get over it."

"Don't you ever feel just a *little* bit guilty?"

Wallace threw up his hands. "Jesus, what is this?" He looked at Nate. "I'm in a Frank Capra movie all of a sudden. Now, don't let me down and turn out to be some loser."

"Ira, I'm not trying to let you down. I know it's OK to expose real corruption, but I don't think you realize that people are complaining about how mean the show is getting. I hear it all the time."

"Sure, you do. The rich and the powerful can't control the press anymore and it's making them mad. But we ain't the villains—they are. Don't shoot the messenger."

"I'm not but these hidden camera things you are doing are pretty iffy."

"Hey—who is going to decide what to withhold? Are you? Is the president? No. Is Howard Kingsley? No. That old craptrap about news being withheld for national security reasons don't wash anymore; we've pulled down their pants and exposed them and they don't like it. That's *why* they're squealing like stuck pigs, and when we catch anybody, and I mean anybody and I don't care if it's the goddamned pope, with their fingers in the till or anywhere else they don't belong, we're gonna report it. Right, Nate?"

"Right."

"You're gonna see a lot more respect for television. We can make or break them and now they know it. You stick with me. Do what I tell you, people will be knocking each other down to get on the air with you. You're gonna be more famous than most of the assholes you interview—and believe me, you'll be working long after these slobs have crashed and burned."

Wallace put his hand up to stop Nate and leaned toward Dena. "You remember that guy that was on top of the building over at Sixty-seventh Street the other day? And a crowd gathered when he threatened to jump and after about thirty minutes the crowd started yelling at him, 'Jump, Jump!' "

"Yes, I remember. Disgusting."

"Yeah, disgusting, but that's your audience, kid, those are your so-called nice people. So when you're doing an interview, remember they're down there just waiting for something to happen. They want action and I've got the ratings to prove it. You think Winchell had guilt? Hell, no, but people remember his name, not those country club snobs who thought they were better than him."

"Ira, all I am asking is why we have to hit so hard all the time. We're not at war, it's just a television show. Can't we even try to do a few human interest stories for a change?"

"You wanna preach? Get a church. This ain't *The Waltons,* this is the news."

"So I take it the answer is no, no teacher stories?"

"Only when the teacher," Wallace said, signaling Nate to resume, "is also a child molester. Now, that's a story."

There was no way to argue with Ira, of course. He was right. And he had the ratings to prove it. He had been the first to jump on the trend of ambush interviews and perfect the sensationalized sound bite. In the beginning, everyone had laughed at him, then hated him, but not now. The world of what they called television news was changing and changing fast. Now they were all scrambling to change their own formats.

And as Ira liked to say, "Hey, it was gonna happen—I just came up with the idea first."

Appointment

Dena woke dreading her doctor's appointment that day but she had to go. He would not prescribe any more medicine unless he saw her. It was just her bad luck to have picked out a doctor who was completely thorough. After her examination she sat in his office dying for a cigarette while Dr. Halling went over his findings and read the results of the GI series tests he had forced her to go through again. He did not look happy.

"Dena, your ulcer is not healing as it should. In fact, it looks worse." He looked at her. "And you're not smoking?"

"No."

"No coffee, no alcohol?"

"No."

"And you are watching your diet?"

"Oh, absolutely." She had eaten a bowl of oatmeal last week.

He sighed. "Well, I'm baffled. The only thing I can figure that is causing this is just plain old stress. So all I can do at this point is to put you on complete bed rest."

Dena's alarm system went off. "Bed rest! What does that mean?"

He looked at her again from over his glasses. "Dena, it means just what you think it means. I'm going to put you to bed for at least three weeks. I have a feeling that's the only way I'm going to get you to slow down. We are approaching a dangerous stage as it is. You don't want to wind up with a bleeding ulcer and have to have emergency surgery. Or worse, bleed to death."

"But it's not bleeding yet, is it?"

"No, but that's what we're headed for if it gets any worse. And I am not going to let you kill yourself."

"But I have to work. Really. I'll lose my job if I stop now. I'm just getting my foot in the door."

"Dena, this is your health."

"Look, I promise. I'll come straight home and get right in bed and drink milk shakes and eat mashed potatoes—really take it easy. I promise. I've worked all my life to get to this point. Can't we just do something . . . isn't there some sort of medicine I can take?"

Dr. Halling shook his head. "No. You're taking everything I can give you and it's not helping."

"Look, I think that now and then I might have not eaten like I should have. And I smoked a little. I have been running around, maybe too much, but I promise I'll do better. The next time you see me I will be a hundred percent better. Please?"

He sat back. "This is against my better judgment but I'll make a deal with you. I want you back here in two months . . . and if it's not better, I'm going to order you into the hospital, do you understand?"

"Oh, yes. I understand."

"But in the meantime, I want you to talk to a friend of mine. See if he can't do something to help you try and figure out what's causing all this stress. You're too young to be in this condition. Talk to this fella and let's see if he can't find out what's . . . eating you. It might be more than work."

He took out his pen from the holder and wrote a name and address. Dena was relieved. "Fine. I'll see anybody you say."

When he finished writing he held out the paper. Before he let her take it he said, "I want you to *promise* me that you'll go to see this man at least twice a week—or I'll put you in the hospital now."

"I swear I will. I'll call as soon as I get home."

She would have *run* out of the office if she could have.

She called this O'Malley that afternoon and three days later she walked into his building and looked on the wall directory in the lobby. DR. GERALD O'MALLEY, PSYCHIATRIST. 17TH FLOOR.

Dena was appalled. A psychiatrist! What in the world was Dr. Halling thinking about? She wanted to turn around and leave. But she was stuck. Halling would find out if she didn't show, so she might as well go on in and humor them both.

She got out on seventeen, knocked on his door, and heard a voice say, "Come in." Dena walked in the office and a young man, not much older than she, stood up and shook her hand.

"Hello, Miss Nordstrom, I'm Dr. O'Malley."

He was a neat, preppie-looking man in horned-rimmed glasses. He had blue eyes and fair, almost baby skin. He looked as if his mother had dressed him and combed his hair before he left this morning.

"You're the doctor?"

"Yes. Won't you have a seat?"

"I don't know why," she said, sitting down, "but I was expecting an older man with a beard."

He laughed. "Sorry to disappoint you but I haven't had much luck with beards."

He sat down, took out a pad and pen, and waited for her to speak. This was something she would soon find out he did a great deal.

Finally she said, "Umm, I'm not here to see a psychiatrist. I mean, I'm not here because I think I need a psychiatrist, believe me."

He nodded. Something else he would do a lot.

"I have an ulcer, and this was Dr. Halling's idea. I just have a little stress, job related."

He nodded pleasantly and made a few notes. She sat back and waited for him to speak.

He didn't.

"Anyhow, that's why I'm here, because of job-related stress."

"Uh-huh," he nodded, "and what is it you do?"

"About what?"

"What is your job?"

Dena was taken aback. "Television!"

"What do you . . . do?"

"I'm on it."

He nodded and waited for her to continue. There was a longer, more awkward pause. "You might have seen me. I do interviews on an evening news show."

"No, sorry. I'm afraid I don't get the chance to watch much TV."

Dena was thrown. "Oh, well. Anyhow, it's an important job and . . ."

Suddenly Dena felt irritated at having to explain who she was and what she did. "I'm sure you spoke to Dr. Halling about my ulcer. He thinks that I should talk to somebody about stress." Dena glanced over at the couch. "Should I lie down . . . or something?"

Dr. O'Malley said, "Not unless you want to."

"Oh. Well . . . can I smoke?"

"I wish you wouldn't."

Dena hated this already. "Are you allergic or something?"

"No. But it's not a very good idea for someone with an ulcer to smoke."

Dena, more and more irritated, began to bounce her right foot up and down, legs crossed. This guy was a real jerk.

"Look, the only reason I came was because I promised Dr. Halling I would."

He nodded.

"So, I don't know what I'm supposed to say. Don't you want to ask me some questions or something?"

"Is there anything you'd like to tell me?" he said, in that maddening noncommittal way.

"I told you. I am under a lot of stress and I am having a hard time sleeping and I thought you might prescribe something to help, that's all."

"Suppose we talk a little first."

"What do you want to talk about?"

"Is there anything in particular bothering you, anything *you'd* like to talk about?"

"No, not really."

He looked at her and waited. She looked around the room. "Listen, I'm sure you are a nice person and I don't want to hurt your feelings, but I don't really believe in all this stuff. All this whining and bellyaching about what your mother and daddy did when you were three. It may be all right for some people but, really, I'm the least screwed-up person I know."

Dr. O'Malley continued to listen.

"I know exactly what I want, I knew from the time I was twelve what I wanted to be. I'm not weird or have some strange sexual attraction to my mailbox or something. Nothing is bothering me, I just have a small stomach problem."

He nodded again. She continued.

"I'm not depressed, my job is going great. I have no desire to jump off the Brooklyn Bridge, I don't think I'm Napoleon. My parents didn't beat me—"

Dr. O'Malley, making more notes, said, "Tell me a little about your parents."

"What?"

"Your parents."

"They're fine, they're dead, but they didn't tie me to a bedpost or anything. I'm very well adjusted. One of the things people have always said about me is that I am confident and mature. People come to *me* with their problems. In fact, everybody says I'm the most normal person they have ever met—and believe me, in my business that's hard."

"Any siblings?"

"What?"

"Brothers or sisters?"

"No. Just me."

"I see," he said and wrote *only child*. "How old were you when your parents died?"

"My father was killed in the war before I was born."

He waited. She looked around the room. "How long does it take to become a psychiatrist?"

Dr. O'Malley said, "A long time. And your mother?"

"What?"

"How old were you when your mother died?"

"I forget. Does it take less time to be a psychiatrist than it does to be a real doctor?"

"No, it doesn't. What was the cause of death?"

Dena looked at him. "What?"

"Your mother."

"Oh, hit by a car." Dena began to rummage around in her purse.

"I see. How did you feel about that?"

"Just like anyone would feel if their mother was run over. But you get over it. Do you have any gum or anything?"

"No, I'm sorry."

He waited for her to continue but she did not. After a minute she became more agitated. "Look, I'm not here to be analyzed. I don't need it. I'm sorry to disappoint you, Doctor, but I basically am a very happy person. I have everything I want. I'm in a very nice relationship. Things couldn't be better; all I have is a bad stomach."

He nodded and made notes. What *was* he doing, playing tic-tac-toe? When the session ended, Dena couldn't wait to leave. She wondered what the hell was she going to talk to this cold fish about for the next two months. How could she possibly talk to this guy? He was an idiot, a Neanderthal.

He didn't even watch television, for God's sake!

Meanwhile, Back at the Springs

Elmwood Springs, Missouri
1974

Norma, Macky, and Aunt Elner were having dinner in the dining room. Norma passed the rolls. "Poor Tot, here she spent all morning baking that cake and then to have it ruined. I tell you, she has the worst luck."

Aunt Elner's face was sad. "Poor Tot."

Norma said, "Imagine, of all days for Blue Boy to do such a thing. Here she had made this beautiful spice cake for the church supper."

"She makes a good spice cake," Aunt Elner said. "You have to give her that."

"Oh, yes, nobody can make a spice cake like Poor Tot."

Macky asked, "Who's Blue Boy?"

Norma said, "He's the one who ruined her cake. She said she went to put it on the cake plate and lo and behold she looked down and noticed there were bird tracks all over it. He had walked all over it."

Macky asked again, "Who's Blue Boy?"

"That stupid parakeet of hers."

Aunt Elner said, "It's not blue, it's more of a green if you ask me. On top of everything else, poor Tot is probably color blind as well."

Norma thought for a moment. "I don't think women can be color blind. I think it's only men. . . . Anyhow Poor Old Tot, married to that drunk and now this."

"Why does she call it Blue Boy if it's green?" Macky asked.

"I don't know why, that's not the question. The question is, what was it doing out of its cage? She said she had to throw the thing out and start over."

"The bird?"

"No, Macky, the cake."

Aunt Elner said, "Well, I don't know why, a few bird tracks never hurt anybody."

Norma looked at her with alarm. "I don't know about you, but I sure wouldn't want to eat a cake that some germy bird has stomped all over. You don't know; that thing could have done his business on that cake. That's all we need is for everyone over at the church to come down with some bird disease and then to have that happen to her hair the very next day. She said when Darlene got her out from under the dryer and started combing her out, it came out by the handfuls. She said she was lucky to have a hair left on her head."

Aunt Elner said, "Birds walk all over my table and I'm not dead yet. I think she should have just smoothed it out and gone on."

"Well, remind me never to eat at your house. Anyway, she said Darlene used too much bleach and kept it on too long or something. She did the same thing to Verbena's niece last year, remember?"

Macky said, "Why do you keep going back to her is my question."

"Well, Macky, how would you like to raise four children all by yourself? That's what she's doing thanks to your dear friend, who just took off into the wild blue yonder with that dental assistant and left her stranded with four young children."

"My dear friend? Norma, I bowled with the guy a few times. He was twenty years old. I couldn't even tell you what he looked like."

"I'll tell you what he looked like, he looked like a criminal, that's what, with all those tattoos. And those little pea eyes. Why you would want to bowl with somebody like that and socialize with a criminal type, is beyond me. Don't character count in bowling?"

"How did a conversation about hair turn into a conversation about me bowling?"

Aunt Elner, who by coincidence just happened to be helping herself to another serving of English peas, said, "Those children got those pea eyes from their daddy's side of the family."

Norma agreed. "Yes, but the oldest one is not too bad." She turned back to her husband. "Anyway, Macky, what do you *want* her to do, not work? Let those children starve to death?"

"No, of course not. It just seems to me all I hear are complaints about how bad she is at fixing hair. Can't she get another job, something she'd at least be good at? A waitress or something?"

Aunt Elner said, "She's not smart enough to be a waitress, bless her heart."

"How smart do you have to be to be a waitress?"

Norma said, "Well you have to be smart enough to spell to write up orders. She said this is the only job in town that doesn't require spelling. I read the label on everything before she puts it on my head, I can tell you that."

Aunt Elner was still sad. "Poor Tot . . . her hair was thin enough without this happening. Her mother had thin hair, you could see right through it."

Norma said, "I read that ninety-nine percent of criminals have tattoos; did you know that, Macky?"

"No."

"Well, they do. Show me a tattoo and I'll show you a criminal!"

"I'll be sure and tell the Reverend Dockrill that. He's got one."

Norma was shocked. "The Presbyterian preacher?"

"Yeah."

"Nooo. Where?"

"On his arm."

"What does it say?"

"I don't remember."

"You're making that up. He does *not* have a tattoo."

"He does. Do we have any more butter?"

Norma got up and went to the kitchen. "Macky Warren, you are too making that up. Just to irritate me."

Macky laughed and looked at Aunt Elner. "I'm not. He does."

Norma said, "When did you see it?"

"Last summer, when we were building the new firehouse. He had his shirt off."

"Where on his arm?"

Macky pointed to the top of his arm. "Somewhere around here."

"Oh, I don't believe it. I've never heard of a Presbyterian preacher with a tattoo in my life. You are making that up."

"Norma, I'm not making it up. I don't care one way or the other if he has a picture of Marilyn Monroe tattooed on his behind but I'm telling you he does—"

"Are you going to sit there and tell me that Reverend John Dockrill has a picture of Marilyn Monroe tattooed on his behind?"

"I said I wouldn't care if he did. I'm sorry now that I even mentioned it."

Norma glanced at him with suspicion. "Which arm?"

"Oh, I don't remember. What difference does it make?"

"Well, was it big or little?"

"His arm?"

"No, the tattoo."

"I don't remember."

"Macky, you are the most unobservant person I have ever met. You are the only person in the entire world that could look at a tattoo on a preacher and not even pay attention to what it was."

Aunt Elner piped in, "Maybe it was a religious tattoo. Was it a cross or the Last Supper?"

"Aunt Elner, I really don't remember. I wasn't paying all that much attention."

"I'll tell you why he can't remember, Aunt Elner, because he never saw it, that's why! You better be careful, Macky, or I'll tell John Dockrill that you said he had a tattoo."

"Go ahead."

"I know Betsy Dockrill and I know she would never marry a man with a tattoo."

"Whatever you say, Norma."

"Betsy . . . is she the one that went off to Bible school?"

"No, honey, that was Patsy."

"Who?"

"Anna Lee's friend, Patsy."

"Who?"

"Patsy Henry. They ran the nursery school on Neighbor Dorothy's back porch. Dorothy's *daughter,* Anna Lee?"

"Oh, Anna Lee's friend. Over at Neighbor Dorothy's. Yes, I remember her, had a pug nose."

"That's right." Norma turned back to her husband. "Macky, I'll bet you a month's worth of back rubs that John Dockrill does not have a tattoo."

"You don't want to do that, because you'll lose."

"See, Aunt Elner, he won't bet. I told you he's making the whole thing up. He knows I can call Betsy right now and ask—"

"Go on," said Macky.

"Don't dare me; you know I'll do it."

"Do what you want. You want to give me a month's worth of back rubs, who am I to say no?"

Norma looked at Aunt Elner. "Should I call her?"

"Well, I wish you would. Now you've got me curious."

"All right, I will." Norma stood up. "Here I go . . . I'm going . . ." She waited but Macky looked at her and kept on eating. She walked into the kitchen and called out: "Last chance, Macky. I have the phone in my hand . . . here I go . . . I'm dialing."

After a moment of silence they heard Norma say, "Hello, Betsy . . . it's Norma; how are you? Good. How's your mother? Good. Oh, nothing. We were just sitting here, having a little bite to eat. Aunt Elner is here. . . . Macaroni and cheese and ham, baked apple, English peas. Well, I know this is a perfectly silly question to ask—and you are going to think I'm crazy—but I was reading this article about tattoos . . . tattoos . . . yes . . . and, well, John doesn't have a tattoo, does he? Oh. Well, that's what I thought. Oh, no reason, we were just wondering if we knew anybody that had one. Uh-huh. Well, I'll let you run on. I know you're busy. I'll see you Thursday. You take care now."

Norma came back to the table and sat down and continued eating.

Macky waited. Then he said, "Well?"

Norma did not look at him. "Well, what?"

Aunt Elner said, "Does he have a tattoo or not?"

Norma reached across and picked up a dinner roll.

"Macky Warren, I could kill you."

"Me? Why?"

"I made a complete fool out of myself and it's all your fault."

"My fault?"

"The one time you're not making something up . . . and you let me go in there and make a complete fool of myself. You knew darn well that he had a tattoo."

"I told you he had a tattoo. Didn't I, Aunt Elner?"

"Yes, he said he did."

"You should have stopped me. You deliberately let me go in there and—"

Aunt Elner said, "What's it a tattoo of, is it a lamb?"

"No."

"Well, what is it?"

"It's just a heart with a name inside."

"What does it say?"

"It says 'Wanda.' "

Aunt Elner was taken aback. "Wanda . . . I thought his wife's name was Betsy. . . ."

Norma glared at Macky. "Macky, I could kill you."

"I wonder who Wanda is?" Aunt Elner mused.

"I don't know and I certainly didn't ask."

"Poor little Betsy."

Norma looked up at Macky, who was smiling. "What are you so happy about?"

"I believe I'll have my first back rub after dinner."

Norma shook her head. "See, Aunt Elner, see what I put up with? Well, that's what I get for ever fooling with his silly bets."

"Maybe his mother's name was Wanda."

Macky chuckled. "No, Aunt Elner, I don't think that was his mother's name."

She was baffled. "Norma, did she offer any hint as to who it was?"

"No, and she did not seem thrilled about me asking, either. It was extremely embarrassing for both of us, thank you very much, Macky!"

"I don't know why you didn't believe me."

"Because what person in their right mind would ever think that a Presbyterian, particularly a minister, would have a tattoo? You can't tell me that's a normal occurrence."

"Maybe it's from the Bible?"

Norma said, "No, Aunt Elner. I don't think there's anybody in the Bible named Wanda."

"She wasn't one of the apostles' wives, was she?"

"No, honey." Norma frowned at Macky. "I'll tell you one thing, you can thank your lucky stars you didn't have some other woman's name tattooed on you when I married you."

"What?"

"You didn't have that Annette girl's name written on you or I would have divorced you the first day."

"Oh, for God's sake."

Aunt Elner asked, "Who's Annette?"

"Nobody," Macky said.

"Don't let him fool you, Aunt Elner."

"I had one date with this girl and she's turned into some big romance."

Norma got up and started clearing plates. "I happen to know you had two dates."

"How do you know?"

"I just know, that's all; never mind how I know." Norma headed for the kitchen to get the rice pudding out of the refrigerator.

Macky winked at Aunt Elner. "I tell you what . . . tomorrow I'll go down and get your name tattooed right across my chest, OK?"

Norma was squirting Reddi Wip on the pudding and called out, "Don't you dare. That's all I need is for you to get yourself tattooed all up. Next thing you'd run off and join some motorcycle gang and be robbing banks. That's all I need is to be married to some criminal."

Macky looked at Aunt Elner, who already had her spoon in her hand waiting for dessert. "The woman is insane."

"Yes, but she sure makes a good rice pudding."

Shrinking

New York City
December 15, 1974

For months Dena had dragged herself to Dr. O'Malley's office two times a week, and two times a week she sat there bored to tears. He too just sat and waited for her to say something interesting or something he could analyze. When she did talk it was about the weather, current events, or her job. Today, fatigued with her own conversation and staring at the ceiling as usual, she decided to use her skills.

"So, why don't you tell me a little bit about yourself. You seem a little young to be a doctor. Where are you from? Are you married? Children?"

He looked up from his notebook. "Miss Nordstrom, I'm the doctor and you're the patient. I'm here to talk about you."

"What do you want me to say? Tell me what you want me to say."

"Anything you want, Miss Nordstrom, this is your time."

"I find this very uncomfortable." He was jotting down something on the pad. *Uncomfortable.* "You just sit there, and ... I mean ... I'm paying you. Shouldn't you be the one who's talking to me, asking questions? I came here for you to help me get rid of stress, not to get it."

He smiled but continued writing. After a moment she decided to try another tack. "You know, Dr. O'Malley, you are a very handsome man, did you know that? Are you married?"

Dena thought she saw a faint blush but he put his pen down and said matter-of-factly, "Miss Nordstrom, you have tried everything that patients usually try but we will eventually talk about you. We can either start today or next week or the week after. It's up to you."

"I *have* been talking. Every time I come here I talk," Dena said, full of frustration.

"Miss Nordstrom, you only talk about what you *do*. I am interested in how you feel."

"How do I feel about what I do? I like my work. It's what I have wanted since I can remember."

"No, how do you feel about you—outside your work?"

"What do you mean?"

"I'm not getting a clear picture of you, unrelated to your work. I need to know how you relate to people, how you feel people relate to you."

"But they relate to me . . . about my work."

"I think you are mistaking a profession for a personal identity. Who are you *other* than what you do, that's what I'm trying to get at."

"I think you are trying to fit me into some box. What I do is not that simple. It's who I am. I am not a plumber or a construction worker who quits at five o'clock. What I do is a twenty-four-hour career. I think it's hard for people to understand. Wherever I go, I'm on television; that's how people 'relate' to me."

"I'm not saying that other people may not be able to separate you from what you do, I'm wondering if you can."

Dena looked out the window. Snow was falling, luminous against the yellow glow of the streetlights. It reminded her of another late snowy afternoon when she and her mother had walked in the streets of New York, all the way from midtown to her mother's apartment building, but she quickly pushed it out of her mind. She did not like to think about her mother. And it was certainly not something she wanted to discuss with O'Malley. It was none of his business.

At the end of the session, he closed his notebook. "Miss Nordstrom, I am afraid we have a problem." He corrected himself. "Well, no, I'm afraid I have a problem, a scheduling problem. A former patient of mine is in a serious crisis and I am going to be forced to give up your time."

Hooray, thought Dena.

"But," he continued, "I've spoken to Dr. Halling and—I am sorry—I am going to have to transfer you to another doctor, one I think can help you a lot more with your immediate problems. You know, sleeplessness, nervousness; she specializes in hypnotherapy and—"

"Hypnotherapy? I don't want to be hypnotized, for God's sake."

Dr. O'Malley said, "Before you balk, I think you should consider giving it a try. We are finding that hypnotherapy can be very helpful with deep-seated . . . ah . . . relaxation problems can be treated quite successfully with hypnotherapy."

Dena made a face. "I'm not crazy about the idea of going to a woman, either. Don't you have a man you can recommend?"

"No, Dr. Diggers is the one person I can recommend with complete confidence." At last O'Malley seemed to loosen up a bit. He confided: "As a matter of fact, she was my therapist."

"What's the matter with you? Why would you need a psychiatrist?"

He smiled at her sudden concern. "It's required. All doctors have to go through analysis before we get our degree. Most of us need it, anyhow."

"Oh."

"I've already spoken to her and she will see you on Friday at our time. Her name is Elizabeth Diggers and I think you're going to be quite pleased with her." He handed her Dr. Diggers's card.

"Oh, well . . . all right. Whatever."

He stood up and shook her hand. "Well, good-bye, Miss Nordstrom—and good luck."

❧   ❧   ❧

Walking home in the snow, Dena felt as if she had been let out of school, yet at the same time strangely sad and a bit rejected. It couldn't be the thought of not seeing Dr. O'Malley again; she was happy about that. Maybe it was just that Christmas was coming up. She hated Christmas. It was always the same, so many people pulling at her. Being single at Christmastime was a pain. She had to make up so many excuses, so many lies. J.C. was already badgering her to go home to Minnesota with him, but she had no intention of spending Christmas in the bosom of somebody else's family. She usually slept through Christmas, and then had to lie about what a great time she had over the holidays. It was getting harder and harder.

By the time she had reached Forty-fifth Street the snowfall had turned into a blizzard and she could barely see three feet in front of her. Two blocks later she looked up just in time to see a large brown mass looming before her that nearly scared her to death. Startled, she stopped and suddenly realized that she had almost walked into a camel. A huge, live camel was being led from a truck into a side door at Radio City Music Hall.

As she stood there and waited for it to pass, she caught a quick glimpse of the darkened backstage. It reminded her of something she did not want to remember so she crossed the street quickly.

Later, at Fifty-sixth, she started to laugh to herself. Ira's early lead would have been "TV personality trampled to death by camel. Details at ten."

And Ira would have loved it.

Passing the Torch

After Dena had left his office for good, Gerry O'Malley sat back down, feeling ill. Sending her to someone else was the last thing in the world he wanted. But ethically and professionally he had to do it. He had fallen hopelessly head over heels in love with Dena Nordstrom, and could not be objective if he tried. That first day when she had come into his office, her beauty had almost taken his breath away. But he had treated beautiful women before and it was not beauty alone that made him constantly want to get up and hold her. It was the Dena he saw under that gorgeous Nordstrom exterior, that vulnerable, terrified girl, the girl inside the woman he wanted to put his arms around.

Letting her walk out that door was the hardest thing he ever had to do in his life. He looked at his watch, and dialed.

"Liz, it's Gerry."

"Oh, hi, doll, what's up?"

"I just wanted to let you know she'll be there on Friday. So I'll send my notes on over, all right?"

"Good. How are you doing?"

"Other than feeling like a complete idiot, wanting to leave the profession and throw myself at her feet, I'm doing just great."

"Poor guy."

"Yeah, I finally found someone as sexy and beautiful as you and she turns out to be a patient. I fell in love with my therapist; why didn't she?"

Elizabeth Diggers's laugh was low and hearty.

"Seriously, I appreciate you seeing her on such short notice. Liz, you are the only person I would trust with her."

"Happy to do it. And Gerry—want some highly technical professional advice?"

"Yes."

"Go out and have a few drinks."

"You tell an Irishman that?"

"On second thought, don't. I'll have the drink. And Gerry?"

"Yes?"

"You're one of the good guys."

"Thanks, Elizabeth."

❊ ❊ ❊

Dena had made an appointment with Dr. Diggers. She sounded nice, as if she might have a little more personality than O'Malley. Her office was on Eighty-ninth and Madison Avenue. The doorman who sent her up recognized Dena. Oh, great, she thought, now everyone in New York is going to know I'm seeing a shrink. And a hypnoshrink, at that. If her next test with Dr. Halling was better, she would stop going.

Dena rang the bell of the apartment and after a few minutes the door opened. A small Hispanic woman said, "Come right this way," and led her down the center hall to Dr. Diggers's office. The woman knocked lightly. "Dr. Diggers, your five o'clock is here."

"Come in."

Dena was surprised. Dr. Elizabeth Diggers was a large black woman in a wheelchair.

"Hello, Miss Nordstrom. I'm Dr. Diggers." She smiled. "Didn't Gerry tell you I was a big black woman in a wheelchair?"

"No."

"I see. He tends to be short on small talk." She pushed a plate of candy toward her.

"Yes, I know," Dena said. "No, thank you."

"Is that going to be a problem for you?"

"Excuse me?"

"How do you feel about my being black?"

Dena, who could lie like a dog, was caught off guard. "I'm surprised, that's all. You didn't sound black on the phone." Dena realized that was the wrong thing to say but it was too late. "How do I feel about it? I couldn't care less. I'm the one who should be worried. I'm the patient . . . does it bother you that I'm white? If so, tell me and I'll be happy to leave."

Dr. Diggers was opening the ever-present notepad and did not answer.

"Look," Dena said, "if this is some sort of test, I don't care what color you are but you might as well know I don't want to be here. But I promised my doctor I would—so here I am."

"I see."

"I just want to start off being honest."

"It's a good start," Diggers said. "And by the way, it was not a test but you passed."

"If it did bother people that you were black, would they tell you?"

"No, not really, but I can get a pretty good idea if it is a problem by the way they answer."

"So it is a test!"

Dr. Diggers laughed. "Yes, I guess you're right; it is a test of sorts. Have a seat."

"Is the candy a test, too?"

"Ah, now you've caught me again."

Dena finally sat down.

"I have a few notes from Gerry but if you don't mind, I'd like to find out some basic information. And by the way, I have seen you on television and I think you do a wonderful job."

Dena liked that. "Oh, thank you."

"Now, Gerry mentioned you seem to be having some biological effects from stress."

"What?"

"Stomach problems."

"Oh, yes. But I tried to tell him it's from my job. But I don't think he gets it. He doesn't know what television is."

"I see. And Dr. Halling is your physician?"

Dena nodded and looked across the room. It was a nice room with light beige carpeting and windows that went all the way across the front. She was glad to see a wall filled with diploma after diploma.

"How long have you had physical problems?"

"With my stomach?"

"Yes, or any other."

"Oh, a long time. Since I was about maybe fifteen or sixteen. You're not going to hypnotize me, are you?"

"Not today."

"Oh, well, I'm a little nervous about it, that's all."

"Now, Miss Nordstrom, tell me a little bit about your history."

"Well, I started in local television in Dallas when—"

Dr. Diggers stopped her. "No, I mean your family history."

"What?"

"Tell me about your parents."

"Oh." She sighed. "My father was killed in the war . . . and my mother's dead."

"How old were you when your mother died?"

"Ah, fourteen or fifteen, I think; it's hard to remember."

"Hard to remember her death or how old you were?"

"Both. She was sick for a long time and I was in boarding school."

"I see . . . and what was it?"

"Sacred Heart Academy; it was a Catholic boarding school."

"No, what was her illness?"

"Oh. Tuberculosis."

"I see." Suddenly Dr. Diggers remembered something from Gerry's notes. "Wasn't somebody in your family hit by a car?"

"Yes, she was, on her way to the hospital for treatment. She got hit by a car. Actually, a car hit her bus. Anyhow, the reason I'm here is I am having terrible trouble sleeping. I wondered if maybe—"

"Do you have living relatives?"

"One or two distant relatives. On my father's side. A distant cousin and an aunt, I think—but I don't see them much."

"On your mother's side?"

Dena leaned over to look at her pad. "Are you writing this down so if I go completely insane you can call them?"

Dr. Diggers laughed. "No, just making a few notes for myself. And on your mother's side?"

"No."

She looked up. "No?"

"No. All dead."

"I see." The doctor made a note: *patient agitated, kicking foot.*

❀ ❀ ❀

Later that evening, when Elizabeth Diggers had finished her dinner and had put the dishes in the sink for the housekeeper in the morning, the phone rang. She wheeled over to the wall phone. "I wondered how long it would be before you called."

"Well, did you see my girl today?"

"Oh, yes."

"Well?"

There was a pause. "Mercy, son, you are either the bravest man I ever knew or the dumbest."

He chuckled.

"Are you sure you want to take all that on?"

"No, but I don't have much of a choice. I am absolutely so crazy about that woman that I can't see straight."

"I'll do my best to help her, Gerry, you know that, but at this point I'm not even sure if she will come back."

"Isn't she the most beautiful thing you have ever seen?"

"Yes, she is a good-looking woman but—"

"And smart."

"Oh, yes, and smart. Next thing you'll be asking is what she wore."

"What did she have on?"

"I don't remember."

"Oh, you do, too. You just enjoy torturing me. But, really, isn't she just a classic natural beauty?"

"Yes, Gerry, she puts the moon and the stars to shame. Does this girl have any idea how you feel?"

"No. I mean, I don't think so. And now is certainly not the time to tell her. She has enough problems, don't you agree?"

"Absolutely. You've got it bad and that ain't good. I think you need to put some distance between you two and see how you feel down the line."

"I can tell you right now, Elizabeth, I'm not going to change. It's just a matter of giving her some time. So, I'll only ask one more thing and then I promise—from now on I'm out of the picture, OK? What do you think—was I off on my evaluation?"

"Not much; I think you pretty much pegged it. Shut down. Definitely symptoms of some sort of severe rejection trauma."

"Yeah. It could be around her mother's death; she wouldn't let me get near that. But it's in your hands now."

"Well, OK, buddy. Now that you've passed the torch on to me, and I do mean that in the real sense, I'll do my best."

"Thanks."

"But in the meantime—it could be a long meantime—I suggest you see other people."

"Oh, really? So, what are you doing this Saturday night?"

"What I always do, boogie till I drop."

He laughed.

"Good night, Romeo."

She had tried to keep it professional but after she hung up, she let her heart go out to him. She knew that being in love all by yourself was the loneliest, most painful experience known to man—or woman—and there was nothing she could do to help him.

Who Are You?

New York City
December 19, 1974

Dr. Diggers was somewhat surprised when Dena showed up for her second appointment. She strolled in five minutes late and flopped down in a chair.

Dr. Diggers smiled at her. "Back for me to have another crack at you?"

"Yes," Dena said, with little enthusiasm.

"Then I will proceed with the torture."

"You might as well. What are we supposed to talk about today?"

"Well, I would like to continue to try and get to know you a little better, find out at least about your background. Where are you from?"

"Where are you from?" Dena asked.

"Chicago. And you?"

"Me? I'm not from any place in particular."

"Strange. That's not my experience."

"What do you mean?"

"It has been my experience that everybody has to be from some place."

"I was born in San Francisco, but we moved around a lot."

"What is your heritage?"

"My what?"

"Your heritage. Where do you come from . . . your roots?"

"My roots? Like the book. You mean my ancestors?"

"Yes, what was their nationality?"

"Oh, I don't know. My father was Swedish . . . or Norwegian or something like that."

"And your mother?"

"Just plain old American, I guess; she never said. Her maiden name was Chapman so I guess she's what?—English? I don't know."

Dr. Diggers was always astonished at how so few people cared about their heritage. "Aren't you curious to find out more?"

"Not really. I'm an American; that's all that matters, isn't it?"

"Well, then. How would you describe yourself . . . other than as an American?"

"What?"

"How would you describe yourself?"

Dena was puzzled. "I'm a person on television."

"No, you personally. In other words, if your job ended tomorrow, who would you be?"

"I don't know . . . I would still be me. I don't see what you're getting at."

"OK, let's play a little game. I want you to give me three answers to this question. Who are you?"

"I'm Dena Nordstrom, I'm blond . . . and . . ." She was having a hard time. "And I'm five foot seven. Is this another test?"

"No, it just helps give me a little better idea of your self-image. It gives me an idea about what we have to work on."

"And did I pass or fail? I'd like to know."

Dr. Diggers put down her pen. "It's not a question of that. But think about how you answered. All three answers describe your image."

"What was I supposed to say? What else is there?"

"You're not supposed to say anything specifically. Some people say, I'm a wife, I'm a mother, I'm a daughter. In all three answers you did not connect yourself with a personal relationship—and that usually indicates you may have an identity problem. And some of our work here will be to find out why. See what I mean?"

Dena felt alarmed. Identity problem?

"It is just something to think about down the line. Right now let's talk about your immediate problems. You say you're not sleeping well."

"No, I'm not. But let's go back to the other thing. Again, I don't want to hurt your feelings but that test or whatever it was is dead wrong. I know exactly who I am. I always knew exactly what I wanted and what I wanted to be. I already told Dr. O'Malley that once."

"As I said, it's not a test," Diggers said. "It's just a question."

That night, when Dr. Diggers was going over her notes, she remembered the first time she had been asked, Who are you? Her answers had come immediately and without difficulty. I'm female, I'm black, I'm crippled. She wondered, after all these years if, asked again, her answers would still be the same and in that order. Dr. Diggers turned out the lights in her office and rolled down the long hall to her kitchen, where her dinner was waiting.

That night Dena picked up the phone and called her friend.

"Sookie, it's Dena."

"Well, hey! How are you?"

"Are you busy?"

"Nooo. I wasn't doing a thing except flipping through my *Southern Living Cookbook* trying to figure out what in the world I can serve two hundred people. I could just put Earle Poole in a paper sack and throw him in the river. What's going on with you?"

"Nothing; why are you mad at Earle?"

"Oh, you don't want to know."

"Yes, I do."

"Every year, around Christmas, I have a little holiday luncheon for all my close girlfriends around here. Just us, nothing big . . . just fifteen or sixteen of us. So I handed the invitations to Earle and told him to have Melba down at the office Xerox them and send them out and she sent it to everybody on our Christmas card list, including all of Earle's patients. So Lord knows how many people will be showing up here next week."

"What are you going to do?"

"Make a lot of cheese grits and hope for the best; what else can I do? It's in God's hands now. But enough about me. I hope you're calling to tell me you're going to get to come and spend Christmas with us this year."

"No, it doesn't look good. I think I'm working the whole time."

"Oh, that's what you said last year. Can't you get off? The girls will be so disappointed. They are dying to meet you. Just think about those poor little things, tears running out their eyes, their little hearts broken."

"Sookie, stop it. You're shameless."

"But it's true! They watch you every time you're on television and they even named a pet after you, Dena the hamster."

"You're kidding!"

"No, your namesake is up there right now, running around in circles on its wheel."

"Well, tell them I'm flattered . . . I think. That's quite an honor."

"Yes, you are officially in the Hamster Hall of Fame."

"Listen. The reason I called is that I want to ask you a question."

"Oh! OK . . . what?"

"I want you to give me three different answers to the question, all right? That's all you can say, don't think about it, just say the first three things that come into your mind."

"OK."

"Are you ready?"

"Yes."

"Who are you?"

"What? Oh, don't be silly. You know who I am."

"No, that's the question. Who are you?"

"Who am I?"

"Yes. Three descriptive facts."

Sookie thought aloud. "Oh, all right . . . Let's see, who am I? Who am I?"

"Don't *think* about it, just answer off the top of your head."

"Well, I have to think! I can't just say anything."

"Yes, you can, that's the point. Hurry up."

"Well, all right. I'm a Simmons on my mother's side, a Krackenberry on Daddy's side of the family, a Poole by marriage. I'm a Southerner. I'm a Kappa."

"OK, stop," Dena said.

"I'm the mother of three daughters. I'm a wife."

"Sookie . . . I just need three."

"Well, Dena, I'm more than just three things! I'm past president of the Junior Auxiliary, a past Magnolia Trail Maid—"

"It's over, you answered the question."

"Well, this is the silliest question I ever heard of. I have a lot more. What is this for, a program?"

"Nothing. It was just a game some people were playing."

"Who?"

"Oh, just a bunch of people at a party. It's a party game."

"Did they ask you who you were?"

"Yes."

"Well, I hope you told them you were a Kappa!"

"That was the first thing I thought of, Sookie."

"What else did you say?"

"Oh, let's see . . . I remember. I said I was a communist and a child molester."

Sookie screamed, "You did not!"

"No."

"You better not have. Those people up there might not know you are kidding."

❖ ❖ ❖

The next morning when Earle Poole came down to breakfast, Sookie sat down and stared at him. He looked at her. "What's wrong?"

"Who are you?"

"What?"

"Who are you? Give me three answers."

Earle put the paper down. "Look, Sookie, if this is about those invitations, I told you I am sorry."

"No, it's not about that, Earle. Just answer my question. Be serious, now."

Earle sighed. "I'm a dentist . . . I'm a husband . . ."

"One more thing."

He looked at his watch. "And I'm late!"

After Earle left, still caught up in the game, Sookie called her mother. Her mother immediately answered in a loud, booming voice, "I'm Lenore Simmons Krackenberry!"

"I need *three* answers, Mother."

Her mother said, "Sookie, that is three answers!"

Neighbor Dorothy's Christmas Show

Elmwood Springs, Missouri
December 15, 1948

Neighbor Dorothy hurried into the living room and sat down, just as the red "on-air" light went on. "Good morning, everybody, and a happy December the fifteenth to you. It's another pretty day over here in Elmwood Springs and I hope it is just as pretty where you are. Looking out my window this morning, I can see that the temperature is a chilly thirty-eight but it's warm and cozy inside my house. Is there anything worse than a cold house? Thank goodness Doc gets up and puts on the fire. I'll tell you, we all pile in the kitchen like chickens on these cold mornings. It's hard to keep the biscuits cooked fast enough. . . . My canary birds are so pretty and yellow they look just like two scoops of banana pudding. Well, I have a news flash. Jeannette and Nelson Eddy are expecting—no, not what you think. It's another big hit movie, called *Blossom Time,* and it will be coming to the Elmwood Springs theater soon, so be sure and look for it at a theater near you. . . . Do you have a winter garden in your window? I tell you, nothing is prettier or cheerier on dark winter days than to see ivy in the window . . . a little touch of spring all year round. If you don't have ivy, get yourself a little dirt in a pot and just drop a lemon, an orange, or grapefruit seed in it and you will have a grand little plant. However, if you are interested in something more substantial, Victor the florist offers this advice: Fuchsias will dangle bells of many shapes and colors. Dieffenbachias' cream-splashed leaves are good in any window and come in several sizes. Grape ivy is fairly pest resistant . . . likes sunlight. . . . English ivy needs acid soil and shade and an African violet is always a delight. So go on down and get yourself a plant today. . . . Let's see . . . what else do I have this morning, Mother Smith?" (Mother Smith played a few strains of "Santa Claus Is Coming to Town.") "Oh, that's right . . . Santa Claus *is* coming to town, and he's going to be in the back of Morgan Brothers department store, right next to the toy department, so everybody that wants to get their picture made, or tell him what they want for Christmas, be sure to go on down. Princess Mary Margaret is going right after the show today and have her picture made with Santa, and all the members of the Princess Mary Margaret fan club will be receiving one this year. . . . Oh, I don't know about you, but Christmas has just come around so fast this year; I am hardly over Thanksgiving and here it is. Isn't time just the oddest thing? Some days I don't know where it goes. I look up and it's suppertime and I feel like I just finished washing the breakfast dishes. . . . I've got to start thinking about baking my gingerbread men, and gumdrop cookies for our Christmas open house . . . and also don't forget we are making a mitten tree this year for all the poor children that don't have any. I hope all of you out there will get a chance to come to our open house—we always have a big time—we have so many exciting things planned. Dixie Cahill is bringing by some of her girls to dance for us, and the handbell choir from the Methodist Church will be here, and we are so glad that they have finally gotten their E-flat bell—it makes a big difference—so you don't want to miss that . . . and food, food, food, and a present for everyone. Oh . . . and Ernest Koonitz will be joining us with his tuba. He'll be playing 'Joy to the World.' Now that's December twentieth down at the VFW. Doc informed me that we are going to put up our tree tonight, so after the show I've got to climb up in the attic and pull down all the Christmas decorations . . . and I'm not looking forward to that, so if any of you see Bobby, tell him I said to come straight home after school. I need him to help me.

"Now, let's see . . . I had a few facts for you. . . . Oh, here's a timely one . . . a fun fact about the Christmas poinsettia. Poinsettias come to us all the way from Mexico. A man named Joel Robert Poinsette brought them to South Carolina and hence the name . . . and we are mighty glad he did. But don't forget, they are poisonous, so don't eat them or let your pets chew on them. . . ."

❦   ❦   ❦

Late that afternoon, Dorothy, Anna Lee, and Bobby met Doc downtown at the Rexall and they all walked over and picked a tree out from the vacant lot where the Civitan Club was selling them. At home Mother Smith was popping corn and all the Christmas decorations had been dug out of the attic, the back closet, and the cedar chest in the hall and were ready to go. By ten o'clock that night, cream-colored cardboard candleholders with blue lights were in every window, and a string of red cut-paper letters that said MERRY CHRISTMAS hung over all the doors. The tree in the corner was covered with satin balls of apple green and shiny ruby red and blue ones with white frosted stripes around them, silver tinsel, strings of popcorn and colored lights, and an angel with wings at the very top. A white sheet wrapped around the bottom was ready and waiting for presents.

As usual, Dorothy was the last one up and as she stood in the dark living room, the glow of the Christmas lights looked so pretty, she didn't have the heart to turn them off and decided to leave them on all night.

Dena Digs at Diggers

New York City
1975

Dena went back to her doctor, and her ulcer had not gotten much better but it was no worse so she promised to continue seeing Diggers. She hated to keep talking about herself but she would do anything to avoid the dreaded prescription "bed rest."

In Dr. Diggers's office, she sat, as usual, kicking her foot. The doctor had been waiting for her to say something and, as usual, it made Dena uncomfortable. Finally, Dena said, "All right, if you're not going to ask me anything, I'll analyze you. At least one of us will get something out of this."

"We are here to talk about you."

"Let's don't. Please, I'm so sick of talking about myself, thinking about myself; please, let's talk about you for a change. Tell me all about you. You look like an interesting person."

Diggers looked at the clock. Five more minutes left. She was not going to get anything more out of Dena today. "OK, I'll humor you. What do you want to know?"

Dena's eyes lit up. "Ahh, let's see." She rubbed her hands together. "OK, what is it like to be black?"

Diggers smiled. White people always thought that was the most important thing about her. She put her pen down. "That's a question that has as many answers as there are black people. Each person experiences it differently."

"Well, I don't know any other black people. What is it like for you?"

"I do believe I'm being interviewed."

"No, you're not. I'm just curious. I really would like to know."

"What do you think it's like?"

Dena shook her finger at her. "Oh, no, you are not going to trap me, Dr. Elizabeth Diggers, M.D., Ph.D., or whatever you are. All you shrinks are alike; you always answer a question with a question. Would you rather not discuss it, or is it too sensitive an issue?"

"No, of course not."

"Have white people done terrible things to you?"

"I've earned my stripes. I've had my share of prejudice."

Dena winced. "Oh, God, I'm sorry you had to go through that. Are you angry about it?"

"Angry? No, but I understand anger. I would say hurt more than anything. And when I say prejudice, I mean across the board. Prejudice can do terrible things to all human beings, and black people can be just as intolerant with one another as white people."

"Really?"

"Oh yes—I've had to put up with it from white people and from my own people as well."

"Really, like what? Give me an example."

"Well, there are those who call me an Uncle Tom because I have white friends and live in a white neighborhood. Accuse me of trying to be white." She laughed. "Me, as black as I am, there is no way I'm ever going to be white, right? Now, there are some that think I should give up my career and devote my life to helping the cause of the black man. Light blacks think I'm too black, some blacks think I talk too white; it never ends. No matter which way you turn there is always somebody at you." She suddenly smiled. "Next I'll be breaking into a chorus of 'Ol' Man River,' won't I? But I have a lot more problems than merely being black."

Dena said, "You mean your—"

"That I'm in a wheelchair? Yes, but besides the fact that my patient is trying to analyze me, the fact that I'm a female in a male profession has been my biggest problem. I've experienced a lot more prejudice because I'm a woman than I ever have because I'm black. Don't forget, black men got the vote in this country long before any women, black or white, and men are men, no matter what color they are. It could drive you crazy if you let it."

"Is that why you became a psychiatrist?"

Diggers laughed and looked at the clock. "Ah-ha, saved by the bell. You're time's up! And good riddance. You never stop inter-viewing, do you?"

As Dena left, she said loud enough for Diggers's housekeeper to hear: "You're responding to treatment extremely well, Doctor. Just keep it up and I'm sure we will be able to get to the root of your prob-lems. Just keep writing those dreams down. See you next week."

Diggers had to laugh. She usually didn't let her patients get around her like that. But she could not help being impressed with Dena Nordstrom. She could see how Gerry could be in love with her. There was something very appealing about her, very sweet, really.

What a shame she was so shut down.

A Much-Needed Breather

Selma, Alabama
1975

For the past six months Dena had been working at a breakneck pace and almost every night J.C. had her going from party to party, from one event to another. Lately she was having a hard time trying to keep up with what seemed to be his boundless energy. Her stomach was beginning to hurt again and she could not face the several parties that he had lined up for them this weekend. She needed a rest, but she knew she would not be able to hide from J.C. in New York. She had to get away, make up an elaborate lie about something and go somewhere far off the beaten path.

But where? Where would be the last place on earth she could go without a chance of running into any of his crowd? Then it came to her.

❋   ❋   ❋

"Hello."

"Sookie, it's me."

"Hey, how are you? What are you doing?"

"Listen, Sookie, will you be home next Friday afternoon?"

"Of course. Why?"

"You've been asking me to come for a visit and I thought I would."

Sookie screamed, "*Really?* You mean to Selma?"

"Yes."

"Oh my God, I'm about to faint. I can't believe it. How long can you stay?"

"I'll fly down for the weekend. Is that all right?"

"All right? It's wonderful."

"Look, Sookie—I'll come but you have to promise me one thing."

"Of course. What?"

"You won't tell anybody I'm coming."

"Why not?"

"Sookie, I am exhausted, really. I need to rest. I need to get away from people for a few days."

"Oh, well, of course. Can I tell Earle?"

"Oh, sure. I just mean the press, anybody I don't know. I just want to visit with you."

"Do you want me to send the girls to Mother?"

"No, I mean just you and Earle and the girls. I just don't want to see anyone else."

Sookie was disappointed. "Wouldn't you know? My one famous friend turns out to be a recluse. And I don't know why, everybody just loves you. They all think you are just the nicest, friendliest, smartest person, and that you would just love to meet them. I don't tell them the truth, naturally, that you couldn't care a thing in the world about meeting them."

"You should be glad they won't meet me. If they did, they'd find out that I'm not very nice these days."

"Oh, you are too nice. Now, how can everybody think that and be wrong? You were voted the most popular female on television just last month. Did it ever occur to you that you might be wrong and everybody else is right? No, it's just silly . . . but I'll do it."

"Thank you."

"But just remember, this is a small town—so you'd better fly in with a sack over your head."

Dena laughed.

"I really am excited, and if you need to rest, then that's just what you can do. I won't let anybody bother you. I'll even wear a muzzle."

❋ ❋ ❋

As Dena stepped off the plane in Selma, a gush of hot, almost tropical heat engulfed her. The sun was blinding but she soon saw Sookie, wearing a large black hat and dark sunglasses. Sookie quickly called out, "Miss Smith, oh, Miss Smith, over here." Dena had to laugh at Sookie's idea of keeping a low profile. As they walked to the car Sookie went down her list. "Now, Dena, I have done everything you said. Not a soul knows you are coming, except Earle, and Toncie— she works for us—and the children have been instructed not to say a word. So I promise you, you are going to be left alone. I want you to rest. Tonight we'll have a quiet dinner. Tomorrow I'm making Earle go down to the club and you and I will just laze around all day by the pool or you can sleep or do whatever you want to. My wish is your command. . . . I mean, oh, you know what I mean."

"Is it always this hot?"

"Honey, this is nothing. Wait until July and August." They got into an enormous blue Lincoln Town Car the size of a limousine. "Is this yours?" Dena asked.

"No, it's one of Mother's rejects. She bought it and then hated it and gave it to the girls."

"But the girls are still little, aren't they?"

"Yes, but she said it would be nice for them when they grew up. Don't ask. That's Mother."

"Will I get to see her?"

"You *want* to see Mother?"

"Sure, I like your mother, you know that. Didn't you tell her I was coming?"

"No! If she knew you were here an elephant gun couldn't stop her from crashing through the door to get at you. But, all right . . . if you want to see her, I'll call her and let her come over tomorrow for half an hour. But you might be sorry. She's like being hit by a tornado. God knows she will be thrilled."

"Is your brother here?"

"Buck? No, he's over in Saudi Arabia doing some oil thing."

Sookie turned down a road that seemed to run right through the middle of a pecan grove. Dena said, "Are those cows out there?"

"I told you I lived out in the suburbs, honey. We're just old Alabama hillbillies."

After about five minutes of pecan groves, Dena saw a huge house at the end of the road and suddenly realized the road they had been driving on was Sookie's driveway. Sookie pulled up and said, "Here we are."

Dena looked up at the rambling two-story white building with columns.

"*This* is a little house out in the suburbs? Good God, Sookie, it looks like a governor's mansion."

Sookie dismissed it with a wave. "Oh, honey, it's not that big. You should see Buck's house."

They got out of the car and a woman in a white uniform came out. "Dena, this is Toncie."

Toncie beamed from ear to ear. "I know who you are and I haven't said a word, no, ma'am."

"Thank you."

They stepped into the vast entry hall with a grand staircase leading up to the second floor. Sookie said, "Where's my brood? They are so excited you are coming, I almost had to sedate them."

Toncie took Dena's bag. "They're upstairs. I'm keeping them in prison till Miss Nordstrom gets a chance to catch her breath."

At this point three little redheaded girls all starched and pressed with big bows in their hair appeared at the top of the landing, peering through the railing at Dena.

Sookie looked up. "Uh-oh . . . here they are. Too late now—you've been spotted."

Toncie said, "I told them not to come down till you called them."

"Well, you might as well get it over with. Dena, they're just dying to get at you." She called up, "All right, girls, come on down but don't run."

The three wide-eyed girls were down the stairs like a shot and stood staring up at Dena in awe. Sookie said, "This is Dee Dee, this is Ce Ce, and this is the baby, Lenore . . . but we call her Le Le. Girls, this is your Aunt Dena."

Dena looked down at them. "Well, hello, girls."

They all looked at their mother, wide-eyed with excitement.

"Well, go on and say hello."

"May I shake your hand?" Dena said.

They all looked at their mother again, who said, "I can't believe my children have suddenly gone shy. Go on, girls, shake hands with her."

The two oldest were delighted and giggled like shaking hands was the funniest thing they had ever done. The smallest walked over and hugged Dena's leg, then all three began babbling and tugging at her. "Come on and see our room," they said and tried to pull her up the stairs. Le Le had attached both hands to Dena's belt.

"All right, girls," Sookie said, "that's enough. She'll go upstairs later. Let go of her." They disappeared with Toncie.

Off the kitchen in the back of the house was a long, screened-in brick patio filled with white wicker furniture and floral pillows. Sookie said, "Excuse the mess but during the summer we just practically live out here. It's so nice and cool at night." They walked across a courtyard with what seemed like an Olympic pool to where Dena would be staying—a charming, smaller version of the main house, decorated in gentle pastels with overhead fans and filled with fresh flowers. The minute Dena walked in, Sookie started to apologize. "It's not much but I thought it would be quieter out here."

"Sookie, all I ever see is the inside of hotel rooms. To me, this is great, believe me."

"Really?"

"Yes."

Sookie brightened up a little. "Well . . . good. Now I'm going to go, like I promised, and drag myself away so you can take a nap or watch TV or read . . . or whatever. . . . There's iced tea in the fridge . . . and I thought we'd eat around seven. Is that too early?"

"No. That's fine."

"I hope you like fried pig's feet and hog snouts."

Dena looked alarmed. "Just kidding," Sookie said, "you're going to get ham biscuits, grits, and a nice congealed salad . . . and Toncie's made a pecan pie. Hope that's all right."

Dena said, "It sounds delicious," wondering how you congealed a salad.

Sookie left, saying, "Rest now."

Dena unpacked and went out on her screened-in patio and noticed that Sookie had neatly placed a stack of old *Kappa Key* magazines and *Southern Living* on the end table. She turned on the fan and laid down. She closed her eyes and before she knew it, she was in a deep sleep.

Dena did not wake up until eleven o'clock the next morning. She stumbled into the living room and smelled fresh coffee. A note was on the coffeemaker.

> *Come over when you wake up ... or when you feel like it. The*
> *girls are in dancing school until one.*
>
> *Love, Sookie*

After an hour she got dressed, put her sunglasses on, and headed over to the big house. Sookie was in the kitchen. "Sookie, I'm sorry I missed dinner."

"Well, thank heavens you are alive. I was beginning to worry. I could see the headlines, 'Dead Celebrity Found in the Pooles' Pool House'!"

"No, I'm not dead but I swear I feel drugged. Did you put dope in my iced tea?"

"Oh, yes, you found us out. We're doping you up good so we can keep you here with us, and sell tickets for people to come and look at you."

Sookie went over to the refrigerator and pulled out a small, frosty silver cup and handed it to Dena. "Earle made you a mint julep before he left. He thought you might need a drink."

"This early?"

"Yes, you'll need it. I called Mother this morning and she is making her command appearance at two. I had to threaten her with the lives of her grandchildren not to tell anyone you're here. And of course, Earle was furious that I made him leave; he wanted to stay and hang on to your every word."

"I like Earle, he's sweet."

"He is, bless his heart. He wanted to know if you needed any dental work done, said to tell you he'd be happy to do it."

"I'll keep that in mind."

Lenore Simmons Krackenberry was a large, handsome woman who always wore pins and scarves and gave the impression she was wearing a cape even in summer. She had silver-white hair, impeccably styled in a winged backflip, one of the many reasons her children secretly referred to her as Winged Victory. As soon as Toncie opened the door, Lenore swept in with arms outstretched, swooping through the house, leaving a trail of expensive perfume behind her, calling out for Dena in a loud voice dripping with honey.

"Where is that precious thang? I can't wait to get my hands on you; where are you? You'd better get out heah this very minute before I have a fit."

Sookie heard her coming. "We're here on the patio, Mother." She warned Dena, "Prepare for attack." But by that time Lenore was upon them, gushing at Dena, "Oh, there she is, come heah and let me give you a great, big hug!" Dena stood up and winced in pain as Lenore crushed her in her arms, pressing pearls into Dena's chest.

"When Sookie called and said you were heah, I just couldn't believe it but heah you are in person." She squeezed her again.

"How are you, Mrs. Krackenberry?"

"Well, honey, I'm just wonderful! Just wonderful! Oh, let me look at you, still as pretty as a picture. Look *at* that skin. Sookie, that's what your skin would look like if you would have stayed out of the sun like I told you."

Lenore collapsed into a large chair, flipping her scarf with a flair, and calling out, "Toncie, let me have a glass of tea, will you, honey? I'm exhausted from the drive. Dena, can you believe that Sookie and Earle moved so far out in the country? It's practically an overnight trip to get to see my grandbabies."

"Mother, it's twenty minutes from town."

Toncie brought a glass of iced tea. "Thank you ... well, you might as well be living on Tobacco Road, way out heah. I wouldn't be surprised if my granddaughters don't grow up and marry potato farmers. Where are the babies?"

"Upstairs. I had to lock them up to keep them from driving Dena crazy."

Lenore said to Dena, "Aren't they just the cutest things? I'm getting their portraits painted this spring." Then she made a sad face and whispered, "Did you notice their little ears?"

Dena said, "No, not at all."

"Mother!"

"Well, darling, they do have the Poole ears! I told her that before she married Earle but you know she wouldn't listen to me, when every boy in the state was after her."

Sookie sighed. "Nobody was after me, Mother."

"And I suppose she told you about her brother Buck, living halfway across the world with the Arabs and the camels. Poor little Darla. But enough about us, how are you? You little angel, just setting the world on fire. Sookie said she would never speak to me again if I brought this up but I am just literally breaking out in a cold sweat trying not to throw you a party while you are here."

"Mother."

Lenore raised her arm in the air. "I'm not saying a word to anybody, but it just kills me that here you are in Selma and you are not even going to be written up. Just say the word and I can have the mayor here in three minutes with the key to the city."

"Mother, now, stop it—you promised."

Lenore looked at her innocently. "I know . . . but I just think she needs to know how loved she is. It just seems so sad. I could have had the Magnolia Trail Maidens and a brass band out at the airport and everything."

Sookie looked at Dena. "You see, I told you but you insisted."

Lenore said, "What did you tell her?"

"Mrs. Krackenberry," Dena said, "that is so sweet, really, but I'm just here for a quiet visit."

"Oh, I know you are, darling, and I would not intrude on your incognito for anything in this world. You career girls need your rest. I just hate it that we can't show you some of our Southern hospitality;

we are all so proud of you, that's all. I told Sookie the first time I met you, I said, now, that girl is going to go far. I think it's just wonderful the way you young girls nowadays have such exciting careers. My daddy wouldn't let me work . . . you know how men were back then, thought we were all too delicate."

"Mother, I don't know how anybody ever thought you were too delicate."

Lenore's eyes got big. "He did! And your father would never have let me work, and I don't mind telling you, I regret it. If I had had a chance back then, no telling what kind of career I could have had."

"The one you would have wanted was already taken, Mother."

"What's that?" Lenore said.

"There was already a queen of England."

Lenore's laughter was loud. "Oh, Dena, do you see how ugly she talks about me? I'll tell you, nothing hurts so much as an ungrateful child, and I have two."

"Yes, Mother, your poor life is hell. We just treat you so terrible."

Lenore leaned toward Dena. "They accuse me of being a domineering mother, can you believe that? Me, just because I care about them. I hope your children don't turn on you when they grow up."

"Mother, face it, you *are* domineering."

"See how she is; once she gets it in her mind about something, she starts to believe it."

Dena smiled. "Oh, yes, I know."

"See, Sookie, Dena knows how you are."

Sookie looked at her mother and pointed to her watch. Lenore said innocently, "What?"

"Mother . . . you promised."

Lenore sighed. "Oh, all right. Dena, she made me take a sacred oath that I would not stay longer than ten minutes. Can you believe it, throwing her poor mother out in the snow with the wolves."

"Mother, it's one hundred and three degrees outside."

"Well, you know what I mean. I'm going! But, darlin', do come back when you're all rested up and let us go just hog wild over you. I'm just itching to roll out the red carpet."

They walked her to the door. "Now, if you girls need anything, call. I'll have Morris run over and bring you anything you want."

She crushed Dena again and pecked Sookie on the cheek. "Good-bye, you old mean daughter. I love you anyway," and she swept out to her car, where Morris, the driver, was waiting and had kept the air conditioner running for her.

"Now, do you see why I talk so fast," Sookie said, closing the door. "I have to just to get a word in."

"I think she's terrific."

"Oh, she is, but exhausting. Now, you know how hard it was to make her keep her mouth shut. She is *obsessed* with making everybody feel welcome to Selma. Last year one of the Daughters of the Confederacy officers came in from Richmond and she had all the poor Magnolia Trail Maidens stand in heat hotter than this for three hours waiting for her plane. Two of them passed out with heatstroke."

"What's a Magnolia Trail Maiden? Sounds like some sort of flower."

Sookie laughed. "No, they're not flowers, they're girls, silly, all dressed up in antebellum dresses; you know, with hats and parasols. They are darling."

"Do they sing or something?"

Sookie looked at Dena like she had lost her mind. "No, they don't sing, they curtsy."

"Curtsy?"

"You know, bow to the ground, like this." Sookie did a deep curtsy. "When a person gets off the plane or train or whatever, we stand in a line and curtsy to them as a gesture of welcome."

Dena was impressed. "Were you a Magnolia Trail Maiden?"

Sookie opened the door to the back patio and walked out. "Of course, and Buck was a little Colonel of the Confederacy. You know, we love to dress up. Besides, Winged Victory made us do it. Mother had her seamstress make the girls three miniature, little Trail Maid outfits and hats, but don't mention it whatever you do or they will insist on trying them on for you. They wanted to wear them when you got here but I wouldn't let them."

"Why?"

"I didn't want you to think we were any crazier than we are."

They sat out by the pool under the canopy. It was another wonderfully bright day. Dena said, "Everything is so green."

Sookie seemed surprised. "It is?"

"Yes. And it's so quiet here."

"It's quieter anywhere after Mother leaves."

"Oh, Sookie, stop. You're lucky to have a mother, lucky to have lived in one place all your life. I'll bet you know everybody here, don't you?"

"I guess between the Simmonses, the Krackenberrys, and the Pooles, we're probably related to everybody in town."

"What was it like when you were growing up?"

Sookie took a sip of her tea. "Like a three-ring circus, with Lenore as ringmaster. The house was always full of people. The bridge club or garden club always had some kind of meeting at our house and Buck's friends were running in and out. Poor Daddy, I miss him. He was the sweetest thing; he said the only reason he could live with Lenore was the fact that he was deaf in one ear. One time Buck said, 'Daddy, why can't you hear out of that ear?' And Daddy said, 'Wishful thinking, son, just wishful thinking.' He was a scream."

"Did you go to the same grammar school and high school?"

"I had no choice."

"How great. And in high school, were you a cheerleader or majorette or something?"

Sookie looked at Dena in horror. "Dena, surely you don't think I was ever a majorette. A cheerleader, yes, but a majorette? There was never a Kappa that was a majorette, Dena."

"Well, I don't know, what's the difference?"

"If you don't know I'm certainly not going to tell you. Honestly, Dena, sometimes I wonder where you've been all your life."

Toncie came out with more tea. "Those girls are having a jumping-up-and-down fit to get out here, Mrs. Poole."

They looked up at the second story of the house. In the window were little faces pressed against the glass, staring at them longingly.

"Look at that, like three little monkeys." They waved and just as Toncie had said, they were literally jumping up and down.

"Oh, Sookie, let them come down."

"Can you stand it after Mother?"

"Yes. Don't make them stay inside."

"All right, if you say so." Sookie raised her arm and announced to Toncie, "Release the prisoners. Free all the infidels at once."

A minute later, the three girls, dressed in matching bright pink-and-white-polka-dot bathing suits, came running and screaming out the back door headed straight for Dena.

Dena spent the day at the pool with Sookie and her girls and it was not until Dena had been upstairs in the girls' room and had been introduced to seven hamsters by name, looked at every doll, every toy, every dress, and every pair of shoes that Dee Dee, Ce Ce, and Le Le owned that they finally calmed down and went to sleep. All three passed out in one bed, exhausted from the day's excitement.

It was after nine when Sookie and Dena went back downstairs so they could relax.

Sookie handed Dena a glass of wine. "I hope you realize that you have ruined my children forever. From now on they will ignore me, think I'm just some old frumpy housefrau."

"Don't be silly. I hope I was all right with them. I don't know how to act around children."

"Are you kidding? They adore you. I know what's going to happen. They'll grow up and run away to New York to live the glamorous life with you and I'll wind up just like poor Stella Dallas, old and broken, standing hiding in the yard, watching my children through the window get married to rich and famous men."

"What are you talking about. You *are* rich."

"I am not, stop saying that. Honey, Earle's daddy was nothing but an old country doctor and Mother's practically given away all our inheritance to the poor."

"Really?"

"Well, not really, not all of it. She's set up a trust fund for the girls. She didn't run off and join the Peace Corps like Jimmy Carter's mother or anything. Believe me, Mother lives well, but since Daddy died, who knows what she's liable to do next. She can come up with the craziest things."

"Like what?"

"Just crazy stuff. Five years ago so many new people started moving here and she didn't think the Welcome Wagon and the Newcomers' Club were doing enough to suit her so she formed the Welcome to Selma Club . . . and I feel sorry for the poor people who move here. As soon as they hit town, Lenore's troops make a beeline over to their house and swarm all over them like ants before anybody else can get to them. I said, Mother, it's a wonder you don't scare them to death. I know if I looked up and saw Lenore Krackenberry and her gang storming up my driveway with ribbons and balloons, singing at the top of their lungs, 'Welcome to Selma,' I'd move back where I came from."

"Singing what?"

"Some old stupid song that one of her friends wrote. " 'Welcome to Selma, Selma, Selma . . . can we help ya, help ya, help ya.' It's just *awful,* but God knows people know they are welcomed."

Sookie got up. "Promise me you won't let me have more than two glasses of wine. Earle says I'm a cheap drunk and I get silly and talk too much if I have more than two glasses. I'm liable to get drunk and reveal all the family secrets."

"Do you have any?"

Sookie sat down and threw her legs over the side of the chair. "Secrets? Are you kidding? In Selma, honey, we couldn't have a secret if our lives depended on it. My life is an open book. Everybody in town knows that Buck is a big goofball and that Mother is a card-carrying crazy . . . and I'm probably not operating with a full deck myself."

Dena was unwinding and the feeling was pleasant. "Sookie, tell me about your life down here."

"My life? It's just a plain old normal life. You're the one who hobnobs with the stars. We are just plain old people, dull, dull, dull."

"No, really, tell me, what do you do?"

"We just do the same old thing just about every day, year in and year out. Dinner at the club once a week, church every Sunday, and brunch with Mother every Sunday at noon . . . that's what my life has been, just the same old thing year after year from the day I was born."

A wave of sadness swept over Dena. Sookie had no idea how lucky she was.

The Little Girl in the Lobby

U.S.A.
1948

Dena's childhood had become a blur. She could barely remember it at all. When she had been four her mother suddenly left Elmwood Springs and after that they had just drifted from one cold city to another and from one set of lonesome rooms in apartment hotels to the next. They were sometimes red brick or gray but they were always furnished with the sparest of furniture. And even though the buildings had fancy names like the La Salle, the Royalton Arms, the Highland Towers, and the Park Lane, they were never what they once were. The chairs and rugs in the lobby were always a little too worn and the halls were always bare. Even the neighborhoods seemed to look dim, with little light, and not quite but just on the verge of going down. These sad apartment hotels were filled with lonely people, the young who had been disappointed in love, had someone and lost them, or never had anyone. The old people in these hotels sat alone in their rooms, leaving only to walk an ancient dog or to buy an occasional can of soup that could be heated on a hot plate. All were living out their lives in these rooms, eating out, sitting at tables for one. Most had developed the habit of reading, and so their only dinner companion was the book from the library, their only tablemates the characters they were reading about at the time.

Usually, Dena was the one child in the building. But they never stayed long enough to really get to know anybody. She passed through people's lives and never became more than that little girl who used to sit in the lobby and wait for her mother to come home. Most of her childhood had been spent in lobbies waiting for her mother or, sometimes, when she had learned to ride the streetcar, she would go downtown and wait for her mother in the ladies' lounge of the department store where her mother happened to be working at the time. She would read or color; she didn't mind. She felt better just being close to her mother and getting to ride home with her. Her mother was her entire world and she adored her. She loved the way she looked, her voice, the way she smelled. She was fascinated with everything her mother did. She loved to watch her put her makeup on, dress, fix her hair. When they went out she could not take her eyes off her; Dena was so proud to be with her. After work, when the weather was nice, they would walk for hours and window-shop and then they would always eat at some restaurant because her mother did not cook. And after dinner Dena used to sit and wonder what her mother was thinking about while her mother drank her coffee and smoked cigarette after cigarette. When they walked down the street her mother frequently walked very fast, and if you had seen the two of them you would have noticed the little girl, just a few steps behind the woman but trying her best to keep up with her.

Hawaiian Good-bye

New York City
1975

Dena woke with tears running down her face. She wondered what that was all about. Then she remembered her dream, that same old dream that had popped up again. She would be on a merry-go-round and see a white house but lose sight of it as she went around, then it would come to her that her mother was dying and needed her. She would rush to the phone and try and get the number to call her but she would dial the wrong number over and over. Or the phone would not work. Then she would start to panic and wake up crying, lost and helpless. That was not a feeling she could understand. She was a person who was not lost or helpless. As a matter of fact, she was one of the most unhelpless, self-sufficient people she knew. Ask any man who had ever loved her. She did not want to depend on anybody for anything. She had always taken care of herself, didn't want to need anybody, didn't want anybody to need her. She had always been good at almost everything she tried; she was bright, and she was a fast learner.

But the one thing she was no good at was love and she knew it. Last week she had to tell J.C. that she couldn't see him anymore, and it had been hard. She liked J.C. but he had turned out to be like all the rest. They always wanted too much from her, something she could not give. She had told him over and over she would not marry him or ever live with him. But, typical of most men, they always believed she didn't really mean what she said and would change her mind. She never did. Why did they always have to push her into a corner and get so upset? She didn't want to live with anybody. She liked being alone. She hated anybody grabbing at her, trying to smother her. Her job was getting harder and harder, and J.C. had become more and more demanding.

She didn't have the energy to fight him and fight for interviews at the same time, so she told him it was best that he find someone else, that it wasn't fair to him to keep hoping. After she told him, he talked her into going out to dinner just one last time.

They were in a red booth at the Hawaii Kai restaurant on Broadway under a red and green lantern with red tassels. She sat and twirled a tiny paper umbrella while he lectured her on how she would never be happy until she made a serious commitment to another human being, and how he knew her better than she did herself—all the things people say. After two hours of this and several piña coladas, all she could think of to say was "Did you know that there are over four thousand little levers that control the lights at Radio City Music Hall? Not to mention the two hundred and six spotlights. And are you aware that the Rockettes are not all the same height, that it is an optical illusion?"

J.C. finally got the picture, and realized that Dena was a lost cause, and gave up. When he took her to her door for the last time, he hugged her good-bye and held her for a long time. It made Dena feel even worse; Dena did not like displays of emotion or affection. They always made her feel embarrassed and uncomfortable. Her mother had never really been affectionate with her, not like Dena had wanted, and she had always felt so awkward around her mother, all arms and legs, gangly and unattractive. Her mother was so cool, so isolated, so in control at all times. She had never seen her cry. She had never seen her laugh much, either. Her mother had been so beautiful, but there was something about her that was far away, removed, and even as a small child it had frightened Dena. As a little girl, she used to crawl in her mother's lap and take her face and look into it trying to see what was the matter. She would ask over and over. Her mother would look at her and smile and say, "Nothing, darling," but Dena knew something was wrong.

She hugged her mother tightly. Her mother would laugh and say, "You're going to choke Mother to death." And afterward, when she was older, she tried to hug her mother, but when she was seven or eight she had stopped trying. It was awkward to hug her, to kiss her, it was a skill she never learned, and after a while it did not come naturally to either of them.

In her personal life, Dena did not like to get too close to people or have them get too close to her. She was much more at ease sitting across from someone than having to sit beside them on a sofa, much more comfortable speaking to a group of five thousand behind a podium than talking with one person alone. When someone tried to hang on her it made her feel claustrophobic.

When she went inside and closed the door, Dena made a promise to herself: never get involved again. It was too difficult.

Mommies and Daddies

New York City

1975

At her next session with Dr. Diggers, Dena figured she might as well ask her about it and at least get something for her money.

"Let me ask you something, Dr. Diggers. Is it normal for people to keep having the same dream all the time?"

Dr. Diggers thought: *This is the first real question Dena has asked.* "Yes. Why?"

"I was just wondering. I keep having the same stupid dream."

"How long?"

"What?"

"How long have you been having this dream?"

"Oh, I don't know. Since I was a child. I can't remember. Anyhow, it's always pretty much the same. I see this house and it has a merry-go-round in the front yard or sometimes in the backyard, but sometimes it's *in* the house, and I want to go in but I can't find the door."

"Can you see yourself in the dream?"

"No, I just know that it's me, but I don't see myself. Anyhow, I just wonder what the stupid thing means. Or if it means anything."

"I wonder if you wonder," Dr. Diggers said.

Dena said, "What is that supposed to mean?"

"I think on some level you know you just don't want to look at it. How did you feel about losing your father?"

Dena rolled her eyes. Here we go again. Ask a simple question and get some psychobabble questions back. "I've told you a hundred times, I didn't feel anything. I never knew him; it didn't affect me at all. Look, I'm not here to whine about my childhood."

"I know, you just come here for the candy. Now, for the hundredth time, what was your mother like? How would you describe her?"

"Oh . . . I don't know."

"Try."

"It's just a stupid dream."

"Was she a loving mother? Mean? What was your impression of her?"

Dena started to tap her foot, irritably. "I've told you . . . she was just a mother, two eyes, two ears. What was your mother like?"

"My interview. Do you think maybe you left something unsaid—before she died?"

Dena moaned. "Why does everything have to be so damn shrinky? I don't think that you understand that a person can get on with her life without being analyzed to death. I'm not saying some people don't need it, but I'm not one of them. I am not some weak, damaged, little person unable to function. I am just under a lot of pressure at work right now, and it has nothing to do with any deep-seated secrets locked away in my psyche, and you didn't answer my question."

"What question?"

"What was *your* mother like?"

"She had fourteen ears and twelve legs and was polka-dotted. You know, Dena, you are harder than a hickory nut to crack, but I will. You seem determined not to tell me one thing about yourself but I am not giving up. You can bat those big blue eyes at me all you want, I'm *not* giving up. You have finally met your match."

Dena laughed. She liked Dr. Diggers in spite of herself. "Do any of you psychiatrists ever get shot?"

"Oh, yes, I have to frisk my patients all the time."

Later, when she was leaving, Dr. Diggers went with her to the door. As Dena was putting on her coat she said, "By the way ... I broke up with J.C."

Dr. Diggers said, "Oh."

"Yes. He was a nice guy. But he got too serious."

                        ❋   ❋   ❋

As Dr. Diggers locked the door behind her, she almost wished she could call Gerry and tell him, but she couldn't. Dena was her patient. Besides, she knew that he was better off not knowing that Dena had broken up with her boyfriend. It would be better for him to forget Dena. She could not hold out any hope there, at least not at the present time.

Diggers rolled into the kitchen, opened the oven, removed her dinner, and chewed thoughtfully while she ate. She had her doubts if Dena would ever be able to find a man she would allow herself to love. Right now, the girl was still looking for that daddy she never had. Oh, Lord, thought Elizabeth Diggers, daddies—aren't they a dangerous lot? If you love them too much they can ruin you for life, or if you hate their guts, it can mess you up. And in Dena's case, they can mess you up even when they were never there.

Letters Home

San Francisco, California
June 1943

Dear Folks,

I am wishing you were here to see this place. Everything is up and down hills, and they have tons of red streetcars and real Chinese people. It is so funny to see them for the first time, they really do look like their pictures. I am sort of confused about what the difference is between Chinese and Japanese. Never thought I would see either one in person, although I hope when I do meet the Japs in person I can make you proud. We have several guys here from Missouri and some from Kansas. One I had met at a Boy Scout Jamboree once so it is like old home week here. They finally gave me a uniform that fits. They are not used to the corn-fed type, I guess. A couple of the fellows are going to take pictures to send to their folks and I will get one and send it to you. I am sending you some postcard pictures of the Golden Gate and Chinatown. The ocean here is the biggest lake I have ever seen. Ha-ha. We went to a nightclub on top of a hotel and oh boy what a view and I mean the girls here as well, very, very pretty but hard to meet. Too many of us swarming around, I guess. We saw Red

Skelton and Esther Williams in person . . . very, very pretty . . . her, not him. All the guys in my outfit seem to be good guys except for my sergeant, but as he said to us he doesn't like us one little bit either so it evens out, but I suspect he really is a pretty good old guy, though, and I wouldn't mind having him with me when we do get into it for real.

I miss you and will write soon.

Your loving son,
P.F.C. Eugene Nordstrom

San Francisco, California
1943

Dear Folks,

Well, get ready for some big news. Mom, go sit down. Dad, get some smelling salts ready. Here is the big news. I have met the *one*!!! And I don't mean maybe and am I in a tailspin. Boy hidy, are my spirits riding high. Have you recovered yet? I am sure you are wanting details so here is the skinny. Bemis, a buddy of mine, had a date with a girl named Faye and I tagged along to pick her up after work. She works at this big ritzy department store here. Bemis and I were standing outside waiting, having a few smokes, when I looked in the window and saw HER. WOW! She was standing behind the perfume counter and I was almost knocked off my rocker. What a beauty. Faye came out and when I asked her who that knockout was she said her name was Marion and that she was not married and did not have a steady, as far as she knew. Faye asked her if she would join us for a drink or something but she said no. Believe me, Mom, this was *not* a pickup. It took me three weeks just to get a date. This was ten days ago and I have seen her four more times, but I am a goner for sure. All the guys are razzing me ... saying old wheat check is in love. She gave me a picture of her and all I do all night at the barracks is moon over her picture. All the guys are jealous, you bet. Mom say a prayer for me and keep your fingers crossed. Boy, am I lucky. I am the first soldier she has gone out with and with so many wolves in uniform roaming around this town, I wonder what she saw in me?

Your loving son,
P.F.C. Eugene Nordstrom

P.S. Mom, you will be getting some perfume in the mail from me but SHE picked it out.

San Francisco, California
1943

Dear Folks,

It is 2 am here in the Barracks and I am writing from the big pink cloud I am riding on. I am one happy boy. I know you may think this is fast, but I am no hayseed about this. She is the real goods, the whole shebang, the best there is, THE ONE for me, I know for sure, but here's the deal. We don't know when we are being shipped out and I am having to work fast and I need all the help I can get. She says she needs to know more about me and where I came from and all that. I have told her about the two of you and I know she will love you, you two are my ace in the hole. I have told her all about Elmwood Springs and Missouri and how great it is and how much she will love it, but, here's where I need the help. Mom, I can't blow my own horn without sounding like a braggart and I knew she would not like that. She has very high standards, so, Mom, if you could help me out I sure would appreciate it, the United States Army would appreciate it because I am not sure what kind of soldier I will make if I don't get her. I am sending you her address. Could you write her and say how happy you and Dad are that I have met her and that I have told you what a nice girl she is and how I never before had a girl that I loved like I do her and that I am a real nice person, from a real nice family and not just some wolf. Maybe you could mention how popular I was in high school and that I was captain of the basketball team and have my letters in baseball, football, and basketball—I think it might be funny if you sent her my report card, you could pretend it was a joke, but she is very smart and I think it might make a difference. Send the one from when I was a junior and made three A's. Also any cute pictures of me when I was little. NOT THE BATHTUB ONE!!! You might want to say how proud you were when I became an Eagle Scout—no, scratch that—that's too corny. She is a very sophisticated person and I don't think that would impress her, and say that you are looking forward to meeting her. She does not have a family and I think this will mean a lot. I really need your help.

Regards, your loving son,
P.F.C. Eugene Nordstrom

P.S. Mom, would it be too much trouble to send her some of your cookies. Also tell her you liked the perfume a lot. She has elegant taste, don't you think? One more thing, send a picture of you—any picture will do—so she can see what a beautiful mother I have. Please send this as fast as possible to

Miss Marion Chapman
c/o 1436 Grove Street
San Francisco, California

Three Telegrams

1943

MR. LODOR NORDSTROM SR.
DAD, WRITE AND TELL ME WHAT YOU SAID TO GET MOM TO MARRY YOU.
I NEED POINTERS. DON'T MAKE ANYTHING UP. I AM SERIOUS.
GENE

DEAR WOUNDED BUFFALO SON OF MINE,
THREE WORDS OF ADVICE. TELL THE TRUTH.
DAD

DEAR DAD,
TOOK YOUR ADVICE. I DID. SHE SAID YES. PICK YOURSELF UP OFF THE
FLOOR. PACK YOUR BAGS AND BE READY. WILL WIRE DATE.
GENE

·

Letter to Mr. and Mrs. Lodor Nordstrom, Sr.

1943

Dear Mother and Dad,

I am so sorry the way things turned out. I wanted so much for you to have been there with me so I could have introduced you to my bride in person. I wish we could have waited but as it was we only had five days with each other before I shipped out. I am sure Marion has written to you by this time and told you about the wedding. It was just a fast courthouse affair, but Bemis and Faye, my sergeant and a few buddies were there so we had some people with us but it was not the wedding I wished I could have given her so I promised her that when I got back we would do it all over again at home, in church, and I plan to get back, believe me, and with Marion waiting for me I know I will, but if for any reason something happens, if I don't get back, I want you to know that the past weeks she has made your son the happiest guy in the world so please take care of her for me. Her folks are dead and she will need you so much. I know I can count on you and that you will welcome her with open arms that way you have always welcomed all my friends and after a while you might encourage her to try and find some nice guy who will love her. I depend on you to check him out thoroughly for me. I know anything happening is a long shot, but all the guys are making sure to talk about it just in case. I don't know when I will be able to write to you again so I thought I would say a few things to each of you.

Mom, you are the best mom a guy could have and I thank you for everything you ever did, especially for loving me even when I messed up the house like I did. Dad, you are my best buddy and you always will be and if I am one half the man you are, I will be OK. Off of serious things. I want you guys to be looking around town for a place for us. Maybe not too far from you. Maybe the old Darthsnider place is still for sale, check it out, will you? Pat that stupid flea-bitten old canine of mine for me. I guess I better sign off now. If I sound funny it is only because I am feeling scared and proud at the same time. I am scared because I don't know where we are being sent but proud as punch that I am one of the guys that is going. Proud that I am standing up for my country.

Your loving son,
Eugene Lodor Nordstrom

One Telegram

Elmwood Springs, Missouri

1944

The regular Western Union messenger had been drafted in 1942, so at age twelve, Macky Warren had taken over his job. Quite a few boys applied but he got the job because there was only one uniform and he had been the one who came closest to fitting into it. Like all boys who had been too young to join up and fight, the idea of wearing a uniform of any kind appealed greatly. It made him feel proud and important to wear it.

Elmwood Springs was one of the few towns that had a lady telegraph operator. Bess Goodnight, whose sister, Ada Goodnight, was the postmistress, was a small woman with a big sense of humor and Macky liked working for her. He liked his job. It was fun, riding his bike all over town. But after the war had gone on for a time, it was not much fun anymore. Although he and Bess never said so, lately, every time the telegraph machine started clicking a message, they both felt a small pang of dread until Bess would nod at him that it was just a plain old telegram and not one from the War Department.

The telegraph office and Miss Alma's Tea Room were the only two businesses that stayed open on Sunday, and after church Macky would head downtown to work. When lunch hour was over at Miss Alma's, downtown was quiet and deserted until five o'clock that afternoon, when the movie theater would open up. Today, Macky was sitting at a card table working a picture puzzle of Mount Rushmore with Bess Goodnight and they only had one more piece left to finish up George Washington's face. The missing piece was right under his nose, but apparently not exactly under it because they had tried about thirty different pieces and so far none fit. Bess was busy searching through the scattered pieces that were left when the clicking started. Bess went over and sat down and started to write as the clicking continued. Maybe because it was Sunday and there was no activity on the street, the clicking sounded particularly loud, almost angry, clacking away its message like it was mad at the world. Macky could tell by the frown that came on Bess's face that the message coming in was not a good one. Then the clicking stopped abruptly. Bess looked at it. And then she slowly turned her chair around and placed the yellow paper in the large black Royal typewriter and began typing the message.

DEAR MR. AND MRS. LODOR NORDSTROM,
THE WAR DEPARTMENT OF THE UNITED STATES OF AMERICA REGRETS TO
INFORM YOU THAT YOUR SON, P.F.C. EUGENE ARTHUR NORDSTROM, WAS
KILLED IN ACTION. . . .

After she finished typing the complete message, she pulled it out of the typewriter. Macky had already gone over and put his hat on and straightened his tie and stood waiting. Bess placed the telegram in an envelope and sealed it and handed it to him.

"Here, son, you'd better take it on over."

She shook her head sadly, her eyes moist, and said, "I hate this old war."

Macky looked at the address and knew who it was. He went outside and walked over to his bicycle leaning against the building and climbed on. He wanted to get on and just keep on riding and never come back. Gene Nordstrom had been a boyhood hero of his. A lifeguard at the pool, he had taught Macky how to swim. As he rode, people who had a son or husband overseas saw him and held their breaths until he went on by their house and on down the block. A telegram on Sunday always meant bad news. After that first rush of relief that the telegram had not been for them came the pang of sadness and pity for the family it was addressed to. When Macky pulled up at the Nordstroms' house, he laid his bicycle down on the lawn and started up the stairs. Gerta Nordstrom was in the kitchen when he knocked. Her husband, Lodor, was in the backyard working on his victory vegetable garden like he did every Sunday afternoon. Gerta called out, "Just a minute . . ." She was drying her hands on her apron as she came down the hall. When she got close enough to see through the screen door who was standing there, she stopped in her tracks, unable to move another step, afraid to move. In that momentary terror, she thought maybe if she did not open the door, if she did not touch the telegram Macky had in his hand, that maybe the words contained in that small yellow envelope would not be true. She stood, motionless, still holding on to her apron.

Macky saw her and said, "Mrs. Nordstrom . . . I have a telegram for you." People up and down the block who had seen him ride by quietly came out on their porches, one by one. The Swensons, their next-door neighbors, had already been outside and when Macky arrived, Mrs. Swenson had put both hands over her mouth. "Oh, no, not Gene—not that sweet boy."

Her husband said nothing but put his paper down, and got up and walked down the front steps, headed next door. He had gone all the way through school with Lodor and he wanted to be there when the news came. In the meantime Macky stood at the front door not knowing what to do. He knocked softy again. "Telegram for you, Mrs. Nordstrom."

BOOK TWO

❀ ❀ ❀

Book Two

Looking Through Windows

Howard Kingsley and Dena's lunches had become a weekly event and she always looked forward to them. They discussed theater and books and rarely talked about the news business anymore. But as the weeks went by she began to see a weariness that she had not seen before. He never said anything about what was happening at work, but one day as they were having their coffee, he said, "Dena, you know what's wrong with the new bunch that's taking over? There's not an ounce of compassion in the whole lot. They don't like people."

He looked into his cup. "Oh, they may like a few people close to them, their families, but they don't like people in general, people as a concept. They don't have any loyalty except to themselves, and you can't have compassion unless you have a certain loyalty to the human race."

Dena nodded in agreement but felt like a fraud. Howard had just described her to a tee. She didn't know if she particularly liked people, and as far as loyalty was concerned, she really did not know what it was. She had no idea what she could be loyal to, other than herself.

She went home that night and thought about what Howard had said and picked up the phone.

"Sookie, it's Dena."

"Dena!"

Sookie yelled at her husband, "Earle! It's Dena! Dena, hold on, I'm going to take this in the bedroom."

Dena heard Sookie tell Earle to hang up the phone when she picked up. Earle took the phone. "Dena, how are you?"

"Fine, Earle. How are you?"

Sookie came on the line, saying, "Hang up, Earle."

" 'Bye, Dena."

" 'Bye, Earle."

"Dena, come on down here where it's warm; we're in the seventies today."

"Wow. Well, it is pretty chilly here. How are you?"

"Wonderful. Just wonderful. Mother is in Europe on some religious art tour or something but we're fine, how are you? Coming to Atlanta any time soon?"

"I don't have anything planned at the moment. Sookie, the reason I'm calling . . . I want to ask you a question and I'm serious."

"Is this another one of those who-am-I things?"

"No, just something I'm curious about. OK?"

"OK."

"What does it feel like to be loyal?"

"What?"

"I know this sounds crazy but I'm not kidding. I really want to know."

"What does it feel like to be loyal?"

"Yes."

Sookie tried her best to answer truthfully. "What does it feel like? Well, I never thought about it. I guess I don't know what it would feel like not to be. But why are you asking me? You know how it feels."

"No, I don't. I don't think I've ever been loyal to anything in my entire life."

"There you go again with that dramatic temperament. Of course you have, silly."

"I haven't."

"What about me? You've been loyal to me."

"No, I haven't, you're the one who's kept up with me. If you had not kept in touch with me I would have lost you a long time ago."

"Well, I'm not going to believe that," Sookie said, "even if it's true. I'm just not going to believe it of you. Don't forget, I know you. I know you better than you know yourself. And no matter how hard you try not to be, you are a wonderful person. Besides, everyone has to side with something or other. Everybody has to be willing to fight for something . . . I think."

"What would you be willing to fight for, Sookie, right now, today?"

"Oh, my family, my children—Junior League."

"What?"

"I'm kidding."

"No, I'm serious, Sookie. Say if there was another Civil War; would you fight for the South?"

"Well, that's not going to happen. There's so many Yankees moving down here, you can't throw a rock down the street without hitting three of them in the head. But let's say if something terrible happened, I would. I can't help it, I just would. It's my home. But I feel the same way about my family and friends."

"Were you born feeling that way or did you have to work at it?"

"I don't know, I never thought about it. It's just how I feel. Everybody feels loyalty to something, don't they? I'm loyal to my women friends; I'd fight anybody that hurt them."

Sookie laughed. "Earle thinks that's why there are so few divorces in town. He says the men are scared of what we all would do if one of them cheated."

"Have you ever cheated or thought about cheating on Earle?"

"Oh, Dena, why are you asking me all these crazy questions? You're not going to put me on TV in some exposé, are you?"

"Of course not. I'm not trying to be nosy, I really need to know. Have you ever thought about any man other than Earle? You can tell me."

"Do you mean like Tony Curtis?"

"No, I mean someone you know or have met."

"No, I really haven't. Is that unsophisticated of me? Honestly, Dena, I know you think I'm corny and old-fashioned, but after all the fun and all the teas and the showers are over and you stand up there in church in front of all your family and friends and take that oath, it's serious. At least it was to me. I would have been scared to death to swear to something I didn't mean; you know what a chicken I am. I don't know how Letty did it."

"Did what?"

"Divorced her husband not more than six months after she married him. Said she loved the bridal showers and the honeymoon, it was marriage she didn't like. Anyway, back to you. What makes you think that you, of all people, are not loyal? Honestly, Dena, you can come up with some of the kookiest ideas. Have you forgotten you are a Kappa? Of course you're loyal, silly."

After Dena hung up she didn't feel any better. Sookie was wrong. Dena could barely remember any of the girls she went to school with, or at times even the names of the schools. Dena had always been a loner. She did not feel connected to anything. Or anybody. She felt as if everybody else had come into the world with a set of instructions about how to live and someone had forgotten to give them to her. She had no clue what she was supposed to feel, so she had spent her life faking at being a human being, with no idea how other people felt. What was it like to really love someone? To really fit in or belong somewhere? She was quick, and a good mimic, so she learned at an early age to give the impression of a normal, happy girl, but inside she had always been lonely.

As a child she had spent hours looking in windows at families, from trains, buses, seeing the people inside that looked so happy and content, longing to get inside but not knowing how to do it. She always thought things might change if she could just find the right apartment, the right house, but she never could. No matter where she lived it never felt like home. In fact, she didn't even know what "home" felt like.

Did everybody feel alone out there in the world or were they all acting? Was she the only one? She had been flying blind all her life and now suddenly she had started to hit the wall. She sat drinking red wine, and thinking and wondering what was the matter with her. What had gone wrong?

The Phone Call

New York City
1976

Dena was now making more money than she knew what to do with. She actually had a savings account and one of the first things she did was to move to a new apartment in Gramercy Park, where she had always wanted to live. She had been out of town covering the Bicentennial in Washington and in Philadelphia, and had not had a chance to finish decorating. After living in her new apartment for six weeks, she still had not hung her pictures on the living room wall, and so she asked a studio set designer, Michael Zanella, to come over on Friday night to help her. He was now standing on her sofa in his socks trying to place a large mirror in the middle of the wall. Dena was eating a sandwich, guiding him, when the phone rang. She walked backward toward the phone and before answering told Michael, "A little more to the left . . . Hello," she said, not taking her eyes off the wall.

"Dena? Uh . . . Miss Nordstrom?"

"Yes."

"It's Gerry O'Malley."

"Who?"

"Gerry O'—Dr. O'Malley."

After all these months? "Oh, yes, Doctor . . . how are you?"

Dena motioned for Michael to move the mirror just a hair to the right.

"Fine," he said. "How are you doing?"

"Just fine, Doctor." As she made an OK gesture to Michael, "What can I do for you?"

"Well, there is something I need to tell you. Actually, to ask you, really. But before I do, I think I owe it to you to be completely honest and up front with you. I think it's only fair that you know exactly how I feel before you make a decision one way or another."

"Uh-huh," Dena said, only half listening. She walked over and touched the next picture and pointed to where she wanted it.

"You know, all my life I have heard that I would meet someone somewhere and no matter how well I knew them or how much or little time we had spent together, that person would just be it for me."

Dena shook her head when Michael pointed to the wrong picture and nodded yes when he picked up the right one.

"And I have known for a long time that you are that person for me. And the truth is, I am, well, totally and completely mad about you. And have been from the first time you came into my office."

"Oh?" Dena mouthed yes when Michael pointed to the next picture.

"I know this call must seem out of the blue but I have waited to give you some time. I wanted to call sooner . . . would you have dinner with me sometime?"

There was no answer on the other end.

"I'm sure you must think I'm insane and this is really bizarre of me to put you on the spot like this . . . or if you are seriously involved with someone else—"

"Dr. O'Malley," Dena said, "can I call you back in a few minutes?"

"Oh! Well, sure."

"It's just that I have someone here and—"

"Oh—oh, I'm sorry. Sure."

"I'll call you back."

Dena hung up, not really believing what she had heard. It *was* so out of the blue, it was bizarre. Maybe she had heard wrong or he was crazy or drunk or kidding or something. She did not know what to think so she forgot about it for the moment and kept on with the picture-hanging while she still had Michael there.

Gerry, on the other hand, was shaken. He had just made the most important phone call of his life and he had forgotten to give her his home phone number. He was too embarrassed to call back and hoped she would look his number up in the phone book. But she did not call back.

On Sunday night, he arrived at Elizabeth Diggers's apartment with a pint of ice cream.

"Hi, Gerry, come on in the kitchen. I was just finishing my supper."

"Oh, I'm sorry."

"That's all right, glad to have the company."

She noticed the bag. "What did you bring me?"

"Ice cream."

"Oh, boy, just in time for dessert. You know the best way to a woman's heart. Thanks."

Gerry put the ice cream in the freezer and sat down at the table.

"What's up? You sounded pretty upset on the phone."

"Elizabeth, I am afraid I did a pretty stupid thing, idiotic, really, and I think you should know about it."

"What did you do?"

"I called Dena."

"Oh, dear . . . and?"

"I made a complete and total fool out of myself."

"Gerry, I'm sure you didn't make a fool out of yourself." She said it but prepared for the worst. It had been her professional experience that men in love, even the most intelligent, are capable of doing some pretty stupid things.

"Well, ass would be a better word. So I wanted to tell you myself before you heard about it. I really just called to hear her voice. But then, when she answered, I just sort of lost it."

She looked up from her plate. "What did you say?"

Gerry began to pace. "I said . . . I know this call might seem out of the blue . . . but ever since the first day I met you I have been absolutely mad about you . . . and that I had always heard that someday I would meet the one person in the world for me . . . and for me she was that person. . . ."

Diggers quietly put her fork down. "You said that?"

"Yeah."

"Oh," said Dr. Diggers. After a moment of silence she asked, "And what did she say?"

"She said, 'Can I call you back . . . I've got someone here.' "

"Oh."

"That was on Friday and she hasn't called. So God knows what she thinks of me at this point and, of course, like a fool, I didn't give her my home number. Anyhow, shall I drown myself now or wait a few more days?"

"I think you have a few more days left." Dr. Diggers smiled, but thought to herself, Poor Gerry, he's really done it now.

On a Whim

At her next session Dena did not mention that she had had a phone call from Gerry, and although Dr. Diggers was eager to ask about it, she couldn't. She was caught in a hard place, between her patient and her friend. She was extremely fond of Gerry; they had been friends for years. They had first met when he was a student and she was still teaching in graduate school. One day in class she mentioned that she wished she could take part in the civil rights marches that were going on. Two days later, Gerry walked in and announced, "Dr. Diggers, you want to go to the march, and you are going to the march. We leave tomorrow. You may not be able to march, but you can sure as hell roll!" He and two of his friends borrowed a van and drove her all the way to Mississippi. They made a strange pair, this handsome, blue-eyed, blond boy pushing a black woman in a wheelchair, but it was an experience that neither of them would ever forget. Later, when the woman's movement demonstration in New York had been announced, she had called him. "Are you up for another march?" He was and they had a ball, especially Gerry, who got patted on the behind by several very liberated women that day.

Gerry would always be a special person in her eyes and she hated to see him hurt, but there was not a thing she could do.

❖   ❖   ❖

A week after his call, Dena came in from having drinks with a boring PR man who was trying to charm her into interviewing his client, and she looked up Gerry's number and dialed. She left a message with his exchange. "So—you call and tell me you're crazy about me and then I don't hear from you?"

❖   ❖   ❖

When Gerry came in later that night he called in for his messages. He had forced himself to go out; he had waited for her to call for days and had given up. When he heard Dena's message he stood still in shock. At least she was still speaking to him; that was something. But what in the world did that message mean? He was a psychiatrist and even he didn't know. But he was again hoping for the best.

As for Dena, she had called the way she usually did when it came to something personal; she had called on a whim and it didn't mean anything, one way or the other.

On another impulse, Dena decided to have a few people over to her new apartment for a cocktail party on Sunday. Although she did not say so, it was her birthday, a day she would have forgotten if, as always, Norma and Macky and Aunt Elner had not sent her birthday cards.

She had invited Ira Wallace and his wife. She liked Mrs. Wallace; she was a lovely lady and must have seen something good in Ira, God knows what. She also invited her agent, Sandy, and his wife, and a few others, including Gerry O'Malley.

When Sunday came around, Gerry was a nervous wreck. He had changed ties five times and wished he had not gotten his hair cut by that stylist who had parted his hair on the wrong side. But Dena made him feel welcome and acted as if he had never called and made a fool out of himself, and he was grateful. He managed to get through the party without doing anything worse than crossing his legs and kicking a glass of Chardonnay off the coffee table. That was a miracle, considering.

Dena, on the other hand, looked at him several times when he didn't know it and decided he was not a bad-looking guy. She needed somebody she could take places when she needed a date. Someone nice, not in the business. Maybe she would give him a try.

The Verdict Comes In

New York City
1976

Dr. Diggers knew that Dena had been out with Gerry; however Dena had said nothing about it. But today, as Dr. Diggers went down the hall with her to the door, Dena said offhandedly, "Oh, by the way, did I tell you that Dr. O'Malley, who recommended you, called me?"

"No," she said. "I don't believe you mentioned it."

Dena got her coat from the closet. "Anyhow, I went out with him a couple of times. But he doesn't say much of anything. All he does is sit there and stare at me and drop things. He's so nervous, he sort of makes me nervous."

Oh, dear.

Dena put on her coat. "Do you know anything about him?"

"All I can tell you is he is extremely well thought of, personally and professionally."

"Oh, I'm sure he's a great guy and all. He's cute but I guess just not my type. You know, he's . . . well, he's sort of dull."

"Dull? Gerry O'Malley?"

"At least he is to me. I guess we just don't have anything in common. He doesn't even watch television."

"I see."

"He's nice but there's no point in leading him on."

"No, I guess not."

After Dena left, Dr. Diggers wondered how long it would be before she would be hearing from Gerry. It was exactly three weeks and one day.

❖ ❖ ❖

Dena had turned down date after date with Gerry and he was baffled. "I know you can't get in the middle of this but she seemed to like me. We had dinner, went to a couple of shows, but all of a sudden she stopped seeing me and I don't understand what happened. It seemed to be going great. I was a gentleman, I didn't push myself on her, I wanted her to have some time to get to know me a little better. I don't think I said anything out of line, I let her do most of the talking. I just don't get it. I was feeling pretty good, actually; the last time I saw her she even gave me a little kiss good night at the door. She wouldn't do that if she hated me, would she? Maybe she's seeing another guy."

Diggers listened to him go on and on for another twenty minutes. Finally, she had to put him out of his misery. There was no other way. "Gerry, she thinks you're dull."

Gerry was taken aback. "Dull?"

"Dull."

"Oh, du—?"

"Dull."

"The only reason I'm telling you this is because she mentioned it out of session so I'm not betraying patient-doctor privilege. But there it is."

"That's all she said?"

"Gerry, don't forget: she doesn't know you. You are the last person in the world I would call dull. Does she know anything about you at all?"

"No, not much. But what am I going to do, sit there and talk about myself? Give her a résumé? Oh, Christ, Liz, maybe I am dull."

Elizabeth Diggers could have kicked herself for ever getting in the middle of this.

"Gerry, am I going to have to put you back in analysis? What happened to my Mr. Personality Party Boy? You're one of the funniest, most interesting people I know. Tell her about yourself. Now, get with it, boy."

Gerry hung up the phone, wracked his brain, but one word kept playing over and over in his head. Even the clock seemed to be ticking *dull . . . dull . . . dull.* He put his jacket on and his lucky red baseball cap. The first thing he was going to do was buy a television set.

How Do You Get to Carnegie Hall?

New York City
1976

Gerry did not give up, and Dena continued to break date after date. A few times she had said yes and cancelled at the last minute until he finally managed to pin her down for a definite commitment. He had invited her to a concert at Carnegie Hall, and said, rather insistently, uncharacteristically, before he hung up: "Dena, promise me you won't back out at the last minute. These tickets were almost impossible to come by. *Please,* give me your word."

"Listen, Gerry, you better ask someone else. With my work I can't promise."

"Please try. These tickets cost an arm and a leg. OK?"

Dena looked through her appointment book. She hated to be pinned down. "When is it again?"

"Next Friday, the ninth."

"Well, I have a cocktail party at five. What time does this concert start?"

"Eight."

"All right, but I'll have to meet you there."

"Carnegie Hall. At eight. And Dena, if you can't make it, call me and—"

"OK. OK, I will. I'm writing it down."

On Friday the ninth, at about seven-forty, Dena looked at her watch and groaned. Late already. She knew she shouldn't have made this date. He was probably there already waiting for her and she was all the way downtown. She said good-bye to her host and as she was going downstairs in the elevator she made a vow to herself, again, not to ever make plans so far in advance. It was raining. She could always just not show up and say she couldn't find a cab. But when she got into the cab she changed her mind. She loved riding in New York in the rain, the way the colors of neon took on a fuzzy glow through the wet windows, the way the lights reflected on the wet streets. The city looked so soft and so magical, she enjoyed the ride.

But by the time they made it through the theater district and up to Fifty-seventh Street, it was ten after eight when she got out of the cab. The sidewalk in front of Carnegie Hall was deserted. Everybody had already gone in, except for a man in a stocking cap playing a violin and another man standing with a bouquet. She pulled the big brass handle of the glass door and walked into the lobby; the young man with the roses ran after her. "Miss Nordstrom?"

Dena turned. "Yes."

"Miss Nordstrom, I am supposed to take you to your seat."

Dena said, "Oh," and followed him to the left down the stairs into a small auditorium. He held the door open for her. "Right this way." The auditorium was empty but he did not give her a chance to say anything, walked her down the aisle, seated her in the fourth row center, handed her the roses and a program, and was gone.

The stage was empty except for a piano, a bass, and a set of drums. She looked around; she must be in the wrong place. She glanced at the program and then read more intently:

A SPECIAL CONCERT FOR MISS DENA NORDSTROM, PERFORMED BY G. O'MALLEY & CO., WITH HIGH HOPES OF FAVORABLY IMPRESSING THE LADY WITH DR. O'MALLEY'S UNDYING DEVOTION.

At that moment the lights in the auditorium dimmed and the lights on the stage came up and Gerry O'Malley walked out in black tie with two other tuxedoed men. He bowed and sat down at the piano. After a moment, he nodded and the trio started to play an old Lerner and Lane tune he had chosen that said exactly what he had been unable to say. And he sang it right to her:

> You're like Paris in April and May
> You're New York on a silvery day
> A Swiss alp as the sun grows fainter
> You're Loch Lomond when Autumn is the painter
> You're moonlight on a night in Capri
> And Cape Cod looking out at the sea
> You're all places that leave me breathless
> And no wonder
> You're all the world to me.

Dena, horrified, wanted to drop through the floor, but Gerry continued, singing in an astonishingly good voice.

> You're Lake Como when dawn is a-glow
> You're Sun Valley right after a snow
> A museum, a Persian palace
> You're my shining Aurora Borealis
> You're like Christmas at home by a tree
> The blue calm of a tropical sea
> You're all places that leave me breathless
> And no wonder
> You're all the world to me.

Among the thousands of things Dena did not know about Gerry O'Malley was that he had worked his way through college with his own jazz combo, playing every weekend at parties. Tonight, he had managed to get both of the other guys, one a doctor and the other with his own venture capital business, to come into Manhattan for the evening to back him up.

Dena sat, as he continued to play every love song he knew and a few really funny ones with lyrics she suspected were his, as well. Dena had no choice but to smile. She also wanted to run. What in the world had she gotten herself into? He was either completely off his rocker or else he thought she could get him on television, but whichever it was, it was very embarrassing. But after a while, she began to relax and to really enjoy herself.

When it was over, she stood and applauded and handed him the roses. He came down to where she was sitting and said, "Well?"

He stood smiling and waiting and she said: "Well, wow! You really can play. Great, what can I say? You're quite a piano player." He introduced the other musicians to her and she told them how much she had enjoyed the concert.

Gerry said, "OK, guys—that's all for this evening. I owe you one. Or two. Or twenty." They said good-bye.

Gerry took Dena to dinner next door at the Russian Tea Room. He had heard that it was a place show business people liked. He was pleased with himself. "I just thought this might be a way for you to get to know me a little better—and give you a better idea of how I feel about you."

"Gerry . . . that was very sweet of you. And don't think I didn't enjoy it and appreciate it. But don't you think this is all a little sudden? I'm really not ready for any kind of serious relationship. My job takes up most of my time and, well, I just can't do it. Right now. At the moment, I don't know how I feel about anybody."

"Dena, I am not going anywhere. You can have all the time in the world, all the time you need. I'm here. If it's one year or five years, whenever you are ready. Believe me, I'm the last person in the world who wants to pressure you. All I want you to know is that I'm here—and I'm in love with you."

"Are you serious?"

"Absolutely," Gerry said. "I told you on the phone. Or tried to."

"Well, to tell you the truth, I thought you were kidding. Or I didn't know you were serious. I mean, you're a psychiatrist. Aren't you supposed to know better or something? I don't know what to say."

"Dena, I am serious. But listen: just because I know that you are the one for me, I may not be the one for you. All I'm asking for is a chance."

At home, she thought about the evening. She had certainly heard many lines from many men, but this one was unique. She had to give him that. But he'd get over it, they always did. She'd heard that J.C. was already engaged to some stewardess. Granted, everyone said she looked like a younger Dena, but J.C. was over her. Give this one some time.

Then a *terrible* thought hit her. What if the network suddenly started looking for a *younger* Dena? She was good but she had better get in there and be the *best,* make sure she was irreplaceable. There wasn't any time to waste. Too many younger and tougher girls were waiting in the wings, waiting for her to make a slip. She didn't have time to get involved with anyone, much less a piano-playing shrink who thought he was in love with her. If she was going to stay on top she had to strike while the iron was hot—and right now she was hot. She had just been on the cover of *TV Guide* and there was talk of an Emmy.

Tour

Dena had been in seventeen cities in seventeen days on a twenty-eight-day promotion tour for the network. They had decided that she was the perfect person to send across the country to their local affiliates because of her increasing popularity. They knew she would charm and interest everyone she met. So the publicity department filled almost every minute of her time in each town with television, radio, and newspaper interviews along with luncheon speeches, other personal appearances, and usually, if they could arrange it, a banquet speech at night. Before she flew on to the next city, she'd try to get three or four hours' sleep and then she would start all over again the next day. It seemed like every town had a local morning show that began at seven. She had known it would be rough but Dena wanted to do it. She wanted to push her TV Que up even higher than it was.

Thank God they had sent their top publicist, Jonni Hartman, with her. Not only did Dena like her, Jonni was a master at getting Dena from one place to another and expert at getting Dena away from fans who wanted autographs for their entire family, or from interviewers who always wanted more time. And she did it without making Dena look bad. Dena had been doing a terrific job charming everyone, until Pittsburgh, when her stomach began to hurt again. She tried to drive herself through it by living on Maalox and Tums.

Right after she finished speaking at a big benefit dinner in Houston honoring the great heart surgeon Dr. Michael E. DeBakey, she and Jonni had to rush upstairs in the hotel, quickly change clothes, and leave immediately for the airport to catch a 10:45 plane to Dallas. They were behind schedule as usual, so when the elevator did not come she and Jonni had to run down ten flights of stairs dragging their luggage. They had made it halfway through the lobby when the pain hit her so hard that she had to stop. Jonni caught her just before she passed out cold.

When she came to, she and Jonni were in the back of a police car with the siren going on the way to the hospital, and before she knew it she was in the emergency room with doctors examining her, talking about the possibility of emergency surgery. After a few minutes, like a parting of the waters, the doctors and nurses stepped aside as Dr. Michael DeBakey, still in his tux from the dinner, walked in and took over.

He smiled and talked to Dena as he examined her. "Well, young lady, it looks like you have decided to stay with us for a while, so we are going to do everything possible to make you comfortable. You know, you were quite a hit at the banquet—you had quite a few doctors who volunteered to take your case. But I said no luck, fellows, she came here in my honor so I'm the one who gets her as my patient. How long have you had trouble with your stomach?"

"Not long," Dena lied.

He continued to check her out thoroughly, then said to his staff, "No need to prep." He took Dena's hand. "You're going to live. And what I'm going to do is give you a little something to help you with that pain and Miss Reid here is going to be in charge of you." An older nurse stepped up, smiling. "We're going to take a little blood," he continued. "Then we're going to take you upstairs and put you to bed so I can keep an eye on you. OK? I'll stop in and see you in the morning."

The next day Dena was still asleep when Dr. DeBakey looked in.

Jonni, tired and frazzled after a night in the waiting room, said, "Doctor, is she all right? It wasn't a heart attack, was it?"

"No, Miss Hartman, her heart is fine. She had a severe attack of gastroenteritis—inflammation of the stomach lining—probably brought on by stress."

"Thank God it happened here, Doctor. And I hate to bother you . . . but I need to know how long it will be before you think she might be back up on her feet. I don't care, but the head of network publicity has already called me a dozen times to see if I can give them an idea when she might be able to continue her tour. They need to know how many cities they have to cancel and how soon she will be able to do at least some phone interviews. They're hoping she can pick up in Denver on Wednesday."

Dr. DeBakey pointed to the paper she was holding. "Is that her schedule?"

"Yes."

DeBakey put on his glasses and studied it. Jonni said, "You can see she has quite a few more cities coming up."

"Oh, yes, I can see that."

"And they need to know as soon as possible."

"Uh-huh. And just who wants this information?"

"It's my boss. I mean, he's really upset and hopes she'll be able to—"

"And who might that be?"

"Mr. Brill, Andy Brill."

"Do you have a number where he can be reached?"

"Yes; 212-555-2866."

"OK, Miss Hartman. I'll get back to the gentleman."

"Oh, thank you, that would be great. He's really coming down hard on me. I told him it was out of my hands."

"Don't worry, it is. You go and get some rest." DeBakey, a tall, thin man, walked down the hall, reached in the pocket of his white coat, and pulled out a few almonds and ate them. He stopped and talked to an intern, checked on three more patients, and then went into his private office. He handed his secretary, Sylvia, the phone number. "Get this guy on the phone for me, will you?" When she buzzed he picked up.

"Mr. Brill, this is Dr. DeBakey in Houston."

Andrew Brill was audibly chomping at the bit. "Great, thanks for calling."

"I understand you are anxious to have a report on Miss Nordstrom's condition."

"That's right, we need to have some idea when she might be able to pick up her schedule. We've got people screaming all over the country. We've already lost Dallas but I was thinking maybe she could do a few phoners this afternoon. Do you think there's a chance she can get back by, say, Tuesday, or maybe Wednesday, latest?"

"Let me ask you a question, Mr. Brill."

"Yes?"

"Are you people trying to kill her? Miss Hartman showed me her schedule. How could you expect anyone to keep going at that pace?"

"Yeah, well, I don't think you understand. This thing has been booked for over six months. We've got commitments here."

"Mr. Brill, I don't think *you* understand. This girl is suffering from extreme exhaustion and serious stomach distress brought on by exhaustion and stress."

"What are you saying?"

"I'm saying that as long as she is my patient, she is not leaving this hospital for at least two weeks. You can expect her back at work in maybe a month. Would you like that in writing? I'll be happy to send it along. And if she does go back any sooner, and if anything happens to her health as a result, I'm perfectly prepared to go on record that your network was forewarned."

"Forewarned? Do you have any idea how much this is going to cost us to cancel this tour? We can't just—"

DeBakey interrupted. "If you have any other questions, please feel free to call my office—collect—at any time."

❖ ❖ ❖

Red-faced with rage, Brill slammed the phone down and yelled at his assistant, who was waiting to find out if Dena would be on the early morning plane, "That son of a bitch says he's gonna keep her there for two weeks. Just who the hell does he think he is?"

Thirty minutes later at an emergency meeting with the network lawyers, Brill was informed that Dr. DeBakey was exactly who he thought he was, one of the most powerful and respected doctors in the world. They knew they couldn't buy him off and they were afraid to cross him, at least in public.

Death of a Cricket

Elmwood Springs, Missouri
February 8, 1976

When Macky and Norma Warren came in from church, their phone was ringing. Norma picked it up, her purse still hanging on her arm.

"Mrs. Macky Warren?"

"Yes?"

"Mrs. Warren, my name is Jonni Hartman and I work with network news public relations and I'm calling to let you know that your relative, Dena Nordstrom, is in the hospital here."

Norma did not let her finish, put her hand over the receiver, and screamed at her husband. "Macky, I told you not to kill that cricket. Baby Girl is in the hospital!" She turned back to the phone. "Oh, my God . . . what's the matter with her?"

"Mrs. Warren, I don't want to alarm you, but—"

"Don't tell me she's been in an accident. Don't tell me she's been hurt; I can't stand it. I'll go to pieces. Here . . . you have to talk to my husband."

She thrust the phone at Macky as if it were on fire.

Macky took the phone, while Norma wailed in the background, "If she's dead, just don't tell me, I can't stand it. I knew something like this was going to happen."

"Norma, be quiet. Hello, this is her husband. What's going on?"

"Mr. Warren, this is Jonni Hartman and I didn't want to alarm you. I just wanted to call and let you know Dena's in the hospital but OK, in case you might hear something on the news. I'm here with her at the Houston, Texas, Medical Center and Dr. DeBakey has just examined her and said she had a pretty severe attack of gastroenteritis."

Macky nodded. "I see. Is this considered life threatening?"

Norma wailed again. "Don't say she's dying!"

"Oh, no, Mr. Warren. It's just a pretty severe stomachache as far as I can tell. The doctor says all she needs is a little rest."

"I see."

"If she's dead"—Norma threw her hands up in the air—"I don't want to know."

Macky said, "Miss Hartman, could you hold on for a second?" He put his hand over the receiver. "Norma, she's not dead. Now be quiet and let me talk to the woman!" Norma covered her mouth with her hands to keep herself quiet. "Miss Hartman, I can be there just as soon as I can get a plane out of here."

"Mr. Warren, I really don't think that's necessary. I think it would be better to wait and see how long the doctor is going to keep her. She might be released by the time you get here."

"I see. Well, how is she doing right now? Can we talk to her?"

Norma couldn't control herself. "Is she asking for us? Macky, ask her if she wants to talk to us."

"Mr. Warren, the doctor gave her something and she's sleeping right now and from what I gather he does not want her disturbed. He put a No Visitors sign on her door. I'm not even allowed in."

Macky nodded again. "I see. What about her family? Should we be there when she wakes up?"

Norma gasped and clutched her purse to her chest. "Mother of God, she's in a coma, I knew it—"

"Norma, she's *fine*. Now, sit down."

"Mr. Warren, I really don't want you and your wife to worry. She has the best doctor in the country, Michael E. DeBakey."

Macky was impressed. "The heart transplant doctor?"

He anticipated Norma's reaction and caught her just before she started to scream *heart transplant*. "No, Norma, it's not her heart, that's her doctor."

"Her doctor? Her doctor has had a heart transplant?"

"Norma, he's *fine*."

Norma stood up. "Oh, I can't stand it, Macky, you're not asking the right questions. Give me the phone. Miss Hartman, this is Norma again. Is this doctor good? Because we have a doctor right here in town that we can get, one that's in good health."

Macky shook his head in disbelief and said in a quiet, steely voice, "Norma, give me the phone and go sit down."

Reluctantly, she handed it back. "Well, you have to ask about these things."

"Miss Hartman, we really appreciate your call and I would also appreciate it if you could call us tomorrow and let us know how she's doing."

Norma said, "Tomorrow? Tell her to call us in an hour; she could be dead by tomorrow."

"I sure will, Mr. Warren, and really, she's OK."

Macky put the phone down and Norma grabbed for it but missed.

"Why did you hang up? We don't know where she is."

"Yes, we do. She's at the Houston Medical Center."

"Houston, Texas? Texas? What is she doing in Texas?"

"I don't know, honey, but she's OK now, just calm down."

"Macky, I don't know how you can stand there and be so calm. Baby Girl is lying up in a strange cowboy hospital with some sick doctor, my God, halfway across the country."

"Norma, it's not that far."

"Well, we can't tell Aunt Elner, she'll get too upset. And she's liable to have a heart attack, too. That's all we need right now, two people in the hospital at the same time."

Macky took Norma by the shoulders and led her over to the sofa. "Norma, listen to me. She's in one of the best hospitals in the country and has one of the best doctors and all she has is just a pretty bad stomachache, that's all. The doctor said she has gastroenteritis."

"What?"

"Gastroenteritis."

"Well, I've never heard of it. How did she catch it?"

"I don't know, honey."

"Is it some kind of Texas thing?"

"Probably not."

Norma jumped up and went to the phone. "Well, I'm calling Dr. Clyde and asking him."

As Norma was dialing, Macky said, "I give up. Do what you want, you're going to anyway."

Norma said, "Macky, get me some vanilla ice cream in a dish, I'm a nervous wreck. Look, my hands are shaking like a leaf. . . . I can hardly dial the—Tootie? It's Norma Warren, is he there? Well, tell him I need to speak to him right away. Yes, it is. Macky, give me two scoops, I'm—Oh, Dr. Clyde . . . this is Norma and I need to ask you a question. Is there a disease called gastro inter-something? Hold on." She called to the kitchen. "Macky, gastro what?"

"Enteritis, I think."

"He says enteritis, he thinks. Macky, did that woman say gastroenteritis? Yes, that's it." She turned away from the phone. "Macky, he says, yes, there is, only it's a condition, not a disease. No, Doctor, we don't have it, it's Baby Girl."

Macky came in and handed her a bowl of ice cream and took her purse from her.

"Thank you, honey. No, I was talking to my husband. What kind of condition?" She repeated everything she heard in a loud voice. "It's an inflammation of the stomach lining . . . uh . . . caused by too much acid. Usually brought on by stress. Did you hear that, Macky? Well, Macky was right, he said she was working too hard and now look what's happened. She can't die of it, can she? Ahhh, he says no, he doesn't think so. Well, thank heavens for that. I was . . . oh . . . OK, yes, in that case you better get on back. Thank you, Doctor." She hung up.

"See, she's not going to die," Macky said. "Now, don't you feel better?"

"Not yet."

An hour later, she picked up the phone in the kitchen and dialed Aunt Elner while Macky made himself a ham and cheese sandwich.

"Aunt Elner, were you taking a nap? It's Norma. Put on your

hearing aid, honey. Can you hear me? Well ... now that we know it's not life threatening, the tale can be told. Are you sitting down? Well, go sit down. Are you seated? I don't want you falling out with a stroke. Well, the whole thing started last night at about ten-thirty. We had been in bed for about an hour when we heard a cricket in the living room and Macky got up without his glasses on and stepped on it and killed it! I *know* it's bad luck to kill a cricket, that's probably the reason Baby Girl wound up in the hospital in the first place!"

The Captive

After Dena had been in the hospital for a few days she began to feel better, and anxious to get out and back on tour. Dr. DeBakey had come to see her every afternoon, and when he came in today, she explained to him why he had to let her out to pick up the rest of the cities. He took her hand. "Honey, I know you are disappointed you can't go back to work. You feel a little better so you think you're ready to get up and start running again. I've heard it from my patients more times than I can tell you. How they can't stop now, how they have to keep going till they get that job, that money or success or whatever it is they are running after, but let me tell you something: *nothing* is worth ruining your health. Most of my patients are sent to me after their doctors have given up on them. If you could see what I see when I open them up . . . I've had some of the richest, most powerful people in the world right here, movie stars, tycoons, kings, begging me to save them, but it's too late. Believe me, nothing in the world is really important except life and death and that's it."

Dena did not give up. "I understand that and I will take it easy from now on, but you don't understand how important this tour is; the network is counting on me. I made a *commitment*. I can't let them down."

"Let me tell you something." He smiled. "Those people in New York may try and make you think they can't do without you but they can. Take some advice from an old man—no amount of success is worth pushing yourself like you are doing. When you came in here your blood count and your blood pressure were so low I don't know how you were able to stand, much less give a speech. I'm not trying to scare you, but I can promise you if you keep on going like you have been, you won't live another five years. This flare-up is a warning that your body just cannot go on at this pace. And once you do permanent damage, you can't get your health back. You have to slow down right now, before it's too late. I called your family and Mr. and Mrs. Warren have already made arrangements to come here on Thursday with a car and take you home and look after you for a while."

Dena was alarmed. "What?"

"The dietician gave instructions to Mrs. Warren as to what you can eat."

"Dr. DeBakey, you don't understand—I don't even know these people. I mean, not well. We are related . . . but I can't go home with them."

"Oh . . . I see. Do you have other family?"

"I can take care of myself."

"No, you can't. You are going to need someone to prepare all your meals, keep people away from you, not let you use the phone. Now, you can stay in the hospital here with us or you can let me arrange to hire a twenty-four-hour-a-day nurse and put you in our aftercare clinic; that's up to you. But one way or another, you have got to rest."

"Why can't I rest in New York?"

"I don't want you anywhere near New York for at least three weeks. It's not that I don't trust you, young lady, it's those people you work for I don't trust. Now, you decide."

And so on Thursday afternoon Dena found herself wrapped in a blanket, lying in the backseat of a brown and tan Oldsmobile, on her way to Elmwood Springs, Missouri, while Norma happily chatted nonstop through the entire state of Texas and on into Missouri about people Dena did not know or care to know, for that matter. She was too busy plotting her escape.

A Cheerful Visit

Elmwood Springs, Missouri
February 13, 1976

That first morning Dena woke up in a strange room with a woman she had never seen before sitting in a chair across the room, staring at her and fanning herself with a small brown paper bag. As Dena opened her eyes, the woman said, "I know you were glad to get out of that old hospital, weren't you, honey."

Dena managed a weak, "Yes," wondering who in the world this old lady was.

"Well, we are sure glad you are home where you belong. I kept saying to Norma, when is Baby Girl getting out of that hospital and coming home? I don't envy anybody in the hospital. Did I tell you about the time Norma carried me up to the hospital for a checkup?"

"No." Dena wondered if she had stepped into the Twilight Zone.

"That bed they had me in was like sleeping on a bunch of cantaloupes. I will say this, that bed could do anything you wanted it to, go up and down, flat or tilted; it did everything but dance the polka and kiss you good night. When they had me up there they looked at me up and down, every which way but sideways from stem to stern, and after they finished, I said to that doctor, I said, 'You're just like that TV show *Star Trek*.' 'How so?' he asked. I said, 'Honey, you've been places where no man has ever dared to go.'"

Norma came into the room with a tray. "Good morning."

"I was telling Baby Girl about my hospital stay, how they checked me out, and how he said all my numbers looked good. Whatever that meant. But it finally calmed Norma down, didn't it, Norma?"

Norma said begrudgingly, "Yes, but everybody needs a checkup once in their life."

The old lady winked at Dena. "She's scared I'm gonna die on her."

Norma placed Dena's tray in front of her. "Here, honey, I want you to try and eat this."

Dena sat up and looked at a bowl of milk with a piece of toast floating in it. Norma went over and opened the windows. "Seriously, Aunt Elner, you could be watering your sweet peas one minute and the next topple over with a stroke. Or, who knows, a 707 airplane on its way to St. Louis could drop out of the sky. You can make fun of me but you never know from one minute to the next."

"All the more reason to enjoy every one of them. You shouldn't waste all your alive time worrying. It tells us that in the Bible. 'Can any of you by worrying add a single hour to your span of life?' Luke 12:25."

"Well, that's fine for Luke," Norma said, "he didn't have you and Macky driving him crazy night and day. Do you want any more iced tea?"

Dena shook her head and Aunt Elner held her glass up. "I'll take some more while you're up."

After Norma left the room Aunt Elner said, "I had that quotation crocheted for her on a doily, but she didn't appreciate it. That girl worries herself into a frazzle over everything. If I don't call her by seven A.M., she has me dead and buried. I said to her, I said, 'Norma, when I finally do go, it's gonna be anticlimactic. You won't even be surprised, you've been practicing for so many years.'" Aunt Elner pointed to the twirling trophies on the shelf that belonged to Norma's daughter, Linda. "You know poor Dixie Cahill died last year."

Dena had no idea who Dixie Cahill was. "No, I didn't."

"Well, she did. Of course, she was well up into her eighties but still teaching when she went. They buried her in tap shoes and with her batons."

Norma came back and Aunt Elner said, "Are you going to take Baby Girl out to eat while she's here?"

"Of course. She can go anywhere she wants. But I have to watch her diet. I have specific instructions."

"You know that catfish place closed."

"Yes, that didn't last long, did it?"

"No," said Aunt Elner. "But I told Verbena, I said, 'They can stick a neon catfish up outside the door but everybody knows that's where the mortuary used to be. Nobody's gonna want to eat fish in a place where they came to see their relatives laid out, no matter how good the food is.' "

Dena could not believe what she was hearing. But Aunt Elner went on. "Baby Girl, since you were last here, Hatcher's mortuary moved outside of town and now they put in a new, drive-through funeral home."

"I'm sorry?" asked Dena, who was trying, in self-defense, to eat.

"They have a drive-by window to view the remains," Norma put in. "It's some lamebrained idea James Hatcher came up with."

Aunt Elner said, "Instead of ordering a burger and fries, you look at a dead relative. No, I believe I'll just get myself cremated, thank you. I don't want anybody looking at me without me knowing it. What if Darlene did my hair funny? You know how horrified we were when she decided to give Mrs. Alexander bangs; everybody forgot about her being dead and just looked at her bangs. Darlene is liable to give me some peculiar hairdo and there won't be a thing in the world I can do about it. At least while I'm alive I can come home and wash it out, but once I'm dead, I'll be stuck for eternity with a bad hairdo. You remember what she did to that poor Church of Christ lady?"

"Oh, yes," Norma said, "it was terrible."

"She always wore her hair pulled back into some big old knot on the back of her head, like a cinnamon bun, and she never wore a drop of makeup, so you can imagine what the other Church of

Christers thought when they saw her lying there with bangs and blue eye shadow."

Aunt Elner added, "I'll tell you, with Darlene around, people are afraid to die. My question is why would anybody want to fix dead people's hair?"

There was a pause. Then Norma said, "Who knows? It's quiet work, I suppose. No complaints. But I guess you never know whether or not your customer is satisfied, do you?"

"No, you wouldn't," Aunt Elner said, "but in her case that might be a blessing. Just the same, I'm not taking any chances. I'm getting cremated. Verbena and I went over there to the new mortuary and talked to James about it. He gave us a brochure to read up on it."

"When?"

"The other day, after I went to my seventy-fifth high school reunion and there were only three of us left. I figured I better start thinking about what my options are."

"Is Verbena thinking about cremation?"

"No, she was up there looking at coffins. She says for fifty years she's been putting Merle Norman cold cream on her face, night and day, so she'll look good, and she says she'll be darned if she's gonna get turned into ashes after all the work she's put into her face. I said, 'Your face may look great, Verbena, but if Darlene does your hair, you're not gonna look good.' "

"What did she say?"

"Nothing. But as for me, I don't care a thing in the world about wasting money on a coffin that you're only gonna use once. I'd rather spend my money over at the mall ... or give it to the Humane Society."

"Uncle Will bought a burial policy for you, Aunt Elner. It's already paid for."

"I know he did but I'd rather have the money now. Do you think they'd give it to me or do I have to die first?"

"Aunt Elner, the subject of death gives me the willies and I am sure Baby Girl does not want to sit here and listen to you talking about getting yourself burned up."

"Oh Norma, you don't burn up, it says so in the brochure. It's like a white light so bright, it's like looking into the sun; you feel the bright light and then you just disappear . . . just one big bright light and you're gone." She snapped her fingers. "Just like that. That appeals to me, much more than a dark coffin. And you still get a headstone and a place over at the cemetery so you can come and decorate me every Easter, so don't worry about that. And when you wonder where I am, just look up at the sun and that's where I'll be.

"Well, guess I better get on home," Aunt Elner said. "I don't want to overstay my welcome. I just wanted to come over and cheer you up." She patted Dena on the hand. "I'll come back tomorrow. Maybe I'll even bring you my cremation brochures, see what you think."

"Come on, Aunt Elner," Norma said. "Let's let her get some rest now."

" 'Bye, honey. Or I could bring my cat, Sonny, if you'd like."

"Aunt Elner, you are not bringing that cat over here and get fleas all over my house."

Dena smiled wanly. " 'Bye . . . thanks for coming."

When they closed the door, Dena thought: *I have to get out of here.*

My Funny Valentine

The second morning Dena had another visitor. At eight o'clock, Dr. Gerry O'Malley arrived at the front door, dressed as a fifteenth-century troubadour complete with pink tights and a plumed hat, and carrying a dozen red roses and a mandolin. Macky came to the door. "Hi. Can I help you?"

Gerry felt like a complete fool now that he was actually here but he was determined to go through with it. "Mr. Warren, I am a friend of Dena's and I wonder if I could see her for just a few minutes?"

"She's upstairs. Can I tell her who—or what—is here?"

"Uh, well . . . it's sort of a Valentine's thing. A surprise."

"OK. Wait just a second. I'll see if I can get her down here."

As Macky passed Norma, who had come out from the kitchen, he said, under his breath, "You're *not* going to believe what's out on the porch."

Gerry spread the roses in front of the door and went down and stood waiting for Dena in the yard. He caught a glimpse of a woman sneaking a look at him from the living room window, but it wasn't Dena.

Dena was still sound asleep when Macky knocked.

"Baby Girl, there is somebody downstairs to see you."

Dena woke up, startled. "What?"

"There is somebody here to see you."

Dena sat up in bed. "Who?"

"He said it's a surprise. He has something for you."

"Oh. Can you just get it for me?"

"No . . . I don't think so. I think you need to go down and get it yourself."

Dena got out of bed and put on her robe. Downstairs, Macky had to pull Norma away from the window. "Come on, Miss Busybody, let's go in the kitchen."

She did not want to move. "One of us should stay here. What if he's a crazy person? He might be dangerous, Macky!"

Macky laughed. "He's crazy, all right, but he's not dangerous."

"How do you know?"

"Because the poor guy's out there shaking like a leaf."

Dena came downstairs and went to the door. She did not see anybody at first but she looked down and saw roses spread out in a big heart-shaped design with a card in the middle. As soon as she walked out on the porch, she heard music. She saw Gerry O'Malley standing in the yard dressed in some idiotic costume playing a mandolin and singing something about love. She could not believe her eyes.

As she stood there in her robe shivering in the cold, as the neighbors started peering out their windows one by one, she could hardly believe what she was seeing or hearing.

After his song he took off his hat and bowed and drove off, leaving her standing, still in a sleepy daze, trying to figure out what Gerry O'Malley was doing in Elmwood Springs, Missouri, at eight o'clock in the morning. Or was she having some sort of hallucination? She reached down and picked up the card and read it.

NO PRESSURE, JUST KNOW I ADORE YOU!
HAPPY VALENTINE'S DAY
LOVE, GERRY

She picked up the roses and went back inside. Norma poked her head around the kitchen corner. "Would your friend like to come in? He's perfectly welcome."

"No, that's OK. He's gone. Here're some flowers if you want them."

"Oh, aren't they beautiful! I'll put them in a vase and you can have them in your room. Well, wasn't he nice to bring you these. He seemed like a very nice person," said Norma, just dying to know who he was but not asking.

Dena started back upstairs. "He's nice, but I'm beginning to think he's a little crazy or something."

Norma shot back into the kitchen and said to Macky, who was having a cup of coffee, "See, what did I tell you. Baby Girl thinks he's a crazy person, too. I told you but you never believe me." She looked at the flowers as she reached under the counter for a container. "But they are pretty roses, I don't care what you say."

"I haven't said a word, Norma."

❅   ❅   ❅

Gerry was about twenty miles outside of Elmwood Springs and still a little nervous and shaky when, going ten miles over the speed limit, he passed a Missouri highway trooper. The trooper slugged down the last of his coffee and took the last bite of his maple doughnut, turned on his siren, and started after the offending vehicle. Gerry heard the siren, looked in his rearview mirror, and his heart stopped. There was not another car for miles around. For a split second, he wondered if he should try and make a run for it, but he was a good citizen so he just groaned and pulled over.

The trooper, a big man, got out, coughed, and walked slowly over to the car. "Good morning," he said pleasantly.

As soon as the trooper looked in, he wondered what in the world he had stopped out here on Interstate 34. Gerry tried to sound normal. "Good morning. What's the problem, Officer?"

"Could I see your registration and driver's license, please, sir."

"It's a rented car. I rented it this morning in Kansas City, and my license is in the backseat in my jacket. Can I get it?"

The trooper was taking no chances. "How about stepping out of the car for me, please, sir."

Gerry got out and opened the back door and took his license out of his wallet and handed it to the trooper, who read it and said, as calmly as possible under the circumstances, considering his white male perp had on pantaloons and shoes that curled up on the ends with bells on them, looking as if he had just fallen off a parade float somewhere: "Wait right here for me while I run a check on your license."

Gerry stood by the car praying that nobody would drive by, but of course they did and all the cars and one truck slowed down while the drivers stared. A few minutes later the trooper came back. "Well, you don't seem to be much of a criminal, other than speeding on the interstate a few minutes ago." He handed Gerry his license.

"Thank you. Could I please get back in the car?"

"Sure. Go ahead."

Gerry's shoes jingled when he got back in.

The trooper said, "We don't get too many men wearing pink tights out here in Jefferson County, so I'd like to know if there is some reason you're wearing that rig or is that just how you guys in New York dress?"

"It's a long story."

"Well, I'm in no hurry. I'm not going anywhere."

Gerry said, "Look, are you married?"

"Yep. Nobody escapes that out here. I got caught and hog-tied just like the rest of them. Why?"

"Then you know today's Valentine's Day."

The trooper looked at him, waiting. "Yeah?"

"I'm sure you must do something special for your wife. You know, to surprise her."

"She gets a card out of me every year but that's about all the fuss I make. If I was to show up dressed in that, she'd think I was two bricks short of a load for sure."

"I just flew down here to surprise my . . . well . . . the one I hope will be my girlfriend."

The trooper nodded. "Yeah. I should have figured right off there was some female involved. You're a thirty-five-year-old man and she's got you dressed up like a circus show dog, son."

Gerry had no defense. "Well, what can I say?"

"That's quite an outfit. Where did you come by that?"

"I rented it."

"Huh. I wonder what she thinks."

"Well, I can be pretty safe in assuming that right now she thinks I'm pretty silly."

"I'd have to agree with her there, buddy. What if she hadn't been at home? That would have been a waste. Why didn't you plan to stay awhile?"

"It's a long story," said Gerry.

"Like I said, I'm not going anywhere."

"I'm trying not to pressure her."

"Uh-huh."

"She is not sure about how she feels about me."

"I see. And what do you think your chances are? Fifty percent, twenty-five percent?"

"I'd say maybe twenty-five percent."

The trooper pointed to the hat on the seat by the mandolin.

"Is that the hat that goes with it?"

"Yes."

"Mind if I have a look?"

Gerry handed it to him. "No. Here."

The trooper examined it carefully. "Is this a velvet of some kind?"

"I guess so. Or maybe a kind of velveteen?"

"What kind of feather do you reckon this is?"

"I have no idea, but I think it's some sort of plume."

The trooper was intrigued. "A plume. Well, I'll be dogged." He handed it back. "What was it that made you decide to dress up in . . . that getup?"

"I don't know. Thought it might be romantic or something. You know women like to be romanced."

"I wouldn't know. My wife told me when we were getting married: there wasn't no romance to it. Did you wear that outfit on the plane?"

"No, I stopped at a gas station and changed." Gerry was losing his patience. "Look, is all this really necessary? Can't you just give me a ticket and let me go? Or put me in jail or whatever it is you are going to do."

"Now, calm down, fella. I ain't gonna give you a ticket." He laughed. "I'll tell you one thing. You wouldn't stand a chance if I was to throw you in jail; dressed like that you might get a hell of a lot more romance than you bargained for. They get pretty lonely in there and you'd probably look cute as hell to some of them, dressed up in them pink tights. No, I was just curious. How long have you been chasing after this female of yours?"

Gerry was relieved he was not getting a ticket, but his nerves were shot by this time. "A year or so. Or more. Do you mind if I smoke?"

"No, go right ahead."

Gerry offered the officer a cigarette.

"No, thanks. I quit them things. Now, here's the deal. As I understand it, all right? You flew in from New York City, drove all the way here, stopped and put on that rig, just to sing one song to a woman who may or may not be interested. That right?"

"More or less, yes."

"You say you rented it. Where?"

"In New York at a theatrical costume shop."

"Are you some kind of actor?"

"No. I'm a . . . well, no, I'm not an actor."

"What's it supposed to be?"

"It's a . . . troubadour outfit. You know, it comes with a doublet and pantaloons. It goes way back in history."

The trooper said, "Like Robin Hood times?"

"No, earlier. Fifteenth century, I think. Or at least that's what they said."

The trooper looked at the mandolin on the seat. "You a musician? Can you play that thing?"

"No, not really. I just learned one song."

"Oh, yeah? Which one?"

"It's an old English madrigal. Do you know what a madrigal is?"

"Sure, I know what a madrigal is. What's it called?"

"You've probably never heard of it."

"Try me."

Gerry mumbled, " 'Thou Art My Fair Lady Love.' "

"Give me that again?"

" 'Thou Art My Fair Lady Love,' " he said a bit louder.

"Nope. Don't know that one. Was she surprised?"

"I'm sure she was."

"What did she say?"

"She didn't say anything. I just gave her the roses, sang the song, and left."

"Uh-huh. And now you are going to drive back to Kansas City, get on a plane, and fly home. All in one day."

"Yes."

"How much is this trip gonna set you back?"

"I don't know exactly."

"Give me a ballpark figure."

"Well, I guess with the plane, the car rental, flowers . . . renting the costume . . . and the mandolin . . . maybe five or six hundred dollars, give or take."

"Whoa. Do you have a picture?"

"A picture?"

"Yeah. I want to see a picture of this female of yours."

"No, not with me. I do at home."

"Is she a blonde, a redhead, or what?"

"A blonde."

"Oh, well, there you go. They'll do it every time."

"She's a beautiful girl but that's not all there is to it. She's extremely intelligent and bright. She's not a dumb blonde by any means if that's what you think."

The trooper shook his head. "You *are* in love, ain't you, buddy? You're not such a bad-looking guy. What's her objection?"

"Well, for one thing," Gerry said, "she thinks I'm sort of dull."

"Dull? You may be a lot of things, fella, but dull ain't one of them."

"Thank you. I appreciate that."

"If it was me, I'd look around for somebody who knew for sure they liked me, date some other gals, play the field."

"I tried that. It didn't work. No, unfortunately, she's the one. I don't know if I'm the one for her, you know? So all I can do is wait."

"Yeah, I see your point."

The trooper put his hands on his belt and looked down the road. "Well ... I'm glad it ain't me. I'm set in the female department. Have been ever since Edna decided I was her intended victim."

Gerry said hopefully, "Can I go?"

"Wait a minute." He took out his pad and started writing.

"I thought you said you weren't going to give me a ticket."

The trooper, without looking up, replied, "I ain't. But you got me curious on how this thing is gonna turn out." He handed Gerry a card. "This is my home address. How about dropping me a line and letting me know what happens. OK?"

Gerry took it and read:

Trooper Ralph Childress
Route 173
Arden, Missouri

"All right."

"Go on now, but watch that speed limit, you hear?"

❖   ❖   ❖

Trooper Childress stood and watched as the man drove away. He thought: I sure would have loved to have taken him in; the boys would never have believed it. He got back in his patrol car and jotted down his report. *February 14, 8:36 A.M. Detained white male. Lovesick fifteenth-century troubadour in pink tights, pantaloons, and doublet.* He wondered how to spell *doublet,* crossed it out, and added, *Hat with plume and shoes that curled up on the end with tiny bells. First offense. Let off with warning.*

The Rescue

It was early Thursday morning and Dena had been in Elmwood Springs almost a week. This was the first time Norma had let her come downstairs to eat breakfast. When she saw Dena she said, "Good morning—you look a hundred percent better. Come on in and sit down. I'll get you some coffee but you have to promise me you'll use a lot of cream."

"Promise."

Norma was happy. "I am so glad to finally see some color back in those cheeks. I will never forget how you looked when we came in that hospital room. I thought for a moment you might be dead."

"I know." Dena laughed. "I remember."

"That was the only reason I screamed like that. I didn't mean to wake you up. I said to Dr. DeBakey, she's always been fair, she got that from her daddy—your daddy was fair—but she's as white as a sheet, so don't tell me she's in good condition. What would you like, pancakes, waffles, or French toast? Or I can make all three if you want, you just tell me. I'm making Macky pancakes but you can have whatever your little heart desires. After all, this is your get-up-out-of-bed breakfast."

"I'll take pancakes too."

"Are you sure?"

"Yes, that would be great. Where is Macky?"

"He's out in the yard fly-fishing."

"Do you have a lake or pond or something?"

"No, he's just out there practicing, and I warn you, as soon as you even look like you might be feeling better he's gonna start pestering you to go fishing with him. So he can show you his so-called skills. But you don't have to go, just remember that. If you don't feel like it, you just say so. First thing this morning he says, 'Don't you think a little bit of fishing might help Baby Girl start to feel better?' And I said, 'Macky, now don't start jerking at her to go off down to that river and stand around in water all day.' I said, 'You just want an excuse to show her your fishing lures,' so if he asks you if you want to see his collection, say no, thank you, unless you want to be bored to death for five hours. Uh-oh, here he is."

Macky was coming in the back door happy to see her. "Well, hey, look who's up."

"I've never slept so much in my entire life."

"Well, you needed it, Baby Girl," Macky said. "You were just worn out. Maybe, if you're up to it, Saturday we can take a run out to the river."

"Macky, will you *let* her eat her pancakes. She does not want to go. Do you?"

Dena was caught. "Oh, I wouldn't mind. It's just that I don't know anything about fishing."

Macky's face lit up. "It doesn't matter. I can give you a few pointers. When you feel like it, come on down to the store and we can pick out a few things."

"Macky—she does *not* want to spend five hours looking at fishing lures. Do you?"

They both looked at Dena.

"Well . . ."

"Of course she doesn't, Macky."

Macky said, "Norma, let the girl answer for herself."

Dena said, "No, I don't mind. That sounds interesting."

"Come on down this afternoon if you feel like it."

"She can't come this afternoon."

"Why not?"

"Because I promised Aunt Elner to bring her over for a visit."

Norma looked at Dena. "You don't mind, do you, Baby Girl?"

❖ ❖ ❖

That afternoon Dena found herself on Aunt Elner's porch. When Aunt Elner handed Dena and Norma their glasses of iced tea, Norma looked at the tea, an unusual shade of brown, dark at the top and lighter at the bottom. "What kind of tea is this?"

"It's instant but it's all I had. I used my last tea bag this morning. I'm sorry 'cause I don't care what they say, instant is nowhere as good as the real thing."

"Don't worry about it, Aunt Elner," Norma said. "This is just fine, really."

"No telling what it's gonna taste like. I've had that jar for a couple of years, or maybe five, but I don't guess it will poison us." She laughed. "And if it does, all three of us will go together. How are you doing, honey? Are you getting a chance to rest up?"

"Oh, yes."

Norma took a sip of tea and tried not to make a face. She caught Dena's eye when Aunt Elner wasn't looking and gestured not to drink hers.

"Nobody's been bothering you while you're here, have they?"

Dena put her glass down. "No, they really haven't."

"And they better not, that's all I can say, or they will have Mr. Macky Warren to answer to. But I tell you, Aunt Elner, you have never seen people act so silly in your entire life. Now I know why those poor movie stars live behind gates. If I've had one phone call I had a hundred, wanting Dena to do this or to do that ... give a speech at some club, wanting to interview her for the paper or take her picture. If this is what you have to put up with every day, I don't know how you stand it. No wonder you are tired; people pulling at me like that would give me the screaming meemies. Even Mary Grace called all the way from St. Louis, wanting her to come up to the phone company and give a talk."

"You remember Mary Grace, don't you, Baby Girl?" Aunt Elner said.

"No, I don't think I ever met her."

Aunt Elner seemed surprised. "Well, you should have, she's your cousin."

"No, honey," Norma said. "Baby Girl's not any kin to Mary Grace. Mary Grace is from Uncle Will's side of the family."

"Oh, that's right. I guess there was no reason to meet her."

Dena took the opportunity to ask a question. "Ah . . . are you my aunt, too? How are we related? I'm a little confused."

Norma answered, "Your grandmother, Gerta Nordstrom, was Aunt Elner's sister, so that makes her your great-aunt. Her other sister, Zela, was my mother, so that makes her my aunt . . . so you and I are second cousins on your father's side."

"What is Macky, then," Aunt Elner wondered. "My nephew?"

"No, honey, he is not related to you by blood. He is your—I guess he's your nephew by marriage. Here, this will make it easier for you, Baby Girl: your daddy, Gene, was my first cousin, so you must be my second cousin, and Macky is your second cousin by marriage. That's right, isn't it? Or maybe you're my third cousin. Isn't that right, Aunt Elner?"

"Oh, Lord, honey, I don't know anymore."

"Well, Gene's mother was my Aunt Gerta so . . . Wait a minute. Aunt Elner, you must be my great-aunt."

Aunt Elner said, "Who's Mary Grace, then?"

"She is your niece on your husband's side."

"Oh, that's right. I can't even think about little Mary Grace without remembering that meal we had up in St. Louis. How old would little Mary Grace be now, Norma?"

"About sixty-seven."

At this point Dena was wondering how fast she could get out of there and back to New York.

"That meal was something, wasn't it, Norma?"

"Oh, yes. A fine Italian restaurant. Gitto's."

"I'll never forget it. Tell Baby Girl what all we had."

"I had the chopped sirloin and onions . . . mashed potatoes, spinach, creamed squash on the side. Mary Grace had fish with nuts sprinkled on top . . . trout almondine."

"That's right," Aunt Elner agreed. "She had fish with the head still on it. And it was looking in my direction. I made her turn it around the other way. For those prices they could have taken the head off, but that's how the Continentals do it."

"Yes, and you ordered liver and onions." Norma looked at Dena, who was still bewildered. "Here she had a chance to eat anything in the world and she orders liver and onions."

"Well, I like liver and onions. How long are you going to be here, Baby Girl?"

"I don't know yet."

"I tell you what. Norma, you and Macky ought to take a trip up to St. Louis while she's here and take her to Gitto's for dinner. I wouldn't mind going back up there, would you?"

"Honey, Baby Girl lives in New York City and I'm sure she has been to plenty of nice restaurants, she doesn't need to go traipsing all the way up to St. Louis to eat a meal."

"Verbena said she and Merle ate out at that new pancake house on the highway and said they got a good meal; maybe we could go there?"

"It's up to Baby Girl; wherever she wants to go is fine with us."

"Well, if you like pancakes, Verbena says this place is the last word."

After they got back to Norma's, Dena said casually, "You know, I think I really would like to see those fishing things. Is the hardware store hard to find?"

Norma laughed. "No, downtown is only a block, you can't miss it. It's right past the flower shop. Do you want me to drive you?"

"No, I'll walk, thanks."

The real reason she wanted to go downtown was not to look at fishing lures. She wanted to get to a phone. As soon as she turned the corner she went into the Rexall drugstore and called her agent in New York.

"Mr. Cooper, you have a collect call from Dena Nordstrom; will you accept?"

"Yes, put her on. Hello! How are you feeling? Are you getting some rest?"

"Get me out of here."

"What?"

"I want you to get me out of here as soon as possible."

"You don't have to go back to work for a couple of weeks."

"I don't care, just get me out of here, now."

When she hung up and came out of the booth, several people were waiting to say hello to her and to say how glad they were to see her home. In a moment she walked by a place that seemed vaguely familiar. At least it smelled familiar. It was the bakery they said her grandparents used to own, still called Nordstrom's Swedish bakery even though there were new owners. She cupped her hands around her eyes and peered inside but nothing looked familiar. It was odd to walk down the street; people kept coming out of the stores and greeting her as if they were old friends. People she had never seen before in her life. Everybody knew who she was but when they spoke to her the older ones referred to her as Gene's daughter, and the younger ones as Norma's cousin or Aunt Elner's niece. It was the first time in her life she had ever been referred to as anything but Dena Nordstrom.

People kept stopping her and telling her about how they had grown up with her father, or that he had once been their paper boy and what a fine fellow he was. It seemed everybody had a tale about her father or her grandparents they wanted her to hear. Finally, what seemed like hours later, she reached the hardware store.

Soon, Macky had shown her all his fishing flies, and explained each one by name and what fish it was used to catch. She said, "Macky, did you know my father?"

He nodded. "Very well. And your grandparents. Fine people."

Today, she had been pleasantly surprised. Elmwood Springs was a really nice little town and all the people who had come up to her seemed very friendly. She suddenly began to wonder what it was that had caused her mother to move away. What had happened?

Even though everybody had wanted to tell her about her father or grandparents or talk about how they used to come into the bakery and see her sitting up on the counter when she was little, no one mentioned her mother. It was almost as if her mother had never been there.

❀   ❀   ❀

After dinner Norma got out her father's high school yearbooks and all his pictures in an album, but again there was not one picture of her mother.

The next morning at breakfast Dena said, "Norma, what did you know about my mother?"

Norma was caught off guard for a moment. Dena had never brought up the subject before. "Well, Baby Girl, not much. What would you like to know?"

"Oh, what she was like when she was here and things like that."

Norma put a plate in the dishwasher and closed it and sat down across from Dena. "Well, I can only tell you what I know. I was in high school, I guess . . . or maybe I had graduated by then. But I certainly remember her. But you know, she wasn't here all that long, and she stayed mostly to herself. I do remember we would go up to Aunt Gerta's house to see you and she was always so proud of you, bought you all kinds of toys."

"Did you like her?"

"Oh, yes, very much. But don't forget I was still young and didn't get to know her all that well."

"What about Aunt Elner?"

"Well, Aunt Elner could probably tell you more than I could. We could talk to her if you'd like."

"Yes, I think I would."

Right after breakfast they were on Aunt Elner's porch again.

"Aunt Elner, I wonder if you remember anything about my mother."

Norma said, "I've told Baby Girl everything I remember."

"Well, honey, let me sit here and tax my memory. . . . Lord, that was a piece ago, wasn't it. But of course I do. I remember the first day she came here. You were just a tiny baby; we went down to the train station to meet Gene's wife. He had written of how pretty she was, but we had no idea she was going to be that pretty. We were all standing there and here this glamorous creature steps down from the train. We almost couldn't believe our eyes. She looked like she had stepped out of a magazine. She had on this aqua wool dress and her hair was swept up on her head and she had this little smart pancake of a hat tilted over one eye. Oh, she was a fashion plate if I ever saw one. Let's put it this way: we had never seen anything like her in Elmwood Springs. Beautiful red hair, and that creamy white skin, and those green eyes—you got Gene's eyes but you got your mother's figure. She was tall and I remember her posture, she held herself just like a queen." She chuckled. "To tell you the truth, I was embarrassed; here we were, her new family, and me so big and fat, wearing a homemade housedress and my old black tie-up shoes, I just wanted to hide. But she recognized us and we were all anxious to get a look at you; you were Gene's baby, you sort of broke the ice. And when we saw you we were all tickled to death. You couldn't miss you were Gene's baby, all right, with that towhead of white hair and those big blue eyes. She had you dressed in the cutest baby outfit, a little pink dress with lace, and she had a big pink bow tied around your head. You looked like one of those baby dolls that Norma had gotten for Christmas, didn't she, Norma?"

"You did, you were the cutest thing."

Dena said, "How did she seem?"

"If anything, she was shy, she wouldn't let anyone take her picture. I said as pretty as you were, you needed to have your picture made—but she wouldn't."

"Did she seem unfriendly?"

"Oh, no, she was very sweet and soft-spoken . . . but sort of reserved, wouldn't you say, Norma?"

"Yes, I guess you could say that. Not that she wasn't perfectly friendly, mind you."

Aunt Elner agreed. "No, she was perfectly friendly and pleasant but you could tell right away that she was not one of those flighty young girls that some of the boys brought home. Not only was your mother pretty, she was refined and well spoken, and she wrote with a beautiful hand. Well educated and from a good family but she never talked about them and we never asked. We didn't want to open a sore spot, we thought if she wanted to talk about it she would, and after losing her entire family in a fire, then to lose Gene . . . I don't know how she lived through it. Do you, Norma?"

"No, I kept thinking that she would talk about it but she never did the whole time she was here."

"It must have been terrible for her, a young girl like that all alone in the world, her whole family gone. I don't know how she stood it but you could tell it had affected her, she always seemed a little sad or something. Even though she never talked about it, you could tell she never got over it."

"I read in the *Reader's Digest* that a person that survives a tragedy goes through all kinds of guilt for being the one left alive," Norma said. "She should have gone for some help. But back then, they didn't have any, not like they do today. She did seem nervous, though, didn't she, Aunt Elner?"

"Well, I wouldn't go so far as to say nervous but she always seemed a little uneasy, looking over her shoulder like something was worrying her—sort of holding her back from really letting go and having fun. You were her only joy, you were the only thing I ever saw her eyes light up over. She never showed her emotions much. She didn't cry or at least none of us ever saw her. She got a job and just went to work every day and came home and played with you at night. Otherwise, she never went out, never saw anybody. And then one day, when you were about four, she just up and left. Packed your things, took you out of nursery school, and left. She said she wanted to get a better job and she couldn't get one in Elmwood Springs, so she just took off and she never came back. It broke your poor grandparents' hearts."

"Did you ever meet anybody she knew?" Dena asked. "Did anybody at all ever come to see her?"

Aunt Elner thought. "No . . . nobody ever did. She never had anybody come and see her, nobody except that Italian man that time."

Norma looked at Aunt Elner. "Italian? You never told me about any Italian man."

"Well, I forgot. I think he was an Italian or Greek or something, some kind of foreigner. I only saw him through a screen door but he had kind of slicky hair. He walked up on the porch and knocked on the door and asked if your mother lived there and Gerta went to get her and I can tell whoever he was she didn't like him much, she didn't even invite him in. Your mother had impeccable manners and that was not like her, but the minute she saw him, she took him way out on the sidewalk and away from the house. I was just sitting there in the living room and I couldn't help but look. I could see right out the screen door. Whoever he was, your mother was not happy he showed up, I can tell you that. It looked like she was mad at him. And whatever she said must have run him off because after about ten minutes he was gone. When she came back in the house you could tell that she was still upset, her face was all flushed."

Norma was amazed. "And she never said who he was?"

"No."

"And you didn't ask?"

"No, Norma, I don't poke in other people's affairs. Just pass and repass, I always say. She didn't volunteer and we didn't ask."

"Are you sure she didn't say anything? I can't believe she didn't say anything."

"Norma, that was some thirty years ago."

"Well, try and remember back."

"She might have said something . . . let me search my memory. I think she might have said, 'I'm sorry' . . . yes, that's right, she did. Like I said, your mother had beautiful manners. I think he may have been some old boyfriend who found out that her husband had been killed and showed up trying to get her to go out with him."

"Did he ever come back?" Dena asked.

"No, not to my knowledge. But your mother left town shortly after that so I haven't any idea if he ever bothered her again or not. But you know, you can't blame the poor fellow, she was a pretty thing."

Norma said, "Couldn't you hear *any*thing? Did you hear what they were arguing about?"

"Oh, I could hear them, all right, but I couldn't understand what they were saying. They were talking in a foreign language."

"*Both* of them?"

"Well, sure, honey, you can't have one person talking one language and the other one talking something else."

"What language were they speaking?"

Aunt Elner said, "Well, now, that was the funny thing. Like I said, he looked Italian. But they were talking in German."

Norma was not convinced. "Aunt Elner, now, think back: Are you *sure* it was German? Don't you think it might have been Italian or maybe Spanish?"

Aunt Elner said, "No. Don't forget your Uncle Will's father was a Shimfessle. All he spoke was German, so I know German when I hear it. It was German, all right, that much I'm sure of."

"Baby Girl knew her mother spoke German, didn't you, honey?"

Dena said, "Oh, yes . . . I knew that." Suddenly Dena began to feel anxious, and she didn't know why she lied. She had no idea her mother had spoke German. She quickly changed the subject and did not bring it up again. The next morning a telegram arrived for her.

AM SORRY TO INFORM YOU THAT YOUR BELOVED AGENT AND SHOW

BUSINESS ICON, SANDY COOPER, PASSED AWAY SUDDENLY LAST EVENING.

PLEASE RETURN TO NEW YORK AT ONCE.

JULIAN AMSLEY, NETWORK PRESIDENT

Later that night when she got off the plane at La Guardia, Sandy said, "Well, how do I look for a dead man?"

Dena said, "Beautiful!" and kissed him, thrilled to be back.

One of the first things she did when she got back to her apartment was to sit down and type a letter.

Dear Gerry,

Thank you so much for your flowers. I know you went to a lot of trouble to bring them to me and I really do appreciate it. However, I think it would be unfair of me to keep you from pursuing a relationship with the kind of woman you deserve to be with. You are too nice a guy to lead on.

I hope we can be friends in the future and I wish you all the best in everything you do.

Sincerely,
Dena Nordstrom

Rumors

New York City
May 1976

As the months went by, Dena was getting better and better interviews. Her agent, Sandy, even heard serious rumblings. They were considering moving her to a coanchor spot on the six o'clock news. But in the meantime, Ira Wallace was happy with her work. The ratings were still climbing and upstairs was pleased, too. Production costs were small compared with the budget for an hour-long drama. News shows were suddenly big business.

Competition was heating up, too, and Dena's interviews were getting rougher and rougher. It made her uneasy, particularly when she remembered that Howard Kingsley might be watching her.

Pete Koski had been elected governor of his state mostly because he had been a championship football star, but after twelve years in politics he had turned out to be a respected member of his party and now there was a lot of talk about him being asked to run for president in the upcoming campaign. Ira briefed her for the interview. As soon as she sat down and saw that look on Ira's face, she knew something was coming, and prepared herself for the worst.

"Your Mr. Macho, hall of famer, Super Governor, has a son that's as queer as a three-dollar bill. Got his little fairy butt kicked out of the army for playing house with some other fairy, but Koski had it fixed so it wouldn't show up on his record. How's that for a nice little cherry bomb to throw in?"

"Oh, God, Ira, why won't you let me just have one interview without trying to turn it into an ambush?"

"It's the truth!" Wallace yelled defensively. "Capello got the god-damn report out of the goddamn military files and he's got a statement from one of his boyfriends."

Dena stared at him.

"Ira, I told you before I wouldn't work with Capello. You lied. You didn't fire him, did you?"

"You think I would quit working with the best son of a bitch in the business just because you don't like him? Whata'ya think, I'm stupid? I got him outta your face, what else do you want from me? Now I'm not asking you, I'm telling you—you work for me, not Howard Kingsley, me! You ask the questions that I tell you to."

"What does Howard Kingsley have to do with this?"

"Don't play innocent with me. Everybody knows what's been going on with you two. Who do you think you're kidding?"

"Ira, I hope you're not serious. You know that's not true."

"Hey, what you do is your own business. Just don't try and con me."

"Ira, you are disgusting, do you know that, a disgusting pig."

"Oh, yeah, I'm terrible. Meanwhile, your sainted governor just got caught abusing his power. He bribed the United States Army, for Christ sakes. That's a crime, kid, so don't get all high and mighty with me. Sit down!"

Dena realized for the first time how utterly ruthless Ira Wallace could be. "You can't be insulted, can you? You really don't care what people think of you, not even me."

"I see people for what they are; you see them for what you wish they were but they ain't. And I'm warning you: if you want to stay on top in this business, you better get over this Doris Day phase you're in or these new broads are gonna kick your ass. Here, read this." He pushed a copy of a medical discharge toward her and an army psychiatrist's private notes.

"See . . . he admits it. What more do you want?"

Dena looked at him in disbelief. "Ira, we can't use this. This is illegal."

"Oh, I know that, for Christ sakes. I just wanted you to see it, you're always screaming about backup. So there it is—your goddamn backup."

"How did Capello get this?"

"I don't ask. I don't care. He got it. Just ask the question."

"Ira, this guy should be in jail—and that's where you are going to wind up if you're not careful. And I'd be going with you. I'm not doing it."

"That's final?"

"Yes," said Dena, and she meant it. She had already ruined one man's political life, she wasn't going to do it again.

Wallace sat back and sadly shook his head. "I don't understand you. I bring you into the bosom of my family, move your career along, and you have no loyalty, none at all." He reached in his top drawer and pulled out a cigar cutter and clipped the end off a new cigar. "You know, kid, you are beginning to worry me. And I don't like that. 'Cause when I worry I start looking around."

"What does that mean?"

"You figure it out."

"I see. That's a threat. If I don't do your on-air dirty work, you'll find somebody who will, is that it?"

"No, no threat. You don't want to do the story, what am I gonna do, force you? I'll give it to Larry, he ain't so particular."

As Dena was leaving, Wallace said, "By the way, I hear your friend Kingsley is retiring."

"What?"

"He's retiring, all right. He's getting his ass fired."

"How—?"

"What is it they say? Old newsmen never die, their ratings just fade away."

"Ira, don't say stuff like that, not even joking. You know that's a lie."

"I hate to break your heart about your boyfriend but he's getting canned. I got it on good authority. I make it my business to know what's going on everywhere in the business."

"Who told you that?"

"Never mind who. They are giving him an ultimatum. Either he retires or gets canned officially."

"I don't believe it."

"Believe it. Do you know what that self-righteous son of a bitch was doing? He was redlining stories, leaving whole segments out. That senile old alligator was trying to control the news." He laughed mirthlessly. "Oh, they'll miss him. About a week or two at most. The man is a joke, and everybody in town knows it. About time somebody knocked him on his holier-than-thou, sanctimonious butt."

Dena went back to her office, sick at what Wallace had said about Howard, and particularly about their relationship. Was he just trying to shake her up and knock her off balance or did everybody else think that, too? She thought about it, then buzzed Arnie, an editor at the network she liked, and asked him to have a drink with her after work.

❖   ❖   ❖

Arnie was a lanky, slender guy with a bobbing Adam's apple, who wore thick, black-framed glasses and could hardly believe his good fortune to find himself sitting with this goddess in a bar high above Fifth Avenue. They had finished their second drink when Dena asked him if he had ever heard any rumors about her and Howard Kingsley.

Arnie became visibly uneasy.

"Tell me. I need to know."

Arnie hemmed and hawed. "Yeah ... I guess ... Well, I guess there was some talk."

"What do you mean some talk? About ... ?"

"Nothing." He cleared his throat and swallowed hard. "You know how things get around; you know, the usual jokes."

"What jokes?"

"Silly stuff, you know."

"No, I don't know," Dena said. "Tell me."

Arnie stammered and turned red. "No, I really don't think I should."

"Arnie, you have to tell me."

He squirmed in his seat and glanced around the room. "Well, things like ... and I didn't say it, but ..." He lowered his voice and said almost apologetically, "There was one ... uh, what's old and wrinkled, has great boobs, and gets laid on Fridays? But, hey, nobody blamed him. Hell, every guy around here would have taken a shot at you if we thought we would have a chance."

Dena sat back in the booth, bewildered, humiliated, and disgusted. Is that what everybody thought? Was that all her friendship with Howard was made out to be? Just somebody's dirty little office joke, some twelve-year-old's bathroom humor?

Arnie saw the look on her face and panicked. "Hey, Dena, you're not gonna be mad at me, now, are you—you asked."

"No, I'm not mad at you, Arnie. And Ira is right. I guess I don't know what people are really like."

Aren't People Wonderful?

Neighbor Dorothy greeted her listeners with a great big "Good morning, everybody ... How is everybody over at your house this morning? We're so glad all our radio neighbors are with us because as Little Annie Rooney says, it's going to be a Grand Dandy day. So pour yourself a cup of coffee and put your feet up. As you know, this is one of our favorite days of the year. Today is our annual Aren't People Wonderful Day and it's devoted entirely to all of you out there who make up this wonderful old world.

"Every year we ask all of you to send in your letters telling us the nicest thing a neighbor did for you and we have received hundreds ... but before we get to our letters this morning, we want to especially thank each and every one of you who sent in money for Bernice's Seeing Eye dog. You know, I'll never get over how sweet people are. So many of you sent in your hard-earned dimes, and I know how hard you work for them; thanks to all of you that held bake sales, sold eggs, and you Scouts who held car washes, and all of the numerous things you did to make this wish come true. And I am happy to announce that on Friday afternoon, Bernice's guide dog was delivered. Her name is Honey, and she is a yellow Lab and was raised and trained by Mr. Dan Martin and family of Elgin, Illinois, and, oh, I wish all of you could have been there. Mr. Martin came up the sidewalk with Honey, and when he walked up those steps with her it was like that dog knew who Bernice was. We were all out on the porch but Honey went over to Bernice and sat down right beside her, just like she knew who she belonged to. Mr. Martin said, 'The Guide Dog Association is proud to hand over your dog . . . and from this moment forth she will be your faithful and loving companion until the day she dies,' and with that he placed the lead in her hands and stepped back, and I wish you all could have seen the look on Bernice's face when Honey rubbed her face against her hand. . . . Well . . . I just don't have the words to describe it. . . . I know it must be hard for Mr. Martin to hand Honey over to someone else—he raised her since she was a puppy—but he will be here with us for a week to train Bernice how to walk with Honey . . . so all of you out there who have been so kind and generous, if you want to see a real miracle, drive by and you can see the three of them walking up and down the sidewalk. Yesterday they walked all the way downtown, past the barbershop, past the theater, down to the corner and back . . . I'll tell you . . . it makes me proud to be a member of the human race.

"And now, we'd better get on with our letters because we want to try and get as many on the air as possible . . . so we will start with this one . . . and it comes to us from Reverend Raymond Rodgers of Sedilia, Missouri. He writes, 'Dear Neighbor Dorothy, when I came back to my congregation after serving four years in the war as army chaplain, I came home not sure I could continue my ministry. I had experienced so many horrible things overseas, my faith had been shaken, and when I came home I was not the same man that had left four years ago. Sadly I expressed this to my congregation and was ready to step down as pastor when to my surprise, the next day I received a telegram that read, "That's all right, Pastor . . . we are not the same congregation that you left behind, either." And it was signed by every member of the church. Needless to say, I am still here. . . .' Well, Reverend, it sounds like you have a mighty wonderful congregation and they have a wonderful pastor as well. . . . The next letter comes from Glaydes Speller of Moorland, Indiana. 'Dear Neighbor Dorothy, six years ago my husband and I were with our daughter, who was deathly ill in the hospital for a heart operation. While we were gone, we heard the news that our farm home had been completely destroyed by a tornado. We were heavy of heart and when we came home to survey the damage, imagine our surprise to see a shiny white, brand-new farmhouse sitting on the same spot where our old farmhouse had been and inside was new furniture, placed in exactly the same place as the old furniture. No one in our little community will take credit for it and deny they had anything to do with it. How joyful it was to bring our daughter home to her new home! There isn't a day I wake up in our beautiful home and don't remember the kindness of my neighbors. I hope you read this so I can say thank you to all my good neighbors.'

"Well . . . I say thank you to all you sweet people of Moorland. You have truly earned stars in your crown. We'll be right back with more of your letters, but first, in your honor, Ernest Koonitz, our Elmwood Springs band director, is going to render a tuba solo played in honor of all the good neighbors out there. So here he is now, with Mother Smith on the organ playing 'How Great Thou Art.' "

The Last Day

Howard Kingsley was becoming more and more agitated as the weeks went by. He was getting tired of having to deal with the latest news director, Gordon, an aggressive thirty-five-year-old bastard who had no respect for Howard and could not wait to get rid of him. Gordon wanted someone he could control. At first he was careful not to upset Howard, but as soon as the ratings started to slip slightly, he began to make Howard's life miserable. Film pieces were switched, TelePrompTers started breaking down, on-air signals were late being called from the control booth, all calculated to make Howard look bad, and they did. But upstairs had a problem. They, too, were anxious to have News go in a new direction, to update it; still, Howard was the grand old man of broadcasting and they could not fire him outright. They did hope to maybe hasten his retirement a bit and seemed not to notice what was happening to Howard on the set. Even if it was at the expense of a few points in the ratings, they first needed something to justify getting him off the air. Yet Howard was stubborn and he hung in there, and fought as long as he could—until he had a little scare with his heart.

As it turned out the problem was said not to be serious, but it was serious enough for his wife and daughter to beg him to quit before it was too late. He hated to do it but he knew he was fighting a losing battle. And so, one Monday morning, Howard went upstairs to the president's office. Ned Thomson III got up from his chair to meet him at the door.

"Howard, why didn't you call me? I could have come downstairs, for God's sake. How are you? Come sit down."

Howard said, "I'm fine, absolutely fine."

"Can I get you coffee, tea?"

Howard sat in the visitor's chair. "No, thanks. I just want to say that I have made the decision to retire and I wanted to let you know, give you a couple of months to get everything in place."

Thomson looked shocked. "My God, Howard . . . are you sure? I mean, this is so sudden. Are you sure—is there anything we can do to change your mind?"

"No, not a thing."

"I don't know; this is quite a blow. I mean, you've been the backbone of this network, hell, you *are* this network. Isn't there something we can do?"

"Yes, there is. I want you to keep this as quiet as possible. I want you to promise me there will be no tributes, no awards, none of that. I want to leave with as little fanfare as possible. Will you do that for me?"

"Of course. Any way you want it handled. We'll respect however you want to do it, you know that."

Howard stood up. "Good."

"Now, when you say a couple of months, do you mean . . . two, three? How long do we have?"

"Two."

"I see. Well, after all these years—you were here before Dad, even—I still can't believe it. But if this is what you want—"

"It is." Howard spoke with certainty.

Thomson walked to the door and put his hand on Howard's shoulder.

"All I can say is, it's going to be hell trying to find a guy to replace you—hell, you can't be replaced. You're an institution. This is going to be tough."

Howard turned to him. "Then why don't you just get on the phone and tell that son of a bitch you hired to get rid of me that I'm out and his boy is in. That can't be too tough, can it?"

Ned watched Howard walk past his secretary and down the hall. He buzzed the control booth. The news director picked up.

"Two months, Gordon. Call David . . . tell him to get ready. I'll get publicity to start the ball rolling. He just walked in here and said he was retiring, whammo, just like that. Yeah, and listen: you might want to lay off of him. I think he smells a rat and we can't afford to have him say anything. He still carries a lot of weight with the board. We want to get out with our noses clean, OK?"

Two months later, exactly, Howard finished his broadcast as he usually did, "And so ends another day." But this night after the sign-off, he continued. In the booth, the news director ordered camera three in for a close-up. Howard took his glasses off, looked into the camera, and said, "As some of you may know, tonight ends for me what has been as exciting and as rewarding a career as a man can have. I have been proud and humbled by the support and trust you have so graciously allowed me throughout the years and I only hope I have been worthy of the task. I wish you well and may God bless you all. Good night and good-bye."

The camera pulled back as he put his glasses back on and gathered his papers off his desk as he had for so many years. Upstairs, in the booth, a crowd had gathered to watch. After the news went off the air, they all stood in silence. It was quiet downstairs on the floor as well. Howard stood up and removed his mike and quietly shook hands with a few cameramen and his makeup woman, who had come up to his desk. Then he walked over to the edge of the set, where his wife and daughter were waiting to take him home.

Celebrity Mail

Elmwood Springs, Missouri
1976

By now, Dena had long forgotten about her stay in Missouri, but they
had not forgotten her. Dena's secretary put a letter on her desk.

Dear Baby Girl,

   I know you get so many requests and I hate to bother you
but being a hometown girl, I thought maybe you would be
willing to help us out.

   I have been named Chairman of the "Revitalize Downtown Elmwood Springs" committee. We are an organization
devoted to saving our downtown area. As you know, so many
little towns all over the country have succumbed to the big
shopping centers. Local merchants are finding it hard to compete with the big Kmarts and Wal-Marts that have opened,
and so many little towns have just shut down and fallen into
disrepair and now, our downtown stores are closing one by
one. Macky's hardware store, the Rexall, the barbershop, and
the Trolley Car diner are all we have left. Everything else has
closed. Since you were here last, Morgan Brothers department
store and Victor the florist have closed. For so many of us who
grew up here it is a heartbreaking sight to walk downtown

and see all the places looking so empty. We are hoping to raise enough money to advertise nationally for small business owners who might be interested in relocating to the midwest. Which brings me to the point of this letter, Baby Girl; on June the 15th, the Lions Club and the Rotary Club are sponsoring an Elmwood Springs Day to be held in the park. We will have a fish fry, rides and booths, arts and crafts, and activities all day with local celebrities and at 6 o'clock we are having a big celebrity auction, and since you are our one and only *real* celebrity, I was wondering if you could send us something. I know it would bring a big price and it is for a good cause.

Anything you could send will be appreciated, an autographed photo, or maybe something you wore on television, a fountain pen, maybe an autographed script of one of your interviews, we will be thrilled with just anything you can send us. I hate to bother you when you are so busy, but it could have been worse. Some of my committee wanted to throw a "Dena Nordstrom Day," have a parade and bring you in as the Grand Marshall. I put a nix on that. I told Macky, that's all Baby Girl needs is to fly all the way here to ride one block.

Love,
Norma

P.S. Wayne Newton is sending us a pair of cuff links he wore on stage in Las Vegas, and Liberace, Phyllis Diller, and Debbie Reynolds have also promised to send something.

Turkey Time

The November after Howard Kingsley had retired, he and his wife, Lee, invited Dena to come and spend Thanksgiving on their farm in Bucks County, Pennsylvania. From the moment she arrived, she could see that Howard was almost a different person. He seemed much more relaxed and looked like a true country squire in his khaki pants and his thick red-and-black-plaid shirt, and after a half day Dena began to relax a little, too. The house was an old stone farmhouse built in 1789 that sat on twenty acres. Dena was helpless in the kitchen so on Thanksgiving Day, she and Howard went for a long walk across the fields, behind the house, and into the woods. There she saw quail and pheasants for the first time in her life. It was a wonderful autumn afternoon.

As they walked Dena asked what it was like for him now that he was retired. He laughed. "Each morning I wake up so stiff and arthritic I can hardly get out of bed. I go into the bathroom and look in the mirror at what used to be a pretty passable mug and what stares back at me is this gray-haired, old, turkey-necked geezer and it's pretty depressing. But then I think, Howard, old boy, today you can say any damn thing you want ... and that puts a spring back in my step, I'll tell you. That's what I wish for everybody, that they get old enough not to have to please anyone, and ornery enough to thumb their noses at all the idiots in the world. It's worth getting old. I recommend it to everybody."

"You look about ten years younger."

"I don't know about that but I can tell you this, I feel better than I have for a long time."

"Do you ever miss it at all?"

"No, strangely enough, I don't. Not a minute of it. As a matter of fact, I wish I had stopped years ago. I'm just beginning to realize how much of life I missed. I can't wait to get out to Sag Harbor for a whole summer. Did I ask you if you sailed?"

"The first time we had lunch."

"Oh."

"But I've never been on a sailboat in my life."

"Well, we'll have to remedy that, young lady. Yes, I didn't think I would, but I like this retirement. I put in over fifty years and I figure that's enough for any man." He smiled and corrected himself. "Or woman."

"Fifty years. That's a long time."

"Yes, but don't forget, I go a long way back. I started on a little two-hundred-watt radio station in Sidney, Iowa."

Howard suddenly stopped and motioned for her not to speak. He pointed out a doe and a baby deer across the field, who stood perfectly still, looking at them, then, after a moment, ran back into the woods.

Dena was amazed. "Wow! Are there a lot of deer around here?"

"Oh, yes. We put out a salt lick for them in the back. I've seen as many as twenty-five come at one time."

"I've never seen them in the wild like this."

"I thought you were a country girl."

"No, not really. I was raised mostly in apartments in the city. My mother worked in department stores."

"I see. Well, you're going to have to get out here more often, put some color in those cheeks." They walked for a while. "You know, the world has come a long way from that little radio station to where we are today. Television. God, I remember when the damn thing started." He pulled a branch back so Dena could get by. "Murrow and I got so damn excited we could hardly stand it. Hell, we were so naive, we thought it was going to educate and uplift every human being, save humanity from ignorance, stop all the wars. I'm glad he didn't live to see what's happening, and it's only going to get worse, I'm afraid." Then he chuckled. "Since I've retired I found out one more thing about television I didn't know. It's a hell of a lot easier to be on it than it is to watch."

When they reached the stream, Dena looked down at the water. It was so clear that the round, smooth brown and tan pebbles looked as if they were under glass. Howard pulled out a collapsible plastic cup he had in his back pocket and dipped it in the water. "I want you to take a drink of this."

"You can drink it just like this . . . right out of the ground?"

"Oh, yes, it's as pure as it comes. Try it."

She sipped. It was ice cold and the best water she had ever tasted. "That is wonderful."

"Isn't it? Lee says we should bottle it."

"She's right."

They walked over to a log to sit down but Dena was hesitant. "Are there snakes crawling around in there?"

"No. You really are a city girl, aren't you? Snakes hibernate in the winter."

"I'm not going to sit on one and wake him up, am I?"

"You're safe."

They sat and listened to the sound of the stream for a while. "We had a little farm about ten miles from town and my father used to say, 'The minute a man gets too far from nature is when he begins to get into trouble.' He was right, of course, but I didn't think so at the time. Back then I just thought he was an old fogey, a country bumpkin that didn't know anything. I just couldn't wait to shake the dust off my shoes and head for the big city. See the world, be a big shot. But every day I'm out here, I think about him. I realize my old man—who I thought had never amounted to much—had lived one of the best lives a man could live. He was never cruel to a living soul, raised his children, loved his wife, and worked the land."

Howard seemed lost in thought. "He didn't talk much about himself. But right after Pearl Harbor, I came home for a visit before going overseas and we took a walk out on the farm. We started talking about the war and he told me something I never knew, something that had happened to him in World War I. He said one night he was in the trenches all by himself, waiting for his replacement, when all of a sudden he heard something and looked up and saw this young German soldier come crawling over. When he saw that German uniform he said it scared him so badly that he just closed his eyes and pulled the trigger. And the next thing he knew that boy had fallen right on top of him. He had hit him in the side of the neck. Dad said he was just a kid—couldn't have been any older than sixteen or seventeen—and was as scared as he was. My old man said he sat there all night with that boy while that boy bled to death and there wasn't a thing he could do for him but to hold his hand and try to comfort him.

"Neither one of them understood what the other one was saying but they talked all night. The only thing he could manage to find out was that the boy's name was Willy. And just as the sun was about to come up, the boy called out for his mother and died right there still holding on to my old man's hand. That was the first time I ever saw him cry. He cried over some boy he had killed over twenty-five years ago. But . . . I was so revved up and gung-ho about getting into the war, all I could think was to ask him if he got a medal for killing a German. He said, yes, he got a medal, but the first thing he had done when he got on the boat coming home was throw it overboard. He said there were no heroes in war, just survivors. I didn't know what he was talking about at the time, until I got to see the glory of war for myself. And years later, when he was dying—he'd been in a coma for a couple of days—I was sitting beside the bed holding his hand and all of a sudden he opened his eyes and smiled at me. He said, 'Hello, Willy.' I think he saw that German boy."

"Really . . . do you really think so?"

Howard picked up a rock and looked at it. "I don't know for sure but you hear all these things about death, people claim they see. . . . It could be that he just had that boy on his mind. But my old man thought he saw him and he went out peacefully."

Howard looked at his watch. "We'd better start heading on back. Lee's been cooking for three days and if we're late, she'll kill me."

"Wouldn't it be great if it were true, that we really did get to see the people we knew after we die? My father was killed before I was born. I sure would like to get a chance to meet him. I've seen pictures of him but he has no idea what I look like. He probably wouldn't even know who I was if he did see me. I'd probably just be a stranger."

He smiled at her. "Well, speaking for all fathers, I'm sure he would be very proud of you."

When they were almost home, Dena said, "Thank you for showing me this . . . it's just great. In New York you forget there's a whole different world out here, not more than just a couple of hours away. The air is so different. What smells so good out here . . . what is that?"

"Wood smoke. Lee has a fire going."

"Oh."

Howard said, "I'll tell you, if I hadn't had this place and my boat in Sag Harbor to keep me grounded all these years, I don't know how I could have done it. You have to get out of that rat race every once in a while or you begin to lose perspective. We start to believe that New York and Los Angeles and the inside of a television studio is all there is to this country. You need to get out among the people, talk to them, find out what they are thinking. I've heard more common sense from a bunch of old guys sitting around drinking coffee than I have from some of the smartest, most educated men in the world. If you want to know what's really happening in this country, ask them and they'll tell you."

At that moment, Howard's grandchildren ran out of the house, excited to see them.

"Grandpa, hurry up, they won't let us eat till you get here."

"I'm here," he laughed. "I'm here."

Born Again

Selma, Alabama
1977

Sookie had called Dena at work and said that she needed to talk to her as soon as possible and that it was extremely important but that she could not discuss it over the phone. "It's something I need to tell you in person."

Dena was somewhat alarmed and asked if she couldn't at least give her a hint as to what it was about. Sookie would give her no clue except that something had happened that she needed to share with her and she could only do it face-to-face. "Can you plan a trip here anytime soon?"

"Well, I can try, Sookie; let me call you back." Dena got on the phone with her secretary and they rerouted a trip she was making to Seattle, Washington, to include a stopover in Atlanta for one night, which was hard to do but they did it. Dena was concerned. Whatever it was, it sounded serious.

The trip was going to be extremely inconvenient but for the first time in her life, Dena was making an attempt to be a good friend. But she also wished that Sookie would get over her silly refusal to travel north of the Mason-Dixon line. By the time she got into Atlanta, she was exhausted.

Sookie had reserved a quiet table for them at the hotel's dining room, a lovely formal room that was almost empty. They sat across from each other at the dining room table. After the waiter had taken their dinner order, Dena said, "All right, Sookie, what is going on? What is it?"

Sookie looked somber as she began a speech that she had either rehearsed or had given many times before.

"Dena, there is something about me that you should know."

"You know you can tell me anything, Sookie, whatever it is."

"Dena, on May the twenty-second, I invited the Lord to come into my life and I have completely accepted Him as my Lord and Savior."

"What?"

"As my best friend I wanted to share with you that I now have a personal relationship with Jesus Christ."

"Sookie, surely you're not serious?"

Sookie leaned toward her. "Of course I'm serious. I would not joke about a thing like this."

She was not kidding and was waiting for Dena to say something, but Dena was at a complete loss for words.

"Oh . . . well, uh . . . I hope you two will be very happy. I mean, what can I say? Is this what you had to tell me?"

"Part of it. Dena, the other thing I wanted to share with you is that two weeks ago Jesus spoke to my heart and told me that you needed to be saved and I would like the opportunity to personally witness for Christ and introduce Him to you."

Dena was horrified at the prospect and desperately began looking around for the waiter to bring her a drink.

"You know what, Sookie—that's great, and if that's what your thing is, fine—whatever floats your boat. But I don't go in for all that Bible stuff."

The waiter was there in a second and Dena ordered a double vodka.

Dena looked at Sookie. "Do you still drink or what?"

Sookie gave her a coy little look. "Of course. I'll have a glass of Chablis. Even Jesus drank wine."

"I can't believe you dragged me all the way down here to tell me this. God, Sookie, I thought it was something important."

Sookie's eyes got big. "Well, it *is* important. To me."

"I can't believe you're serious."

"I thought you would be happy for me. You don't seem happy for me."

"Gee, you're right, Sookie," Dena said. "I guess I should just be thrilled to find out that my best friend who I thought had good sense tells me all of a sudden she has some hot line to heaven and is chatting on the phone with Jesus Christ every day. And when did you get so religious all of a sudden?"

The waiter brought their drinks. "Dena, I was always a Christian. You knew that, don't you remember? I always went to Kappa Bible study on Wednesday nights, you forget, and I always went to church. You would just never come with me. I tried but you had all that theater stuff going on. It's not anything new. It's just that I have really made a commitment to live as a true Christian and help spread the Gospel to others."

Dena continued to stare at her in disbelief.

"After all, Dena, it was Jesus Himself who said that unless a man is born again he cannot enter the Kingdom of Heaven and I don't want you not to be there with us. I care about you. I worry about your soul."

Strangely enough, at that moment the waiter brought their meals and Dena's entrée just so happened to be filet of sole. As Dena tried to enjoy her meal, Sookie kept at her.

"You do believe in God, don't you? Don't tell me you don't even believe in God?"

"Sookie, I love you, but let's don't talk about this. You are going to make me say things I don't want to say. Let's talk about something else. How are the girls?"

Sookie was clearly disappointed but she gave up gracefully. "All right. I promise I won't talk about it anymore. But I'm not going to give up on you, Dena; no matter what, I'm going to pray for you."

"Don't."

"Well, I will. I am not going to heaven without you ... and I have my sneaky ways."

On the plane back to New York, Dena was still somewhat astonished at Sookie. She must have been brainwashed. When Dena landed she jumped into a cab and headed for the studio. Opening her purse to pay the driver she saw the pamphlets that Sookie had slipped into her purse. One said, "Are You Saved?" and the other, "Jesus Wants You for a Sunbeam." The only other thing that made the trip worthwhile was the look she imagined would be on Ira Wallace's face when he found them on his desk.

But the minute she walked into the office in New York, her secretary handed her a news report that had just come in over the wire.

SAG HARBOR—Howard Kingsley, the retired newscaster and "conscience of broadcasting," died at his home of heart failure last night. He was 68 years of age.

Good-bye

Lee Kingsley had called Dena and told her they were going to scatter Howard Kingsley's ashes in a quiet ceremony from his boat, the *Lee Anne.* "We want you to be there. I know Howard would have liked that, he thought so much of you. So please come." Dena said she would. They met at the house in Sag Harbor and went aboard the boat around four—Lee, Howard's daughter, Anne, her husband, and their two children, Howard's close friend Charles and his wife, and six or seven friends of theirs she didn't know. Dena had never been to a funeral of any kind before and was frankly nervous about how to act or what was going to happen, but, Lee took over with her usual grace and made everyone feel comfortable. Anne had come up to her right away and said, "I'm so glad you could come and be with us. Dad thought the world of you."

They rode out and the water was calm and quiet except for the seagulls following the boat. When they dropped anchor, Lee served champagne. A little later, as the sun was beginning to set, Lee stood up. "As you all know, Howard loved this place from the day we came here thirty-seven years ago. He fell in love with the town and the people, and this boat was where he spent some of his happiest hours. When he was particularly troubled he would get in it and just ride around out here for hours. We never talked much about death but I somehow think this is where he would want to be buried. I asked him once why he never went out any further. And he said, 'Lee, I love to look for miles across the horizon and clear my head and think about what's beyond but I never want to lose sight of home.' And I think that's how he lived. With his eyes on the horizon but never losing sight of home."

One by one, those present said a few things about Howard. Dena was too moved to say anything. A friend, John, spoke last. "You know, I thought of hundreds of things I could say, things I'd like to say about Howard. About the kind of man he was, the kind of friend. But you know—even now I can hear that old bastard saying, Get on with it, John, we don't want any of your overblown sentimental schoolgirl prose. So I'll just say, Good-bye, and safe harbor, old friend."

The sun was beginning to fade as they watched the mild wind that had suddenly come up blow the ashes across the water and Lee played Howard's favorite record. For such a serious man, most people would not have guessed the Cole Porter tune was the one he loved to sing. As the last of the ashes disappeared, Fred Astaire sang:

> *You're the top . . . you're the coliseum*
> *You're the top . . . you're the Louvre museum*
> *You're a melody from a symphony by Strauss*
> *You're a Bendel bonnet, a Shakespeare sonnet*
> *You're Mickey Mouse.*

Everyone held up their glasses to toast Howard, except Dena, who totally and unexpectedly lost complete control. She burst into tears and began to sob. She tried to stop but she couldn't; watching those ashes disappear had triggered something inside her. It was so *final*.

If anyone was surprised by her sudden burst of emotion, they could not have been more surprised than Dena, who prided herself on control at all costs. She was a master at sidestepping feelings, batting them away, avoiding them. She was horrified. *What must they be thinking? I am the one person on this boat who knew him the least.* Several people came over to her and she kept saying, "I'm sorry, I don't know what's the matter with me." One man put his arm around her shoulder and held her up. She knew she was making a fool out of herself but she couldn't stop. Finally, Lee came over, sat her down, and tried to comfort her. But she was crying harder than she had ever cried in her life, trying not to make noise, trying to stop. Her nose was running and she didn't have any Kleenex. Oh, God, she wanted to die. They were all going to think she really had had an affair with him, the way she was carrying on.

As they turned and headed home, they saw that boats of many shapes and sizes had lined up behind them. The boats sat silently, motionless in the water, their owners flying their flags at half-mast as a tribute to their neighbor. The boats remained still until after the *Lee Anne* had passed, then they all rode out in single file and made a slow circle around the area where Howard's ashes had been scattered and headed back to harbor.

When Dena saw that, she sobbed even more. By the time they got to the house, Dena had to be put on a bed in a room off the living room. Lee brought her a cold, wet washcloth and put it across Dena's eyes, now red and swollen. "Sorry . . . I don't know what's the matter with me. I'm sorry, really."

"You just lie here and try and relax," Lee said. "I'll be back."

As Dena tried at last to calm down, she could hear them out in the living room, talking and even laughing, glasses clinking. It was so strange; everyone was working so hard to keep up a brave front, talking about everyday things, as if that would lessen the loss. Dena heard the children in the den throwing a ball to the dog, who was excited to have playmates. It all seemed so unreal. Howard was gone but life went on and all that was left was an empty chair. At that thought she started to cry again.

Lee came back in after a while, sat on the bed, and took her hand. "How are you doing?"

Dena shook her head. "I don't know . . . I'm sorry."

"It's perfectly OK, Dena, it happens. Something touches you and sets off old memories, some old loss. It's OK. You just take your time and come on out when you feel like it."

After Lee left, she tried to think. What in the world was she crying about, so deeply sad about? Could it all be Howard's dying? She had not cried when she heard the news. She had been upset, but she had not cried. She liked him, she respected him, she would miss him, but not enough to break down like this. Was it something about saying good-bye? Was it about her own father? She didn't think so; she had not even known him.

What was wrong? Maybe she was just weeping about living in a world without Howard.

Two Letters

New York City
1977

Dena arrived home from Howard Kingsley's memorial service at about twelve-thirty that night and the minute she came in the door she opened a bottle of vodka, put her nightgown on, and drank much of the bottle. At about 4 A.M., drunk as a loon, she got the idea that she would finally tell Ira Wallace what she thought of him. She went to her typewriter, sat down, and started typing.

Dear Scumbag,

How dare you even say all those terrible things about Howard Kingsley. You aren't fit to wipe his shoes, you scumbag. You think nice people are chumps. You laugh at anybody who has integrity ... you belittle everybody, strip everybody of any dignity. If anyone should get respect and be looked up to in this country, you have to throw dirt on them ... pull them down in the gutter with you. You don't care who you hurt. You are not loyal to anyone but yourself ... you worm ... people are going to learn to hate and suspect each other just like you do and when it's not safe to go out your front door, what do you care? Don't forget I know where your money is, you scumbag, *tax evader,* bald-headed scumbag and I don't think you are a good American either, you fat buttermilk-pancake-face scumbag. I quit. So long, good-bye, auf Wiedersehen ... and good riddance. I don't know why I ever liked you, you rude cigar-smoking little worm.

Sincerely,

Dena Nordstrom

P.S. Howard was the top.

You're the bottom!

Dena finished writing at about five-thirty in the morning and felt a great weight off her; she felt free, went to bed, and slept like a baby for the first time in weeks. At around one o'clock that afternoon she woke with a new hangover from hell and a terrible stomachache. She made herself coffee, had Maalox and three aspirins, and read the letter she had typed. What a pile of sanctimonious crap. Who was she to point the finger at anyone? Who did she think she was to imagine herself in the same category with Howard Kingsley? Such a bunch of holier-than-thou, self-righteous drunken babble ... Then a wave of panic hit her when she realized she might have gone out and put it in the mail chute. Thank God she hadn't mailed it. Last night she had been so sure she believed all this stuff, but today she realized all she was doing was spouting off some of Howard's thoughts. Last night the vodka convinced her that she really believed all she had written. Today she had no earthly idea of what she really thought or felt about anything anymore. Who in the hell was *she* to judge? Did she really care about anybody but herself? Ira Wallace at least loved his kids and that was more than she could say; at least he loved something. She ripped the letter to shreds and threw it in the wastebasket. A fresh sheet of paper was in the typewriter. She typed a few sentences before she went back to bed with a Valium.

> *To whom it may concern and to those who don't give a damn ... Who the hell am I? Help! Help! Help! Fireman save my child. Blab blab blab, who cares, who cares, who cares. Leave me alone!!!!!!!!!!!*

Across town Gerry O'Malley was leaning over the center-island counter in his kitchen, wearing his red baseball cap, scribbling out another one of the many letters he had started.

Dear Dena,

There are so many things I want to say to you, but mere words are not enough to convey to you what I feel in my heart. I am like a painter who visualizes a beautiful painting full of vivid colors but is only given sticks and mud to work with. I wonder how I can reach you. I don't want words that skim lightly over the top of what I feel for you. There are too many words that are spoken from the mind and like a roomful of firecrackers pop and are gone. I want words that will produce a long deep boom of explosion, that will jar you to your very bones and stay ringing in your ears forever. That's how I want to talk to you. I want you to hear me through your skin. I want you to drink my words in like rich red wine, to reach down in every part of you until there is not a place left untouched. I want to be in your bones, your muscles, all the way to the ends of your hair. I want you to know I love you in every cell of your brain, in every sleeping and waking thought. I want it to be in the air you breathe . . . so with every breath you will know there is someone on this earth that is yours, knows who you are, loves you forever and if there is anything after forever . . . even after that.

Gerry stopped writing and reread what he had just written and thought: That's the most sickening, most embarrassing pile of hooey I've ever read in my life. And wadded it up and threw it in the trash can along with the others and started a new one.

Dear Dena,

I know this might come as somewhat of a surprise to you but since the first day I saw you I still have not been able to get you out of my

He stopped, tore that up, and said out loud, "God, why don't you just call her, you idiot!" He went to the phone and dialed her number. But she had unplugged the phone.

True Love

One of the hundreds of things Dena did not know about Gerry O'Malley was that he believed in true love. His father and mother had been madly in love with each other so he knew that it did exist and what it looked like. His father had been in the military and had a big job at the Pentagon and his mother usually left their home in Middleburg, Virginia, to go to Washington to be with him during the week. They hated to be apart even for a few days. Gerry and his father adored her. She was so bubbly, so alive, so much fun to be around, until his sister was born, with cerebral palsy. After that their lives had changed. His sister needed constant care and his mother, who had been the toast of the Washington party circuit, almost never left the house anymore. Gerry was sent to military school at the age of twelve.

As she got older, his sister's condition grew worse, and as hard as his mother tried to take care of her, she could not. His sister finally had to be put in a special school in another state where she could receive twenty-four-hour medical care. It devastated his mother when she was forced to let her go. Each time he came home from school he noticed that his mother was drinking more and more, and his father would come downstairs to breakfast alone, saying his mother was sick that morning. He and his father had never discussed it then and so it was not talked about.

A year later, she never left her room.

The only time he had ever seen his father cry was one day after he and his father had been to visit her in the convalescent home. After they left, his father put his head on the steering wheel and sobbed. Gerry knew that he was crying over having to leave first his daughter and now his wife, who had slowly retreated into another world and had left him so alone.

His mother died of acute alcoholism the first year he was in college. His father had become so despondent from years of watching his wife slowly destroy herself and feeling helpless that he too withdrew from the world and left Gerry feeling helpless, not knowing what to do to reach him. The feeling of wanting to help but not knowing how or what to say was what caused him to change his major from music to psychology. Years later, his father remarried. It was nice. He had someone, but it wasn't love. He never got over his first wife. Gerry knew it took courage to love like that. He knew firsthand how painful and dangerous it could be, but as it turned out he didn't have a choice in the matter. Gerry recognized the woman he loved at once, remembered her as one remembers an old dream, and he was at once lost, at once found. His life was as changed as if he had gone to bed in one place and the next morning found himself clear across the world, a world vaguely familiar but new and full of wonder, as bright and fresh as the world had seemed as a child after a rain when the sun came out, a place of endless possibilities. He had all but forgotten that old dream of finding her. But dreams have a way of crashing through the darkest of places, the thickest of walls, and there it was, and her name was Dena.

From the moment she walked in his door that first day he had felt his former life, the one that had been so carefully planned, all behind him, barely remembered. He knew he would follow this woman wherever she wanted him to go. And there was something almost merciful about that moment; he didn't have to fight it, or struggle, or regret, because he was as sure of this as he had been of anything in his life. He knew that trying to stop it would have been as futile as trying to stop himself from sliding down a glass mountain. He felt himself falling but there was no fear, no terror, only the sweet, burning anticipation of landing beside her, in her arms.

On the other hand, the object of all this earth-shattering activity was unaware of it. Dena Nordstrom did not believe in love, true or not. It almost killed him when he read in the paper that Dena was now dating Julian Amsley, the president of her network. Every time he saw their picture together in the paper, which was often, it almost broke his heart. But there was nothing he could do.

What Are Friends For?

Atlanta, Georgia
1978

Six months after Howard's death, Dena spoke at the Mississippi College for Women, and Sookie had driven her back to Atlanta. They were driving around looking at houses, killing time before Dena had to get the plane back to New York.

"I wish I had paid more attention to current events when I was in school," Sookie said. "Then maybe I wouldn't be so surprised at what's happening now in the world. I was busy trying to be liked."

"You *were* liked."

"Yes, but I had to work at it. You didn't have to. People just liked you automatically, I don't know why, you didn't have to lift a finger. Not me. I had to run around like a chicken, smiling, joining this and joining that. I never got a good rest until after I was married."

"Sookie, you're still running around joining everything in sight."

"I am not! You'd be surprised, the things I haven't joined. And the things I do belong to I enjoy. Listen, don't forget, it's good for Earle's practice to have a wife out there in the community, doing things; besides, what else would I do, sit home and stare at the walls? Look at that house! Are those not the most gorgeous boxwoods you have ever seen?"

"What?"

"Oh, you missed it. My boxwoods are just puny this year."

Dena had no clue as to what she was talking about. "Sookie, have you ever spent any time alone? I mean really alone."

Sookie thought about it. "Why would I want to?"

"Don't people get on your nerves?"

"No."

"Ever?"

"No ... not really, except for Mother, of course." Sookie suddenly spotted something. "Look at that! Now, why would anyone paint their house that color, will you tell me?"

Dena looked at the lavender house with the dark purple shutters. "God only knows. But seriously, Sookie, I'm really interested in knowing why."

"Why? New money, honey. Atlanta's full of it. No taste, bless their hearts."

"No, I mean why do you like people?"

"What a silly thing to ask. Because, why shouldn't I like people? You're supposed to like other people; everybody likes other people, don't they?"

"I don't know if I do or not."

"Of course you do. You always liked people."

"I did?"

"Yes. Very much."

"Maybe I'm just tired of people now."

"Don't tell me you've gone Bohemian, like Margo?"

"Who?"

"Oh, I told you about Margo, that girl from Selma who went to school up north."

"I don't remember."

"Yes, you do. She came back home all warped and weird? She acted so bored with everybody, wore black all the time?"

"I can't ..."

"Well, anyway, she wouldn't join anything, not even Junior League. She just wanted to sit around and read or something. So finally, one day I went over there to see her and I said, 'Margo, what in the world is the matter with you? Have you just given up on humanity?' She closed her book and looked up at me and do you know what she said? She said, 'I haven't given up on humanity, it's man that I'm disappointed in!' And with that, honey, she just marched back in the house and left me standing there on the porch like a fool! And I guess by man, she must have meant woman too, because she never has gotten any nicer. She bought some little dinky house way out in the woods and raises those ugly little pug dogs. I hate to say it, but I think she's peculiar."

Dena smiled. "Well, then, I must be peculiar. I wouldn't mind living in a house in the woods, all alone."

"If you ask me, you are alone too much as it is. You need to have somebody to talk to, to share your innermost thoughts with."

"Don't worry. I have a psychiatrist I pay a lot of money to share my innermost thoughts."

Sookie, alarmed, almost ran the car off the road. "A psychiatrist? Don't tell me you're going to a—Oh, my God, see, I knew something was wrong."

"There is nothing wrong. A lot of people go to psychiatrists. And it's not really psychiatry, it's hypnotherapy."

"What?"

"Hypnotherapy. She hypnotizes me."

"Oh, my God, Dena! I hope you know what you are doing. Earle says most of those New York psychiatrists are card-carrying communists. You don't know what he may be telling you when you're hypnotized."

"She."

"Well, she, then. She may be turning you into a spy or something. You just better be careful, there are a lot of subversives everywhere now."

"Sookie, where do you come up with this stuff?"

"I read."

"Oh, Sookie."

"Well, they are trying to get rid of Christianity and once they do that, then you watch. Our taxes will go up and they'll take all our guns away and the next thing you know, a communist or a socialist will get in the White House and then it will be all over."

"Sookie, surely you don't believe that."

"Honey, they are trying to outlaw prayer in the schools, right now, as we speak."

"I think it has something to do with separation of church and state."

Sookie turned the corner. "Oh, listen, that's just some lame excuse they're using to try to turn us into a Godless nation and corrupt our children."

Dena was getting a headache. "Whatever, I don't care that much."

"You should care. It's your country, it's your children and my children we are talking about. Do you want them to come home from school someday and murder you in your bed?"

"I don't have children."

"Well, you'll want to get married someday and have children. You have to think about those things."

"I'm not getting married."

"Oh, sure. You say that now. But someday you'll meet someone and fall head over heels. And I better be your matron of honor or I'll never speak to you again. You're my big claim to fame, so don't you dare ask one of your movie star friends to show up and take my place."

"You don't have to worry because there isn't going to be a wedding."

"Don't you want children?"

"No, I really don't."

"Oh, I can't believe that. Every woman wants to get married and have children."

"You have them and I'll enjoy them, OK? I don't feel the need to procreate."

"Why not, for heaven's sake?"

"Because any idiot can get married and have children; that's no great accomplishment."

"Well, thanks a lot!"

"Oh, I'm not talking about you. You know what I mean."

Sookie's face was all amazement. "I can't believe you don't want to ever get married. I thought I knew you better than that."

"Believe it, we are just two different types of people. I keep telling you that—we always were."

"No, we weren't!"

"Yes, we were."

"How so?" asked Sookie.

"For one thing, you were always boy crazy."

"I was not!"

"Sookie, don't tell me that. You used to go to bed with a cold rag on your head if some stupid boy didn't call."

"I did not. Once, maybe. What does that have to do with you not wanting to get married?"

"Haven't you heard of women's liberation? Not everybody wants to get married."

"I know that but you don't want to be alone the rest of your life, do you? And wind up raising a bunch of ugly dogs somewhere in the woods. You don't need to go to some psychiatrist, Dena Nordstrom. I can tell you what's wrong with you absolutely free. You think you don't like people but you do; and you're just scared of them, so you stay alone."

Dena sighed. "Sookie, I have so many people around me all day, believe me, I am not alone."

"I mean when you go home at night. And on holidays, for instance. Who are you with on Christmas?"

"God, not this again. I don't need to have children just to have someone to spend Christmas with. There are plenty of places I can go."

"Ah, but you *don't* go and that's my point. You sure won't come to Selma to spend it with us. You know what I think? I think you sit up there in that apartment of yours all by yourself, that's what I think."

"Sookie, I'm not like you. I like to be alone. I really do. Anyhow, let's get off me. I am under enough pressure as it is without having to listen to your lamebrain, *Good Housekeeping* theories about how miserable and all alone in the world I am. Why can't we just have a nice visit without you constantly badgering me?"

Sookie kept driving. For a long time she did not answer. "Dena, I have something I have to tell you."

Dena could tell by her tone that it was going to be something she did not want to hear and moaned, "Oh, God, this isn't going to be about some new religious experience, is it?"

"No." Sookie looked worried and glanced into the rearview mirror, then pulled over to the curb and turned off the engine. She stared straight ahead, took a deep breath. Her eyes were closed. "Dena, I know about your mother."

Dena, startled, said, "What?"

"There, I've said it and I'm glad. I know I'm taking a chance of losing you as a friend, but before you get furious at me, I didn't mean to find out. It was an accident."

"What are talking about?"

"It was a stupid thing to do but . . . we . . . well, all the girls in the house used to think you had a secret boyfriend. And . . . they put me up to looking to see if you had any love letters stashed away . . . and I accidentally read the letter from your grandfather by mistake."

Dena felt her face getting hot and flushed and her heart was racing.

"I know I shouldn't have done it . . . and I'm sorry. . . ."

Dena did not say a word.

"Are you just ready to kill me?"

Before Dena could answer, a woman with short brown over-permed hair in a green cotton housedress came out of her house and looked at them with curiosity. Sookie smiled and waved at her. The woman smiled and waved back and headed down the stairs toward them. Sookie mumbled, "Oh, Lord," and rolled down her window.

The woman came over to the car and looked in at Sookie. "Are you here to give me an estimate?"

"No, ma'am, we're just sort of lost."

"Oh, I thought you might be looking for my house. I'm waiting on some people from Sears to come and give me an estimate on some indoor-outdoor carpet. But I guess you're not them, are you?"

Sookie said, "No, ma'am." The woman looked over at Dena. "No, ma'am. We just . . . stopped here for a minute. We're headed on now. But good luck with your carpet."

"Oh," she said. "Well . . . would you like to come in anyway? If you're lost you can use the phone, and I can show you the back room where I'm thinking about putting it. You can tell me what you think."

Sookie, realizing that they had to leave, reached to turn on the ignition. "Thank you but that's OK."

The woman said to Dena, "You look familiar to me . . . are you any kin to the Larkins?"

Sookie jumped in. "No, she's not from here, she's just passing through. On her way to a plane. She's a complete stranger."

The woman was mildly disappointed. "Oh." She stepped back from the car. "Well, let me get back on inside in case they are trying to call me. Nice talking to you."

"Nice talking to you too . . . good luck with your carpet."

"I just hope it's not an arm and a leg, that's all I hope. But I guess they'll tell me, won't they, if they ever show up."

Sookie pulled away and waved good-bye. They drove awhile and Dena lit a cigarette but was silent. Sookie was miserable. "Dena, if you don't say something I am going to have a heart attack. You're going to have to say something eventually. I don't know what gate your plane leaves from. . . . Look at me; I'm so nervous I'm breaking out in hives."

Dena spoke. "Who else did you tell?"

"Nobody!" Sookie was emphatic. "Do you think I would tell anybody else? I didn't even tell you until now! I wanted to but I was a coward. I wanted you to like me and you kept telling me you were spending all your holidays with your mother and what a wonderful time you had. I couldn't very well just come out and say I knew you were lying, could I? I kept inviting you to come home with me but you never would come. I didn't know what to do. You know I was addle-brained back then; I could barely figure out what to major in, much less something like that. I didn't know what the right thing to do was so I didn't say anything."

Dena took another drag of her cigarette. "Have you told Earle?"

Sookie reacted in horror. "Earle! Why in the world would I tell Earle? *No,* I haven't told anybody. Do you actually think I would betray a friend? I am a good friend, Dena, you know that. And if you don't know that by now, then you must not trust anybody. Didn't all the Kappas come to me and tell me everything? And the Pi Phis too? And did I ever repeat one word, even when I was dying to? No, I would never betray any of my sisters, and believe me, I know plenty. I'd rather have my tongue ripped out. You say I don't know you, the truth is you don't know me. I am your friend whether you like it or not."

Sookie's chin began to quiver and she was on the verge of tears. "I'm sorry I read that letter . . . but I would never betray you and it hurts my feelings that you think I would."

Dena put her cigarette out in the ashtray. "You were spying on me. What do you call that?"

"That wasn't spying. I thought it was just boyfriend stuff. That does not count for serious spying . . . and you know it."

"What if I had been going with some married man?"

"Oh, don't be silly. I knew you weren't going with some married man, for Lord's sake."

"How do you know that?"

"I know."

"How?"

"You're not that kind of girl."

"How do you know?"

She looked at Dena as if she had suddenly lost her mind. "How do I know? Because you're a Kappa, that's why!"

Sookie looked up and saw the Varsity Drive-In sign. "Can we pull in here a minute? I'm a nervous wreck."

"All right."

Sookie parked and turned her engine off. A girl came up and Sookie ordered a large Coke. Dena ordered nothing. Sookie said, "Listen, Dena, I know you're mad at me but you want to know why I worry about you and badger you. That's why. I think you still lie to me about where you go and what you do on holidays. You spend too much time alone and that's not good for a person. I don't care what you say. And I didn't get that out of *Good Housekeeping,* either."

"Sookie, you knew about my mother; then why do you insist on babbling on and on about how happy and how great everything was back then when you knew better?"

Sookie threw her hands up in the air. "Oh, I know, I know . . . don't ask me why. I always felt so guilty about it. I guess I couldn't face the fact that I knew, that I let you down, because I couldn't deal with it myself. Or maybe I could have helped you or something. I don't *know* the reason; you're the one seeing the psychiatrist! Ask him. I'd like to know myself. But don't give him my real name."

"Her."

"Well, her, then, or just kill me. I'm flawed, what else can I say? I am just a weak, flawed person like Mother says. All I know is that I did the best I could . . . even though it wasn't much. But, Dena, you really don't know how badly I've felt all these years, and if you never speak to me again as long as I live, I'll understand. I'll kill myself and my children will be orphans, but I'll understand. Give me a cigarette."

"You don't smoke."

"Well, I'm going to start. I might as well, I've just lost my best friend."

"Oh, Sookie, you haven't lost your best friend."

"I haven't?"

"Of course not."

"Thank heavens . . ."

"After all, I was lying to you, too."

"That's right!" Sookie turned to Dena. "Why did you lie to me? I was your best friend."

Dena reached for Sookie's glass. "Give me a sip of that."

After she drank, she said, "Because I was embarrassed."

"Embarrassed? But why? It wasn't your fault. Besides, Dena, it's nothing to be ashamed of."

"I'm not ashamed."

Sookie took her hand. "Don't you think we should talk about it? It must have been terrible for you."

"There's nothing to talk about. I don't even think about it anymore. That was a long time ago."

"Did you ever find out what happened?"

"No."

"Listen, Sookie—there are only a few people who know anything about it. And I'd like to keep it that way. It's not something I want out in public. It's not that I'm still upset over it or anything, it's just something I don't want to talk about with strangers, you know? Can you understand?"

"Of course," Sookie said. "First of all, it's nobody's business. Second of all, you don't want people to feel sorry for you or pity you. I understand perfectly, and as far as I'm concerned it's forgotten. And you know you can trust me with your life."

An hour later, when they arrived at the airport, Sookie hugged her good-bye. Dena paused a moment before she left, and even though it was hard for her to express her feelings she said, "Sookie, you really are a good friend."

"That's what I've been telling you for years, goofy!"

A Greek Bearing Gifts

New York City
1978

Julian Amsley, the president of Dena's network, like Ira Wallace, was born on the lower east side of Manhattan and had grown up as the poor son of first-generation immigrants. Both men had been ambitious and driven, determined to claw their way out of the dirty streets one way or the other. Only their methods had been different. Wallace wanted money and power for money and power's sake and did not care what people thought of him. Amsley wanted money and power to acquire the things he wanted most, to be accepted into society, to get as far away as he could from the seedy Greek coffee shops where his father had been a dishwasher. By the time he was eighteen, he had changed his name from Julio Andropulous to Julian Amsley, worked, and saved enough money to take speech lessons. He married the daughter of a network vice president, took a job at the network, and using his father-in-law's contacts and name, moved up the ladder fast until he eventually got the old man's job.

At night he studied the so-called society people as if they were a college course. He learned how they dressed, where they bought their clothes, how they named their children, where they went to school. He found out where they lived, how they lived, and what they liked. He learned French, studied art, music, drama. Amsley hired the darling of the right set, Sister Parish, to decorate his apartment and his "cottage" in the Hamptons, hired experts to buy a collection of art. He paid a down-and-out, drunken son of one of the best families to make sure he was invited to the right parties. He needed the right address and the right wife. He divorced the first wife, married another, and mysteriously managed to get an apartment in a building that would have never allowed anyone to move in who was not approved of by the board, and certainly not a person in the entertainment business. He had to buy the building but it was worth it. It had taken him decades to do it, but eventually he was rich enough and smooth enough to marry beautiful and elegant women, thinking that somehow what they had would rub off on him, change him, magically make him one of them. But self-hatred had a way of ruining the world for you. After he pursued and married the first two women from the "best families," he had nothing but contempt for them. And eventually they left him. He had all the trappings—the money, the company of attractive women, the parties—but still that thing he wanted, class, had always eluded him, stayed just beyond his reach. He had tried to buy it, to marry it, to imitate it but nothing he did worked. It was like trying to grab smoke.

Still, his black valet had more true class in his little finger than Amsley had in his whole body and he knew it, and was baffled by it. Julian sat one night at a small white table in the middle of his huge, cold kitchen surrounded by the best stainless steel appliances that money could buy. He sat alone at 3:00 A.M., drinking a glass of milk, staring at the wall, wondering what to pursue next to try and fill that black, empty hole in his gut. He was dressed in eight-hundred-dollar black silk pajamas, a fifteen-hundred-dollar cashmere robe, soft leather slippers, and his two-hundred-dollar haircut, but underneath, he still felt like that hungry little boy from Third Avenue, still running, still desperately trying to grab an apple off the cart as it passed by. And lately Dena Nordstrom was the shining apple he was trying to grab.

The game show hostess he had been going with for two years had struck him in the head with a huge onyx ashtray while he was asleep because he wouldn't marry her. That week she had gone back to Texas and married the man who had the second largest Cadillac dealership in the Dallas/Fort Worth area and who had always hoped she would. Amsley was looking for another beauty to take her place, and who better than Dena Nordstrom? She was just what he liked. She had class and she was hard to get.

The next day Dena received what he always sent and what had always worked before, diamonds, and she sent them right back. She turned his invitations down, week after week, but finally he said something that changed her mind. "Going out with me will give you more stature, more clout. I can introduce you to everybody who is somebody. Think of it as business, if nothing else."

That appealed to Dena. It wasn't love. But it wasn't easy; Amsley was an older man but he was not harmless. He was trying to prove that he was still a virile Greek man and it came to be exhausting having to fight him off.

But by dating him, and moving in his circles, there was a feeling in the air that she was moving up. The pressures mounted. His friends had the mistaken idea that because she was at their parties she was one of their crowd. She wasn't. She was a working girl. Her social life was work to her. When the wealthy wives were busy the mornings after, shopping, getting their faces lifted, sleeping late, Dena was at the studio—and she was getting worn out. Again.

At first she had been impressed with all the so-called beautiful people with whom Julian Amsley brought her in contact. They were for the most part active people, restless, always on the move, seeking pleasure, seeking possessions and publicity ... always running in packs from place to place, from Palm Beach to Paris to Monaco or Morocco, anyplace that was the next, new In place. But after a while she found out that most of the so-called jet-setters were as boring as they were bored—and as cynical as she felt herself becoming.

The truth was that ever since Howard had died it seemed like a light had gone out inside her, and she felt more lost and lonely in the world than ever. She needed someone to inspire her. Someone who could excite her. But who?

There was one person in the world whom she had not met whom she really would like to know. She had never had the nerve. One particularly gloomy Monday morning she felt at the end of her rope and picked up the phone and called his agent. Her reply astounded Dena. "Miss Nordstrom, he usually will not meet with people, or give interviews, but our mutual friend Howard Kingsley thought so highly of you, I will do the best I can."

Dena put the phone down. It was like a gift from heaven, if she had believed in heaven.

The Court of Two Sisters

New Orleans, Louisiana
1978

Dena flew into New Orleans in the late evening and checked into the Bourbon Orleans Hotel but she did not sleep. The next morning the phone in her room rang. A high, thin voice said, "Miss Nordstrom, I understand you have traveled to the Crescent City for the sole purpose of engaging in a scintillating conversation with me, is that correct?"

"Yes, Mr. Williams, I have."

"Well, I cannot guarantee you how scintillating it will be. All I can do is to assure you that as of this morning I still have a heartbeat, so I will call for you at around eleven-thirty. Will that be convenient?"

"Yes, sir, I'll be downstairs."

She hung up. If someone had told her that one day she would be getting ready to meet Tennessee Williams she would not have believed them. At eleven, she was downstairs, sitting in the lobby under a palm tree, looking out on Orleans Street, hoping to see him first. She wore a thin white silk dress and was starting to freeze in the air-conditioning when a voice startled her. "Miss Nordstrom, I'm Robert, and Mr. Williams and I are here to take you to lunch."

Tennessee Williams was standing by the front desk. He looked like a smaller version of the Count of Monte Cristo, as if he had wandered in from another century. Even his manner seemed to be that of another time. But when he spoke he was very much in the present.

"Miss Nordstrom, welcome to New Orleans. You've met Robert, who will accompany us through the streets, just in case I have a spell. I hope you don't mind?"

"Oh, no, not at all."

"I though we would take a little walk and then have a bite to eat, if that's agreeable."

"I would love to. This is my first trip to New Orleans." They walked out into the brilliant sun, and the day was as humid as it was overlit.

While they walked he explained Robert's presence.

"Robert is my clean-up man."

Dena appeared to be puzzled and he laughed.

"After Mardi Gras they have clean-up men to pick up all the debris off the streets left over from the parade. That's what I am, just debris left over from some past parade, and if I fall in the streets, Robert picks me up." He cackled at his own joke.

Dena could tell he was shy with her so she tried to keep it light. "Do you tend to fall down a lot?"

His eyes twinkled. "Miss Nordstrom, I'm down now, but not out. Not quite, not yet this morning, at least. But I cannot vouch for this afternoon."

The three of them walked down the street, one tall, cool blonde; one short man in a straw Panama hat and sunglasses; and Robert, a medium-sized young man in gray slacks and a maroon jacket. Everyone they passed recognized Williams. They walked over to St. Louis Cathedral and Bienville Square as he provided her with a short history of New Orleans. But Dena was more anxious to talk about him.

"Mr. Williams, I know this is a stupid question, but you are clearly the most famous living playwright in America. How does it feel to be so famous?"

He pointed to St. Peter's Street, and an upstairs veranda. "That's where I live. I have just a small place." He walked her past the old Cornstalk Inn Hotel and showed her the wrought-iron fence that surrounded it. She realized that he might not want to answer her idiotic question.

He pushed his glasses up on his nose and gestured to a restaurant down the street. "Let's go in the Court of Two Sisters; don't you love that name?" They walked into a long, dark room leading to the restaurant and the maître d' was pleased to see him. When they were escorted to a lovely outside courtyard, three waiters came over immediately. He knew them all. Williams and Dena ordered screwdrivers and Robert ordered iced tea. Williams explained to the waiter, "He's driving," and giggled. After his drink came he seemed to relax.

"Mr. Williams, getting back to ... what we were talking about . . ." She took out her notebook.

He looked amused. "Oh, yes. You wanted to know about that mean old whore, fame." He lifted his glass and stared at it.

"Yes."

"Fame is like a shark with a thousand eyes, waiting to eat you, gobble you up. Eat and swim, eat and swim. Fame kills, baby. Fame is an uneasy place; people are either running toward it or running away from it but it's not a place where anyone can live comfortably. No one enjoys it."

"Don't you think there are some people who like being famous?"

He took a sip of his drink. "I suppose there are some insensitive people out there who don't mind living their lives out in full public view. But I don't know of a true artist who can survive or create without some privacy. One must be allowed to break away from the herd and form different ideas. Don't you agree?"

"Oh, yes," Dena said, "completely."

"But there are those determined to destroy privacy, to kill individual thought. Robert thinks I overstate my case but it's a case that needs to be overstated. There must be privacy, even among the well known."

"What did you expect being famous would be like, Mr. Williams?"

"I didn't expect anything. I just wanted to write plays. I was not prepared for fame; nothing prepares you for that, baby. You struggle along for years, unnoticed, then you wake up one day and suddenly everybody in the world wants to meet you. But you soon find out they don't want to meet you, they want you to meet them. All these pretty boys." He nodded slightly toward a table full of unusually graceful young men over in the corner, who had been staring at him and whispering. "They don't want me. It's a piece of that hot fame they want. It's shocking, the number of young men who try everything to catch my attention, like male birds strutting around the female, flashing their plumage." He laughed. "And I do mean flashing. All thinking, mistakenly, of course, if I were to fancy them, *they* would become stars overnight. They have long ceased to consider that one ingredient called talent. And who can blame them? Look around. It's the untalented hiring the untalented, all desperate for fame at any cost. But at any cost, the price of fame is too high, baby, way too high." He raised his hand and a waiter was there. "Two more screwdrivers, please, and bring mine without the orange juice. I wish to donate my orange to some person in need."

"Mr. Williams, I appreciate your seeing me for this interview."

He smiled. "I've been assured that you were not out to do me harm. I rarely give interviews anymore. Of course, now it really doesn't matter; they write them anyway." Their drinks arrived. "I call them the Masturbation Pieces. They do it without me."

His eyes changed as he began to stare across the courtyard at a brick wall.

"One such interview was particularly disturbing. This person wrote the most atrocious lies about me and some sailor! Afterwards I had young toughs riding by my home in Key West, throwing rocks and calling out the most ... well, let's just say it was a most hurtful and unpleasant experience to be stoned for something out of another's warped imagination. But what can you do?"

He shuddered. "Today, public life is as unforgiving as heart surgery; one slip, one mistake and you're dead. Fame for the strong and the invulnerable can be hard, but when one has a secret or a perceived weakness, living in constant fear of public exposure can be devastating; it can kill you, baby. I know, I was literally sick with fear at what certain printed information would do to my family, my mother, my sister, and my worst fears came to pass, of course. But no one is safe now. There are numerous unscrupulous people offering to pay for private information on anyone well known. Every person you have ever come in contact with is a time bomb waiting to explode and do you harm, even strangers who don't know you." The waiter replaced his drink. "There's nothing one can do. People claim to have met me, or slept with me, claim to have been in my home . . . and that's while I'm alive, baby. Imagine what will be written after I'm gone."

Suddenly he seemed sad and put his drink down. "I don't even *know* half the people who write those books. But when friends start trafficking in your life for money, it is a wound that will not heal. I am like a dog that has been hit too hard, too often. I don't trust anything human anymore. I am completely baffled." He looked at her. "What would cause someone to betray another and speak publicly of private and deeply personal matters? It is the ultimate betrayal, don't you think?" He looked away. "It sickens me. But it happens every day now. Lovers betray lovers, children betray parents. I once said nothing human disgusts me but I was wrong. This disgusts me—and I am equally disgusted with the writer, the publisher, the so-called journalist, and the public who ultimately buys. No wonder the celebrity becomes deranged and confused. They see on one hand a large group of worshipers, and on the other a large group of people who have nothing but jealousy and contempt for no reason except that you are recognized and they are not. It wasn't beauty that killed the beast, baby, it was fame."

"What about your real fans, the genuine admirers of your work?"

"I suppose there are some, of course, but I rarely see them. They are not the kind to push themselves in front of anybody to get to you. I might be in a restaurant and such a person could be at the next table but they are not going to invade my privacy. The kind of people I would like to meet, I don't, while the others push in front of them, shielding me from the gentle and shy people I would want to speak with."

Dena felt uneasy. "Mr. Williams, did you ever have an idol?"

"Oh, yes, many, but it would never occur to me to run up and ask for an autograph. It never occurred to me to do anything but appreciate and enjoy their work. Work, baby—that's what is offered, not his life. Two different things. Now the recognizable are being shot at, sued, or built up by public relations factories to some fevered, frenzied pitch, and when their time is up they are pulled down off their pedestals and eaten alive by interviewers asking rude questions. Oh, it's worse than feeding Christians to the lions. . . . Mercy, I need a little more fortification for this conversation." He raised his hand and immediately another drink was in it.

Now he seemed cheered. "You know, the Indians wouldn't let you take their pictures. They thought people were trying to steal their souls. And they were right!" He repeated in a loud voice that could be heard across the room. "The Indians were right!"

"I think we should order some food," Robert said, and waved at a waiter.

Williams squinted at him, then back at Dena. "Robert is concerned about my health. Or else he is trying to fatten me up for the kill."

A waiter announced, "Mr. Williams, we have some awfully pretty oysters today."

Williams's eyes lit up. "Pretty? Well, this is a phenomenon. I have never seen a pretty oyster in my life. You see, Robert, beauty is in the eye of the beholder." He turned back to the waiter. "Bring me eleven pretty oysters and one old ugly one!" He screamed with laughter and they all ordered oysters Rockefeller. Dena thought he might be drunk, but he picked up the conversation precisely where they had left off.

"The line between the public life and the private life has been erased, due to the rapid decline of manners and courtesy. There is a certain crudeness and crassness that has suddenly become accepted behavior, even desirable. But you are talking to a relic left over from the war before the cannibals took over. I'm just an old barnacle still clinging to that shaky, rotten pier of civility."

The waiter brought their lunch, and when he put the plate down, Williams said, "Point out the ugly one, Louis." Louis pointed and said, "There it is, Mr. Williams."

"Fine. I'll save it for last."

After he left, Williams said, "Louis has soul. Any man who can perceive beauty in an oyster is a poet. Leave him a large tip, Robert; he must be rewarded."

After he had eaten, he said, "Ahh, just like in life. Sometimes the ugly ones are the most delicious." He sat back.

"Mr. Williams, do you believe in God?" The question surprised her and after she asked, she wondered why she had.

He seemed amused. "God? Well, he's either the meanest bastard that ever lived or the most careless. He certainly has an uncanny talent for looking the other way, turning a deaf ear. But I'm still trying to hold on to a thread. Trying not to get mean and bitter, like little Truman. I wouldn't be surprised if Capote doesn't start biting people any day now." He laughed. "And that would be a poisonous bite, baby! All I know is that our civilization is a result of struggling and defining the ultimate truth."

"What is that?"

"We must be kind and forgive one another or we won't survive. But even among the most religious there seems to be a great blind spot covering the world, an inability to learn from past experience. Civilization is as precarious as a sand castle. All the care and effort it took to create it can be knocked down in a second by some bully or another. And the world is full of bullies. But I suppose we have got to keep trying. Who knows, maybe one day . . . but don't look to me for answers, baby. I'm looking myself, in every nook and cranny. People come here year after year looking for answers, but I have none. The body and soul have already been stripped. Nothing left but a few old bones for you to rummage around in. You got here too late."

Dena slowly closed her notebook. "Mr. Williams, I lied to you. I really didn't come here to interview you. I don't know why I came here . . . except that I love your plays. I guess I wanted to ask you how to survive. How have you survived?"

"How?" He sat silent for a long moment. "By a concerted effort on my part to develop some small milieu of insensitivity. And then there's sex, and booze, drugs, anything to soften the blow, to dim the glare and muffle the noise—anything to keep the world at bay. I've even resorted to insanity, of course; in or out of the loony bin, we are all insane. But at least the ones in the bin are being watched. That's something. It's the ones who are loose that you have to worry about, the ones making the bombs to blow the world up eight times over. Now, if that isn't a valid enough reason for confinement to a mental institution, I don't know what is."

His voice began to drift off. "The earth, baby ... sometimes I think it's just a holding pen for crackpots. Who knows what planets have discarded us as factory rejects, unfit to live among more civilized planetary societies. We may be living on the dark side of the moon and don't know it."

He seemed a million miles away and Dena realized he was tired. She did not want to overstay her welcome. She reached for her purse. "Mr. Williams, I can't thank you enough for your time. I really appreciate your seeing me, I really do."

When she stood up Williams tried to stand, but he was unsteady and Robert had to help him to sit again.

He looked up at her. "Miss Nordstrom, I find myself in the embarrassing position of not being able to accompany you back to your hotel, but Robert will be your gentleman escort. Do you mind?"

"Oh, no, that's all right, I can find my way."

"I wouldn't hear of it. Robert can pick me up on his return. I have enjoyed our luncheon. I'm afraid I don't look at television, but I'm told that you are headed in the direction of fame and success, so I suppose our meeting has been like two strangers passing one another on a narrow road, one coming from the front lines, the other walking toward it."

He started to say something more, then hesitated. "But you probably don't want to listen to the drunken babbling of a failed playwright."

"Mr. Williams," Dena said, "first of all, you are not a failed anything. And I would listen to anything you said."

His eyes suddenly became watery and he looked away. "Then I would warn you, I would say, run, baby—turn around and run for your life before it's too late."

As she and Robert left the restaurant, Dena could see Williams's reflection in the mirror in the hall, a small man, alone, with his hand raised to order another drink. It broke her heart because she could see that his heart had been broken.

That night she had the same dream again about trying to find her mother.

The next morning she sat up in bed in the hotel room in a cold sweat remembering what Tennessee Williams had said. When one has a secret, fear of public exposure can be devastating.

BOOK THREE

* * *

Sookie's Secret

Dallas, Texas
1963

After Dena's photograph had appeared on the cover of *Seventeen* she had been offered drama and speech scholarships to colleges all over the country, but her favorite teacher had advised her to accept the one from Southern Methodist University in Dallas. And from the moment Dena had walked on campus, she was a star. Everywhere she went, people would stare and all the sororities fought to get her. But Dena herself did not seem to notice or be fully aware of her impact on others. The boys and the male teachers tripped all over themselves when she passed by, and the girls secretly longed for what they mistakenly thought to be her sophistication and maturity. In truth, Dena was shy and uncomfortable with people her own age. She was always friendly and pleasant but not someone who was easy to get to know. A part of her always seemed distant and removed. She had only one really close friend, her roommate, Sarah Jane Krackenberry, but even with Sookie, Dena did not talk about herself. All Sookie had ever been able to find out was that Dena had attended several different schools and her mother was a career woman who worked as a buyer for a big department store in Chicago and traveled a lot. She had mentioned a few relatives in Missouri but Sookie never met them.

Dena could be fun at parties but as a rule, she lived in her own little dream world and walked around unconscious of the fact that she was viewed by most as some sort of enigma, some sort of mystery to be solved. She took little interest in boys and spent most of her free time alone, at movies or working over at the college theater. Her date-crazed sorority sisters were baffled as to why she would turn down the best-looking boys on campus to work on sets or watch a rehearsal of some stupid play. Pretty soon everyone came to the same conclusion: she must have some incredibly handsome, secret boyfriend. Sookie and Margaret McGruder had even followed Dena over to the theater late one night, but Dena was alone on stage, apparently rehearsing. This secret-boyfriend speculation went around like wildfire and curiosity peaked to the breaking point, especially with Margaret McGruder and Sally Ann Sockwell, who were now so wild to know who he was and what he looked like that they could no longer contain themselves. One Saturday afternoon, when they were sure Dena was at a rehearsal, they sneaked down the hall at the Kappa house in sunglasses and raincoats and knocked on Sookie's and Dena's door.

Sookie appeared in a green chenille robe, her red hair rolled up in bubble-gum-pink sponge rollers. She was in the middle of giving herself a facial and looked like she had just dipped her face in a pan of cement, but the girls were used to such sights. Sookie tried to speak without disturbing her mud pack. "What is it?"

"Sookie," Margaret said, "come on, we just know Dena must have some love letters or some clues or a picture of him in there. We want to see if we can find any."

Sally Ann, who was dating Sookie's brother, Buck, said, "Please . . . we are just dying to know who it is and what he looks like. I'll bet he's a Greek god!"

"She won't know, I promise," said Margaret McGruder, "we'll never tell a soul."

"Nooo! I'm not going to let you come in here and spy on my roommate."

"Please. We'd do the same for you. Please, we won't mess up anything; she won't even know we were here."

"No, I can't. She'd kill me if she ever found out."

Margaret stuck her foot in the door before Sookie could close it.

"We are not going away until you let us in. You know you are just dying to know who it is, too. Come on, Sook, we won't be but a minute."

Sookie, usually easily manipulated, stood her ground. "No. If anybody is going to spy on her, it will be me, not you. I'm her roommate."

"All right," Sally Ann said, "we'll wait right here. We'll be your lookout. And we won't tell anyone. It will just be between us."

"Promise?"

"Of course, on our Kappa honor. Do you think we would betray a sister?"

Sookie looked up and down the hall. "Oh, all right. But you stand right there and knock if you see someone coming. If I get caught I'm going to kill you."

Sookie hated spying but she was dying to find out herself. Now at least she had two accomplices. She went over and quietly opened Dena's top drawer. She felt around for paper. Nothing. She went through all five drawers and came up empty-handed. She looked under the bed, under the pillows; nothing.

Then she remembered: Dena kept some papers in a box on the top shelf of her closet. She pulled a desk chair over, got the box down, and started shuffling through the papers. No letters, just grade transcripts, a couple of Playbills, classroom notes, a newspaper article on Tennessee Williams, a typed letter from the scholarship board. Then, down at the bottom, she found a personal letter and her heart started to pound. It was postmarked just last week; it looked like a man's handwriting. She opened it carefully, excited and full of guilt.

And was riveted by what she read.

1420 Pine Street
Kansas City, Mo.
Sept. 21, 1963

Dear Dena,

I hope this letter finds you well. They have got me here at the VA Hospital for some therapy. I am staying in an outpatient home run by the VA. I know this has been a bad year for both of us. Baby Girl, I wrote to tell you I do not have good news about your mother, but it is not terrible news either. I have just received the final report from the Pinkerton fellow and he informs me that after two years he can go no further in his investigation but can say with some certainty your mother is alive and still in this country. As long as she remains listed with the Bureau of Missing Persons there is always a chance she will be found.

Don't ever let yourself get old. Mrs. Watson is a good nurse and puts me on a leash and walks me, so it's me and all the other old dogs that go round and round the block every afternoon. I miss home, but Aunt Elner keeps me well supplied with news and fig preserves. Do well in your studies. Keep your powder dry. I have enclosed a check for a little dough I have managed to squirrel away.

I remain your loving grandpa,
Lodor Nordstrom, Sr.

Sookie carefully folded it and put it in the box and back up on the top shelf. Sookie was not the brightest of girls, but she knew it was something she should never have seen. She felt like a traitor for having read it. She waited a moment, then went to the door to the waiting girls and reported that she could not find a thing. Sally Ann and Margaret were extremely disappointed and went down the hall. After Christmas, when Dena came back from the holiday break and told her all about the wonderful time she had spent with her mother, Sookie said nothing.

Letter in a Tin Box

Elmwood Springs, Missouri
1963

After Dena's grandfather died, Macky went through his papers, looking for a burial policy and anything else as executor he needed to know about. He had to pry open a tin box.

Dunbar & Straton
Resource Tracing Inc.
Chicago, Illinois

Re: Marion Chapman
White, female
Born: Dec. 1920
Washington, D.C.
#8674

Dear Mr. Nordstrom,

Using all the information at hand from your daughter-in-law's marriage certificate, her social security number, and the birth date and place given, we have not found a Marion Chapman born on that date in Washington, D.C., listed in any official records. We have repeatedly checked and rechecked all

our national research sources and have found only eleven
Marion Chapmans born on or around that date, all of whom
have been located and accounted for. According to our files
and the census taken, no such person exists. If you have any
further information, we will be happy to assist you in the
future.

Yours truly,
A. A. Dunbar

Macky talked it over with Norma and they both decided not to tell
Dena. As Norma said, "What good would it do for her to know the
person she thought was her mother didn't exist?"

A Dish Best Served Cold

New York City
1978

Dena Nordstrom had ruined Sidney Capello's one chance to be big in network television, but like a rat in a maze he had quickly scurried in another direction. In the tabloid business, where speed does count, Capello had shot to the top like a silver bullet. He had tired of being a freelance. It was too much of a hassle dealing with editors for a good price, so he cut out the middle man and started his own paper. Stripped of the dead weight of ethics, a conscience, or fear of the law, combined with his willingness to do anything to get a story, Capello and his paper were soon way ahead of the pack. Not fussing over facts was an economy. In less than a year his cheaply produced paper outsold everything on the supermarket rack and his readership was growing stronger every day. And he intended to keep it number one despite growing competition.

He had no qualms about stealing mail, tapping phones, and bribing or even placing maids, gardeners, or chauffeurs in the homes of the well known. His appetite for access to private information was boundless, and FBI files read like first-grade primers compared to his. He knew who was sleeping with whom, when, where, and how they did it, and could come up with one or two "witnesses" and, if necessary and for enough money, he could provide the "other person" involved, whether that person had been there or not. He had access to medical records, bank statements, private phone conversations. He knew how almost any half-fact could be blown up into a scandal at a moment's notice. But the main reason for Sidney's success was his ability to look to the future, to put away something for a rainy day. He had his "insurance" file chock-full of tidbits, photos, documents he could use when that rainy day came. If it had been a slow news week, he simply pulled something out that had been on hold, added a few factoids, and ran it. One aging movie star lost a lead in a movie when her before-and-after plastic surgery photos showed up in color on the cover of Capello's sheet, for no reason other than it had been a slow week. He liked being on top and he also had what he called a Hot File, ready to go, his get-them-before-they're-famous time bombs. He sent his staff out gathering information on anybody he even *suspected* might become newsworthy one day—kid actors, musicians, public servants, do-gooders. It was expensive, but what was thirty or forty thousand dollars when one story might sell millions of papers? He wanted to have a head start program of his own: as soon as someone hit it big he wanted to be ready. This is how the Dena Nordstrom file had come into being and now sat, ticking away, waiting for the right moment. Capello was usually strictly business, but he took a personal interest in her story. If it had not been for Nordstrom he might be producing television today. He had put his most expensive, tough-digging researcher, Barbara Zofko, to work on this one. It had been worth it. What she had dug up exceeded even his wildest dreams. Now all he had to do was sit back and wait for the right moment, and he was a patient man. It was a dirty business. But it wasn't blackmail. Ask him and he would tell you it was simply entertainment news, and news as entertainment, and there was much more money in the tabloid business than there ever had been in blackmail. And it was legal. It sort of made you proud to be an American.

❖   ❖   ❖

If Sidney Capello was the queen bee, Barbara Zofko was the perfect drone. She served him well. A lumpy, misshapen sort of woman with thick, slightly pockmarked, shiny white skin, not ugly, not pretty, she had the kind of face that could walk past a thousand people a day and not one would remember her. This characteristic worked in her favor. In fact, she was perfect for her job: she had no human relations to interfere with her work.

Barbara Zofko did not mind eating alone. She preferred it. She was totally focused on her work and the next meal. Her appetite was insatiable and she could eat a bag of cookies, an entire cake, and a dozen doughnuts at one sitting. And, if there was one characteristic that had made her what she had become, it was that hunger. Zofko had come from a small coal-mining town outside of Pittsburgh, one of seven children. The daughter of a taciturn miner and a mother who had been old at thirty, Barbara had never had enough of anything, love, money, or food, and now, no matter how much she ate, she never felt quite full. She was always left feeling just a little bit hungry and that's why she was Capello's top bird dog. She had been on this case for several weeks now and so far all she had been able to turn up on Dena Nordstrom was that she had attended schools all over the country and everyone remembered her but few people remembered much about her. It was turning out to be difficult. The hardest target to hit is a moving target and from the age of four, this TV woman had done nothing but move from one place to another. She had not stayed in college long enough to graduate, and when Barbara had gotten a list of the names of her sorority sisters and tracked them down all over the country, it had been a waste. Not one would say anything bad about her and a few said how wonderful she had been. Not only that, the woman in Alabama who had been her roommate in college had almost talked her ear off. She had gone on and on for hours with glowing accounts of what a fabulous girl Dena was. She had a hard time getting the woman off the phone. Zofko figured there must be some kind of conspiracy. She had tracked Dena's career from one local television station to another and nothing. They all said the same thing. Nice girl. We knew she would do well. Another blind alley.

Time to start on the immediate family. When Barbara made her reservations at the only place in Elmwood Springs to stay, her first thought was "fried clams." She always liked the little fried clams at Howard Johnson's, so she was not terribly upset at having to spend some time there. When she checked in that first day, she was disappointed that they did not have room service, but her spirits lifted when she saw the brochure for the International House of Pancakes and learned it was not too far off. She dumped her bags and did what she always did in a strange town. She drove to the nearest supermarket, got a basket and circled the bread and pastry section like a great white shark, and snatched a variety of sweet supplies to get her through the night. The next morning she knocked on Norma Warren's front door.

"Mrs. Warren?"

"Yes?"

"You don't know me but I'm here from the governor's office in Jefferson City and I wondered if I might talk to you about something concerning your cousin . . . Dena Nordstrom?"

Norma was surprised and caught off guard as Zofko knew she would be. "It's a confidential matter."

"Oh . . . well, of course. Come in."

They went into the living room.

"Mrs. Warren, this year the state of Missouri is setting up a Missouri Hall of Fame and your cousin has been picked to receive the first Missouri Woman of the Year award."

Norma drew in her breath. "Ohhh really? You don't mean it!"

"Yes. But we aren't announcing it to the press until next month so I have to ask you to keep it under your hat."

"Yes, of course. I understand. What an honor."

"We want it to be a surprise."

Norma whispered, "Even from Dena?"

"Yes. Especially her."

"I understand. Mum's the word. Will there be a dinner or anything?"

Zofko was getting her tape recorder and notebook out of her satchel. "Excuse me?"

"Will there be a dinner . . . or an awards banquet?"

"Oh, yes. Now, what we need from you, Mrs. Warren, is a little background information for the official bio."

"Will it be formal, do you think?"

"Yes, I believe it will be, and if you have any photographs we could use, school pictures or—"

"Where will it be? Here, or will it be in Jefferson City?"

"In Jefferson City."

"Oh. Do you think we'll be able to go? Is the public invited?"

"You'll be sent invitations."

"When is it?"

"The date has not been set but we'll let you know."

"Oh, I'm so excited I am about to faint. Do you think we could get an extra ticket for Aunt Elner? We'll be happy to pay for the ticket. She's her great-aunt, actually, she would just be thrilled to pieces. Will the governor be there?"

"Now, as I understand it, her father was born in Elmwood Springs..."

Norma stood up. "I'm so excited, I haven't even offered you a thing. Would you like some coffee or anything?"

"No, I'm fine, thank you. Well, I will take a Coke if you have it."

Two hours later Norma was still talking about what a darling little girl Dena had been. "Her mother was working so I took Baby Girl up to nursery school at Neighbor Dorothy's house and picked her up every day and she was the sweetest little thing. I remember her fourth birthday party, we had a big birthday cake for her. Her mother had her dressed up like a little doll."

Zofko responded to the word *cake,* realized she was starving again, and tried to cut to the chase. "Mrs. Warren, you say her mother was from where?"

"I couldn't say. I really don't know."

Zofko's ears perked up. "Didn't she ever say?"

"No. But she was a lovely person."

"And you say she's deceased?"

Norma nodded and changed the subject. "And of course, when we actually met Wayne Newton in person, we were beside ourselves. Baby Girl arranged it. She has been so good to us."

"Mrs. Warren, when did Dena's mother pass away?"

"Oh, I really couldn't say for sure."

"And when did she leave Elmwood Springs?"

"She was about four and a half—I think."

"Dena, you mean. Where do you think I could get some more information about her mother?"

"Well, really, all you need to say is that she was not from Missouri."

Zofko decided to drop it for the moment. She could check that out later.

"Mrs. Warren, I think that's enough. We'll get the pictures back to you as soon as we make copies. You've been very helpful."

"I hope so. You know what? I'm sorry but I never got your name."

"Barbara." She stood up and shook hands with Norma and said, "Congratulations."

Norma walked her to the door. "I just wish her daddy was alive to see this day. Tell the governor that we are just thrilled. Oh, and Barbara, you'll be at the dinner, won't you?"

"I'm sure I will."

"I hope you'll be at our table!"

Norma ran back to the kitchen and called him at work. "Macky," she said, "I know a secret. But I can't tell. Just wait till you find out, you are going to be so excited. I can't talk anymore, I have to go."

❀　❀　❀

After talking in circles with Dena's great-aunt, Mrs. Elner Shimfessle, Barbara Zofko left Elmwood Springs without anything more than two jars of fig preserves, a few good fried clam dinners under her belt, and several school pictures. Other than that the trip had been a bust. The family had been dull, typical small-town, churchgoing, well-liked people. Nothing she could use. The father, Gene, had once gotten in trouble for swimming inside the town's water tower with a bunch of other boys. Certainly nothing that even Capello could work up a good smear over. The only item where there might be something was the mother. She had noticed that both Mrs. Warren and Mrs. Shimfessle had been extremely sketchy and seemed reluctant to talk much about her. Both had answered the questions about her with the same phrase, "I couldn't say for sure."

All she had to go on was that when the mother left she had gone to work in some department store. Somewhere. But Zofko had her resources. She got the mother's Social Security number and began tracking her from the first job she had down to the last. She tracked down every state employment record on her and was able to get copies of her job data. They were always the same: Name: *Marion Chapman Nordstrom*. Born: *December 9, 1920, Washington, D.C.* Parents: *Deceased*.

Her record of employment was odd. She had first applied for a Social Security number in 1942 and had gone to work in a dress shop in New York City and remained at that job until 1943, when she went to Gumps in San Francisco. From then on she seemed to go from one job to the next, from one town to another. Through store records Zofko managed to find the names of several women who had been employed at a department store still in existence in Chicago, flew to Chicago, and found one still living in the city and still employed. She was a thin, pale woman named Jan, who smoked too much and was happy to talk. "I'll tell you what I can . . . but it's been years now since we worked together . . . but I always wondered what had happened to Miss Chapman. The last thing I heard she had moved to Boston, but yes, I surely do remember her. Oh, Miss Chapman was the last word."

Zofko asked what she meant and she laughed. "I mean she was It. Yes, Miss Chapman was a walking fashion plate if there ever was one, impeccably dressed. I tell you the rest of us used to marvel at how she kept herself. Not a hair out of place, makeup perfect. She wasn't stuck up or anything like that, she was perfectly pleasant, but she, oh, I guess you could say she held herself back—or apart—from us, in a way. Of course, I was young—I don't think I was even eighteen—but I remember all of us younger girls wanted to be like Miss Chapman, dress like her, walk like her, talk like her. But she was one of a kind. We always wondered why somebody like her had to work. You know, with her looks, her style . . . If it had been me, I would have hooked me a rich one and quit, put my feet up for the rest of my days."

Zofko was surprised that she used Nordstrom's maiden name. "Do you know if she was married or not?"

"No, I never heard if she was. She never talked about it if she was. She wasn't social. I don't think she ever went anywhere but to her job and home. Not that she didn't have offers. Some of those society women, and I mean rich women, were always inviting her to parties, but she never went. She was very polite but she never went. She dressed some of the wealthiest women in Chicago. Yes, Miss Chapman was the last word. If she said a dress looked good on them, they bought it, no questions asked. And you say she has a big check coming from the government?"

"Yes."

"Oh, my, well, I just don't know what to tell you about finding her but if you do, tell her Jan in the shoe department says hello. She probably won't remember me but tell her anyway."

A week later Zofko located a Mrs. Eunice Silvernail in Birmingham, Michigan. She and her sister were now living together in a retirement home. Zofko explained that she was trying to find out information that might give the Internal Revenue Service a clue as to her whereabouts. People were always willing to help if there was money involved. Mrs. Silvernail and her sister sat in the small living room, they all ate cherry pie, and the sisters chatted away about the good old days and showed Zofko the watch Mrs. Silvernail had received from the department store when she had retired. Zofko finally reminded them of the purpose of her visit. Mrs. Silvernail said, "You know, when you called I went back through my things and I thought I had a picture of Miss Chapman; we had employee pictures taken every year. I found the year but she wasn't in it. I can't imagine why—maybe she was sick that day. I know she was working there then, and I certainly remember her. What kind of information are you looking for?"

Zofko took another bite of the pie they had put out on the coffee table. "Anything, anything at all you can remember."

Mrs. Silvernail closed her eyes. "She always wore Shalimar—I know that because I was behind the perfume counter that year, before I moved to lingerie—and she got the employee discount. You know, I've worked with so many people, it's hard to pinpoint details but I do remember that. And she was a pretty woman, had a lovely voice; she worked in Better Dresses. You know, we have a lot of rich women here and they all shopped in her department and I'll tell you something—she was just as elegant as her customers. More so than some; she held her own."

Zofko had heard all this before. "Do you know if she had any boyfriends?"

Mrs. Silvernail said, "No, she was not interested in men. I can tell you that for a fact. The owner's son, Marcus, a good-looking man, had his eye on her and she wouldn't so much as give him a tumble. He was just crazy about her, followed her home, and found out she had been married and had a child. Begged her to marry him, said he would put a hundred thousand dollars in that child's name, buy her a house, a car, anything she wanted, just name it, but she just gave him his walking papers. But you know men, if they think they can't have you, then they go crazy trying to get you. But he never did. Lord, if it had been me, I think I would have married him. I mean, how many chances like that come along? Of course, that was before I met Mr. Silvernail, but she was having no part of it and I don't mean maybe. And she left shortly after that. I wouldn't be surprised if that didn't have something to do with why she left. But he finally got married. He married that girl from . . . handbags, I forget her name, but . . . that's all I know."

A day later Zofko sat in her own apartment eating a bag of Fritos, studying the chart she had made. She was not going to give it up. She read and reread the copies of all the employee records and job applications she had managed to get hold of and this time noticed something she had not caught before. A Lili's dress shop had been listed in all her references, then suddenly, after 1946, did not appear on any more applications. Why had she left that job out? Could something have happened there that might be the reason she was running? What had happened on that job that she did not want checked? Why had she left? Had she been fired? Maybe for stealing? Maybe for having an affair with a married man? Zofko was hopeful. She went to the New York City library newspaper reference room searching through the 1937 and 1938 advertisements in the New York area and she found it. Lili's Exclusive dress shop, "clothes for the discriminating woman," 116 Park Avenue. She went to the city records and looked up the address and the list of owners. It showed that the building at 116 Park had been purchased from a Rickter, William J., and sold to Steiner, Lili Carlotta, in 1935 and sold back again in 1944 to Rickter, William J., the original owner. From there it was easy. She called a woman who worked for the New York Census Department and was on Sidney's payroll as well and told her to send everything she had on Lili Carlotta Steiner. Then she went back to her office and waited. The information came by messenger. Zofko ripped open the envelope as if it were a bag of M & M's and devoured the contents with about as much relish:

> Steiner, Lili Carlotta
> Born: Vienna, Austria, 1893
> Moved to New York, resided in Yorkville section at 463 East 85th Street. Owned and operated fashionable dress shop until the time of her arrest. Closely associated with American Nazi Party members and accused of spying and on December 13, 1946, was convicted and served ten years in prison. Died in 1962 at the age of sixty-nine in Milwaukee, Wisconsin.

When Capello read the information she handed him, he looked at her. "What can I say? It doesn't get better than this. You're the best." Barbara Zofko was happy. She liked to please her boss.

"How long did she work for Steiner?"

"About eight months."

Capello nodded. "It's enough, more than enough. Write it—Hitler, holocaust, death camps, the whole deal."

Zofko went back to her office, sat down, and knocked out a few sample headlines and phrases:

Dena Nordstrom's Shameful Nazi Past . . . mother war criminal . . . leader of American Nazi bund . . . Daughter of Nazi spy now in American broadcasting. Mother close friend of Hitler, a source revealed . . . aided the Nazi cause . . . Nazi war criminal confesses, names top American broadcaster as the daughter of Nazi spy . . .

She would finish a full rough draft later. Right now she needed lunch. After all, there was no rush. Nordstrom was not quite a big enough star yet. They had time, time to embellish, add "evidence." Certainly time for a nice lunch. She deserved a reward, she had worked hard, and she had come up with the nucleus of a great story. It wasn't airtight, it wasn't complete, it might not be true, but it would do the job. When she finished, she put it in the file with the rest. This little hand grenade would wait for a time when Sidney Capello decided to pull the pin and throw it at Nordstrom, the all-American girl.

The Banquet

Kansas City, Missouri
1978

After the visit from Barbara, Norma drove all the way to Kansas City to shop in the Plaza for a formal for herself and Aunt Elner. She figured they could rent Macky a tuxedo in Jefferson City. As the capital of the state, they certainly had a rental place but she called and checked anyway, and they did and had several tuxes in Macky's size. Keeping a secret like this was hard for most people, but it was hell for Norma, who had to practically strangle herself to keep from blurting it out to Macky. She was terrified that she might talk in her sleep and she had promised Barbara that she would not breathe a word about it to anybody.

Every day she scoured the papers, looking for the announcement that Dena had been named Missouri Woman of the Year. And every morning she grabbed the mail hoping the banquet invitation would be there.

After several months she began to wonder if maybe they had made the announcement and somehow it had not made the Elmwood Springs paper, so she decided to check. She called the governor's office in Jefferson City and asked to speak to Barbara. The voice on the other end said, "Do you have a last name?"

"No, but she works for the governor."

"In what capacity?"

Careful not to give anything away, she answered, "She's in charge of awards."

"I don't know who that would be, ma'am."

"Oh. She didn't tell me her last name. Who's in charge of banquets?"

"Catering?"

"No, of writing up the programs."

"I don't know who that would be, ma'am."

"Well, do you have anybody named Barbara working there?"

A pause. "Ma'am, I'm going to connect you with Public Relations. I have a Barbara Thomas listed."

"Is she a heavyset girl?"

"I don't know, ma'am, I'm just the switchboard operator."

Someone answered, "Public relations."

"May I please speak to Barbara."

"May I ask who's calling?"

"Ohh, if you don't mind, I don't think I can tell you. . . ."

"Hold on."

A woman picked up. "Hello. This is Barbara."

Norma whispered, "Barbara . . . is that you?"

"Yes, it is. Who's this?"

"It's me, the lady in Elmwood Springs. You know, the relative of . . . you know who."

"I'm sorry. Who is this?"

"Is there anybody else on the line? Can I speak freely?"

"Yes."

"It's Norma Warren, the cousin of you know who, in Elmwood Springs."

"Where?"

"Elmwood Springs. You paid me a little visit about six months ago."

"I don't think so. I've never—"

"Yes, don't you remember—about the—" and Norma spelled out A-W-A-R-D.

"What award?"

"Don't you remember coming about the bio?"

"I'm afraid you must have the wrong person."

"Are you a heavyset girl with black hair?"

"No."

"Oh. Well, do you know a heavyset girl with black hair named Barbara?"

"No."

"She works there. She's in charge of the big banquet."

"What big banquet?"

"Well, if you don't know, I can't say. Would you put me back to the operator? I seem to have the wrong Barbara. Sorry. And please don't mention that I called."

"I won't."

Norma spoke to the only other Barbara who worked in the governor's office but she was not the right one either. Norma was completely confused. She called Aunt Elner and asked if a woman named Barbara had ever come to her house.

Aunt Elner, also sworn to secrecy, answered cautiously.

"Who wants to know?"

"I do."

"Well, I can't tell you; all I can tell you is that don't be surprised if you get an invitation in the mail any day now and that's all I can say on the subject."

Aunt Elner and Norma both waited and waited but nothing ever came.

Marion Chapman

The La Salle Dress Shop in Philadelphia, where Dena's mother now worked, was unlisted in the phone book. Those who needed to know the number knew it. Under its long blue and white canopy strolled customers who peopled the best homes, schools, and clubs in Philadelphia, the Main Line, Palm Beach, or wherever they happened to be. Mrs. Robert Porter, one such customer who wanted and could well afford only the best, always insisted that Miss Chapman was to wait on her. She had picked Chapman out from the first as a woman who knew what she was doing. Today, Mrs. Porter was seated on the edge of a large round tufted ottoman in the center of the mirrored showroom, choosing a wardrobe for a daughter-in-law's trip to Europe. As always, she was impeccably dressed in a black designer suit that showed off her small, neat figure to best advantage. Her thin, black, T-strap shoes called attention to the fact that although she was in her early seventies, she still had the legs and perfectly shaped ankles of good ancestry and the very rich.

As her daughter-in-law, Margo, modeled each outfit, selected by Miss Chapman, Mrs. Porter approved by a simple nod. She was really more interested in studying Miss Chapman, something she had been doing for some time now. It began when her middle son,

Gamble, who was at present between marriages, started to pursue Marion Chapman but to no avail. Over the ensuing weeks Mrs. Porter had observed that Miss Chapman handled herself very well indeed at all times. She was never overly friendly, always pleasant, but still there was always something slightly reserved, slightly removed about her. She was a tall, extremely attractive woman with flawless, almost porcelain skin, and wore her light auburn hair in an upsweep that emphasized an aquiline nose and a perfect profile. At first glance she had the exact look of the professional woman, but upon closer inspection, the one feature that did not fit the picture of the cool, emotionless saleslady was her eyes. There was something in her eyes that told another story. A certain expression, a sadness, almost a preoccupation with something that had nothing to do with the present.

After her daughter-in-law had finished her fitting, Mrs. Porter said, "Margo, wait in the car for me, will you? I'll be out in a few minutes."

When Margo left, Mrs. Porter patted the space beside her on the ottoman. "Miss Chapman, sit down. I'd like to talk to you."

Miss Chapman seemed rather reluctant. "Mrs. Porter, if this is about Gamble, I can assure you—"

Mrs. Porter waved her hand. "No, of course not. You are perfectly right to stay away from him. He's a fool where women are concerned. On the contrary, I'm surprised he had the good sense to go after you. Most of his women are brainless." She snapped open her cigarette case and placed a cigarette in a small black cigarette holder and lit it. Miss Chapman sat down. "Is it about the clothes? Is—"

Mrs. Porter interrupted again. "The clothes are excellent. Margo is a big girl and you did a magnificent job of minimizing it. No, it's you I want to talk about."

A look of alarm crossed Miss Chapman's face but she did not flinch. Mrs. Porter took a drag from her cigarette, turned and blew it out the other side, then looked at Miss Chapman squarely. She said, matter of factly, "Miss Chapman, I'm too old and too rich to beat around the bush. Why are you here?"

Miss Chapman blinked. "Pardon me?"

"You don't belong here. I know it and you know it. I've been watching you for quite some time now. And frankly, you fascinate me. You're no ordinary shop girl; nobody speaks French like you do on a high school education. It's obvious you have breeding so don't try to tell me your parents were just plain working folks. I raise horses, Miss Chapman, and I can spot a Thoroughbred a mile away."

Miss Porter saw her blush. "Please don't misunderstand, I would never presume to pry into your personal life; I find that sort of thing distasteful. But this much I do know. You could probably have any man in town if you wanted him, but maybe you don't want a man, for whatever reason; I couldn't care less. But in the meantime I also know you have a daughter to raise. I also know what they pay you here and it can't be easy." She took another drag of her cigarette. "What I am proposing is this. I have plenty of money and God knows I have clout and contacts. Let me buy you a shop of your own. Anywhere you want, that's up to you, but at least allow me to put you in a position where you are not working for somebody else."

Miss Chapman looked concerned.

"And you needn't worry that this has anything at all to do with my son; this is strictly between you and me. You have talent, style, and you know your business. There is no good reason on earth you shouldn't have your own shop. I'm sure in a matter of a few years you could be very comfortable. There are enough clotheshorses in my family alone to keep you busy."

Miss Chapman looked as if she were about to speak but Mrs. Porter stopped her. "Don't decide today. Take some time to think it over. You can give me your answer at the end of the week." She removed her cigarette from the holder and crushed it out in the large crystal ashtray between them. "But I'll tell you as I would tell one of my own daughters. Don't be foolish and not accept my offer. You can pay me back or not. It doesn't matter."

❖ ❖ ❖

Marion Chapman was still rattled as she hung up clothes in the dressing room. Of all her customers, she had always liked Mrs. Porter more than most, but this proposal had caught her off guard.

Dealing with Gamble had been tricky, but she had handled such situations before. This was different. Maybe it was because there was something about Mrs. Porter that she trusted, that even allowed her to entertain the idea. If only she could. It would mean a new life, security; she would be able to do so many more things for Dena, buy her anything she wanted. It would give her a chance to get them out of those seedy apartment hotels. They could have a lovely home, a place where Dena could bring her friends.

When she got home from work that night, Dena was in the lobby waiting for her. They went to dinner around the corner at a small restaurant, and Dena asked what was wrong, what she was thinking about. But she said, "Nothing, honey, I'm just tired, that's all." After they came home and she put Dena to bed on the sofa in the living room, Marion Chapman sat across the room in the dark and watched her daughter as she slept.

The streetlight shining in the window bathed Dena in an almost silver glow and she could see her hair and white skin. Lately she had begun to see a lot more of her father in her. She looked more and more like Gene every day, same blue eyes, same hair. As she sat and smoked in the dark, her mind drifted back to 1943 and San Francisco. A girl who worked with her was dating a marine, and his friend had apparently seen her through the window and was dying to meet her, but that year the town was crawling with boys desperate to get a date before they were shipped out, and she was not interested. But the girl badgered her for weeks to at least meet him and finally, as a way of getting the girl to leave her alone, she agreed to meet him at the Top of the Mark for one drink and one drink only. That night when she got off the elevator at the Mark he was standing there waiting for her holding a cellophane-wrapped box, tied with a purple ribbon, containing an orchid. "Miss Chapman, I'm Gene Nordstrom," he said. "I didn't know what to buy; the lady at the flower shop said you might like this."

He was certainly not what she had expected. He looked as if he had just stepped off a marine recruiting poster. He was at least six foot three with blue eyes and white-blond hair. The place was packed with servicemen and their girls, and they had to fight their way through the crowd to get to their table by the window. He said, "I hope this is all right. I got here early to get a really good one. I've been here for a couple of hours; this place fills up fast."

She looked around. "Yes, it certainly does."

"I ordered a bottle of pink champagne, is that all right? I figured this might be the only time I get a chance to drink some." As soon as the waiter poured, he pulled out his wallet and took out a picture. "That's my dad's bakery and that's my mom and dad standing in front of it."

His father was a tall man standing beside a plump, smiling woman. He handed another picture across the table. "This is my Aunt Elner and this one is my dog, Tess. I don't suppose you have ever heard of Elmwood Springs, Missouri, have you?"

"No," she said. "I've heard of St. Louis. How far away is that?"

He laughed. "Pretty far. But you would like Elmwood Springs. Have you ever heard of Neighbor Dorothy?"

"Who?"

"Neighbor Dorothy . . . on the radio? I guess you don't get her show all the way out here. Anyhow, that's where I'm from, Elmwood Springs. It's not very big but we have everything you need. We have a movie theater and a lake. I wish you could see it sometime. I bet you'd like it. I don't know why I'm going on and on about Elmwood Springs; I guess I must be homesick or something. I'm probably boring you to death."

"No, you're not."

She had not meant to fall in love and get married but his joy and enthusiasm for life had been so infectious that she actually began to think that maybe her life could be different. Maybe she could leave her past behind and really live happily ever after, in a small town in the middle of the country, making a fresh start in life.

But it had only been a momentary dream. After Gene was killed she realized how foolish she had been to even consider it for a moment. And when their daughter, Dena, was born, she made up her mind what she was going to do. She had every intention of taking Dena to Elmwood Springs and leaving her with Gene's parents and simply disappearing from her life.

It had not turned out that way. When she stepped down from the train that day, it was already too late. As hard as she tried to leave Dena, she could not. Every day that passed, she knew she should go, but as the days went by life in Elmwood Springs had somehow begun to make her believe that maybe she was safe here. The Nordstroms asked no questions, accepting her with open arms.

She had almost begun to forget who she really was and what she had done when suddenly her worst nightmare had come true. Right after Dena's fourth birthday, Theo had found them, had come knocking on the Nordstroms' front door.

She should never have married, never have had a child; she should have left Dena that first day. What had she been thinking of? What was she thinking of now? She could not stay in Philadelphia or anywhere permanently. She had to keep moving. She could not take a chance again, not with Dena's future.

A week later Mrs. Porter called the La Salle and asked to speak to Miss Chapman. The owner said, "I'm sorry, Mrs. Porter, but she's no longer with us. Can I be of service?"

"You mean she doesn't work there anymore? What happened?"

"I don't quite know, Mrs. Porter. One day she called in sick and the next day when she didn't come to work I called to see how she was, and the man on the desk told me that she had moved and didn't leave a forwarding address. I don't know what to think. I have a paycheck for her but I don't know where to send it. I'm sorry, Mrs. Porter, I know you were fond of her."

"Yes," Mrs. Porter said. "Yes, I was."

A Night at the Theater

New York City
1978

Dena went with Julian Amsley to see the musical *Mame,* a benefit performance for the Actors Fund, and it seemed as if all of New York was there. It was a glittering evening and she admitted to herself that she enjoyed hearing people whispering as she walked down the aisle, "There's Dena Nordstrom." She was dressed with elegant simplicity and stood out in the crowd even without the expensive jewelry and expensive face-lifts of the women who had married well. Seated, Dena was thoroughly enjoying the show when halfway through the first act, she started to break out in a sweat and felt as if she could not breathe. Her heart began to pound and she heard a ringing in her ears; everything became distorted, began to look unreal. The entire audience seemed to be moving in on her ... and she was gasping for breath. She felt as if she was either going to die or pass out.

She stood up and was stepping over people, trying to get to the aisle. Julian turned and half-rose, but she was gone before he had a chance to ask her what was wrong.

Dena made it to the ladies' room, ran to the sink and held on, but her head was still spinning. The attendant was concerned when she saw her face was as white as her dress. "Are you all right, miss?" Dena was still fighting for breath and turned on the cold water and splashed herself in the face. The woman sat her down and said, "Just sit here and breathe as deeply as you can." Dena was still shaky but began to feel slightly better as the attendant kept talking to her and applied cold compresses to her wrists. "You probably just got too hot in there. Just try to relax, you'll be all right."

Dena had never had this happen before. "I don't know what happened. I thought I was going to faint."

"You might have eaten something that didn't agree with you or you might be coming down with the flu. Or you could be pregnant; lots of ladies feel faint when they are pregnant." An elderly usherette who had seen Dena run into the ladies' lounge knocked on the door. The attendant said, "Yes? Who is it?"

"It's Fern . . . is she all right?"

"Yes."

"Does she need anything?"

"I need a drink," Dena said. "Tell her to get me a drink." The attendant called out, "Fern, go to the bar and tell Mike to give you a brandy."

Dena called, "A double."

The thought that she must be pregnant snapped her back from wherever it was and into reality. Julian had been driving her crazy, and last month she had gotten pie-eyed at a party at his place and thought she might have finally gone to bed with him, but she couldn't be sure of the details and the next morning she hadn't asked. She didn't want to know.

The drink came and she drank it in one gulp. She sat in the chair motionless and stared straight ahead. Finally, she turned to the attendant, looked her right in the eye, and made this solemn vow to a complete stranger: "I will never go out with another Greek man for as long as I live."

The attendant, a large, caramel-colored woman who had never been out with a Greek man, nodded at Dena. "I don't blame you, sugar."

Dena got up and tipped her $50 and tipped Fern and Mike the bartender on her way out the door on her way to a taxi and home, leaving Julian in his third-row center-aisle seat, wondering what had happened to her.

❀ ❀ ❀

The next morning she woke up scared to death and for the first time was glad she had an appointment that day with the doctor. She really needed to talk to someone.

She told Dr. Diggers exactly what had happened the night before, including the thought that she might be pregnant. Dr. Diggers listened and jotted notes. Dena was irritated that she seemed so calm and unconcerned. "I'm glad you can sit there doodling or whatever it is you do, while my life may be over. I may be carrying some Greek child I don't even know."

Elizabeth Diggers said, "You're not pregnant."

"How do you know, you weren't there. That man is like a rabbit."

"Dena, you had an anxiety attack."

"A what?"

"What you described is a classic, old-fashioned, ordinary anxiety attack."

"Are you sure?"

"Yes, I'm sure."

"Oh, thank God." Dena breathed a sigh of relief. "Wait a minute—why would I have an anxiety attack?"

Diggers asked automatically, "Why do *you* think you did?"

"I don't know . . . I don't even know what it is, that's why I'm asking you."

"Well, are you unusually anxious about something?"

"No. I'm perfectly fine. Everything is going great. Why would anxiety attack me all of a sudden?"

Diggers did not answer.

"I was just sitting there enjoying myself and then, *wham,* it was horrible. I don't know where it came from or why. Why do people have anxiety attacks?"

"Sometimes it's environmental; sometimes it's subconscious, something repressed trying to get out."

"Great, now my subconscious is attacking me. It's not enough that I have to fight off Julian Amsley every night, now my subconscious is after me."

"Let's talk a little bit about last night. Tell me exactly what you were doing."

"I told you I was just sitting there watching the show."

"What were you watching at the time? Do you remember?"

"Mame."

"What part of the show?"

"Oh, I don't know, the first act; why?"

"Try and remember exactly what was going on at the moment you started to feel anxious."

"What would that have to do with anything?"

"Maybe nothing. But humor me . . . try to remember."

Dena thought for a moment. "It was something about Christmas. They were singing they wanted a little Christmas early and there was a tree. That's all I remember."

"Ah, yes, that was the 'We need a little Christmas' song. I know the show."

Dr. Diggers was busy writing. "Let me ask you this. Does anything about Christmas or a Christmas tree trigger anything for you?"

Dena looked at her blankly.

"Remind you of anything? Did anything happen to you around Christmas that would be upsetting or—?"

"No. I don't even like Christmas. Why are you asking me all these questions?"

"What did you and your mother do at Christmas? Did you go to family?"

"No, I don't remember what we did. Nothing. We just did nothing." Dena started to break out in a cold sweat. Her mouth became dry and she became suddenly panicky.

"Dena? What's the matter?"

"I don't know."

"Are you feeling anxious right now?"

Dena had dug her nails into the chair and was breathing heavily. "A little . . . I don't know why."

Diggers immediately wheeled over to her. "OK, now, just calm down. You're all right; I'm here. Get up and walk. Let's go in the kitchen, put some cold water on your face—keep looking at me, I'm right here with you."

They made it to the kitchen and Dena put water on her face and held on to the sink like she had the night before. The woman who worked for Diggers stood in the kitchen over in the corner, saying nothing. Diggers said, "Louisa, go in the medicine chest and bring me a ten-milligram Valium." She gave it to Dena and made her lie down on the couch, then sat talking to her. "You're OK, just keep breathing, and relax. It will pass, I promise you."

Dena felt herself calming.

"I've been through this myself," Diggers said. "I know how scary it is but you're OK."

"I hate this."

"I know you do."

"Is my time up yet?"

Diggers said, "No. Can you stay here by yourself for a minute? I'll be right back. If you need me just yell."

She wheeled herself into her office, called the doorman downstairs, and told him not to send the next patient up. She would reschedule. She came back in the living room.

"Do I have to go?" Dena asked.

"No. You stay right where you are."

They sat in silence. About five minutes later, Dena said, "Something did happen on Christmas but . . . I forgot it a long time ago. I never think about it. I thought I was over it."

Christmas

When Dena was fifteen, her mother was living in Chicago, in a large red-brick apartment building called the Berkeley. Dena's boarding school was outside Baltimore and she couldn't wait to see her for the holidays. She had called and called her mother from school but each time she missed reaching her at home. She called the department store where her mother worked and they told her that her mother was no longer working there. Her mother changed jobs quite a bit and sometimes forgot to tell her, so Dena wrote a letter and told her what time her train would be arriving. All the way across the country she was humming with excitement. She loved riding through the small towns and seeing all the Christmas decorations and looking in the windows of the houses. When her train finally pulled into the station, Dena was the first person off. She looked up and down the platform but her mother was not there. She waited almost two hours. She didn't know what to do. Maybe her mother had not received her letter or had to work late. So she went outside and took a cab to her mother's apartment building. Her heart jumped with joy when she saw her mother's name written on the small strip of paper next to the buzzer. She pushed the button. But there was no answer. The air was freezing and the wind was so cold it hurt. It was getting dark when a man came, took a key, and opened the big glass front door leading into the lobby. Dena said, "Excuse me, could you tell me if there is a superintendent or something? I need to get into my mother's apartment. I don't have a key and she's not home yet." The man let her in and pointed her to the brown door. "Ring that bell." Dena saw that it said MRS. F. CLEVERDON, MANAGER. A middle-aged lady in an apron opened the door. "Hello. I'm Mrs. Nordstrom's daughter and I just got here and I was wondering if she left me a key."

The woman smiled. "Well, no, dear, she didn't leave a key. But I'll take you up and let you in. Your mother's on the sixth floor. Hold on while I go get the key."

"Thank you. Guess she's working late . . . you know, because of Christmas."

"I imagine so," Mrs. Cleverdon said, "they keep the stores open late. Thank heavens I don't have to get into that mess. I've done all my shopping—well, all the shopping I am going to do."

They took the elevator up and she followed her down the hall to apartment 6D and opened the door. "Here we are. I know your mother will be glad to see you. You have a nice visit, now."

"Thank you."

Dena walked into the apartment and switched on the lights and noticed unopened mail lying on the floor. Her letter was right on top. Then it dawned on her. Her mother must have gone out of town on a buying trip for the store. She often did that; she was probably on her way home right now.

The minute Dena walked into the bedroom it smelled familiar— her mother's Shalimar—and she felt at home. She liked this apartment. It had a little kitchen and a nice-sized living room. The furniture was pretty much like the furniture in all of the furnished apartments they had lived in, a trifle worn and tired but comfortable. Then she noticed that her mother had put a small white ceramic tree on the dining table in the living room by the front window. It had tiny, little colored lights. She plugged it in and it lit up in red and green and blue. She decided to keep it on, and if her mother happened to look up when she came home and saw it, she would be surprised.

After unpacking her things, she opened the front closet to hang up her coat. Four beautifully wrapped Christmas packages were on the floor. Each one said: *To Dena. From Mother*. She put her gifts for her mother by the little tree and sat down to wait for her, wondering what was in the packages, especially the big one. That night, every time she heard the elevator door open and heard someone come down the hall, she held her breath; she just knew it was her. But it never was. They all walked on. At about ten o'clock she was starving and there was nothing in the refrigerator, so she wrote a note and propped it up against the Christmas tree. *Mother, I am here! I have gone to get something to eat and will be right back.*

She put her coat on and had to leave the door unlocked because she didn't have a key. She went down the street to a coffee shop and got a grilled cheese sandwich and a Coke and a piece of chocolate pie to go, but when she got back to the building it was locked and she couldn't get back in. She buzzed her mother's apartment, hoping she would be home by now. There was no answer so she had to push the manager's buzzer again.

The next morning she woke up and got dressed and fooled around the apartment all day, killing time. Each time she went out she left the same note in the same place. Two days later she called her school until finally someone picked up. Dena asked if her mother had called and left her a message. They said she hadn't.

Christmas morning she got up early and made a pot of coffee. She combed her hair and put on her good dress and sat by the window and waited for the phone to ring. Every time she heard the elevator door open, her heart jumped. She knew it was going to be her mother this time. And her heart sank again as whoever it was walked on down the hall. She sat there all day. The window was ice cold but the apartment was warm. At about six o'clock she went in the kitchen and heated up the frozen turkey dinner with mashed potatoes she had gotten at the store and sat down and ate it. She watched the Perry Como Christmas special on the old black-and-white television set in the living room. She waited until eleven o'clock and then she went into the closet, got her presents, and put them in the middle of the floor and opened them. She saved the big one for last. She cleaned up all the paper and went to bed.

All through the rest of the holiday, she waited. Each day, Dena was convinced that her mother was going to walk in the door at any minute. With each day that passed, the feeling drained out of her body, until at the end of the week she was numb. On her last day she packed, called a cab, put on her new blue wool pea coat that her mother had given her for Christmas, went over and turned off the lights on the Christmas tree, locked the door behind her, and went downstairs to wait in the lobby for her taxi. Mrs. Cleverdon came out to see about a hall bulb that needed replacing and saw that Dena was leaving. "Did you have a nice visit?" she asked pleasantly.

"Yes, ma'am."

Upstairs in apartment 6D a note was on the table. *"Mother, I was here. Love, Dena."* Three weeks later the note she had left on the table in the living room was still there. Mrs. Cleverdon told her so on the phone. Her mother did not come back. Her mother had disappeared off the face of the earth. But Dena did not cry. Not once. Back at school, if anyone asked how her Christmas had been, she lied. She pretended it had never happened. It took years for Dena to really believe that her mother was not going to come back.

That next Christmas her grandparents wanted her to come and be with them, but she took a train to Chicago and spent the holidays alone in a room at the Drake. The first day she got in a cab and went over to the Berkeley and stood outside the building for a long time and then went back to the hotel. Christmas Day she dressed up and went downstairs and had Christmas dinner in the Cape Cod room. She sat at a table by the window and ordered a lobster. She had never had one before so she decided to try one. People looked over at the pretty girl sitting all by herself with a lobster bib, trying to crack the shell and figure out which part you were supposed to eat, but she did not see them staring at her because she spent most of her time looking out the window as though she was expecting to see someone she knew.

Me and My Shadow

New York City
1978

"And you never heard from your mother after that?" asked Dr. Diggers.

"No. Nobody did. Anyhow, that was a long time ago and has nothing to do with what's happening now."

"Wait a minute. So you don't really know if she's living or dead."

Dena dismissed it. "I don't know and I don't care. Really, it doesn't matter to me one way or another."

"Why didn't you tell me this before?"

"Because—" Dena looked up "—it's not anything I'm particularly proud of."

"What do you mean?"

"I don't know, it's just embarrassing."

"Let's talk about it."

"Let's don't. I am not interested in the past. I don't even remember most of it; what's the point? Look, I'm a little old to sit around hugging a teddy bear, whining about my mother. I don't have time for that; it's all I can do to keep my head on straight without spacing out or getting myself whipped up about yesterdays. You get one mother and one father and if you're lucky, you grow up and it's over, get over it, and become an adult. I didn't have a great childhood but I'm not going to dine out on it. I hate whiners. And I don't need anybody to feel sorry for me."

Diggers rolled over closer to Dena. "Sweetie pie, I do feel sorry for you. And you have a right to feel sorry for yourself. That was a *terrible* thing that happened to you."

It was the first time Dr. Diggers had called her anything but Dena and it caught her off guard.

"You are going to have to talk to someone; it might as well be me. OK?"

Dena heard herself say, "All right."

"Good girl. I know it's hard for you to talk about but we have to. We have to look at this thing head on and not sweep it under the rug, because until you face what really happened and deal with it, you are not going to know what you are feeling about anything. I won't lie to you; it is going to be a long, hard process ... but we have to start somewhere."

Dena was really listening to her for the first time.

"Are you willing to start and work with me now?"

"Yes."

That night, Elizabeth Diggers thought more about Dena. She had grown very fond of her. She could still look at her with a cold, trained, professional eye, but there was more there—something more beyond the usual patient-doctor relationship. Lonely people have a way of recognizing each other. She could see past that beautiful face, past those eyes that did not reveal. When she looked at Dena, she saw that fifteen-year-old who never got out of that room. She was still sitting there, looking out the window, still waiting for her mother to come home. Diggers's job was to go inside that room, take that girl by the hand, and bring her out. Get her out into the sun and fresh air so she could continue to grow. Diggers knew all the clinical names, all the medical and psychological terms for what was bothering Dena, but it could be summed up in simple, human terms. Her heart had been broken and she had never gotten over it.

Session after session, Dena would close her eyes and try to remember, but she seemed to have a block. What was she like? Dena was even having a hard time remembering what her mother looked like. She tried her best but she was unable to come up with anything but the shadow of a person, darting in and out of the picture. She remembered apartment buildings, smells, long halls, names—the Sheridan ... the Royal Arms ... the Bradbury Towers—eating alone in big cities—the Windsor Arms ... the Drake—afternoons in ladies' lounges in department stores, reading, coloring, waiting for her mother to stop work when she would have her all to herself, where she could sleep next to her. The Altamont, the Highland Towers, the Hillsborough. She remembered walking past city windows full of warm, soft sofas and easy chairs and rich, dark, shiny tables and chairs; beautiful mannequins in the latest fashions, shoes, hats, gloves, dresses, fox furs. Park Lane, Ritz Towers, Ridgemont. She remembered standing, shivering, waiting for the streetcar in front of a window where tuxedos, tails, and top hats were displayed. Windows with a hundred different glass bottles on display, blue, green, and clear, full of amber-colored perfumes. She remembered riding a hundred different streetcars across strange cities. But who was her mother? What had she thought about, what had she felt, had Dena loved her, had she really loved Dena? Didn't she know she had a little girl who adored her, needed her? She had faded into the city, disappeared, gone, and as much as Dena tried, the woman she remembered was like someone she had seen in a film, not a real person at all. At times she wondered if her mother had ever really existed, if she wasn't remembering something from a movie. It was all mixed up. It was as if her childhood never happened and she had simply wakened one day, an adult.

But Dr. Diggers persisted, asking her the same questions over and over. "How did you feel when your mother did not come home?" As time went by, Dena lost her patience. "This is so *stupid*! Why do I have to talk about this all the time? I'm so tired of it I could scream. I don't want to *do* this anymore."

Dr. Diggers put down her pad. "Why do you come here, Dena?"

"Frankly—you want the truth—I come here because you won't give me my damn prescription for Valium unless I come here. Why do you think I come here? For the candy?"

"I think you come here because you're scared. You need a place to rant and rave and lash out at someone you feel safe with, someone who can see through your bullshit. I know you can walk right out that door and find a thousand doctors happy to give you all the tranquilizers, the mood elevators you ask for; you can charm your way into getting whatever you want and take all the pills in the world. You can do that. You can either become a dope addict or an alcoholic or you can jump out a window, or go through this and get it over with and hopefully feel better."

"Hopefully?"

"Dena, in life there are no guarantees. But I feel that you are making progress."

"OK, I know my mother didn't love me like she should have. She walked out; so what good does it do me? I still feel lousy. It doesn't make it any better. I don't care anymore—why can't you accept that? Why can't you understand that I just want to forget about it?"

"You can do that, you can put all the Band-Aids in the world on it, but it is still not going to get to the bottom of what is causing your stomach stress and anxiety. And whether you admit it or not, Miss Hickory Nut, you come here because you want to get better. So what do you say we start again, OK?"

Dena, thinking it over, finally said in resignation, "Oh, give me a piece of that rotten candy, then. But you know I hate you."

Dr. Diggers laughed. "Oh, I know."

"No, I really do."

"I'm sure you do. Now, let's get back to where we were."

Weeks went by and then one day, out of the blue, Dena suddenly burst into tears and started to cry uncontrollably. "What is it?" Diggers asked. "What are you thinking about?"

"I . . . always thought she'd come back . . . but she never did," Dena blurted out between sobs, "and I don't know what I did wrong."

✤ ✤ ✤

Finally Dena stopped fighting. Dr. Diggers's hypnotherapy began
to help Dena relax and she was remembering more and more each
session. Today, she put her under a little deeper. Dena had her
eyes closed and could almost see her mother. But she was still
an indistinct figure. Then, Dena said, "She had taken me shopping. I don't know what city we were in . . . New York, maybe. Oh
I don't know, but I remember we walked by this big store and
it had all these pianos in the window. She stopped and we went
in . . . and she walked all around, looking at all the different
pianos . . . and way in the back she saw one . . . she must have
liked. She sat down and opened it up and she had this odd look on
her face. . . ."

"Like what? Describe it."

"Oh, I don't know . . . like I wasn't there or something. And all
of a sudden she started to play a song. I was so surprised. I didn't
even know she could play. She played some sort of waltz, and
I remember she looked so happy. I had never seen her look so . . .
well . . . happy is not right. She looked like she was somewhere else;
transported would be a good word. Then this old man who worked
there opened the door to his office and he stood listening until she
finished. He had some sort of thick accent, and he said, 'My dear
young lady, where did you learn to play like that?'

"He asked her to please play something else but she told him that
song was all she knew, and we left. I said, 'Mother, why didn't you
tell me you could play the piano?' And she acted like it was nothing.
But she must have been good or else that man wouldn't have come
over."

"Did she ever talk about her parents?"

"No . . . just that they were killed in a fire."

"Did you ever see any pictures of them, or of her when she was
growing up?"

"No. She said everything burned up."

"Weren't you curious?"

"She didn't want to talk about them, it upset her. So I just
didn't."

"You spent a lot of time not upsetting your mother, didn't you? Can you remember that?"

"Yes . . ."

"Why?"

"Why? Because . . . I was enough trouble as it was."

"Why do you think that?"

"Well, because she had to look after me."

"Let's go back to your feeling of being afraid. What were you afraid of?"

"I told you, I don't know."

"Was there something that made you think your mother was frightened?"

"No."

Diggers sat back and waited. Then Dena said, "I think she was afraid of that man, one time."

"What man?"

"Some man she saw . . . when we were still living in New York. We were coming home and it was snowing. We turned the corner and when we got to the apartment building she stopped all of a sudden. I looked up at her and saw that she was staring at the man talking to the clerk at the desk. He had his back to us and all I saw was a big man in a black-checked overcoat. I said, 'What's the matter?' Before I had finished, she grabbed me by the arm and almost dragged me down the street. I asked, 'What's the matter, Momma? What is it?' She said, 'Be quiet and let me think.' She was walking so fast that I had to run to keep up with her. I was panicked now. So I said, 'Did I do something, Momma?'

" 'No,' she said, 'come on.' In a minute she told me to go out in the street and get a cab, wave one down.

" 'Me?' I said. 'What do I do?'

" 'Just go and wave; go on.'

"I ran and stood on the corner and waved and waved but nobody stopped. I ran back to her and said, 'They won't stop.' She said, 'Is anybody coming?' I looked up and down and nobody was. She practically ran to the subway and we caught the first one and she sat down and just looked straight ahead. I was convinced I had done something wrong and I started to cry. She said, 'Why are you crying?'

" 'I'm scared,' I said. 'I don't know what's the matter.'

" 'Oh, Dena, it's nothing. I just saw someone I didn't want to see, that's all. Don't be so sensitive.'

" 'Who is he?'

"She said, 'Oh, nobody, just some man I used to work with, nobody important. I just don't want to see him, that's all.'

"I asked, 'Why?' She said, 'He's been bothering me to come back to work for him and I don't want to.'

" 'Why don't you just tell him?'

" 'I would rather not hurt his feelings. Now stop asking so many questions.' Then she looked up for the first time and noticed where we were headed. She stood up and we got off at the next stop and changed subways and we went all the way to the Village. It was really snowing and it was hard to walk but we got to West Twelfth or maybe Eleventh Street. We stopped at a coffee shop and she made a phone call. After she came back she seemed a little more herself. She said, 'We're going over to see Christine.' "

"Who was Christine?"

"A friend of my mother's who was a dancer at Radio City. She said, 'She's invited us to come and spend the night with her; won't that be fun?'

"She lived in a basement apartment on St. Luke's Place and was very glad to see us. She let me play with her cat, Milton, and then Christine put me in this long gown of hers and I slept on a pad that she made up for me, and Momma slept on the couch. At about daybreak I woke up. I looked over and saw that my mother was sitting by the window. I remember having that cold, scared feeling in the pit of my stomach again. I knew she was unhappy and I didn't know why. I was scared to ask her because I thought maybe it was me. Maybe she wished she did not have a little girl. I don't know why I thought that but I did."

"Dena, I'm going to count to three, and when you wake up you will feel rested and peaceful. . . . One . . . just like you have slept for hours . . . two . . . feeling calm and serene . . . three."

Dena slowly opened her eyes.

"How do you feel?"

"Fine." She yawned. "Hate to disappoint you but I don't think I was hypnotized. I remember everything you said."

Diggers smiled. That's what everyone she hypnotized said.

Wall-Cap Productions I

New York City
1978

Ira Wallace was listening to an idea Capello had for a television news show. Although Wallace did not trust Capello as far as he could throw him, the more he heard about the idea, the more he liked it. Capello elaborated. "We cover all the Hollywood stuff; I can feed you enough material from my files to keep you supplied for years. We set it up as a news thing—legit gossip, headline stuff, cutting-edge, hard-hitting, red-hot items. I'm telling you, it's a uranium mine. It's what the people want."

Capello threw a copy of his supermarket rag's P&L for the year across the desk. Wallace glanced at it. The profits were impressive. He said, "I don't know, it sounds good, but you know Winchell tried a gossip show like that in the early days of TV and it didn't work."

Capello had an immediate answer. "Of course it didn't. He was too hard. We soft-sell, we get some hair-spray head or some good-looking broad to sit up there, tell them to smile, and I guarantee you got a hit. You just have to package it the right way."

"You talking network?"

"No, I'm talking syndication. That's where the money is. We own it, we sell it, no regulations. We can cover stuff the networks won't touch."

Wallace was suspicious. "Syndication? What do you need me for?"

"Experience. With my story contacts and your TV experience we can flood every major market within five years. Somebody is gonna do it . . . if we get a jump on this and do it right, I'm talking millions, maybe billions, Ira."

Wallace leaned back and relit his cigar. "You may be right. Get some legit, recognizable anchor . . . like maybe a David Thorenson? Have you been anywhere else with this?"

"No, you're the only one . . . so far. I need to move on this thing as soon as possible, Ira."

"How soon?"

"Today."

Wallace looked at Capello. The dirt-digger had not seen the light of day for years and had unhealthy, blue-white skin and lips the color of raw liver. Wallace, who was no beauty, wanted to throw up at the sight of him. But he thought, as he fought back his nausea, You rat bastard: someday somebody is going to slit your throat and I wish I could be there to see it. But in the meantime, Wallace was smart enough to know a damn good idea. "What's the deal?"

"Sixty-forty."

"Jesus," Wallace said.

"Hey, without me, you got no show."

Two months and what seemed like forty-eight lawyers later, Sidney Capello and Ira Wallace were, as they say in the business, in bed together and Wall-Cap Productions was formed. As the thing took shape, looking good, looking very good, they again discussed talent. Capello dropped his bombshell. "I want Dena Nordstrom."

"Yeah, and I want the queen of England but she ain't available."

"Why not? She's got the following, she's got the looks, she's got the class; we'd have a built-in audience. She'd make it legit. Mass plus class."

"Sidney, she's now the most popular female newscaster in the business. Nordstrom would be anybody's first choice. But you are dreaming. I know her and she ain't gonna do it. First of all, she hates your guts. Second of all, she hates your guts, so forget it, we'll get some other blonde."

"It doesn't hurt to ask, Ira. You never know, people change."

"Yeah, but they don't change that much. Besides, she's on some goddamned scruples kick. She got mixed up with that asshole Howard Kingsley and he screwed up her head. I'm telling you we don't have a chance."

But Capello would not give up. For years now he had thought long and hard about the day when Dena would be working for him, and he relished the idea. After a week, Wallace gave in. "All right, we'll ask. I guess it can't hurt to ask."

❊ ❊ ❊

Dena's agent, Sandy Cooper, sat wide-eyed. "Executive vice president in charge of production?"

Wallace smiled. "That's it, kid. You're in charge of all the talent, you'll have a staff of a hundred if you want it. What say? I've got to move on this thing."

Cooper was busy figuring out how much money he might make in five years. Wallace helped out. "We're talking a guarantee of five million for two years with options and bonuses. And that could be just the beginning. What do you say? You want to be a penny-ante small timer all your life?"

"No. But—"

Capello, sitting in a corner, spoke up. "Tell him the best part, Ira."

Sandy looked over at the man who he had not been introduced to. Wallace said, "What Sidney is talking about is it's a package deal. We want your client, too."

"Dena?"

"Yeah, and we are prepared to offer her a contract that will make her the highest-paid female on television. Look, we know it's gonna take some negotiation to get her away from the network, and we're willing to do a profit share, over and above salary. She *owns* a piece of the company. I know it's probably a bad move on our part, but—"

Wallace shrugged his shoulders. "Call me crazy, call me sentimental, but I wanted to come to her first with this. You know, not that she *owes* me. But I have a soft spot, what can I say."

"Why do you need me in this?" Cooper asked.

"Well, we might have a little problem."

"Besides the network, what little problem?"

Wallace poked his thumb at Capello. "She don't like my partner."

Sandy Cooper was no fool and got the picture. "So, in other words, I deliver her or I don't have a deal, is that it?"

There was no answer.

After Cooper left, Wallace warned Capello again that she would most likely turn them down, but Capello did not look concerned. "It may take a little more persuasion . . . but I think she'll take the offer."

He didn't tell Ira but he could almost *guarantee* it was a done deal. He knew how to negotiate.

❖   ❖   ❖

The next day, Sandy Cooper asked Dena to meet him after work. He had an offer that had come in for her. She said, "Can't you just tell me over the phone?"

"No, this is too big, too important. This is something that could change your life."

At seven o'clock that night she met him across the street at a restaurant on Sixth Avenue. They ordered drinks, Dena specifying chocolate milk because her ulcer had been giving her trouble lately. Cooper ordered a gin and tonic because he was nervous. He took a gulp. "So, Dena, how would you like to be a millionaire by the time you are thirty-five?"

Since she was now thirty-four, he had her attention.

"Just hear me out before you say anything, OK?" And he went on to tell her all about the new show she had been offered, what the deal would be, that she would own a piece of the show, what the floor on her guarantee was. Dena knew how much money there was to be made in syndication, and was intrigued.

"Who's producing this? Do they have the money?"

"It's a new company, just formed. But they have the money and the experience." Cooper looked around the room and confided, "I'm not really supposed to tell you until it is announced, but it's Ira Wallace . . . and a partner."

"Ira?"

"Yes, he's handing in his resignation to the network and forming his own company. And you know he knows what he is doing and has the money behind him, but the best part is, and I don't want to let this influence your decision one way or another, but he's offered to make me executive vice president."

Dena sat back in her chair. Something was off. She knew Ira thought Sandy was a fool; why would he need to bring Sandy in? "Wait a minute. What's the name of this company?"

Cooper couldn't hedge; he'd have to tell her eventually.

"Uh . . . Wall-Cap Productions."

"Wall-Cap Productions? Who is Cap?"

"Well, that's the one thing Ira thought you might have a little problem with. He said you didn't like this guy but, hell, Dena, where this much money is concerned, you don't have to like them. I hate, loathe, and despise Ira Wallace—who doesn't—but that wouldn't stop me from working with him."

"What guy? Who are you talking about?"

"A guy named Capello."

Dena reacted with horror. "Capello, Sidney Capello? Are you serious?"

Sandy nodded sheepishly.

"Forget it. Absolutely not."

"OK, so he doesn't have the best reputation. But we are talking about a *lot* of money here. Couldn't you just try?"

"Sandy, there is nothing, and I repeat *nothing* in the world that could make me work for that sleazebag."

Sandy could see by the look on her face that the odds of his becoming a vice president had just gone from slim to none.

Plain Manila

New York City
1978

Barbara Zofko wandered down the hall in a lump and went back to her office. She sat down and pulled the sleeves of her gray cable-knit sweater up on her plump forearms, kicked off her shoes, and rolled a sheet of paper into her typewriter. She reached into the drawer and pulled out a chocolate chip cookie.

> Dear Ms. Nordstrom,
>   I could lose my job for doing this but I can no longer stand by without warning you ... Sidney Capello is a dangerous man. Please do not cross him. He will destroy you. I know what I am talking about. He is an evil man and *he will print this information*! I beg you to reconsider your decision.
>   A Friend

She picked up a plain manila envelope and put a copy of the Dena Nordstrom file in it. She searched for her shoes under her desk, found them, and went back to Sidney's office. He nodded his approval.

That Friday night, her doorman handed her the envelope. "Miss Nordstrom, a lady dropped this by for you earlier." She took it, with thanks.

As she rode up the sixteen floors she wiped a few raindrops off the sleeve of her coat and opened the envelope.

All her life she had lived with some low-grade dread, a fear of something unknown, and now here it was. That elusive shadow that had been chasing her like a big black dog had finally caught up with her. When the elevator doors opened on her floor she was almost unable to move. Terrified, her heart was pounding so hard she almost fell. When she somehow reached her door, her hand was shaking badly and she could hardly get the key in the lock. The door open, she walked in and slid down to the floor, leaning back against the wall. She could not believe it. Maybe this was someone's bad idea of a joke. Surely this could not be true. But there it was in black-and-white and with Capello's name attached to it.

As she sat there and the more she thought about it, she slowly began to realize this might not be a joke.

Maybe it was true. Maybe it *was* the reason her mother had been so frightened, had kept moving so much. Then Dena remembered what Aunt Elner had told her, about her mother speaking German. She felt sick and she was soaked with sweat. It was as if someone had opened a trapdoor and she was falling into space.

NORDSTROM . . . MARION CHAPMAN

MOTHER OF AMERICAN BROADCASTER DENA (GENE) NORDSTROM,

1939 NEW YORK CITY

SUSPECTED OF HAVING NAZI TIES

EMPLOYEE AND CLOSE ASSOCIATE OF STEINER . . . LILI

CARLOTTA, HIGH-RANKING OFFICIAL, AMERICAN NAZI PARTY

CONVICTED OF SPYING DEC. 13, 1946

SERVED TEN YEARS, DIED IN 1962

CHAPMAN HAD CLOSE CONTACT WITH KNOWN MEMBERS OF THE AMERICAN NAZI PARTY, SUSPECTED OF SPYING.

CHAPMAN/NORDSTROM REPORTED AS MISSING PERSON, JAN. 1960

WHEREABOUTS UNKNOWN.

It was happening to someone else. Nothing seemed real. After a moment she got up off the floor and called downstairs. She asked the doorman what the woman with the envelope looked like. He said, "I don't remember, exactly, she was just a, well . . . nondescript-looking kind of person." Dena sat down on the sofa, still in shock. She realized that even if this weren't true about her mother, it didn't matter. If the implications of this ever got printed, her career would be over. Just like that, everything she had worked for gone. She had seen it happen to a newscaster friend in Kentucky. A paper printed the fact that his father had been a member of the Ku Klux Klan and her friend's career was ended the next day.

Dena knew what Capello could do to her and the awful power he had. With this information, saying no to him would be playing Russian roulette with her life.

All night she struggled with herself, wondering what to do, trying to figure out a way to somehow compromise, to save herself. Maybe she should take the job. Maybe she could work for him.

But she knew that however hard she tried, and as much as she wanted a career, or did not want her name or her mother's dragged through the mud, she could not work for him. She could not let herself become a part of the garbage she knew that Sidney and Ira would be pushing on television to get ratings. Howard Kingsley had warned her, and he had been right. She couldn't do it, not only for her sake, but for Howard's sake. He had had too much faith in her. Besides, the real truth was, even if she were to take the job, Capello would never stop threatening her. He would own her for life. And she would rather be dead than have that happen.

When Sandy called again, on Capello's orders, Dena was particularly brave. She was as terrified as she had ever been but she still said no.

As always, there was a price to pay.

Secrets Can Kill

On Monday morning when the cleaning woman let herself into Dena's apartment, she was not prepared for what she saw. Blood was everywhere. Smeared on the walls, on the floor, in the hall. It looked as if a massacre had occurred. When she saw her employer lying on the floor in the doorway to the kitchen in a pool of dried blood, she ran out of the apartment screaming, "Missus Nordstrom's been murdered!" She ran down sixteen flights of stairs, shouting, "There's been a murder!" The doorman immediately called the police. He was reluctant to go up alone, worried that the murderer was still in her apartment. When the police arrived, they entered with guns drawn but nobody was there except her dead body, or at least what looked like her dead body. But when the doctor came and started to examine her, he looked up and said, "Call an ambulance. This girl is still alive."

The paramedics felt a weak pulse. She had lost so much blood the emergency room doctor did not hold out much hope, but he started a transfusion anyway. They checked her for bullet or stab wounds but could not find any. Later, they discovered that she had bleeding ulcers, one had hemorrhaged, and she had almost bled to death. They got her into emergency surgery.

As sick as Dena was, being unconscious was at least some relief from what she had been going through. She had tried not to think about the letter, but it had haunted her. She kept wondering when it might happen, would it happen. When she had gone to the market, she had been too frightened to look at the papers displayed right by the cash register. Would she wake one morning and it would be all over? At night she was haunted by the fact that what she had read might be true. How could it be true? But there were so many unanswered questions. Why did her mother even speak German? Who was that man in Elmwood Springs? Who was the man in the lobby her mother so feared? Why did her mother never let anyone take her picture? Why had her mother never told her she played the piano? She kept going over everything, like a movie that ran again and again. She could not get it out of her mind. Suddenly it seemed like everything about her mother that she had worked so hard to remember became suspicious. She cancelled all her appointments, including Dr. Diggers. The only way she could get any sleep was to drink until she passed out. At four o'clock in the morning on Monday, she sat up in bed and started to throw up blood and could not stop. She tried to crawl down her hall to buzz the doorman but became unconscious.

For days it was touch and go. She remained in the intensive care unit and on the critical list. Nobody knew if she would pull through but her doctors felt that after all the blood she had lost, it was a miracle she was alive at all. And Dena, who did not believe in God, much less in prayer, had the most unlikely people praying for her in the most unlikely of places. When it was announced on the news that she had been rushed to the hospital and was on the critical list, Peggy Hamilton called her husband, Charles, who was in Russia on a world crusade. That night, five thousand or more Russians, who barely spoke English, bowed their heads and prayed for a woman in New York they did not know. Elizabeth Diggers and the entire congregation of the AME Baptist Church on 105th Street said a prayer for her. Sandy Cooper did what a lot of people do when they are terrified of losing something; he started to make a lot of promises and vows he would keep if she lived. When Norma heard about it she was so frightened that she completely bypassed hysteria. She immediately picked up the phone and called her minister. That night in Elmwood Springs, people in all three of the churches came to do the only thing they knew to do. They prayed for her. Calls were made to the Unity Prayer Hot Line for Dena. In Selma, Alabama, Sookie, who was now on a first-name basis with Jesus Christ, had a lot to say, and just to be on the safe side, alerted all the Kappa Bible study groups in the country to say a special prayer for their sister. Sookie's mother, Lenore, instructed every board member of the local chapter of the International Coalition of Christians and Jews to pray and to get everyone they knew to pray for her as well, and as an afterthought, went right over poor Archbishop Lipscomb's head, saying to Sookie, "This is too serious to fool around with. We need to go straight to the top." The next day, a telegram arrived in Vatican City:

DEAR YOUR HOLINESS,

I NEED YOU TO PRAY FOR A FRIEND OF OURS WHO IS GRAVELY ILL. HER NAME IS DENA NORDSTROM AND I NEED YOU TO DO IT IMMEDIATELY IF NOT SOONER. THANKING YOU IN ADVANCE.

MRS. LENORE SIMMONS KRACKENBERRY

SELMA, ALABAMA

If God had been listening, it is most likely the prayer that might have done the trick was Aunt Elner's, who talked to God every day. She went out into her yard and looked up and said, "Please don't take her now, Lord. She's just getting started and that poor little thing has had so many hard knocks. And if you need a family member, just go ahead and take me. I'd be tickled to death to see you and I don't have a thing planned except for putting up some preserves. Other than that, I'm free as a bird to come on up."

After three days, Dena was taken off the critical list. Whether or not it had been all those prayers or the skill of the doctors, nobody could say for sure. But to put it in Elner's words, "It sure didn't hurt her any."

A lot of things went on during those long days that she was totally unaware of. Visitors came and went. Reporters and fans tried to get in, but were turned away. As usual when a celebrity gets sick, rumors spread that she had tried to kill herself, that she had overdosed on drugs, that she had suffered a nervous breakdown, that Julian had caught her in bed with another man and fired her. None were true, but it did give the gossips, professional and amateurs alike, something to talk about.

Julian Amsley had called several times and sent flowers, and he had come to the hospital once. But Gerry O'Malley came every day. He had been sitting outside Dena's room when an intern he had not seen before came down the hall and went into it. Gerry wondered what he was doing in there, and when he saw a flash of light go off, he knew. That son of a bitch had taken a picture. The "intern" came out and hurried down the hall toward the stairwell, but Gerry jumped up and grabbed him just as he hit the first step. Gerry said quietly, so as not to disturb the other patients in intensive care, "Hey, buddy, how about letting me have that camera?"

"Screw you," the guy said and he kept going. Gerry pulled him by the back of his smock down the stairs to the landing, where a nurse passing by heard a loud snap that sounded like someone had stepped on a twig. A minute later Gerry came back up the stairs with a camera and went over and sat back down.

Five minutes later, the fake intern, who was out a lot of money he could have made from the sale of that picture, was informed that he had a broken arm. He was lucky. When you attend military school, as Gerry had, you learn a few things. The guy should have been glad it had not been his neck.

And Dena never knew Gerry had been there.

Wake Up and Live

New York City
1978

When Dena woke, she wondered where she was. She could not quite figure it out. Then she heard a familiar voice.

"Well, hello there, Miss Hickory Nut." Dr. Diggers was sitting in the wheelchair by her bed. She smiled. "You sure scared the hell out of a lot of people."

Dena was groggy. "I did?"

"You did. Do you remember what happened?"

"No . . . kind of . . . no."

"You hemorrhaged and you passed out. Do you remember that?"

Dena was still confused.

"You just go on back to sleep and rest. You are going to be fine."

Macky and Norma had been packed, waiting for the doctor to tell them they could come, but he asked them to wait a little while longer until she was stronger. Sookie paid no attention to the doctor. The next day her brother, Buck, flew her to New York and when she walked in the room she burst into tears. Dena looked like a ghost. She had lost fifteen pounds in the past few days. After a while, when she had composed herself, Sookie sat by her bed. "Dena . . . you have just got to get better. If you die on me after I have crossed the Mason-Dixon line to come up here and see you, I'll just be furious!"

Sookie had cheered her up, but at night when Dena was all alone in her room, she was still filled with that old black dread. Dena knew she could not stay in New York. She had to get out, get as far away from Capello as she could. She needed time and distance to try and figure out what she was going to do. She had to do something or the fear would eventually kill her. Sookie begged her to come back to Selma for a while, but Dena found herself saying the oddest thing, something she had never even thought of saying. "Sookie, that is so sweet. But I really want to go home, can you understand? I really need to go home for a while."

She asked Dr. Diggers about it and she had agreed. "Dena, I think that's the best possible thing you could do right now." And, like a good omen, the next morning a telegram arrived:

YOUR ROOM IS READY. WHEN ARE YOU COMING?

LOVE, NORMA AND MACKY

The day before she was to leave, she heard a knock on her door. Gerry O'Malley came in the room with an enormous bouquet of roses.

"Hi. How are you doing?"

"Hi, come on in. I'm fine. Or nearly fine."

"I heard you were pretty sick."

"Yes. I was ... but I'm leaving tomorrow, going to Elmwood Springs."

"Yes, that's what I heard." He put the flowers down on a chair.

"Thank you, they're beautiful. I'll get a nurse to put them in some water."

Gerry was happy to see that she looked a hundred percent better than the last time, when she was still unconscious. Color had come back into her cheeks and the sight of her sitting there in bed looking like her old self took his breath away. He was suddenly nervous.

"So, I heard you were pretty sick."

"Yes, I was. Bleeding ulcer."

"That's what I heard. Elizabeth Diggers said you were really sick."

"Yes, I was."

"Well, you look good. How do you feel?"

"Much better."

"I just dropped by to see how you were doing. When do you think you're coming back?"

"I don't know. I'm really not sure."

"Ah . . . well. If there's anything I can do for you while you are gone, just let me know. You have my number. Just call . . . and, uh, call me and let me know how you are doing. If you think about it. Or call Dr. Diggers. Keep us posted, OK?"

"I will."

❖ ❖ ❖

Gerry left the hospital, aching. He knew by looking in her eyes that she was a hundred miles away. He had no idea when he would see her again or if he would ever see her again, and there was not a thing he could do about it. He had the feeling it was hopeless, but so much in love, he still hoped that maybe someday, some year, she might give him another chance.

That night Dena could not sleep. As she lay in the room, waiting for daylight to come, she thought about what Elizabeth Diggers had asked her that first time. Who are you? She thought she had known then. But who was she now? She had no idea. She had lost herself somewhere along the way.

She was like the front of a bombed-out building, still standing but empty inside. All she knew was the truth of what Dr. DeBakey had told her. If she didn't slow down, she'd be dead. She had come close.

The next morning, good old Buck flew to New York again and picked her up and flew her home. To Elmwood Springs.

Good-Luck Clover

It was good to be here. It was quiet in her room. The weather was warm. She went to sleep with her windows open and slept soundly all through the night. On the fourth day she awakened at seven and felt strong enough to get up. She went downstairs to the kitchen. Norma said, "Baby Girl, what are you doing up so early?"

"I couldn't go back to sleep, but I feel better."

"Well, the kitchen is a mess, but come on in if you can stand it."

Dena noticed one cup and a saucer in the sink; other than that it was, as usual, spotless, but Norma, horrified, quickly rinsed them off and put them in the dishwasher.

"Sorry the place is such a wreck but I got a little behind this morning. Aunt Elner has already been on the phone three times wanting to know how you are doing. She wants you to come over there and see her. She's all excited because she found a four-leaf clover in her front yard and she wants to show it to you, as if you have never seen a four-leaf clover before in your life."

Dena sat down and a red and white plastic mat was placed in front of her. "Actually, I don't think I ever have."

"Really? Well, she's all worked up about it." Norma opened the icebox and pulled out the eggs and milk. "I don't know how she can see well enough to find one. Imagine, at her age. I couldn't find one even with my glasses on, but she has eyes like a hawk. She keeps saying she doesn't need glasses, but I wanted her checked so last year I carried her to see the eye doctor, Dr. Mitton. He sat her down and said, 'Mrs. Shimfessle, just how far can you see at a distance?' And she said, 'Well, Doctor, I can see all the way to the moon, how far away is that?' "

After a big breakfast, Dena decided to walk over to Aunt Elner's house. People waved to her as she went by and said, "Good morning." As she paused on the porch, she could hear Aunt Elner in the kitchen singing away. She knocked on the screen door. Aunt Elner and Sonny, the cat, came to the door.

"Well, hey, there, Baby Girl, come on in!"

Elner was wearing a faded floral blue and white housedress and white mesh tie-up shoes. The house smelled like bacon.

"Have a seat if you can find one. Let me go in and turn my bacon off."

Dena went into the living room and sat down. Elner came back. "Would you rather go out and sit on the porch? I'm a terrible housekeeper; Norma says it looks like someone had an epileptic fit in every room. She won't come over here anymore, says it makes her a nervous wreck. She says if I won't let her clean the house, she won't come, but whenever she cleans up I can't find anything for a week. I'd offer you bacon but I have strict orders not to feed you. But I do have something I want to give you."

Aunt Elner came back with a little white bowl full of water with a four-leaf clover floating on top.

"I found it this morning and I said, I'm giving it to Baby Girl, for good luck."

"Thank you, Aunt Elner, that's very sweet."

"Well, that's all right, honey, bless your heart. You need a little good luck to come your way. How are you doing? You look good. But I worry about you; are you getting enough to eat? Is Norma feeding you?"

"I'm getting plenty to eat, and more."

"Well, good. I was worried about that. I can fix you a biscuit."

"No, I'm fine, Aunt Elner."

"Norma doesn't eat enough to keep a twig alive, and on top of it she runs around all day cleaning and scrubbing and sweeping."

"She's a good housekeeper, all right."

"Too good, if you ask me; she's a neat-aholic. I told her, I said, 'Norma, if you were to have a heart attack before you'd done your breakfast dishes, you'd wait until you did them to call the ambulance.' I'll tell you, when the chips are down, you want to get in her boat. Little things drive her crazy, but in a natural disaster, she calms right down when everybody else around her is falling apart. That's when Norma is at her best."

"What kind of natural disaster?"

"Any kind, you name it. A while back when we had all those terrible floods and so many people lost their homes, Norma went down to the high school auditorium and had it organized into a shelter and a hospital in no time. She had it up and running. Set up a hot line for people to call, organized groups of men to go out in boats and find everybody that wasn't accounted for, handled all the food supplies and medical supplies, saved all kinds of lives."

"Really?"

"Oh, yes. When the Red Cross finally were able to get in, she had it all under control. She got awards but she won't tell you. But take my word for it: in a natural disaster, Norma Warren is who you want to be with. She has an earthquake kit that you wouldn't believe."

"Are there earthquakes here?"

"There was one a hundred years ago but if there is ever another one, Norma's ready. She's prepared for a tornado, a drought, floods, the atomic bomb, germ warfare; you name it, she's ready for it!"

"Well, that's good to know."

"You're not gonna run off back to New York, are you?"

"I'm not sure."

"I wish you'd stay here with us. Nobody's gonna bother you; Macky Warren has seen to that. In fact, the whole town is gonna see to that. This is your home. You don't need to be pestered to death in your own hometown."

❖   ❖   ❖

As Dena walked home with her four-leaf clover she wondered to herself just what she was going to do. So many people had offered her a place to stay. Lee Kingsley had offered her their guest house in Sag Harbor for the summer, the Hamiltons had a place on Sea Island, Georgia, and Sookie's brother, Buck, and his wife had offered her their house on Mobile Bay. She had thought it might be good to be alone, but now she was finding that it was ... sort of nice to have relatives around. She began to toy with the idea of maybe staying in Elmwood Springs for a while. Maybe she would even find some place she could rent for a few months.

When she got back to Norma's she looked in the phone book and saw an ad in the small, two-page business section. It had a picture of a woman in a hat, talking on the phone, that said FOR ALL YOUR REAL ESTATE NEEDS, CALL BEVERLY. Two weeks later, when Macky and Norma had gone out of town for a hardware convention, she called Beverly.

❖ ❖ ❖

Beverly showed up wearing a huge hat and driving a big blue Lincoln. The passenger seat was cluttered with brochures, newspaper ads, signs, and listings books. She was elated to have a potential customer, especially Dena, and quickly made room for her by tossing everything into the backseat.

"Well, am I happy to meet you. When my husband and I first moved here, we heard this was where you were from and I always hoped you'd come back."

Beverly was a dynamo and within an hour they had seen everything. They looked at a duplex, even a condo, and several new apartments way out by the mall, but Dena did not warm to any of them. They were too cold and sterile. Beverly was stumped. "We just don't have that many apartment rentals here."

Dena said, "Do you have any houses?"

"Houses? Would you want a whole house?"

"I don't know, maybe. Are there any for rent?"

"Let's see. I do have a little one ... but it's way out in the country. And you don't want that. I have one in town. I can show you that if you like. Now, I don't know what kind of shape it's in but we can look."

They drove to the older section of town. Large elm trees lined the street and Beverly stopped and parked in front of a white frame house with a green and white awning around the front porch. Beverly rummaged around in her large black purse, searching through what looked like hundreds of keys. "The other girl in the office has the listing. The owner's a friend of hers. . . . I'm sure that key is here somewhere. Anyhow." She rattled on about the place as she continued looking. "The house stayed in the family. The daughter and her family lived here up until a couple of months ago, but her husband got emphysema so bad they had to move to Arizona—I'll kill myself if I have lost that key—anyhow, they said they would rent it. . . ." She finally gave up. "I don't have that darn key but I'm sure we can get in." They got out of the car. "It might be a little big for you but it's in a nice old neighborhood. You don't see many houses these days with two swings, do you?" As Beverly tried the door, Dena noticed something written on the front window that she could barely read. She walked over to look closely and could just make out WDOT RADIO STATION, NUMBER 66 ON YOUR DIAL. Beverly, who was rattling furiously and pushing on the door, noticed what she was looking at. "They say a woman who used to live here had a radio show but that was before we got here." Finally, with one more push the door opened.

"Here we go. I didn't think she locked it. Come on in." It was dark inside, all the curtains drawn, and as Beverly quickly went around the front room opening them, Dena noticed a certain smell, a sweet smell, as if someone had been baking. The house still had the original venetian blinds. The curtains in the living room were thick and floral, green and yellow and maroon, with what looked like palm leaves. There was some furniture left. A small desk was in the living room over by the window; and a little telephone table in a small alcove in the hall off the living room; and several old Aladdin lamps, yellow with white flowers; and a stand-up lamp in the living room that still had the original shade, maroon, and with a maroon silk ruffle around the top and the bottom. Beverly switched it on and the old lamp gave off a soft yellow light, almost golden in color, not like the harsh blue white glare of all the new lamps.

As Beverly turned on more lamps, all the light seemed to glow in a soft, muted way that somehow Dena found soothing. They walked down the hall and Beverly turned on the single hanging lightbulb. "Look at that old cedar chest. I just love the smell of those things, don't you?" They had walked into a bedroom and Beverly had some difficulty opening the closet door, but a pro, she made light of the wobbly, old glass doorknob that had come off in her hand by cheerfully pointing out another feature. "One of the wonderful things about these old houses is that all the closets are cedar, too." Dena looked inside and the closet was huge and dry and the mothball smell was still there, fresh after all these years. Beverly pointed to a small white saucer with a dozen large mothballs in it. "Look at those, I haven't seen those in years." It was obvious that Beverly had never been in this house but was doing such a good job of faking it that Dena had to admire her for trying. "The great thing about these old houses is that they built them to last."

"When was this built, do you think?"

"Oh, I'd say probably around 1925, no later than the thirties, I would guess by the transoms over the doors and the wallpaper. I think this is the original wallpaper. I remember my grandmother had this same paper so it had to be somewhere in the twenties." There was one chest of drawers in the second bedroom. Dena opened a drawer and the scent of old-fashioned talcum powder came to her. The ceilings were about twelve feet high. Dena had lived in apartments and hotel rooms so long she had forgotten about high ceilings. It seemed so strange to have all that space up there. The floors were in excellent condition, a beautiful oak. All the rugs were gone but she could see where they had been. She noticed a few brown stains on the wallpaper in some of the bedrooms, but other than that the house was in pretty good shape. The bathrooms all had the huge claw-foot bathtubs and large pedestal sinks.

The dining room's brass chandelier had four milk-glass shades with Dutch scenes on them, and the living room had a round, pink glass ceiling fixture that Dena liked.

They walked to the back of the house. As soon as they entered the kitchen, Dena said, "Smell that? Someone has been baking a cake or something in here." Beverly sniffed a few times. "No, I don't smell anything." The kitchen was huge; a lone lightbulb hung over the white wooden table. There was a big white enamel sink and drain board with a floral-print skirt around it, a huge icebox, and a 1920s white O'Keefe & Merritt stove in perfect condition. "Look at this pretty stove," Beverly said, and she turned on one of the burners. The flames popped right up. "And it works, too!" Dena looked in a drawer and there was an old O'Keefe & Merritt cookbook still there. They walked out of the kitchen onto a large, screened-in back porch and saw that beyond the backyard there was a field. Beverly said, "Oh, look, there's an old sweetheart swing. I just love those, don't you?"

"Oh, yes," said Dena, not having any idea what a sweetheart swing was.

"They say there used to be a big radio tower out in the backyard and that people could see it for miles around."

"Really?" Dena went back to the front porch and sat on the swing by the window with the writing on it and waited for Beverly to finish locking up. When Beverly emerged, Dena said, "I'll take it."

"Oh. When would you want it?"

"Today, if possible."

"Oh," said Beverly.

❖ ❖ ❖

That afternoon after Dena had signed the lease, she went through the house again. She still could not believe she had actually rented an entire empty house, never having lived in a house that she could remember. She went from room to room. She opened the cabinets in the kitchen and found a few white cups and saucers, and three little plates that had TROLLEY CAR DINER around the edge. There were several pictures hanging on the walls and a few small blue glass violin-shaped vases in the windows that had some sort of dried-out plants hanging over the sides. On the wall outside on the back porch was a 1954 calendar with a picture of a little boy in his pajamas holding a tire and small candle, and the name of the sponsor, Goodyear Tire Co. In the living room was a picture of a cottage with flowers covering a white picket fence, and in the room off the front porch there was hanging a movie-magazine picture that someone had framed of Dana Andrews. Down the hall was a print of an Indian on a pony sitting on the top of a cliff with his head hanging down, captioned END OF THE TRAIL.

Up in the attic was a dog's bed, boxes of Christmas decorations, and a few diving trophies that read, FIRST PLACE, CASCADE PLUNGE, 1947, 1948, 1949. Other than that there was little trace of the people who had once lived there, only the smells that had somehow permeated the walls and the floors. The back porch still retained the pungent, sweet smell of grape Kool-Aid. Dena sat in the living room in a chair she had found and looked at the stripes of sunlight on the floor, shining through the old venetian blinds. She sat there until it got dark and turned on a lamp. She hated to leave. There was a feeling, an atmosphere, something in the air that calmed her. The house smelled familiar, it felt familiar, almost as if she had been there before. The air inside that house held the faint memory of a dream she might have had.

A New Friend

The next day, Aunt Elner's friend, Merle, brought over a couple of old mattresses and a hideous brown sofa that Dena had bought at the Goodwill store out on the highway just so she'd have something to sleep on and sit on until she figured out what all she wanted to put in the house. She borrowed some sheets and a few pillows from Norma's linen closet. After Merle left, Dena walked down to the grocery store and bought coffee, cream, milk, eggs, and a few frozen dinners, and came home and wandered around the house. Beverly had left her a coffee pot, a box of cornflakes, and some bananas. Dena found a bucket and Octagon soap under the sink and started cleaning the venetian blinds. They were in perfect shape and still had the original plastic bell-like pulls on the ends of their thick cords. While she was cleaning, she looked up and saw a black-and-white cat sitting in the window glaring at her. Dena walked to the front door and opened it and the cat shot by her into the house, like a person trying to get the best seat in a crowded bus. There was a green, tin wastebasket with a picture of a cocker spaniel on it in the living room that had tipped over, and the cat ran over and curled up inside of it and went right to sleep, highly indignant that it had to wait so long to get in the house. Dena was a little afraid of it and left it alone.

A few minutes past three, Dena heard a knock on her door. "Yoo-hoo." Dena saw a tiny woman of about sixty-five standing at the door. "I'm Tot, your next-door neighbor. I'm not going to bother you. I'm just going to drop this off and run. I know you are busy."

Dena opened the screen door. "I'm not busy. Was just doing a little cleaning; please come in."

"Well, I'll just stick this in the kitchen for you. I figured you might not want to go out so I brought you this just to have in case you get hungry. I know you have a bad stomach so I made you a cream-chicken-noodle ring. If you need anything, anything at all, just holler." Tot was in the kitchen by now and was putting the food in the refrigerator. "Just heat it up a little when you're hungry. I'm not going to bother you, I promise, but I just wanted you to know that we're right next door." As she walked back through the house she looked in the living room. "Oh, I see B.T. is here." She laughed. "That's one of my crazy cats. I hope she's not a bother. She doesn't like everybody but she seems to have taken a liking to you. That's good luck, you know, but if she gets in your way just throw her out. But I can tell you right now it won't do a bit of good. I hope you like this house, it's a friendly old place." Tot was at the door. "I just hated to see it standing here empty. Anna Lee and her husband had to move to Arizona."

Finally Dena got a word in. "Yes, I heard."

"All the neighbors are thrilled you are here and we're not going to bother you. You don't remember me but I remember you when you were just a tiny thing. Well, come over if you need anything."

Dena watched as Tot walked back to her house. Then she went into the sunroom and went back to the blinds. She opened them and she could see the outline of the round rug that used to be on the floor and evidently a sofa. At about six-thirty, she was tired. She went out in the yard and sat in the swing and watched the sun go down over the field. When she came back in, she remembered the casserole, turned on the oven and heated it up, and ate almost the entire thing.

As she sat at the table she noticed how quiet it was in the kitchen. All she could hear was the ticking of the clock on the stove. When she felt something under the table brush against her leg, she almost jumped out of her skin. She looked down and saw the cat, rubbing back and forth on her leg, looking up at her and meowing. Dena said, "Good God, cat—you better go home." She went to the back door and opened it. "Go on, kitty, go on home, go on . . ." The cat just looked at her. Dena stood there with the door open but the cat would not budge. Finally, Dena closed the door and sat back down and tried to finish eating but the cat kept staring at her and meowing so Dena gave the cat what was left. After the cat ate, Dena opened the door again. "Don't you have to go to the bathroom or something?" But the cat cleaned its paws and ignored her.

Dena walked around the house turning on all the lights. The four milk-glass shades of the little brass chandelier in the dining room had turned slightly yellow with age and gave off the most beautiful glow. The dining room had a bay window with white sheer swag curtains that looked pretty at night. She walked from room to room thinking about furniture she might put in them. It was so quiet. After a while she went out on the front porch and sat in the swing. The cat appeared at the front door and pushed her way out and went down the stairs and into the yard. A few minutes later the cat came back and sat on the porch with Dena. It was a warm and balmy evening but a small breeze kept the air moving and she could smell the flowers that were just starting to bloom on the side of the house. A few cars drove by; other than that, there was no activity.

At about eleven o'clock she and the cat went inside. She went in the bathroom and ran the water for a bath. The deep white tub had a round white rubber stopper on a beaded metal chain. It took a long time to fill up and when she got in and sat down, the water was almost up to her neck and she had to laugh. It was like getting into a small swimming pool. After her bath she went into the bedroom and took her nightgown out of the chest of drawers. It had picked up just a slight aroma of talcum powder. She bent down to pull her bed covers back. The cat jumped up on the bed and crawled under the sheet. A minute later, she felt something pushing at her arm and heard the cat purring away, happy and contented to have her for a bed partner. She reached over and petted it. She had not slept with a cat since that night so many years ago at her mother's friend Christine's apartment, when Christine's cat, Milton, had slept beside her in the living room. It felt good.

The Circus Cake

Elmwood Springs, Missouri
1978

In the morning she went over to pick up a little ivy plant for her window that Aunt Elner wanted her to have. Aunt Elner was overjoyed she was going to be so close by. "I'm just tickled to death you are going to be living in Neighbor Dorothy's old house. Oh, honey, many is the broadcast I heard from there."

"Was there a studio there or something?"

Aunt Elner sat down at her kitchen table. "I don't know if it was a studio or not, it was just in her living room. That's where the show came from, every day from nine-thirty to ten, like clockwork. I never missed."

Dena reached over and took a fresh biscuit. "What was it, a kind of news show?"

"A news show? I guess you could call it that. But she had all kinds of things on there. She had music—there used to be an organ in the living room that Mother Smith played, but after Mother Smith died they gave it to the church. And all kinds of people used to sing or play or do whatever they had a mind to. She gave out household hints, recipes, and had talks."

"What kind of talks?"

"Oh, all kinds—Ruby Robinson, the radio nurse, would give

health talks—and Audrey would give religious talks. Anybody that wanted to come on and talk on the radio could. People used to stick their heads in the window and chat about things."

"Things like what?"

Aunt Elner laughed. "I don't know, somebody might have lost a dog or wanted to announce a pot luck or something."

"What's a pot luck?"

"Don't you know what a pot luck is? Don't they have them in New York?"

"I don't know, what are they?"

"It's just a dinner where everybody brings something. We have one up at the church the first Friday of every month. Why don't you come? It's a lot of fun. You never know what all they might have to eat; it changes every month. One time Bess Truman came."

"To the pot luck?"

"No, on the 'Neighbor Dorothy' show. All kinds of people would come on, people would send in letters. She had contests where you could win a sack of flour. She put out a real good cookbook. I lost mine but Norma may still have hers."

"What was she like?"

"Who?"

"Neighbor Dorothy."

"Oh, she was just a nice lady, had two children . . ."

"What did she sound like?"

"Real sweet, like she was glad you were listening. It's too bad they didn't have tape recorders back then, I'd love to hear one of her old programs again. I sure do miss not hearing her. I got used to hearing her. Neighbor Dorothy was a lot of company, I can tell you that. Not that I didn't love living on the farm while Will was alive, but one of the bad parts about living way out in the country is I'd get so lonesome for people. My closest neighbor was twelve miles up the road. Will wasn't much of a talker and I used to be starved for the sound of another person's voice. If it hadn't been for Neighbor Dorothy's show, I would have been twice as lonesome for sure. It was like having a next-door neighbor to visit with every day. Made it easier to get through the days all by yourself out there. And at night, you could see the red light on the radio tower she had in her yard all the way out at the farm. I don't know what kind of a show you'd call it but it always made me feel better. Eat all the biscuits you want, honey, I was just going to give them to the birds."

Dena took another one and put butter and jam on it.

"Did you ever meet her, Aunt Elner? Neighbor Dorothy?"

"Oh, lands, yes. She was a good friend of your grandmother's." She looked at Dena. "Come to think of it, you met her, too; don't you remember?"

"No. When?"

"Oh, lots of times. Anna Lee, her daughter, and her friend, Patsy, ran a little nursery school out there on the back porch. That's where you used to go to nursery school. Don't you remember going there?"

"Are you sure it was me?"

"Yes, I'm sure. I can even remember one time, you must have been four, and you had your birthday party there with all your little nursery school friends. Your mother dressed you up like a china doll; she was working at Morgan Brothers department store, and kept you in the cutest dresses. Your grandparents came, your mother got off work early so she could be there, I came, Norma came, we all came."

Dena was surprised. "Really?"

"You were so happy, a happy little child, and you were such a sweet little thing, not one bit spoiled."

"I was happy?"

"Oh, yes. I think that was the happiest time of all our lives when we had our Baby Girl with us. We sure hated to lose you, I can tell you that."

"I don't remember ever having a birthday party."

"You sure did. You know, I might have a picture in Gerta's things. I think we took a picture that day if I'm not mistaken. Hold on and let me go get that box. I'll go look in my bottom drawer, see if I can't find it."

Dena could hear her opening and closing drawers.

Then she said, "Here it is!" and came back into the kitchen and handed a photograph to Dena. "Looka there. Now if that isn't you, a happy child, I'm a monkey's uncle."

Dena looked. It was a picture of a little blond girl sitting at the end of a small table full of other children. The girl was her and there was her mother, leaning against the wall with her arms behind her. Her head was turned toward Dena and she was smiling and looking at her with love in her eyes. The photograph had captured her mother in an unguarded moment. Dena had never seen her mother look at her like that; she had never felt that love she saw now.

Something else in the picture caught her eye. It was a cake with what looked to be a miniature merry-go-round on top.

"What's this?"

"Neighbor Dorothy made you that. She made you one of her famous carousel cakes. It was pink and white; you remember that, don't you?"

On the way home Dena tried to remember what it was. There was something familiar about that cake and yet she couldn't quite place it. It was something she had seen before. Then, all of a sudden, it hit her. She knew what it was.

When Dena got to the house, she walked out on the back porch and stood there, staring at the picture in her hand, and cried. This was the same merry-go-round she had been dreaming about for years. This was the place she had been trying to get back to, where she had once been happy.

Welcome to the World, Baby Girl!

Elmwood Springs, Missouri
1944

"Good morning, everybody. It's another beautiful day here in Elmwood Springs and we have hardly been able to contain ourselves waiting for this morning.... We are so full of good news today, you will think I made it all up. First of all, I want to start by saying a great big welcome to the world to little Miss Dena Gene Nordstrom, who entered into the human race yesterday afternoon at four-twenty. The baby girl is the brand-new granddaughter of Lodor and Gerta Nordstrom and the daughter of their son, Gene. We all remember what all we went through when we lost Gene in the war ... but by some miracle we have a little piece of him back, a part of him lives on ... and we couldn't be happier. Gerta says that as soon as baby Dena is able to travel, her mother will be bringing her to Elmwood Springs and we can't wait to see you, so hurry up and get here so we can all give you a proper welcome. Also, yesterday we received a letter all the way from Canada. Last month a Mrs. D. Yeager said she was switching her dial when she heard us as clear as a bell ... it was such good radio weather. Don't faint, but Bobby actually got an *A* in deportment. Don't ask me how, and we have lots more good news. We have a big winner in the Who's the Most Interesting Guest You Ever Had in Your Home? contest. Wait until you hear this one—

and I know it's not nice to toot one's own horn but—Mother Smith and I are so proud of Doc. He has won the Rexall award for proficiency in dispensing drugs for the second year in a row. So if you are listening down there at the drugstore . . . Doc: we are mighty proud of you.

"And now here are the Goodnight Twins to sing for you that old favorite, 'I'll Keep a Light Burning in the Window, Dear, 'Cause I'm Still in Love with You.' "

Not Yet

As the days went by, Dena sat with the cat, whose name turned out to be Bottle Top III, wondering what she was going to do with the rest of her life. She had not thought much about life other than her work and pushing for success. It had never occurred to her what she could do without either. What was left? Who was left? She had even forgotten why she had wanted to succeed in the first place, and why was she so devastated to think of life without success? What difference did it make anyhow? What difference did it make if she lived or died, for that matter? Nothing lasts, what's the point?

After the first week in the house, Norma had brought over an old copy of *The Neighbor Dorothy Cookbook*. Lately, Dena had spent hours staring at the picture of the smiling lady on the cover. Her eyes seemed to be looking right at Dena. She looked so alive—but she was gone. Where had she gone? She was here, she was gone, and nothing was left, just a place where she used to live. Dena began to wonder about the past. Was it gone forever? Or late at night, when all was dark and still, did it come back? When the house stood empty, did the past suddenly come flooding back into the rooms? Was Neighbor Dorothy still there somewhere, her voice still up in the air? Dena didn't know. All she knew was that she felt the presence of something in that house. She did not feel alone. Maybe it was someone there or maybe, thought Dena, she was slowly losing her mind. But whatever it was, it did not scare her and that was some relief, not to be afraid.

In the meantime she waited and listened. And, sometimes, she thought she heard things. It had happened the first week, early in the morning. At about four-thirty she sat up in bed and she could have sworn she heard someone rattling around in the kitchen. She looked over and Bottle Top was in bed with her, so it wasn't the cat. She got up and as she walked down the hall, she could have sworn she smelled coffee brewing. But when she got in the kitchen and turned on the light, no one was there. There were times she thought she heard someone singing or the screen door slam or a sound like someone bouncing a ball against the house, but when she went to look, there was never anyone there. As the weeks went by, New York and the Ira Wallaces and the Sidney Capellos of the world seemed farther and farther away. When she had arrived in Elmwood Springs, her nerves were in such bad shape that any loud noise caused her to jump. But now, she felt safe here, a million miles away from the real world with its harsh lights and loud noises. As her ears adjusted to the quiet she began to hear other sounds—birds, crickets, and at times the sound of children playing. She could hear the church bells and lately she could even tell which bells were ringing, the Unity, the Methodist, or the Lutheran. Each had a distinctive sound.

She would sit for hours late at night with nothing but the orange glow of the radio light in the room, listening to the pleasant voices of strangers talking about God or the weather or crops. There was something so intimate about being in the dark with this talk about God that she almost began to be seduced into believing that they were telling her the truth. Her days were long. She had not known days could be so long. She woke up with the sun and watched the sunsets and the moon and the stars come out, amazed each time.

She sat in every corner, looking at the light from every angle. At night she began experimenting with the lighting in each room. She loved to put lamps against the honey-colored pine walls of one room; it looked so inviting.

Sometimes, she would go outside and stand on the lawn, looking in at the house with the lights on, and a wave of homesickness would sweep over her, a feeling so powerful it brought tears to her eyes. She would stand alone and cry, not knowing what she was crying about, or what she was homesick for. She began to feel like she did after she had been to the dentist and the Novocain started to wear off; it was painful, but a bittersweet pain. Slowly she was beginning to feel like the girl she used to be, the one that had gotten lost along the way.

❊ ❊ ❊

Fall approached and the network kept calling Sandy, wanting to know when she was coming back. She sent him a telegram.

DEAR SANDY,
TELL THEM I'M SORRY BUT THEY WILL HAVE TO START THE FALL
SEASON WITHOUT ME. I FIND THAT I CANNOT COME BACK AT THIS
TIME. NOT YET.
LOVE, DENA

The Middleman

Elmwood Springs, Missouri
1978

Dr. Diggers had told Dena to take her time making any decisions about her future, but as the weeks went by and she began to feel stronger, it became clearer and clearer to her what she had to do first. She had to find out the truth about her mother. She had to find out for herself what had happened. As painful as it might be, she had to know before she could make any decisions about what to do next.

But she needed help. She needed someone she could trust. Someone who was not in the business, someone who wouldn't turn around and sell information or talk to the press or simply talk. God, how she wished Howard were still alive.

On September 21 she was sitting out in the yard in the sweetheart swing, when a name popped into her head: Gerry O'Malley. The more she thought about it, the better the idea became. She didn't know him all that well, but she trusted him. He certainly was not connected to the television business. She had been his patient; anything she told him should be privileged information, shouldn't it? That night when Dr. Diggers called Dena asked, "You know Gerry O'Malley very well, don't you?"

"Yes, why?"

"Do you trust him?"

"With my life. Why?"

Dena told her that she had decided to find out about her mother. Dr. Diggers was pleased; this was what she had hoped for. "Good for you. Is there anything I can do?"

"Thank you, but the problem is I can't look for her myself, for obvious reasons. What I need is to find someone to be a middleman who would be willing to say that it was *his* relative he was looking for so my name would not be involved. Do you think Gerry would help if I asked him?"

Diggers thought that Gerry would probably jump off the Chrysler Building backward if Dena asked. She said, "Call him. Now."

❧ ❧ ❧

He answered right away.

"Gerry, it's Dena."

"Well, hello," he said again. "Are you back?"

"I'm still in Missouri."

"Are you coming back soon?"

"Gerry, that's just it. I don't know. I have a problem. Well, a big problem—and I need some help."

"Oh," he said and reached over and put on his lucky red baseball cap. "What's going on?"

She told him everything about her mother disappearing and read the letter she had gotten from Capello. Gerry said, "Who is this idiot?"

"He's a man I know and he's dangerous."

"But that's just a bunch of stuff he's trying to scare you with. You know it's not true. Why can't you call his bluff?"

"Because I don't know if it's true or not."

"What do you mean?"

"Well . . . my mother did speak German."

"So?"

"And she didn't like to have her picture taken."

"Dena," Gerry said, "a lot of people don't like to have their picture taken. Don't let this creep freak you out. Your mother was no more a spy than I am."

"Gerry, you didn't know her. *I* didn't know her, really. I always felt that there was something . . . wrong. Why else would somebody just run off like that?"

"There could be a thousand different reasons. Maybe she met a guy. Maybe she just didn't want to be a mother anymore; it happens all the time. Who knows what her reason was. But Dena, you can't let this jerk drive you out of your job. If you don't want to go back, that's one thing, but this is blackmail! You can't let him get away with it."

"I have to," Dena said. "I don't have a choice."

"Sure, you do. Come on, there has to be something. Talk to a lawyer. Sue him for defamation of character."

"You don't know Sidney. He would love for me to sue him, get it on public record."

"But it's not true."

"It doesn't have to be true. Besides, I don't want my mother's name dragged through the papers. And my name would make it news. There is nothing I can do, believe me. Don't you understand? I can't fight him. It would kill me. I don't have the strength to do it anymore."

Gerry realized she was right.

"No, of course you can't. What am I thinking about? Sorry, it's just that I'd like to kill this guy. But don't worry, we'll figure out a way so you won't be involved. You just forget about this sicko, he's not worth your getting ill again. Let's concentrate on what we can do for you so you won't have to think about this anymore. The first thing we need to do is to find out what happened to your mother. And then we'll figure out what to do about this character. Dena, do you trust me?"

"Yes."

"OK. I want you to sit tight and let me handle this thing for you. I have a friend in Washington I can call, somebody I went to school with who will know exactly what to do. And I promise you, you can trust him, too. The sooner we find out, the better, so you never have to guess or wonder, you'll know once and for all. OK? Are you up for that?"

"Yes . . . I think I am."

"Here you have been living with this thing all these years, all by yourself, but you're not alone anymore. I'm with you, do you hear me?"

Dena felt as if a hundred-pound weight had been lifted off her chest. "Yes."

❀ ❀ ❀

Macky, Norma, and Aunt Elner were in the living room when Dena told them that she had decided to try and find out more about her mother. Aunt Elner's response to that news was "Well, she was a pretty thing, I can tell you that. When she stepped down off that train . . . we all said that, didn't we, Norma?"

Norma looked at Macky with a horrified expression.

Macky slowly leaned forward in the chair and said, thoughtfully, "Baby Girl, if that's what you want to do, then that's what you need to do." Norma became very nervous and stood up and said, "I think we should all take a walk. I don't know about all of you but I'm stuffed; they say it's good to walk after a big dinner."

"Sit down a minute, Norma," Macky said. "Dena, is there any particular reason other than I'm sure you'd like to know what happened to her?"

She had not told them about Capello's threat. "I just think it's time I found out. I'd like to know if there's a chance she's still alive. I know my grandfather hired some people and they didn't find her but that was what? Twenty-some years ago? They have all kinds of new ways to track people now."

"So you're definitely gonna go ahead with this thing?" Macky said.

"Yes, I think so. Unless there's some reason I shouldn't?"

Norma wailed, "Oh, I just knew we would make the wrong decision, no matter what we did. I told Macky that at the time. Now look what's happened."

"Norma, calm down, nobody's made a wrong decision. Just go get the box."

Dena appealed to Macky. "What's she talking about?"

Norma stood up and started for the bedroom, muttering under

her breath, "I am going to have a complete nervous breakdown before I die, I just know it."

Aunt Elner, not really clear what was going on, smiled. "I'll tell you one thing about your mother, she was a pretty thing, had that little hat sitting on the side of her head. It looked just like a little pancake with a net on it."

Norma came back in and handed Macky a tin box. "Here, you give it to her, I can't."

"What is it?" asked Dena.

"It's a letter, Baby Girl," Macky said, "from the detective agency your grandfather hired. I didn't think it would do you any good to see it at the time but now, if you're gonna go ahead with this thing, you need to know about it." He took the letter out of the envelope.

Norma said, "Does anybody else besides me want any more coffee? I know I shouldn't have any but I've got to have something."

Dena skimmed the letter. One sentence jumped out at her: *According to our records, no such person exists.*

"Macky, what does that mean?"

"It means that for some reason she was using a different name than her own."

Aunt Elner said, "Maybe she didn't like her real name. I know if I hadn't married a Shimfessle, I would never have called myself that. I would have changed it to Jones . . . but I didn't tell them that!"

❈ ❈ ❈

The next afternoon, Dena's phone rang.

"Miss Nordstrom?"

"Yes?"

"This is Richard Look with the State Department."

Dena's heart pounded. "Yes?"

"I understand from Gerry O'Malley that you might need a little help locating someone?"

Dena found herself relieved he had not called to tell her anything specific. She was not as ready to find out the truth as she had thought. She sat down and the cat jumped up in her lap. "Yes, what has Gerry told you?"

"Miss Nordstrom, just so you know, Gerry informed me of the entire situation and I understand completely the need for confidentiality. I can assure you, your name will be kept out of the investigation."

The word *investigation* made her uneasy but she said, "Thank you, I really appreciate that. Did he tell you about the letter?"

"The German spy stuff? Yes, but don't worry, we've handled these kinds of things before. We'll get to the bottom of this and we'll do it without involving you, I can promise you that. All I need you to do for me is to send whatever you have—papers, letters, photographs, the names of any friends or anyone who might have known her. Sometimes they can tell you much more than records. Can you do that?"

"Yes, I can do that."

"Fine. Then we'll go from there."

All there was to send him was the one photograph, plus the letter Macky had given her the night before, the letter that had come about Capello's file, and the first name of a woman who had been a Rockette. Other than her, her mother had no friends that she knew of.

The minute she mailed the letter she regretted it. Walking home she began to wonder again why her mother had changed her name. Had she been a spy? What if she were still alive somewhere? What if they found her and arrested her? What if they executed her? What if she would be responsible for killing her own mother? By the time she reached the house she was in a full-blown panic and was so rattled she could hardly dial the phone.

Gerry was with a patient and she left a message. She looked at the clock. She had to wait twenty-one more minutes until he would pick up his messages and call her back and for twenty-one minutes she threw cold water on her face and walked the floor. By the time he called she was almost hysterical and was too panicked to sit up and was lying on the floor with the cat walking all over her thinking it was a game.

Gerry said, "Dena, just calm down. Listen to me. It's not too late . . . nothing's happened. I can call Dick right now and stop it right now."

"I don't want to do this. I've changed my mind."

"Fine. You don't have to. Nobody is holding a gun to your head."

"Will you call him?"

"Of course, whatever you want."

"Will you call right now? Tell him to forget it, please . . . before he does anything. Tell him not to open the letter."

"All right, I'll call him now."

Five minutes later Gerry called back. "OK, everything is fine. He's not going to proceed."

"Does he think I'm crazy?"

"No."

"Is he mad at me? What did he say?"

"He said whatever you wanted. When and if you ever need his help, he's there. OK?"

"Gerry, I'm sorry. I guess I'm not as ready as I thought. Are you disappointed?"

"Of course not. You called me, didn't you?"

"I don't know what I'm so afraid of. I just can't do this right now."

"It's taken care of."

"Gerry, are you mad at me?"

"I'm not mad at you, Dena. But I want you to get some help with this. You should talk to Elizabeth."

Dena set up a phone session with Dr. Diggers for the next afternoon and told her everything that had happened.

Dr. Diggers said, "But from what you tell me, Gerry's friend assured you that he could try and get some answers and you wouldn't be involved, right? Don't you *want* to know?"

"Yes. But . . . it's more than that. I just feel it's wrong, that I shouldn't pry into my mother's past, whatever it was she didn't want me to know. I feel like I might be betraying her or something, you know? I feel guilty about sneaking around trying to find out things, it makes me feel dirty or slimy or . . . I don't know, bad . . ."

"I see," Dr. Diggers said. "You are going to spend the rest of your life being miserable because you don't want Mommy upset with you or to get her in trouble. Dena, face the facts. Your mother walked out on you. You were a fifteen-year-old child. Stop trying to protect her. She was a horrible, despicable human being. You should hate her. She didn't love you, she walked out on you, she didn't care about you, she just left for no reason. She was a cold, heartless bitch."

Dena felt her face flush. "Hey, wait a minute, you don't know that. Nobody knows that for sure . . . she could have had a very good reason."

"Dena, that's exactly my point! Nobody knows and you will never know because there is a part of you that does not want to know. And sweetie pie, whatever you find out, either way, is not going to be easy. We can't go back and change the past. All we can do is to try and make the present as pleasant as possible."

"So you are saying I should just go ahead?"

"I can't tell you what to do. That's up to you. All I can do is tell you that if you do, there is no reason in the world to feel guilty. You are not a stranger or somebody trying to hurt her or expose her, you are her daughter. You have a *right* to know. And no matter why she left you, and whatever she did or didn't do, that woman was your mother. And let's be realistic: even if she is still alive, what do you really suppose the chances are of finding out she had been a spy?"

Dena did not answer.

"I can tell you. About one in a million. But in the meantime, don't beat yourself up for getting cold feet; just take one step at a time. Do whatever you think you can handle. Are you smoking?"

Dena put her cigarette out. "No."

A week later, Dena, to her own surprise, called New York. A woman answered, "Radio City Music Hall. Personnel Office."

"I wonder if you can help me. I am trying to locate a woman named Christine . . . I think her last name was Whitten, or something like that. She was a Rockette and she worked there around 1950 or '51. I know she lived in Greenwich Village at the time and I was wondering if you had a present address or any way that I might get in touch with her?"

"I'll have to look in my files and get back to you."

"May I hold on? I'm calling long distance."

"It might take me a while."

"That's all right, I'll hold."

After some minutes, the woman came back on. "I found a Christine Whitenow but we don't have a current address on her, just the one she gave us at the time, Twenty-four St. Luke's Place."

"I see. Would you have any idea how I might find her?"

"No, but there were a few of the gals that used to keep up with one another. One of them might know. They had some club."

"Do you have a number?"

"Try calling Hazel Fenner, in East Lansing, Michigan. Her number is 517-555-9785. She might be able to help you."

A cheery woman picked up and after Dena explained, Hazel Fenner repeated the name. "Christine Whitenow? Christine Whitenow? Was she a pretty blonde?"

"Yes."

"Oh, yes, I remember her. She came in the line right after I left. Lots of fun . . . Wait a minute, I used to know her married name; what was it? Well, I used to know it; we all just sort of lost touch with her. Oh, I can't remember that girl's name to save my life. I can't tell you, dear, but it seems to me that Dolly might remember. I think they kept in touch for a while. Anyhow, ask Dolly. Call her—and tell her she owes me a letter."

Next Dena called Mrs. Dolly Berger in Fort Lauderdale, Florida, at the number Hazel supplied. She said, "Oh, you know we used to send each other Christmas cards but we stopped. If you can hold on, I might can find it on one of my old lists. Hold on."

After a moment Dolly picked up in another room. "Hello, are you still there?"

"Yes, I'm here."

"You are going to have to bear with me while I go through this. I'll tell you, sweetie, you know you are getting old when half of your Christmas card list is crossed off. It seems like people are dropping like flies."

Dena had a sinking feeling. It had never occurred to her that Christine could be dead. Then Dolly announced, "Here it is! I found it! I thought I still might have it. Now, I'm not sure if she's still living there but this is the last address I have on her; do you have a pen?"

"Yes."

"It's Mrs. Gregory Bruce, 4023 Massachusetts Avenue, Washington, D.C. The zip is 20019. And when you talk to her, tell her that Dolly is still alive. And, as we all say, kicking."

"I will, Mrs. Berger. And thank you so much. Oh, and by the way: Hazel says you owe her a letter."

It was a small step but at least it was a step.

The Neighborhood

Washington, D.C.
1978

A week later Dena was in a car, watching the rain hitting the windshield, listening to Gerry talk but not really hearing him. He was telling her to knock on the door and if the woman was at home, he would either wait for her in the car or go in with her, whatever she wanted. They were parked across the street, where according to Richard Look, who had checked it out, a Mrs. Gregory Bruce was still living. Massachusetts Avenue was a wide residential street in what looked to have been a nice upper-middle-class neighborhood at one time but was now beginning to decline. A few houses here and there were showing that forlorn, uncared-for look and had wrought-iron bars on the windows and doors. Number 4023 was set back a bit from the street with a long, deep yard that led up to a red-brick two-story house. Washington was cold and dark and everything looked depressed, including the trees, some nothing but bare black sticks against the gray sky. They had driven up and down the block once or twice before they parked but had not seen a living soul. Richard Look had advised Dena to show up unannounced. He had said that on the off chance Mrs. Bruce might know about her mother's employer having been convicted of spying, she might not be so eager to discuss old times with Dena. She had agreed with Look at the time but now that the moment was actually here, Dena was anxious.

Gerry looked up at the sky through the windshield. "I don't think it's going to let up any time soon. Maybe you should go on and get it over with. What do you think?"

"Yes, guess you're right." She turned to him. "What's the signal again? I forgot."

"If it is her, and you feel like you need me to come in with you, turn around and wave and I'll come. Otherwise, I'll be here waiting for you."

She opened the door, repeating, "Wave if I want you, don't wave if I don't. Wish me luck."

As she started up the four cement steps, she thought, a coward dies a thousand deaths, a hero dies but one. This is just another interview, that's all.

She reached the front door, took a deep breath, and pushed the bell. She stood there in the rain and waited. Nothing. She rang again and waited. Nothing. She could see the lamp on the table inside the hall was not lit. Maybe she was not home. Relieved and disappointed at the same time, she gave the bell one more short push and waited, then turned to leave, when she heard the sound of footsteps coming toward the door. A figure she could not make out switched on the lamp and opened the door halfway, leaving the barred outer door closed. In the dim light Dena could see it was a dignified-looking woman who wore her silver-gray hair pulled straight back from her face, and was wearing a coat.

"Yes?"

"I'm sorry to bother you but I'm looking for Mrs. Gregory Bruce."

The woman said, somewhat leery, "Yes, I'm Mrs. Bruce. What can I do for you?"

Dena was caught off guard for a moment. "Ah . . . I believe you used to know my mother, Marion Chapman?"

The woman frowned slightly. "Who?"

"Marion Chapman; you knew her around 1950 or 1951?"

The woman did not respond. Dena continued, "She had a daughter and they came to see you at Radio City Music Hall."

The woman did not give any indication of remembering.

"And one time we spent the night at your apartment in the Village on St. Luke's Place? You had a cat named Milton?"

Dena heard the sound of a loud iron lock clicking. The woman opened the door and stood staring at her in amazement.

"Dena? Are you Dena?"

"Yes."

Her entire demeanor changed. "Oh, for heaven's sake. Well, come in, come in."

Dena stepped inside. "Do you remember me?"

"Of course I do. I just can't believe it. I thought you were somebody trying to sell something. How did you get here?"

"A friend brought me." Mrs. Bruce glanced out at the car across the street.

"Don't you want to have him come in?"

"No, he's just going to wait for me."

"Here, let me have your coat. Go on into the living room and have a seat. I'll be right in. Can I offer you some coffee or tea?"

"No, not a thing, thanks."

"Look at me, I'm still in my coat. I just got in from a church meeting and when I came in the back door I thought I heard the bell. Let me run back in the kitchen and lock up. I left my keys in the door. Be right back."

"Take your time." Dena went into the living room and sat down. It was a dimly lit, rather formal room, furnished with furniture that looked as if it had been there for a long time. Christine came in, smoothing her hair. "I wish I had known you were coming. I don't have a thing to offer you as far as food goes. Here, let me put some lights on in here. What a surprise. I thought you looked familiar but couldn't place where I'd seen you before."

As Christine went around switching on the lamps, Dena was able to get a good look at her. She was not at all what Dena had pictured. She was conservatively dressed in a gray dress and pearls. Somehow Dena had expected her to still be blond and somewhat jazzier. This woman was reserved in speech and manner. Her features could have been Greek or Italian and she had aged well and was still quite attractive. Christine sat down across from her and asked the inevitable question: "Now, tell me, where is Marion? I was beginning to think you two had just dropped off the face of the earth. And how is she doing?"

A good interviewer, Dena wanted to let her talk a little longer before she answered, and answered her question with another question.

"How long has it been since you two have seen each other?"

"Oh, too long. We just lost touch with—" She did not finish her sentence. This was the first moment it dawned on her. "Wait a minute . . . I know you. You're Dena Nordstrom!"

Dena smiled. "Yes."

Christine sat back on the sofa. She put her hand over her heart. "That's you? You grew up to be Dena Nordstrom? You mean to tell me that it's you I've been looking at all these years. Oh, I can't believe it." She laughed. "No wonder you looked familiar. Here I've been looking at you and didn't even know it was you." Christine kept shaking her head. "And you remembered me after all these years. Well, I'm flattered."

"Of course I did. How could I forget meeting you, a real Rockette? That was a big event for me. You may not remember but I do."

"Oh, I do and I remember when your mother brought you backstage. You were this high." She held out her arm. "Your mother had you dressed up so, little bows in your hair, but all you wanted to do was look at the light board. The lighting man got the biggest kick out of you asking him all those questions."

"Do you remember that time when we came and spent the night with you?"

Christine's expression changed at the mention of that night and she gave Dena a sympathetic nod as if they shared the same memory. But she did not offer anything more. "How in the world did you find me after all these years?"

The phone in the kitchen started to ring. Christine made no attempt to get up.

"Believe it or not," Dena said, "I called Radio City Music Hall and they told me to call a woman named Hazel, who told me to call a woman named Dolly Berger, who had your married name and address."

She smiled. "Dolly Berger, how is that crazy thing?"

"She sounded fine, and she said to tell you to write her."

The phone continued to ring. Christine said, "Wouldn't you know it, right when I have company. Excuse me. Let me get rid of whoever that is."

Dena glanced around the room. Christine had photos of foreign-looking people sitting on the mantel, but other than that the room was cold, almost austere.

Christine came back. "That was my neighbor; her furnace is out so I told her she could come over here and watch TV in the basement. She has a key so she won't bother us." She sat down. "You still haven't told me about your mother. Is she all right?"

This was going to be the tricky part. Dena needed to see what Christine knew.

"Actually, the reason I'm here is about my mother. I was wondering if you could tell me when was the last time you saw or heard from her."

Christine thought. "Oh, I think it must have been, well, I know it was before I got married. I got married in 1953. I remember I wrote her at the last address she gave me—I think you and she had moved to Boston or Philadelphia by then—and I never heard back from her. Why? Is she all right? Did something happen to her?" Christine looked anxious. "She is not . . . dead, is she?"

Dena could see by the genuine concern in her face that she was not hiding anything, or if she was, Christine was the best actress Dena had ever seen.

"That's just it. I don't know. I don't know where she is or if she is still alive."

At that moment a short, black woman in a windbreaker came in the front door and waved and said, "It's just me." As she headed for the stairs leading to the basement room, Christine's eyes never left Dena, waiting for her to explain. After Dena told her the whole story about that Christmas in Chicago, Christine looked stricken. "Oh, no. And she didn't leave a note or anything?"

"No, nothing. Just my gifts—and she just vanished into thin air."

Christine's eyes filled with tears. "Oh, no, that poor girl." She sat sadly shaking her head. "That poor girl." Dena handed Christine a

Kleenex. Christine wiped her eyes. "I'm sorry. It's just so terrible, it just breaks my heart to hear it. But I'm not surprised. I always worried something like that would happen."

Dena spoke as calmly as possible. "You're not surprised?"

"No. From the very beginning, she was scared to death somebody might find out who she was. That you might be disgraced or thrown out of school." Dena's heart began to pound. Christine folded and refolded the Kleenex. "A lot of them just disappeared like that, just dropped out of sight, couldn't stand the pressure. Always looking over their shoulders, never trusting anybody." She looked at Dena. "But to leave your child . . ." She started to cry again. "Oh, that poor girl, what she must have been going through."

Dena's face became chalk white and she felt as if she might faint. This was not what was supposed to be happening; it was a strange sensation. The worst things that people imagine almost never come true, but her worst nightmare was unfolding before her eyes. She was surprised to hear her own voice saying, "But she trusted you."

Christine blew her nose. "Oh, yes, she knew I would never have told anybody. Listen, how she wanted to live her life was her business but there were a lot of people who didn't feel that way, couldn't wait to hound you down and expose you."

Dena, who was now on automatic pilot, nodded as if she had a clue as to what Christine was talking about.

"And after all that mess about Theo hit the papers, she almost went crazy, she was so scared. She was convinced she was next." Christine looked away. "I think she may have even been afraid of me after that."

Dena was pulled back into reality. "Theo? Who is Theo?"

"Her brother Theo," Christine said, matter-of-factly, as if Dena should know.

Dena stopped her. "Wait a minute. My mother had a brother who was also a Nazi?"

Christine frowned at Dena. "A Nazi? Theo wasn't a Nazi, he was a violinist. Where did you hear that?"

"Well, isn't that what you said?"

"What?"

"Didn't you just say my mother was a Nazi spy?"

Christine was completely taken aback. "A spy? I don't know what you're talking about. Your mother was not a Nazi spy; who told you such a thing?"

"Didn't my mother work for a woman named Lili Steiner, who had a dress shop in New York?"

"I remember when your mother first got to New York, she worked for some woman named Lili something. But what does that have to do with anybody spying?"

"Lili Steiner was convicted for spying and spent ten years in jail."

Christine said emphatically, "Well, I don't *care* what that woman was convicted of, your mother was not a Nazi. My Lord, I've known your family almost all my life. Whoever told you that must have been pulling your leg. Your mother was no more of a Nazi than I am."

The phone in the kitchen rang again. Christine stood up. "No, she hated the Nazis. Your poor grandfather had to get out of Vienna, leave everything he owned just to get away from them." The phone rang again. "Let me run and get this. She's expecting a call from the furnace people." She called back over her shoulder. "Not only that, if they hadn't gotten out of Europe when they did, you might not be sitting here talking to me today."

Dena's mind was reeling. She felt as if she had just been pulled by the hair through a knothole at a hundred miles an hour. So that was it—her mother was Jewish! That's why she changed her name, why no such person as Marion Chapman existed. This was the last thing in the world she had expected to hear . . . but what was the big deal about that? Why had her mother not told her? Why was she so afraid? Something was still not right. It didn't make any sense; there had to be something else. Her mind raced in a hundred different directions. If she had not been a German spy, who was she running from? Then, another thought . . . maybe her mother had something to do with the *arrest* of Lili Steiner. Maybe the reverse was true, maybe her mother was an American spy! Maybe the postwar Nazis were after her for revenge. Maybe that's why she had to change her name; perhaps she had been in a government protection program.

Christine walked to the top of the basement stairs. "Lucille, he said he'd be here in half an hour."

Lucille called, "Thank you." Christine said, "Are you sure I can't get you some coffee or tea?"

Dena was so distracted that she did not respond. "I don't understand. Why did she change her name?"

"A lot of people did. I did."

"But why? It just doesn't make any sense to me. I mean, to change your name and your entire life over something like that . . ."

"I know, but you have to remember, things were very different back then. It was not easy for any of us. I know."

Dena looked at Christine, now that she knew. She did look somewhat Jewish.

"You couldn't get a job, you couldn't even get in most places. Your mother wasn't the only one. There were thousands of people doing the same thing. I did it myself for a while. Whitenow was not my real name. If anybody looked at me funny I used to tell people my mother was Spanish. During the Depression, when people were desperate for jobs, you'd be surprised how many Spaniards and Cubans showed up looking for work."

"Do you think my father knew?"

"No," she said. "I know for a fact he didn't."

"Would it have made a difference to him?"

"You never knew if it would or not. No, I think your mother just wanted to get married, have a baby, and forget it. It just broke poor Dr. Le Guarde's heart, first Theo, and then your mother—"

"Who's Dr. Le Guarde?"

"Your grandfather."

Dena tried to recover. "Oh, I knew about my grandfather, but I didn't know he had been a doctor."

"Yes," Christine said, almost reverently, "your grandfather was one of the most respected doctors in Washington."

"Really?"

"Oh, yes, he was chief of staff at Freeman Hospital right over here and head of the medical school at Howard College for years. He was very well known."

Another "Really" was all that Dena could manage.

"That's what made it so sad for him, to lose both children like that."

Dena was half listening; this was the first time she had ever heard her mother's real name and she kept repeating it in her head.

"Your grandfather was a good-looking man. Of course, so was Theo."

Dena looked at Christine. "Le Guarde. That doesn't sound like a Jewish name to me. Why would they have to change it?"

Christine was puzzled. "Jewish?"

"Yes, why would they change it? It sounds more French than anything."

"Jewish?" Christine said with an even more puzzled expression. "Dr. Le Guarde was not Jewish."

"He wasn't? Was it my grandmother?"

"No, neither one. Where did you get the idea that they were Jewish?"

Dena felt herself getting ready to be pulled through that knothole again. Either she had completely lost her mind or Christine was purposely trying to confuse her. "Didn't you just get through telling me that my grandfather had to leave Vienna to escape the Nazis or am I crazy?"

"Yes, I said they had to leave but not because they were Jewish."

"What are you talking about, then?"

Now it was Christine's turn to be confused. "Didn't you tell me you knew about your grandfather?"

"I said, I knew I *had* a grandfather. But all my mother ever told me about her family was that they all burned to death in a fire."

"A fire? What fire?"

"Was that not true?"

All of a sudden Christine realized what had just happened and a look of near-horror came to her face. She put her hand over her mouth and gasped, "Oh, my God in heaven, I thought you knew."

"Knew what? I think we must be having two conversations at

the same time. I thought you told me that you and my mother were Jewish. Isn't that what you just told me?"

Christine shook her head. "No."

"Then you're not Jewish either."

"No."

"You're not." Dena scanned her face once more, looking for some answer. "Are you Italian? Is that why you changed your name?" Christine did not answer her but Dena reacted to the word *Italian*. "Is that it? Does it have something to do with the Mafia? Was my mother involved with the Mafia, is that why she was afraid? Were she and her brother criminals or something? Look, I'm completely lost here; you've got to help me. I'm not trying to pry but I need to know. It's not just for me, there's somebody out there that's trying to blackmail me. I'm not trying to put you or my mother at risk, I just need to know for myself. What happened to her . . . why she left."

Christine was clearly torn. "Dena, please don't ask me anything else. I promised your mother."

Dena's eyes got big. "Then she *was* in the Mafia!"

"No, your mother was not in the Mafia."

Dena's head began to throb. "Then what is it? I can't imagine what it was that was so terrible . . . that she would just leave like that. . . . What didn't she want me to know that—"

Dena suddenly stopped talking. Slowly, it began to dawn on her, what Christine had assumed she knew all along. What had been right before her eyes, and had been so obvious from the start. Something she had missed completely until this very second. All at once everything began to clear and things started to fall into place one by one, like pool balls dropping into pockets . . . and everything began to make sense: the neighbor, the odd photographs she had seen around the house. Christine was not Italian or Greek or anything else. Christine was a light-skinned black woman. Dena was in a black neighborhood, and had not even suspected it.

Dena and Christine sat there for a moment staring at each other, both in shock but for different reasons. After a time, Dena went outside and motioned to Gerry to roll his window down. "Gerry, I think you'd better come in."

Gerry got out of the car quickly. "Did she tell you anything?"

"Oh, yes. You're not going to believe this—"

"What?"

"Wait."

Tilt-A-Whirl

Washington, D.C.
1978

When they got back to the hotel late that afternoon, Dena was worn out. She felt as if she had been riding a giant Tilt-A-Whirl at the carnival for the past five hours, whipped first one way and then the other. Even after she had taken a hot bath and was lying in bed, her mind was still spinning. Gerry registered them under his name but had gotten a suite with two bedrooms. At eight-thirty he called her from his bedroom. "How are you doing? Sure you don't want me to order you some dinner?"

"No, I just want to sleep." Then she asked, for the twentieth time, "Do you *believe* this?"

"Well . . . it's different from what we expected."

Later, Gerry was rereading *What's Doing in Washington* magazine when the phone rang. He jumped up and ran into the bathroom and picked it up as fast as he could, so it would not wake Dena. It was Macky Warren, wanting to know how things were going. Dena had said he might be calling and to let them know what was going on. Gerry whispered, "Well, we found the woman we were looking for."

"Great. What did she say?"

"Mr. Warren, could you hold on a moment?" He went into his bedroom, closed the door, and picked up the phone. "She told Dena that her mother was a black woman."

"A what?" Macky was quite sure he had not heard right.

"A black—you know, like Lena Horne. Light but black. She didn't know what happened to her, but at least now we know the mother's real name; that's a start. Dena's asleep in the other room but I'm sure she'll call you when we know more."

Macky walked slowly back into the living room, where he had left Norma and Aunt Elner cracking pecans. Norma sat, waiting for news like a bird waiting for a worm.

"Well?" she asked, her eyes wide.

Macky sat down in his BarcaLounger and picked up the paper, hoping to avoid conversation.

"What did she say?"

"I didn't talk to her, I talked to her friend. She was asleep."

"Yes . . . and?"

"And he said they found the woman."

"They found the woman. Yes—and?"

"And what?"

"What did she say about her mother?"

Macky tried to sound casual. "She said that Dena's mother was a black woman."

She looked at him incredulously. "What?"

"Black."

Norma closed her eyes. "Macky, why do you do this? You know I'm a wreck over this thing. Now tell me what she really said."

"I told you."

"Macky, you are not funny. What did she *say*?"

"Norma, I am not trying to be funny. She said her mother was black."

Norma squinted at him. "What do you mean, black?"

"Just like I said. Black."

"You mean Amos and Andy black?"

"No, he said more like Lena Horne black."

Norma waved him off. "Oh, you are making this up. You probably didn't even talk to him."

He looked over the top of the paper at her. "I'm telling you, he said she was black. That's what the woman said. I'm just repeating."

"Oh, don't be ridiculous, she was no more black than I am!"

Norma cracked a pecan to make her point and threw the shell in the green bowl in her lap.

"Norma, you asked and I told you."

"Well, he's wrong. Don't you think somebody would have noticed if Gene had married a colored girl? Don't you think one person would have looked at her when she got off the train and commented, 'Oh, look, Gene married a colored girl'? Not one person said that, did they, Aunt Elner?"

"Not that I recall."

"Of course they didn't, she was a white person, for God's sake. That woman has her mixed up with somebody else. How can you be black if you are a white person? It makes no sense at all, I've never heard of such a crazy thing. Lena Horne, my foot."

Aunt Elner looked up, confused. "How did Lena Horne get in this? Was she there?"

"Oh, she's not in it, Aunt Elner," said Norma. "He's making it up just to get my goat. He is determined to drive me insane. Keep it up, Macky, and when I'm down at the state hospital foaming at the mouth, then you'll finally get your wish."

Macky heaved a sigh. "Have it your own way, Norma. I've told you the truth and you don't believe me, so forget it."

A few minutes passed. Norma cracked two more pecans. "The very idea of saying a white person is black. I knew her, you didn't."

"Norma, I'm not saying it. The woman said it. I don't know!"

"Well, you shouldn't be passing that kind of false information along. How can you be black if you have green eyes? Answer me that."

"I don't know, Norma."

"No, I didn't think you did."

Aunt Elner said, "Well, whatever she was, she was a pretty thing. Isn't that what they say? That black is beautiful?" She emptied her bowl of shells into the paper bag at her feet. "And I'll tell you another thing, they ought to put Amos and Andy back on the radio. Where did Amos and Andy go, is what I want to know."

Who Was My Mother?

The next day after their first meeting, Dena went back to see Christine. They sat in the kitchen drinking coffee. "Last night after you left," Christine said, "I racked my brain trying to think of someone who might know where Theo is. I called my brother, and a few other people that knew him, and they all said the same thing. They have no idea. And your mother? Well, God only knows. I know I'm the only one besides Theo who knew that she was passing." She sipped slowly. "I just don't know what to tell you. I wouldn't even know where to start. I'm as baffled as you are. All I know is that your mother adored you; she used to call me up and tell me all about what you were doing, how pretty you were. . . . You were the only thing that kept her going. After your father was killed, you were the only thing she cared about."

"If she cared about me so much, why did she just leave? How could she do that?"

"I don't know." Christine sighed. "Your mother was a complicated girl, even when she was young."

"What was she like?"

Christine weighed her words. "Well, she and Theo were both different. When I say different, I don't mean in a bad way; it's just that they both had been raised in Vienna."

"What were they doing in Vienna?"

"Your grandfather went there to study medicine, that's where he met your grandmother."

"Was my grandmother black?"

"No, she was a German, a doctor's daughter, came from plenty of money. I don't think your grandfather would ever have left Vienna if it had not been for the war. He may have had blond hair and green eyes but his visa still said Negro and don't forget Hitler didn't like blacks any more than he did Jews."

"How old was my mother when they came back?"

"Theo was already fourteen or fifteen, so she must have been ten or eleven. So you can imagine what a shock it must have been for them. I don't think either of them had ever seen real Negroes before. It must have been hard for them. One day they were little white Viennese children and the next thing they knew they were colored children living in a colored neighborhood. But your mother was such a little lady, she spoke perfect French and German, played the piano; both she and Theo were so well behaved." She smiled. "Not like me. I was more or less your mother's age and I think she wanted to play and have fun, but she just didn't know how. A lot of people used to think she and Theo were stuck up but they weren't, they had just been raised in a different culture. And, oh, how they loved their father. He was so proud of his children."

"Do you remember him?"

"Oh, yes, Dr. Le Guarde and my daddy were good friends, they were in the same clubs. We used to love to go over there all the time. It was a beautiful home, so tastefully decorated; when you stepped into that house it was like going into another world. I remember your grandfather and grandmother both loved music and always had music playing—Brahms, Schumann, Strauss—and the parties they had. A library that was second to none, as my daddy used to say, and the art. They brought a lot of wonderful paintings from Europe. They almost never went out; their home was their haven."

"What did my grandfather look like?"

"Oh, he was a good-looking man, tall, very distinguished."

"I see." Dena wanted to ask the next question but was concerned about not making it sound like an insult. "Well, just how dark was he?"

Christine was not offended. "About as dark as you with a tan; he was a real blue vein."

"A blue vein?"

Christine laughed and turned her arm over. "So light you can see the veins. His mother had been one of those light-skinned quadroons from New Orleans and had married a Frenchman. My mother was a blue vein. My sister, Emily, is as white as you. I got my color from my father and he wasn't happy about it, either. In the summer, if I would come home with just a little tan, he would be furious with me. 'Sister,' he'd say, 'you get any blacker, I'm sending you to Harlem with the rest of the darkies.' He didn't like dark skin."

"Why not?"

"Oh, I don't know. He just didn't. That's the way he was. The first time I brought my husband home to meet Daddy he almost had a fit. 'Too black, too black,' he said." Then she laughed. "But I didn't care, I think I might have married him just to spite Daddy."

"What did Theo look like?"

"Theo? Oh, well, if it's possible for a man to be beautiful, then he was. I was in love with Theo. He looked more like his mother, with those big brown eyes and those long lashes. I used to sit and watch him practice his violin for hours." She dropped another cube of sugar into her cup. "But he never looked at me or any girl as far as I know. All he cared about was playing that violin."

Dena sat there trying her best to keep up. "If my mother's mother was full-blooded German and her grandfather was French, how much black blood did my mother have?"

"About a drop, if there is such a thing as black blood, which there isn't. All blood is red or blue. But it was enough. Back then, one-sixteenth of a drop of Negro blood was one drop too much. You were still Negro under the law."

"Do you think my father would have cared?"

Christine shrugged. "I don't know. But that was just it, you never knew how people were going to feel. And don't forget that was in the forties, and it was all illegal in some states for a person to marry outside their race. People were still being put in jail for it. Things were very different then. But me, I was lucky. When I was young I never took the race thing all that seriously. I even changed my name to Whitenow—it was a big joke to me. I was just out for some fun, and I had it, too. I wanted to be a Rockette and I wasn't going to let a stupid law stop me. If they felt better thinking I was Spanish, let them."

"Why didn't she tell me? It wouldn't have made any difference to me."

Christine's smile was sad and weary. "Oh, yes, it would have. Maybe not as much as your mother thought, but your mother figured you were better off not knowing about her, and it would have made a difference because—don't kid yourself—there were people back then who if they had known about your mother would have looked at you with an entirely different eye."

Dena was astounded. "Me?"

"Yes, even you. It would have been a stigma. To a lot of people it didn't matter how small the amount of Negro blood your mother had, all that mattered was that she had it no matter how far back it went."

"But that's idiotic!"

"Maybe so, but you have to think of all the advantages you might not have had if people had known. Everywhere you went they would be whispering behind your back, and she knew it. Think about it: Could you have gone to the same schools, dated the same boys, walked through the same doors? Oh, you might have made it eventually because of your looks and talent, but everywhere you went they would have been looking at you with that in mind. They might not have said anything but they would have been thinking it."

"I wouldn't have cared, it wouldn't have changed the way I felt about my mother."

"No, maybe not, but it would have changed the way you looked at the world. And how the world looked back. You would always wonder what people were really thinking, no matter how nice they were. You'd wonder what they *didn't* say around you. It changes you. Believe me. I've had to deal with it all my life. Your mother was just trying to spare you the same heartache."

"Did my mother ever tell you why she decided to pass for good?"

"No, but I just figured that she felt the same way Theo did. I couldn't blame either one of them, really; they never really fit in from the beginning. Especially Theo. He was pulled one way and then the other till he didn't know what or who he was. Finally he was just pulled apart. He had to choose between his daddy and his music. He didn't want to be the great new Negro musician, he just wanted to be a musician. And believe me, they weren't going to let a Negro in any symphony orchestra, not back then. You still don't see all that many today."

"No, you don't."

"I could have passed for good if I had liked it, but I just felt more comfortable with my own people. But I don't judge those who did. When you get as old as I am you realize that life is hard, and if you can get a break in this world, why not take it? But even so I can tell you passing was not an easy thing to do. I don't envy those who did. It was like going to another country and never being able to go home again. They couldn't even come back to their own daddy's funeral, and in your mother's case passing was particularly hard. She couldn't pass into rich white society, you had to be born into that; she had to take a step down. Why, with her background and education, that girl shouldn't have been working in any department store. I didn't even know she was passing until that day I ran into her."

Christine got up from her chair and went over and shut the kitchen door. "I had this cute white boyfriend at the time and we go waltzing into Saks Fifth Avenue to shop for my birthday present. He wanted to buy me a nice dress so I figure, why not? So I'm sitting there and up walks your mother to wait on us. Well, I looked at her and she looked at me, and I knew who *she* was and *she* knew who I was but neither one of us said a word. The next day I went back and that's when she told me all about you and what had happened to your father. We kept up with each other for a few years, then after that I just lost touch."

Christine sighed again. "I tell you the truth, I'm so tired of this race thing I don't know what to do . . . the things it does to people." She looked away. "You just don't know the insults my poor husband had to take all his life because of color. He was one of the sweetest, most refined gentlemen that ever walked on the face of this earth, and then to be treated so badly, even by my own father. I don't know what happened to your mother; she may have just been worn out from the whole thing. I wish I could be of more help to you, but I guess none of us will ever know what's in another person's mind. I don't know what caused your mother to run off like that, but whatever it was, she must have had a good reason. Because I know she loved you."

❖   ❖   ❖

After Dena's morning with Christine, she got in the car and Gerry looked at her. "How are you?"

"Fine." But she wasn't. She had been strangely touched by Christine. There was something about her that made Dena deeply sad. It was a look in her eyes. She had seen the same look at times in her mother's. She started to cry.

"I'm sorry, I don't know what's the matter with me."

"That's all right, Dena, you're going through a lot right now. It's OK."

"I really liked her."

"I know."

"I don't know why I'm crying over it."

She had learned much in two days but she still had not found out what had happened to her mother that Christmas. But at least they had a little more information to pass on to Richard Look.

That night as Gerry was walking her to the plane, he reassured her: "Richard said this is plenty to work with, more than he had hoped for, and I promise the minute he finds anything I'll call you."

When they reached the gate she shook his hand. "Gerry, I don't know how to thank you for everything; you've really been a good friend. I couldn't have done this without you—and I just want you to know I really appreciate it."

He shrugged it off. "Hey, that's what I'm here for." He smiled and waved back as she went through the gateway.

He wanted to get on that plane with her so badly it almost made him dizzy, but he knew he had to let her go. Gerry thought of nothing but Dena as he drove back to New York.

On the plane home, Dena could think of nothing except a family she never knew she had until yesterday.

A Brief Family History

Washington, D.C.
1913

The neatly dressed young man with the polished shoes and fresh haircut had been waiting in line at the employment office for over two and a half hours, and when his turn finally came he eagerly stepped forward, hat in hand, his blue eyes bright and hopeful, and said, "Good morning!" The woman who sat behind the desk did not bother to look up and responded to his cheerful greeting with the flat, dull, monotone voice of boredom and indifference so prevalent among civil servants, a voice guaranteed to extinguish even the smallest human enthusiasm as effectively as a bucket of cold water.

"Name."

The boy tried to recover. "Uh . . . James Alton Le Guarde."

"Spell it."

"Oh, *J-A-M*—"

The woman closed her eyes. "Last name."

"Oh, I'm sorry. Capital *L, E*. Capital *G, U-A-R-D-E*.

"U.S. citizen?"

"Yes, ma'am, but I've been living in—"

"Place and date of birth."

"New Orleans, October 11, 1895."

"Education."

"High school, but I plan to—"

"Experience."

The young man shifted his weight and cleared his throat. "None, really—this will be my first job if I get—"

"Race."

"Pardon?"

The woman repeated the word, somewhat louder, as if he were deaf. "Race . . . what is your race?"

The young man, confused by the question, was desperately trying to come up with the right answer. "Uh, I'm not quite sure what you mean. Human race, I guess? Is that right?"

The woman looked at the clock. "Negro or white."

"Oh, can't you tell by looking?"

She looked at him with tired, dead eyes. "That's not my job, sir. Negro or white?"

The young man wiped his sweaty palms on his pants. She waited. "Sir, I'm going to repeat it one more time. Negro or white?"

The young man began to flush. "Well, it's just that I don't think I'm either one. Can't you just put down neither one?"

The woman was losing what little patience she had. "Look, there are fifty people behind you. Make up your mind, one or the other."

She waited.

"Well, I think my grandmother had some Negro blood but—"

"How much?"

"Oh, I don't know, not much. Just a little, I think."

"Half, more than half?"

"Maybe half, I'm not sure . . ."

The woman stamped the letter *N* by his name. "Any known health problems?"

"Uh, no. But wait a minute. I think that's not right. I think you need to put down white, I'm more of a white person than anything else—my father is white."

"I don't make the laws. I just work here." She stamped his application again and held it out. "Section D, take a seat and wait for your name to be called."

She looked around him. "Next."

"Wait, where do I go?"

"Section D, in the back. Step aside, please."

James turned to look at the large board that said SECTION D, where ten or twelve Negro men dressed in worn and tattered work clothes were sitting. He felt his body start to break out in a clammy sweat.

"Miss, I think there's a mistake. I've always been a white person. This is—"

She did not look at him. "If you want a job, go wait in Section D; if you don't, fine. I don't care one way or the other. It's up to you. Move on, please."

"But isn't there some other place, a place in between where I can wait?"

She pushed his application to the right side of the desk and motioned for the man behind him to move up. "Next! Move up, please!" A spare, older man in a brown suit stepped up and looked at him.

"Name?" she droned.

The young man moved aside and looked down at his application. It had fallen off the desk and was now lying on the floor. After a moment, he bent over and picked the paper up and walked slowly back to Section D and sat down on the wooden bench beside a Negro man who earlier that morning had tipped his hat to him. The man began to grin. "Well, lookie here. Look who's a nigger just like me. You a dressed-up, white nigger but you a nigger," he said, for the benefit of the other men sitting there. "Them fancy clothes and them blue eyes didn't help you none." He laughed. "You ain't nothing but a nigger . . . just like me . . . nothing but a white nigger."

A few men nodded and laughed. The young man looked straight ahead and gritted his teeth and tried to hold back the hot tears he felt forming in his eyes.

❖ ❖ ❖

The set of circumstances that had placed James Le Guarde in Section D had all started on June 17, 1808. His grandmother, a mulatto woman from the West Indies, had fled from Santo Domingo to escape the many political upheavals. She escaped with the family she had been working for and she came into the port of New Orleans carrying all she owned in a cloth bag and carrying the unborn child of the white planter.

Upon entering New Orleans, a free black, she was given the title of *femme de colour,* which automatically placed her above the black slave population.

Her daughter, Marguerite Delacroix, James's mother, grew up to become one of the beautiful red-haired quadroons of New Orleans. She in turn married a young Frenchman from Alsace-Lorraine named Philipe Le Guarde, who had met her and fallen in love with her at one of the world-famous quadroon balls held on Bourbon Street.

When their son, James, was five, they had moved to France. A bright boy, by the time he was eighteen he was determined to go back to the land of his birth and become a great doctor, make his parents proud. He had read of all the wonders of America and had stars in his eyes and the hope of a great future before him. He went on scholarship, and when he arrived at the school he did not have much money and was told that there might be a small job on campus for him. All he had to do was to register with the employment office and get a work permit.

He hadn't even thought about race. In France, he had not been a Negro. His mother had barely mentioned it.

Two days later he was called into the admissions office. A man sat with a copy of his work permit before him.

"Mr. Le Guarde," he said somewhat apologetically. "I'm afraid there is a problem. I have looked over your records that were sent and there was no mention of you being a Negro."

"No, sir, that's wrong, I'm not. I tried to tell that lady that my grandmother had a little Negro blood but not me. She made a mistake. I tried to explain it to her but she wouldn't listen."

The man looked at the young boy. He hated this part of his job. This sort of thing had happened before and it was never pleasant.

"Mr. Le Guarde, I'm sorry but we don't accept Negroes here. That's our policy. But I'll tell you what I will do. I will write a letter to my friend at Howard College and see if they won't be able to take you."

James was baffled. He had just come from France, educated like his father before him in the strictest of Catholic schools, and had been trained to believe that to lie was a sin against God. He had not been told what the letter *N* beside your name meant, how it would become the most important fact about you. He didn't understand that in America, one sixteenth of Negro blood canceled out all your white blood and made you a Negro under the law. How could anyone understand that? "But I was *accepted here,* I wanted to study here."

"I'm sorry, but that's all I can do for you. Howard is a fine school and I think you'll find that you are happier with your own people. Your grades are excellent and I know you will be a credit to your race one day."

James walked out the door with his records, a letter of recommendation, and the words "a credit to your race" ringing in his ears. He did not know what to do. He did not have the money to return to France. A few weeks later, he entered Howard College and found there were a few light-skinned, blue-eyed Negroes there and he eventually accepted his fate as God's will and made the best of it.

After graduation James applied to study with a doctor in Vienna whose papers he had admired, and was elated when he was chosen out of a field of over a hundred young men. On his application, the word *race* was missing. They did not ask, and James did not volunteer; after all, Europe was not America. He trained in Vienna for two years, working under his mentor, Dr. Theodore Karl Lueger. When he was not at the General Hospital of Vienna, he was often a guest at Dr. Lueger's home. Sometimes on Saturdays he would join the Luegers' daughter, Gisele, and a group of her friends to take the streetcar around the Ringstrasse and ride the giant Ferris wheel and see all of Vienna. It was a splendid city, a splendid time to be young, and they fell in love. Gisele was madly in love with the young American doctor and wanted to marry him. James had not meant to have this happen because he knew he did not want to take her home to a segregated America. He tried to explain the problems they might have. But Gisele, who had black hair and dark eyes and skin darker than his, laughed when he told her. He could not be a Negro. He had blue eyes and light, honey-colored straight hair. He could not make her understand. When he tried to explain to her father that because of his race, he would not be able to work in a white hospital or live in a white neighborhood. Dr. Lueger sat and listened, and after James had finished he slowly took off his glasses and wiped them with his handkerchief and said in a quiet voice, "Dr. Le Guarde, if you do not wish to marry my daughter, be a man and tell her so, but do not subject her to such a fantastic falsehood."

James was miserable, guilty about letting it get this far with Gisele. It was too late to turn back without breaking both their hearts. He walked the streets of Vienna all night, agonizing over what to do. Along the Danube, he stared at the bright stars reflected in the dark water, despondent and confused. But by the time the sun came up over the city, he had made a decision. He knew what he was going to do. After all, he had told them he was a Negro, hadn't he? He had been honest. But he would not take Gisele home to America. No, he loved her too much. He would not subject her to that. He would marry her, and they would stay in Vienna and raise their children there, where they would be safe from prejudice. But James had not counted on Adolf Hitler.

❖   ❖   ❖

When Dr. Le Guarde returned to Washington to take over as chief of staff at Freeman Hospital, he immediately found himself listed among what W. E. B. Du Bois named the "talented tenth." He soon belonged to the Urban League, the NAACP, the Columbian Education Association, the Music and Literary Society, Boule, all the clubs and organizations of elite black society. He was certainly thought of as one of the leading black aristocrats of Washington, who vacationed in the exclusive holiday spots—Sarasota Springs, Highland Beach, Maryland. They moved in rarefied air.

But his wife and children had not been happy. Over the years Dr. Le Guarde had come to believe that he had a duty to try to be a credit to his race, to help his people; his children held no such beliefs.

Dr. Le Guarde often thought about that morning when the letter *N* had been stamped on his work permit. It had only taken a second, but that one second, that one letter, had changed the course of his life, and of his children's lives. And even today, as he sat in his office so many years later, he still wondered if he had done the right thing by telling the truth. Having seen his wife die an unhappy, misplaced woman, and his children so tormented, he wondered if he had the chance to go back and lie, would he?

He was a deeply religious man, but he still did not know. All he knew was that he had lost his beloved son. His beloved Theo was gone, and now he might be losing his daughter, Marguerite, as well. He could feel her slipping away, withdrawing.

He opened his desk drawer and pulled out the only thing he had left of Theo and reread it, as he had almost every day for the past five years.

Dear Daddy,

Please forgive me but I can no longer be your son. I have tried to feel the way you do but I am not like you, I feel no kinship with the Negro race and to champion a cause I do not feel in my heart would do them no good and would clearly destroy me. Let others who feel strongly and have deeper convictions speak out and set examples. I must have a chance to prove myself on my own and not be forced to carry an entire race on my back.

Don't you see, Daddy, I would not be just a man who plays the violin, but a colored man who plays the violin. A curiosity, my every move a political cause. Music does not judge who plays it, but people do. You tell me it is a sin to lie but, Daddy, my whole life is a lie. I am caught between two lies. I am not a Negro, I am not a white man, I am nothing, a thing in between, fitting in nowhere. I tell one lie only to stop the other lie, but I lie no matter what I say. You say God's will be done but I do not believe in a God that says I must sacrifice my chance in this life because of some man-made law. It is not you I leave, it is the Negro race, who has never done anything but resent my white skin and cause you nothing but heartache. These are not my people, Daddy. They do not own my talent. It is mine and mine alone. I am going where I can be free. Please do not look for me. Forget about me. I will love you forever.

Theo

Tears came to the old man's eyes. Poor Theo. As if he could just forget about the boy he loved, the boy he had held as a baby. He folded the worn page.

It was not an unusual story. Thousands of people had buckled under the pressures of segregation and had quietly slipped into the white world, but it was not an easy life, either.

Dena Nordstrom, Girl Reporter

Elmwood Springs, Missouri
1978

The minute Dena walked in the door, she called Dr. Diggers and told her about her mother.

Diggers sounded as surprised as Dena had been. "Well, I must say of all the things I suspected, this was not one of them, and I should have guessed. *Me* of all people! When I first started in practice, half of my patients were passing. Oh, yes, unfortunately I know all about it and I tell you, it was a bitch. I don't care if you were a Jew passing for Gentile or black passing for white, it was a tricky business no matter how you slice it. The point is: How do you feel about it?"

"Betrayed, I guess. Confused. Lost, like I never really knew my mother."

"Sweetie pie, there was a big part of her you didn't know. But at least now we have a pretty good explanation of why she seemed so remote. No wonder you felt she wasn't there for you. She was probably worried to death twenty-four hours a day. Passing is a complicated issue, with a lot of serious problems that go along with it. Guilt, confused identity, feelings of isolation, deception, abandonment. It's very stressful; I've seen it drive people right out of their minds."

"I understand all that, but I just can't understand why she didn't tell me. I could have helped her."

"I can't be sure of the exact reason, but I can tell you it wasn't because she didn't trust you; it was just plain fear. When you live a lie like that, people tend to start to get paranoid. She probably was afraid to trust anybody."

"But I wasn't anybody. I was her daughter."

"Yes, but don't forget you were the closest thing to her. She might have been afraid of losing you, afraid if you knew, you wouldn't love her. I've seen it happen before. People push away the very ones they don't want to lose trying to hold them. Listen, I'm not saying what your mother did was right, but in her defense, she had good reason to be afraid. You have to understand how things were back then; when she was a girl, there was no such thing as integration. Black and white were still two very different worlds."

"I know, but it was 1959—couldn't she see things were changing? New laws were being passed?"

"No, I don't think so. From what you've told me about your mother, I suspect she was not able to see much of anything going on around her. People who are passing are too busy looking over their own shoulders, trying to cover their tracks, to notice much else. She was probably stuck in the same old fear, with the same old tape running around in her head, and couldn't see past it."

"Do you think it had anything to do with her just disappearing like that?"

"Maybe. People who have disappeared from one life often do it again."

"But why *then*? Why at Christmas? Why couldn't she have waited?"

"Oh, sweetie, it could have been one of a hundred different reasons. She may have met someone or she may have just reached a breaking point, living with that much stress every day. You know, everybody handles stress differently. But a good possibility is that it just built up over the years and she couldn't take the pressure any longer and one day she had some sort of psychic break, lost touch with reality. In plain English, one day she may have just snapped and took off. You hear about it all the time. People leave for the store and never come back home, just disappearing off the face of the earth."

"Is that what you think happened?"

"Well, that would be my guess, based on what we know. But the important thing is for you to finally come to terms with the fact that her problems had nothing to do with the way she felt about you. She gave you all the love she was capable of giving under the circumstances. It wasn't as much as you needed but there it is; it's unfair and it's lousy but that's life, and at least now we know the basic cause of your problems. The next thing for us to do is to try and get beyond them and get on with your life. All right, now, when are you coming back to New York?"

"I'm not sure, I haven't thought about it yet."

"No, you are probably still in a state of shock. Do me a favor and take some time before you make any decisions about anything, OK?"

That night Norma and Macky brought her a hot supper.

When Dena told them what Dr. Diggers thought had happened, a look of relief came over Norma's face. "I am so glad to finally find out what was the matter. I was always afraid it was something that we had done, or maybe it was just us she didn't like."

For the next three days Dena still felt dazed. But a week later, as her mind began to clear, she woke in the middle of the night and sat straight up in bed. Something was wrong. Something did not add up. She was too good a reporter not to know when a piece was missing from a story. Dr. Diggers's theory had sounded good at the time, but it was too simple, too pat.

Her mother had loved her, she knew that now; she would not have left unless there had been something terribly wrong. Her mother had been a strong woman. There must have been another reason beyond stress. Something else her mother was afraid of. But what? There were still too many unanswered questions.

Why had her mother left Elmwood Springs so abruptly in 1948? Who was the man who spoke German?

As soon as the sun came up she made her first call.

"Christine, it's Dena."

"Oh, hello. How are you!"

"I have a question for you. You mentioned that there had been something in the papers about my mother's brother, Theo, and I was wondering if you could tell me what year that was and the name of the newspaper."

"Oh, dear, it must have been in the early forties, but I don't have any idea what the newspaper was. I know it was one of the big ones. But I do remember the name of the woman who wrote for it; would that be of any help to you?"

"Yes."

"Ida Baily Chambless."

"Who was she?"

"Oh, just some stupid woman who set herself up as a society columnist of sorts. I never read it. But Daddy said she was nothing but a Georgia nobody who thought she should be invited everywhere. She had some run-in with your grandfather years before and she just went after poor Theo with a vengeance. Pretended she was on some crusade but she was just jealous. If she couldn't pass, by God, nobody was going to pass. Honey, I was lucky she didn't come after me."

"Is she still alive?"

"No, thank heavens. Daddy said she finally got herself murdered."

Dena's heart skipped a beat. "Murdered . . . when?"

"Oh, a long time ago. I was still living in New York. It must have been 1948, somewhere around then."

Dena's heart skipped two beats. 1948 was the same year she and her mother had left Elmwood Springs in such a hurry.

A Woman Scorned

Mrs. Ida Baily Chambless, the sixth child of a laundress in Smyrna, Georgia, had always had a way with words. Her writing skills were considered "almost poetic," as a teacher wrote on one of her reports, "Plucked from Mother Africa's Bosom and Thrown Asunder." Over the years she had worked her way up until she wound up writing for one of Washington's leading Negro newspapers.

She enjoyed her power and found herself catered to by people desperate to see their names under her newspaper column's banner, SOCIETY SLANTS . . . SLAPS FOR ENEMIES, KISSES FOR FRIENDS.

When Dr. Le Guarde and his family moved to Washington, Mrs. Chambless was chomping at the bit to get to know them. But she had not received an invitation to their home, a fact that she sought to remedy by several glowing mentions of the Le Guardes in her column. Surely they would see that of all the people in Washington, she should be included at their affairs. However, after a year and a half no invitation had arrived, and she was dying to get inside the Le Guarde house. Although the exterior of the big brick four-story was rather plain, she imagined that what she would find inside would be spectacular. She was kept apprised of many social happenings by a certain florist who informed her, among other things, whenever Mrs. Le Guarde ordered floral arrangements for a party.

Eventually, Mrs. Chambless got wind of a musical evening that was planned and she could wait no longer. She decided that, after all, it was her right and her duty to her readers to report on the social life of such a distinguished Negro doctor. She would simply forgive them the obvious oversight of an invitation and attend anyway. And so, on the evening of the party, Ida Chambless, a large, brown woman with a flat, round face, dressed to the nines, complete with ostrich feathers in her hair, waltzed in the door uninvited, and proceeded to take notes. As she floated from room to room she was sorely disappointed. The house was dull, the clothes were dull; as a matter of fact, as the evening went on, even though everyone had been perfectly nice, she began to think this was one of the dullest parties she had ever been to. Only the art and the music were impressive. It was clear these poor people needed her help. In her column the next day she described the Le Guarde home in generous terms. The clothes the women had worn the night before, pale and muted, suddenly became magenta, lime, purple, royal blue, and red. According to Mrs. Chambless, the ladies at the party had been shimmering with jewels and diamond tiaras. Mrs. Le Guarde's single strand of pearls suddenly became twelve strands. Brahms and Strauss were described as lively and toe tapping. She informed her readers that gold-plated dinnerware and polished silver heirlooms from Dr. Le Guarde's family were in evidence everywhere, as were precious art and tapestries hanging on each wall. Mrs. Chambless thought, If that doesn't make them realize how much they need me in their lives, I don't know what will. Several days later a letter arrived from Dr. Le Guarde. Ah, here was that thank-you note and, probably, an open invitation to all their future entertainments. She sliced open the engraved stationery and began to read with a satisfied smile on her face that slowly faded.

> Dear Mrs. Chambless,
>   Although I am sure you meant no intentional harm, your public report of a private gathering was most unwelcome. Your exaggerations and the descriptions of the interior of my home and the clothes worn by my guests may have been meant as compliments, but I must ask you with all politeness and

respect to please refrain from writing any more about my family and friends. The publishing of our address and the listings of the contents, some real and some imagined, has caused me serious concern for my family as there has been a rise in thievery and misconduct of all sorts.

I am a private person. I seek no publicity and have found your several mentions of my name to be an embarrassment. I am sure you will understand this and comply.

Most sincerely,
Dr. James A. Le Guarde

Mrs. Chambless felt as if someone has just slapped her in the face. She had been slapped in the face by a white girl when she was nine and the effect was the same; however, this time she had recourse and could slap back with a mighty blow that would flatten any man. He was telling *her,* Ida Baily Chambless, that *she* was not good enough to be in his home? That *she* was not welcome? Ida Baily Chambless, who had carte blanche in the homes of richer men than he? Who did he think he was dealing with? Did he think he could insult her and humiliate her and tell her she was not good enough? Oh, he would rue this day. She had power and would turn it full force on this man and his puny, pink-blooded, lily-white family. How dare this pseudo-, ginger-cake, yellow-pine-codfish, self-proclaimed negrocrat think he was better than she was? In one moment that letter brought back every insult, every hurt, every slight, every humiliation she had ever been made to suffer. She was in a blind rage and literally ran upstairs to her typewriter, and wrote another column.

Soon Dr. Le Guarde had groups of young men walking by his home yelling and making catcalls and a few, who had had several drinks too many, poured black paint down his front doorstep.

Good. She would never let him forget that he had insulted Ida Baily Chambless for as long as he lived. She would hound him and his family to their graves and beyond!

Carlos Maurice Montenegro

From the moment Carlos began to play, Joseph Hoffman knew at once that the young man before him was one of the most extraordinarily gifted violinists he had ever heard. Hoffman immediately took him under his wing and in less than six months Carlos Montenegro had been named first violinist of the San Francisco Symphony.

Of the millions of musicians in the world, only a handful soar beyond what is written on the page, transcend what seems humanly possible, and Carlos was one such musician. His teacher knew that Carlos was destined to become one of the greats, perhaps to take his place beside Heifetz and Menuhin. All he needed was the right person to guide his career, and Joseph was it. If handled correctly, this boy could change the face of classical music. He had the looks of a matinee idol and the talent of an angel.

If there was one flaw it was that he was almost too pretty, and when he played most women could not take their eyes off him. Carlos had never talked about himself or where he was from, but as such a romantic figure there had been rumors that he was probably the son of a Spanish count. Many went home and dreamed of those beautiful hands and long, delicate fingers and the way the shadow of his eyelashes fell across his cheek. But there was something else that concerned his teacher. Without his violin, Carlos seemed unusually shy and unsure of himself. He seemed content to just play in the orchestra and to compose. But Hoffman was anxious to have such a talent exposed to the world, and took it upon himself to enter one of Carlos's concertos in an international music competition held in Quebec.

He wanted the boy to realize his future, to build his confidence. The winner was assured of a year's worth of concerts around the world. All he needed was this chance to tour. Then the boy would have the world at his feet. A month later, to Hoffman's great joy and to Carlos's great surprise, he won. But there was, shortly, another surprise waiting for Carlos.

SOCIETY SLANTS

by Ida Baily Chambless

There is exciting news today. It came to my attention by way of a little bird that last week's happy headline "American Wins International Music Competition" should have read "American Negro Wins International Music Competition." The celebrated recipient is none other than Theodore Karl Le Guarde, who has of late adopted the melodious nom de plume Carlos Maurice Montenegro, for "artistic" reasons, no doubt, for the name Le Guarde is a proud Negro name. His father is Dr. James A. Le Guarde, a prominent Negro doctor here in Washington for many years.

Despite Mr. Le Guarde's stage name and his absence from our fair city, nothing could keep us from shouting from the highest rooftops that one of us is on his way to the big time. I want you to know that your columnist has been burning the midnight oil, and with much cajoling and powerful string pulling, it is with great glee and salutations to the world that I announce that Theodore Le Guarde, né Carlos

Maurice Montenegro, has just been named "Negro of
the Year" by this newspaper. We are proud of so many
high achievers who share our Negro heritage, and I for
one shall be awaiting his return to our fair city with a
great big welcome home and where have you been?
Move over Cab Calloway, Duke, Jelly Roll, and Louie
and make room for a new genius on the block!

Ida Baily Chambless gloated in her triumph. Dr. Le Guarde's precious, lily-white son was going to be a Negro whether he wanted to
or not. She had known about Theo for some time, but she had
waited for the right moment. Shrewdly, she knew it was much
more damaging to kick people not when they were down, but when
they were up.

When Theo's photograph, along with her press release announcing that he had been named Negro of the Year, appeared in
newspapers around the country, all hopes of a classical career went
down the drain. His colleagues had been stunned by the news. Some
had felt betrayed. Suddenly they saw him as someone who had pretended to be something he wasn't, an imposter who had lied to them.
Others were sympathetic and said that it didn't make any difference
to them but it did. It was still the 1940s in America, and many whites
had never met a Negro other than a maid or a Pullman porter. Yesterday he had been the charming and incredibly beautiful young
man of obviously aristocratic Spanish descent. Today he was something of an odd curiosity. They began looking for signs, hints of
Negro blood, and began to see them, even when they weren't there.
Even the young woman who had been so in love with Theo the day
before looked at him with different eyes today. She felt that she had
been made a fool of. His father was probably nothing more than a
yard man. He had tried to push his way into San Francisco society on
false pretenses. He must have been secretly going back at night and
laughing about her with his Negro friends.

Of course Theo had never said he was from a wealthy family,
and society had sought him out, but facts changed along with atti-
tudes. Hoffman was devastated for him, and went immediately to his

apartment but found that Theo had locked the doors and would not let him in. He would speak to no one. The day after the article appeared Negro newspapers from all over the country sent photographers and reporters wanting interviews. Overnight, he was flooded with invitations from the leading Negro organizations wanting him to entertain and lend his name to every Negro cause and speak at every event. They were proud of him and, as the *Washington Bee* put it, "We rejoice in his victory and add a new star in the crown of Negro accomplishments."

White newspapers took a different tack. The caption under his photograph read: NEGRO CAUGHT MISREPRESENTING ANCESTRY.

The International Music Committee reconvened for an emergency meeting and voted to a man to stand by its decision, but there was a war in Europe, most of Carlos's concerts had been planned for America, and one by one they began to be canceled.

Dear Sirs,

We feel it would be best if Mr. Montenegro were to limit his concerts to halls that can accommodate members of his own race. Our present policy does not do so.

—Atlanta Philharmonic

Dear Sirs,

You have maliciously misled us as to the race of your winner and therefore our contract is null and void. Any attempts to perpetuate the fraud and embarrass our patrons shall be met with legal action.

—Chicago Music Club

After several weeks of similar telegrams and letters, and much pressure all around, this press release was sent:

The International Music Committee has reconvened for the second time and announced today that it has withdrawn its cash prize and canceled all concert dates of recent first-prize winner, Carlos Montenegro. A spokesman for the committee said this decision was made with deepest regrets and was not based on the fact that he is a Negro, but that he withheld that fact from the committee.

His sister Marguerite was working in New York. When she read about what had happened to Theo she immediately went to San Franciso. But by the time she arrived, he had disappeared into thin air.

That Something Else!

After he left San Francisco, Theo wandered aimlessly about the country, going from one dark, dirty bar to another, from one couch in some stranger's place to another. He tried to work at a factory job but in a few days collapsed with what the doctors termed a nervous breakdown and spent a year in a charity ward in a hospital outside of Lansing, Michigan. After he was released, he slowly made his way back to Washington, washing dishes, sweeping floors, anything to get by. Once back, he managed to pull himself together somewhat and made a fair living giving private violin lessons to the children of the wealthy diplomats. He often thought about his sister. The last time he had written her she had been living in New York. He hoped she was safe and happy. He hoped that at least one of them was happy.

For the next four years he lived less than a mile from his father, but as far as real distance, it might as well have been a thousand miles. He wanted to see his father, but he did not want his father to see him. He had shamed his father enough, caused him enough pain, and as much as he missed him, he couldn't face him. He sometimes bought a copy of the *Washington Bee* just to see if it had any mention of his father. It was there he learned of his father's death. The day of the funeral, he stood in the back of St. Augustine Church in a corner and listened to the priest eulogize his father as a great man and a great doctor. No mention was made of his two children. It was as if they had never existed.

Theo left before the service was over, shaking from head to toe with regret, sorrow, anger. He hated himself. How could he have done it? How could he have turned his back on his daddy? If only he could go back. But it was too late. He was completely alone in the world now; all he had left was his sister. But where was she?

Theo didn't know it but there was someone else who was wondering the same thing. Word had reached Mrs. Chambless that someone who had looked like Theo had been spotted leaving the church, but the sister had not been spotted and it confirmed what she had already begun to suspect. Two days after the funeral she wrote:

SOCIETY SLANTS

1948

I have dipped my spoon into the thick, rich soup of Negro history of our fair city and have pulled out a tasty morsel. It has come to my attention that our reluctant Negro musical genius, Theodore Le Guarde, has a sister, Marguerite, who has all but vanished into thin air. Could it be that she too has chosen to take the same traitorous route leading into white society? As the children at play call: come out, come out, wherever you are. It is a sad fact that there are those of our race who simply do not have the decency to come out in the open of their own accord, and if I am the chosen to spur you to acknowledge you to your duty, if this task must fall on my weary shoulders, so be it.

You will not be allowed to sit at the table of acceptance until all Negroes are seated. And a word to the wise to all you *others* out there resting your pretty heads upon the soft white pillows of deception ... Rest not, for your days are numbered. There is an army of the righteous, dedicated to exposing you and bringing you back alive!

✳   ✳   ✳

That night Theo Le Guarde walked with Chambless's column in his pocket to her house in Le Droit park. The house was dark except for a light in a room on the second floor. He went to the front door and knocked. No one answered. He tried the door and it was unlocked; in fact, it swung wide open. Mrs. Chambless rarely locked her doors. She had no fear. What man would dare to rob her? He stepped in and closed the door behind him. He could hear the sound of typing and followed the sound up the stairs to the room where she sat, enormous in a pink housecoat, completely absorbed in her work. He stood in the doorway and looked at her. She did not hear him until he was standing right in front of her. When she saw a man, pale as a ghost, appear, she almost jumped out of her skin. She grabbed at her chest and let out a "Whooo! . . . Good God Almighty. You nearly scared me to death. What do you mean coming in here and sneaking up on me like that? What's the matter with you? What do you want coming here this time of night?"

She peered at the gaunt figure before her and was puzzled. "Who are you? Do I know you?"

Now that he was actually face-to-face with the woman, Theo began to shake all over and struggled to get the words out. "Why . . . why are you doing this . . . why did you ruin my life?"

Suddenly Mrs. Chambless sensed who he was and sat back in her chair with a smug, mocking smile on her face. "Well, well, well. Look who we have here. If it's not the great Theodore Le Guarde himself."

Then her expression changed and her eyes narrowed as she lunged forward and hissed at him with a voice filled with contempt. "Listen . . . if your life got ruined it was you that ruined it, not me. You and that high-and-mighty family of yours. You think you're too good for me? Well, Eleanor Roosevelt doesn't think she is too good for me . . . now, you get out of here!"

She dismissed him with a wave of her hand and turned back to her typing. As an afterthought, she added, "And tell that sister of yours she's next."

At that moment something deep inside Theo broke loose and he heard a roaring in his ears so loud that he could not hear Ida Baily Chambless's screams as he grabbed her by the throat and squeezed. Something was erupting; a terrible, red-hot, boiling rage came rumbling out. He was choking and shaking the very life out of the woman and he could not stop it.

The next thing he remembered he was outside in the cold, wringing wet with sweat. He walked for a mile, not knowing where he was going until he was at the Lincoln Memorial. He looked up at the statue of the man and suddenly heard a woman's screams in his ears and saw the grotesque face of Mrs. Ida Chambless, her tongue hanging out, her huge eyes bulging, and he retched and threw up in the grass until nothing was left but yellow bile. He looked down at his hands, and he began to sob.

He had to make his way to his father's house. He had to find his sister; she would hide him. He would be safe with her.

When he reached the house every door and window was locked. The sun was coming up. Desperate, he went to the back and crashed through a basement window and crawled in. He made his way in the dark up to his father's den. Almost everything was packed in boxes. He went to his father's desk and broke open the lock. He could feel papers and letters still there. He lit a match and found his own letter to his father, and one more envelope. It was addressed to his father, too. Although the name on the return address was strange, he recognized his sister's handwriting. The letter was postmarked Elmwood Springs, Missouri.

Living a Lie

Dena's mother, Marguerite Le Guarde, had not intended to lie about who she was. It had just happened. She had taken a trip to New York to help a friend shop for her trousseau. When she spoke to the owner of the shop in German, Lili Carlotta Steiner recognized at once that the young girl had been raised in Vienna, as she had. Delighted with the pretty young woman who obviously knew about fine clothes, Steiner offered her a job on the spot. Excited, Marguerite wrote her father and asked him if she might stay for the summer. Her father wrote back and said yes. Her mother had just died and he thought the change might be helpful.

The first lie was when she went for her work permit. She gave the made-up name of Marion Chapman, the first name of one friend and the last name of another. Why take the chance of someone recognizing the name? By now her father was well known in medical circles and his name had appeared in the paper numerous times connected with various Negro organizations. Why go through the humiliation of trying to convince people that she was the daughter of a famous Negro doctor? No one ever believed her, and besides, the job was only for a few months.

But as the weeks went by, she found she liked working for Lili.

She liked being Marion Chapman and not having to deal with anything other than being an ordinary working girl. Lili had found her a small apartment in the Yorkville section in a predominately German neighborhood. She ate German food, heard familiar music, and, as she wrote to her father, "it was somewhat like being back home in Vienna."

She had been completely unaware of Lili's political activities. To her she was just a nice woman who had given her a job. All she knew or cared about that summer was that as much as she missed her father, she was happier in New York. She liked being around her own people again. But it was only to last a short time. When she read in the newspaper about Theo losing the award, she was devastated for him. She knew he would be crushed. Music was his life. She loved her brother, but he had never been a strong person. He had always been delicate and high-strung and she was frightened of what he might do to himself. She tried to call, but could not reach him so she immediately took a train to San Francisco. She had to find him, to be with him, but by the time she arrived he had disappeared again. She stayed in San Francisco and, using her previous place of employment as a reference, took a job at a department store, hoping Theo might come back. But he didn't. She finally gave up waiting and was about to go home to her father in Washington. Then she met Gene Nordstrom. She had not meant to fall in love, but from the first time they went out and he ordered that silly pink champagne, there was nothing she could do about it. From the beginning she had every intention of telling Gene about her father and her brother. She wanted to, but after what had happened to Theo when people had found out about him, she was afraid to tell him, and the more deeply in love she fell, the more and more frightened she became of losing him. She did not know how he might feel about her having Negro blood, even if it was only a drop. He was so open, he might not care, but she had learned in matters of race, you could never be sure. Since she had been passing, she had heard people who had seemed perfectly nice say the most horrible things. So she continued to put it off.

She was apprehensive every time they passed a black person on the street or saw a group of black soldiers, concerned that Gene might say something derogatory. But he never did.

Then he proposed. She knew she had to tell him before they married. She had to give him a chance to back out if he wanted, but there was a war going on and everything was happening so fast. The whole city was in a frenzy, boys were shipping out every day now. That year it seemed that everybody in San Francisco was in a mad rush to get married, desperate to have a few days together before the men went off to war, maybe never to return. After they got word that Gene's unit was shipping out immediately, there had been no time to tell him, or so she told herself.

When they arrived at the courthouse the next morning, couples were already lined up around the block, anxious and looking at their watches. She told the clerk she did not have a birth certificate, that it had been lost in a fire. The clerk was annoyed but he issued them a license anyway and passed them through. She should not have lied, but that day she was hopelessly in love, and Gene was leaving. She and hundreds of others were not thinking too clearly about tomorrow; they just wanted to get married today.

It was not until Gene had been gone for a week that she realized the seriousness of what she had done. Then she became filled with remorse. What had she been thinking of? Why had she done it? Had she been in such a daze that she had begun to actually believe that she was Marion Chapman, that there was no such person as Marguerite Le Guarde? Had she been foolish enough to think he would never find out?

Gene had to know, but this was not something she could put in a letter. She thought about just disappearing, but she couldn't do that. She loved him too much for that. She had to tell him herself. She made a vow that she would tell him the minute he came home. But he never came back.

Gene had been dead only a month when she discovered she was pregnant. After many nights of crying and wondering what to do, she finally decided. She could not go back to Washington now. She did not want this child facing what she and Theo had, never knowing in which world or to what race they belonged. She wanted her baby to be raised free of those problems, free of her. It was the least she could do for her and Gene's child. After the baby was born, she would take the child home to Gene's parents in Elmwood

Springs. When she had written and told the Nordstroms, they could not wait for her to come.

So it was settled. She would take the baby and after a few days she would just leave, disappear, and it would be as if Marion Chapman had never existed at all.

Her plan was to go back to Washington to her father and resume her life as it had been. He was old and ill and he needed her. She took her daughter to Elmwood Springs, but the one thing she had not planned, had not realized, was just how much she would love the little blond baby girl with Gene's eyes.

As hard as she tried, she could not leave. Each day that passed she knew she should, but she didn't. Finally, she wrote her father and told him what she had done and why she could not come home. It broke her heart to do it. But her baby needed her. The Nordstroms had taken her in with open arms and without any questions about her past. This was Gene's wife, and Gene's baby; that's all that mattered to them. She found small-town life out in the middle of the country to be as wonderful as Gene had described. She had a job at Morgan Brothers department store and was enjoying seeing her child grow up such a happy little girl. Dena had just had her fourth birthday party when suddenly her mother's world fell apart again.

Five days after Dena's party, Theo was in Elmwood Springs and came to the house looking for her. At first she was upset at him for just showing up like that without any warning; then, Theo showed her the column Ida Baily Chambless had written about her, wanting to know her whereabouts. He then broke down and confessed that he had murdered her, and that the police might be after him. When she heard that, Marion was terrified that he might lead the police right to her door. He begged her to hide him, to let him stay, but she refused and sent him away. As much as she loved her brother, her first thought was of Dena. She could not let the Nordstroms be dragged into a murder investigation, find out who she really was, that she had been lying to them all along. She had implored Theo to please stay away from her, but in the state he was in she could not be sure he would not come back.

The next day, she took Dena and left Elmwood Springs. She had to get them as far away from Theo as possible. But where to run? She could not leave the country. Her Austrian passport was issued under her real name, Marguerite Le Guarde, and she could not get a new one as Marion Chapman. No such person existed. She had no records she could use as identification and she didn't want Dena connected to the Le Guarde name. She was trapped by her own lies. So she and Dena began moving from place to place, so Theo would not find them, but it wasn't easy. Time and time again, he found her. Each time he became more desperate, needed greater sums of money. And each time she told him it was the last time she would give him money, but it wasn't. And as frightened as she was, it broke her heart to send him away. She was all he had now that their father had died. Not a day went by that she did not think of him and she was consumed with guilt. But it was too late to undo the past. She had to think about Dena now. She had done everything she knew how to protect her, including turning her back on her brother and father. She had gone back to using the name Chapman instead of Nordstrom at work, so if there was to be trouble, she and Dena would have different names. She destroyed all pictures of Gene and herself and burned their marriage license.

For the next few years she lived in secret fear that one day her brother would be arrested. She had played out that horrible scenario a thousand times in her mind. Theo would be caught, and all the details of the murder and his family would come out. They would hunt her down and expose her, spread her picture all over the newspapers and the scandal would follow her and Dena for the rest of their lives. She could confide in no one, not to her one friend, Christine, not even her own daughter. She lived in a world all alone and it began to take its toll on her.

Without anyone she could trust or talk to her fears grew worse and worse over the years. Simple, innocent gestures of friendship from coworkers, or anyone attempting to get close to her, frightened her. She did not want anyone to have too much information in case the police might be looking for her brother. She was getting exhausted from continually looking over her own shoulder at things that in reality were not even there.

Her brother, Theo, fared no better. Over the next decade he had fled from imaginary police all over the world. Everywhere he looked he saw them lurking in the shadows, waiting to grab him. In 1953, with money from his sister, he somehow managed to cross into Canada and sneak onto a steamer headed for South America, and after two more years he worked his way back to Vienna, where he was now living, hiding in a damp basement in a seedy part of the city.

Although the brother and sister had no way of knowing, the Washington police had closed the investigation of the murder of Mrs. Ida Baily Chambless two months after it had taken place. The police had no particular interest in the case. As far as they were concerned, those people were always killing each other and as long as they didn't bother any white people, the police couldn't have cared less. There had been a few reports that a white man had been seen in and around the neighborhood that night, but the police had immediately dismissed it as rumor. No white man in his right mind would be roaming around that neighborhood at that time of night, unless he was after one thing. And after they viewed the body, they knew that she had not lured any man, white or black, for that. One of the policemen had remarked to his partner, "That woman is so ugly I'm surprised somebody didn't kill her sooner."

Vienna, City of My Dreams

Marion Chapman had been jumpy and on edge more than usual. The phone call she had just gotten a few days before from a stranger wanting to use Dena's picture on the cover of *Seventeen* magazine had rattled her so that she was having a hard time trying to get things together for Dena's Christmas. It was only a week away but the same nagging questions were gnawing at her: Why did that woman really want to put Dena's picture in a magazine? And why had she mentioned a mother-and-daughter photograph? Was someone trying to connect her and her daughter? And why had the Mother Superior given out her number to that woman? Did she know something? Had she said anything to Dena? Her thoughts raced in a hundred different directions. She was so distracted that she had to wrap and unwrap the last of Dena's presents, something she was usually expert at doing. Lately, even at work, the simplest of tasks seemed so difficult that she could hardly get through them.

She had just put the last box in the closet when the phone rang and startled her. Who could be calling at this time of night? Could it be that woman again?

But it wasn't. It was long distance from Vienna. Theo was in the hospital, dying. The man said Theo had given her name as next of kin, and if she wanted to see him she had better come right away.

When she put the phone down her heart was pounding so hard she could hardly think. All she knew was that she had to get to him. He needed her and there was no time to waste. She quickly packed a bag, ran out in the freezing rain, and hailed a cab for the airport. Thank God she had kept her Austrian passport. Eighteen worried and sleepless hours later, she arrived at the hospital.

When she was led into the ward where they had him, she was shocked to see the person the nurse pointed out. At first she could not be sure if it was her brother. The man lying there was so small, his face was so old and drawn. It couldn't be Theo.

But it was. As she got closer she recognized his hands, his long, delicate fingers. They were the only part of him that was still young, still beautiful. Tears ran down her face as she sat by his bed and held the hand of what was left of her brother. She sat there with him for the next three days until he died.

She could not be sure if he had even been aware that she had been there or whose hand he had been holding, but at least he did not die alone in a charity ward.

For those three days she had felt so helpless, such a sense of deep despair. To think that Theo, of all people, who could have brought such joy and beauty to the world, should have ended up like this. That he would have been so tortured, been driven to murder all because of that one drop of blood. Poor Theo. Every bone in her body ached with regret that she had not done more to help him.

Two days later she stood alone, shivering in the bitter cold in a small cemetery on the outskirts of Vienna, looking down at the small headstone that read:

THEODORE KARL LE GUARDE

MUSICIAN

1916–1959

It was all over. She had done everything she had to do. Now she could go home to Dena.

As she walked back through the cemetery, a sudden wind kicked up and she thought she heard a small limb or twig snap off a tree. She turned to look but she did not see anything. She had not slept for days and was now burning with a raging fever, but as she continued on she began to feel a strange, almost euphoric feeling, an odd sense of relief, almost as if all the stress and tension had suddenly been lifted. At that moment she looked up and suddenly noticed for the first time how blue and clear the sky had become.

She rode the streetcar back past the botanical gardens near Schönbrunn Park, where she and Theo had been taken so many times as children. When she got off near her hotel, she did not go in. Instead she walked.

She had been so occupied with Theo that today was the first time she actually realized: *she was home!* Suddenly it seemed that the entire city had come into sharp focus. Colors looked brighter to her and sounds seemed strange and amplified, almost as if they were coming from an old radio or phonograph.

She walked over to their old apartment house in the Lothringerstrasse, looked up, and remembered the good times, the music, the laughter. She walked over to the Alsarstrasse, past the general hospital, where her father and grandfather had practiced medicine, and along the Elisabethstrasse Promenade beside the Danube, past the Central Café, the Café Mozart, and everywhere she went she heard music. She did not see the bombed-out buildings. She saw only what she remembered. Vienna was now occupied by French, English, American, and Russian soldiers but she did not notice them. To her the aroma of the coffee mixed with the rich, sweet smells of pastries and warm bread were still the same. As she rode the giant Ferris wheel two hundred feet high and looked across the city, she felt ten years old again and happy. She was so glad the war had not destroyed her beautiful city. Vienna seemed almost exactly as she had left it.

It was late afternoon when she walked back to her hotel. As she turned the corner she stopped and could hardly believe who she saw. It was her childhood friend Maria, watching the animated Christmas display in a shop window. She could see her face clearly in the blinking lights. She called out and rushed toward her.

"Maria! It's me, Marguerite!"

The little girl's parents looked at the woman who thought their daughter was someone named Maria and realized she must not be in her right mind. They quickly took their little girl and hurried away into the crowd.

She went into the Hotel Sacher, asked for her key, and went upstairs.

Fifteen minutes later she stepped into the tub full of warm water. Despite the fever, she felt so relaxed and yet so alive. She was back where she had once been happy. She reached up and opened the small window and heard the sounds of the city below. She could hear a soprano rehearsing in one of the rehearsal rooms in the Staatsoper House across the street. She smiled and leaned back and waited until all the water had gone down the drain.

For the first time in years she wasn't afraid. It had come to her this morning at Theo's grave that she was the last of the Le Guardes. The only one left. The one, last drop of blood in her was the only link that could connect Dena with the Le Guardes. That little drop of blood was all that was left. She closed her eyes and squeezed the razor blade in her hand. She knew what she had to do.

It was so simple. Why hadn't she thought of it before?

Where was it, she wondered? Was it on her left side? Where was it lurking? Did it stay in one place or did it travel throughout her body, running and hiding, determined to haunt her year after year? She would just get rid of it once and for all. First the left side, the ankle, then the wrist. She must let it escape. Then the right side. There, it was done. She leaned back and waited. She felt a strange calm come over her as she felt the blood begin to leave and wondered if she would be able to feel it as it flowed out of her, so red against the stark white tub, past her, and on down the drain. Soon it would be gone. Oh, what a relief to finally get it out. Then she and Dena would be free. She leaned back and took a deep breath of the cold, fresh air that blew across her naked body and waited. As she lay waiting, a faint tune began to play over and over again in her head, a sad sort of waltz . . . what was it? She began to softly hum the tune.

What was it? Oh, yes, now she remembered. It was an old waltz, "Vienna, City of My Dreams." A waltz from her childhood. Yes, soon she heard the music, softly at first, and then it slowly became louder and louder, drowning out the sounds of the street and the piano across the way, until the sound of an entire orchestra filled her ears and the words sang to her from so long ago. She could feel herself moving with the music. But where was she? She opened her eyes and looked. . . . Oh, she was dancing with her father in the gold-mirrored ballroom, under the crystal chandeliers, and there was her mother across the way, sitting in a small gold chair, dressed in satin and chiffon. Glittering stones sparkled on her neck and ears and she swayed with the music, smiling at them. Marguerite was ten again and she was waltzing with her father. She glanced up at him, so handsome in his tuxedo and white gloves, and he was young and happy and she was so proud to be his partner, so happy to be dancing again, she felt light, free, as they were sweeping and turning. He lifted her higher and higher, up and up, and as they waltzed they were lifted still higher, twirling and turning, around and around all the way up to the sky; now they were dancing among the glittering stars . . . higher and higher until they danced past the stars and on out of sight. The music lingered for a moment, then softly faded. . . .

She had only been trying to get rid of one drop of blood. She had meant to go back to the little girl who now sat in the apartment in Chicago waiting for her and live happily ever after. She had not meant to kill herself. It had just happened.

A Few Scribbled Words

Three weeks after she had been to Washington the phone rang. "Miss Nordstrom, it's Richard Look."

She closed her eyes and waited for his next sentence. "I have some news about your mother and I'm afraid it's not good news."

She sat down and listened while he read her the report.

Look had said he was sending it. Three days later, when the large, ominous-looking envelope arrived, she put it down on the kitchen table. She did not want to open it. The facts inside were so shocking, so brutal, so final. She knew when she opened it and saw the facts on official paper that she would have to accept them as true.

Her mother had destroyed herself over something that in a few more years might not even matter. It was so unfair that a person's life could be changed so dramatically by just a simple matter of timing. Her mother's life had been ruined by something as stupid and as changeable as the prejudices of the day. If only her mother had been born in a different time, she would have been spared all that unnecessary misery. Just a few years later, and she might have had her mother back.

Dena got up and walked around the block. Her neighbor, Poor Tot, was in her front yard on her hands and knees working in her begonia garden. She had on red jeans, her husband's bowling shirt, and a straw hat, and called to Dena, "Hey . . . isn't this a pretty day? I think we are going to have an Indian summer, don't you?"

Dena had no idea what she was talking about but answered, "Yes, I think you're right." When she came back she sat down and opened the envelope. Inside was another envelope with a letter attached:

Dear Mr. Look,

Pursuant to your inquiry of November 27, we have obtained the following information:

Le Guarde, Theodore: 43 years of age, cause of death unknown. Central Cemetery, plot 578.

Le Guarde, Marguerite Louise: 39 years of age, cause of death apparent suicide by multiple razor cuts, Hotel Sacher.

I am sorry to inform you that after a thorough investigation, the whereabouts of Marguerite Le Guarde's remains have not been located. At the time of her death an attempt to locate relatives was made, but when none were forthcoming, as is policy, she was cremated and most probably buried in one of several municipal grave sites. I am also sorry that our investigation could not have brought you happier news.

As the inquiry was made on behalf of a family member of the deceased, we have enclosed some heretofore unclaimed personal effects.

Please call if I can be of any further assistance.

Sincerely,
Dieter Kleim
Director of Forensic Files
Vienna, Austria

The envelope inside had been closed with a red wax seal. Dena took a deep breath and broke it open. Inside was her mother's passport. Underneath her picture was written *Marguerite Louise Le*

Guarde—born, Vienna, Austria, 1920. A train ticket and about two hundred American dollars and some foreign bills. A few receipts and a folded sheet of Hotel Sacher stationery. Dena unfolded it and read the note her mother had hurriedly scribbled across the page to herself: *Pay hospital bill . . . Call Dena . . . Tell her to wait at apartment.*

Seeing her mother's handwriting again after all these years, and realizing that her mother had intended to return to her again, was a shock.

If only she could have told her mother that nothing mattered, told her how much she loved her and needed her. But she couldn't. All she could do was sit there and cry while the cat, upset because Dena was upset, kept rubbing up against her, over and over.

BOOK FOUR

* * *

Partial to People

Dr. Diggers had told Dena not to make any important decisions for as long as possible, that she needed to take a lot of time to think before she did anything.

After she found out about her mother, she did just that. She had a lot of things to think about. She felt sad, but mostly she felt as if she was not the same person she had been just a few weeks earlier. She realized that she did not know much about life at all. Everything she thought she knew as fact wasn't. Everything she had believed was important wasn't.

Today she was out in Aunt Elner's backyard, walking along with her as she watered her tomato plants.

"Aunt Elner," she said, "do you like people?"

"Oh, lands, yes, honey, sure, I do." She cocked her head to the left. "Come to think of it, I guess you could go so far as to say that people are my pets. They just tickle me to death. There is nothing cuter to me than a pack of Brownies or Cub Scouts or a table full of oldsters. I used to make Norma and Macky take me up to Miss Alma's Tea Room so I could sit there and watch all the little early birds come in for their supper." Aunt Elner moved on down the row and looked up at the sky, which was turning slightly gray over to the west. "You watch, as soon as I water, it rains. Anyhow, I used to go to Alma's and listen to them chattering away, cute as pie." She chuckled. "And now, I'm an oldster and Miss Alma's is gone, closed down ... of course they have an early bird special out at Howard Johnson's ... but, yes, I like people.

"To tell you the truth, I feel sort of sorry for most of them. Some days I could just sit down and cry my eyes out ... poor little old human beings—they're jerked into this world without having any idea where they came from or what it is they are supposed to do, or how long they have to do it in. Or where they are gonna wind up after that. But bless their hearts, most of them wake up every morning and keep on trying to make some sense out of it. Why, you can't help but love them, can you? I just wonder why more of them aren't as crazy as betsy bugs."

"Do you believe in God, Aunt Elner?"

"Sure I do, honey, why?"

"How old were you when you started believing, do you remember?"

Aunt Elner paused for a moment. "I never thought about not believing. Never did question it. I guess believing is just like math: some people get it right out of the chute, and some have to struggle for it." Aunt Elner spotted something. "Hold on a minute, dear." She slowly reached in her apron. "Don't move." She pulled out a lime-green plastic water pistol and aimed it at her cat, Sonny, just as he was about to pounce on a fat robin, busy eating birdseed. She hit Sonny in the back of his head and he took off. "Hate to do it but it's the only thing that works. I can't stand to see him get one of my birds." She put the water pistol back in her apron. "It has a range up to sixty feet. Norma got it for me up at the Rexall. Oh, I know a lot of people struggle, wondering is there really a God. They sit and think and worry over it all their life. The good Lord had to make smart people but I don't think he did them any favors because it seems the smart ones start questioning things from the get go. But I never did. I'm one of the lucky ones. I thank God every night, my brain is just perfect for me, not too dumb, not too bright. You know, your daddy was always asking questions."

"He was?"

"I remember one day he said, 'Aunt Elner, how do you know there is a God, how can you be sure?' "

"What did you tell him?"

"I said, 'Well, Gene, the answer is right on the end of your fingertips.' He said, 'What do you mean?' I said, 'Well, think about it. Every single human being that was ever born from the beginning of time has a completely different set of fingerprints. Not two alike. Not a single one out of all the billions is ever repeated.' I said, 'Who else but God could think up all those different patterns and keep coming up with new ones year after year, not to mention all the color combinations of all the fish and birds.' "

Dena smiled. "What did he say?"

"He said, 'Yes, but, Aunt Elner, how do you know that God's not repeating old fingerprints from way back and reusing them on us?' " She laughed. "See what I mean? Yes, God is great, all right. He only made one mistake but it was a big one."

"What was that?"

"Free will. That was his one big blunder. He gave us a choice whether or not to be good or bad. He made us too independent . . . and you can't tell people what to do; they won't listen. You can tell them to be good until you're blue in the face but people don't want to be preached at except at church, where they know what they are getting and are prepared for it."

"What's life all about, Aunt Elner? Don't you ever wonder what the point of the whole thing is?"

"No, not really; it seems to me we only have one big decision in this life, whether to be good or bad. That's what I came up with a long time ago. Of course, I may be wrong, but I'm not going to spend any time worrying over it, I'm just going to have a good time while I'm here. Live and let live." Sonny started slowly inching his way back toward the fat robin and Aunt Elner pulled her gun out and aimed. "Sonny, one more move and you're dead."

Dena had to laugh in spite of herself.

The Decision

Elmwood Springs, Missouri
1978

The network lawyers had informed Sandy that unless Dena came back within a week they would cancel her contract and replace her. Today was the day she had to make the decision and it had not been as hard as she thought. The decision had been made for her, really. In the end she had no choice.

Her agent, Sandy, was in his office waiting for the call.

"Sandy, I can't."

"Are you sure? You know what this means. Think about it."

"I know that, and I have thought about it. It's just that I couldn't come back even if I wanted to. I wouldn't be any good at it anymore."

"What do you mean? You're the best in the business. You could be back on top in a few weeks. You haven't lost all that time."

"No, but I've lost something else. I don't have the drive I had. I know too much, Sandy. Once you've been on the other side of this thing and know how it feels, you can't ever go back." Dena drew a deep breath. "Before, I was able to do my job and just keep moving and never think about the results. But not now, I'd be too slow, I'd hesitate, I'd think too much. No matter what the person had done, I'd be too soft on them. I couldn't ask the questions I need to ask anymore without thinking about the damage I might be doing."

"What will you do?"

"I don't know. Get out of the way, I guess, and sit down for a while."

"What about your apartment?"

"I'm going to give it up."

"Where will you live?"

"Here."

"In Dagwood Springs?"

"Elmwood Springs, yes."

Sandy hung up and sighed. It was sad, he would miss her. The network would miss her. For a while, maybe a week, until one of the hundreds of new, bright-eyed, blond Dena look-alikes moved into her spot, and then it would be as if she had never been there at all.

❖   ❖   ❖

A month later, on the morning of her thirty-fifth birthday, Norma called her on the phone. "Dena, have you been outside today?"

"No, why?"

"You need to go outside—and look up."

"Why?"

"Just go out, that's all I can tell you."

Dena put on her sweater and walked into the yard. She looked up in time to see a huge gray blimp, its sign spelling out in gold lights the same phrase, over and over: HAPPY BIRTHDAY . . . YOU'RE ALL THE WORLD TO ME. LOVE, GERRY.

She had to grin. She suddenly remembered the look on Gerry's face when he had sung to her at Carnegie and a warm feeling came over her. She went inside and called him.

"Gerry, I got your message. Now here's mine: You are insane. Do you know that?"

"That's not exactly the clinical term I would use, but close enough. How are you?"

"Fine. Listen, Gerry, why don't you come down here, maybe stay the weekend. Can you do that?"

"When?"

"Come this weekend."

"Oh. Is there a hotel in town?"

"You can stay here. I have four bedrooms."

There was a slight pause. Then he said, "I'll be there."

Gerry had been a good friend. They had talked on the phone often since she had found out about her mother and he had been there for her, as he'd promised. It would be good to see him. As a matter of fact, as the few days went by, she couldn't wait to see him. By late Friday afternoon, when he was on her front porch with his garment bag and just as he was about to ring the bell, the door opened and an arm grabbed him by the tie and pulled him inside the house and Dena put her arms around him and kissed him. And she was surprised at how well they seemed to fit together. It was as if they had been kissing for years. She didn't know if it was because she had been alone for so long, but he looked good to her. Better-looking than she had remembered.

It wasn't until sometime after he had arrived that she realized if you have a guest, you have to feed him, so for supper she made the only dish she knew, Franco-American ravioli straight out of a can, heated, and Gerry said it was delicious. After dinner they went out and sat on the porch and talked until one-thirty in the morning. When they got ready to go to bed, he said, "I just want you to know I am fully prepared to sleep in the back room like a gentleman. All right?"

She was relieved in a way because she had suddenly become a little nervous around him. They said good night.

After twenty minutes, she called out, "Gerry?"

"Yes?"

"I think it will be all right if you come in here and sleep with me. We won't do anything, we'll just sleep together, all right?"

Gerry came down the hall carrying his pillow, wearing a pair of blue bunny pajamas with the feet in them, and the minute she saw him she burst out laughing. "You fool . . . where did you get those?"

"Elizabeth Diggers sent them over to my office on Thursday."

He modeled for her. "Like them? Are you sure you can trust yourself around me?"

"You are the silliest man I ever met. Get in the bed."

He took his glasses off and put them on the nightstand and got into his side of the bed and lay down and felt her body next to his. And he was so relieved to finally be where he had wanted to be for so long that he relaxed completely for the first time since she had telephoned and fell sound asleep. The next morning at 7:00 A.M., Dena woke and looked over at him sleeping beside her like a child in his blue pajamas and the next thing she knew they were making love and for two people making love for the first time, it was surprising. She had not expected him to be so unbelievably passionate or that she could be so completely uninhibited. This was the first time in years she had gone to bed with someone when she was stone-cold sober. It was a new experience and she liked it. Gerry, who had been thinking and imagining such moments for a long time, was completely amazed. Making love with Dena was even better than he had imagined, and that was going some. Dena had gone back to sleep but he was too excited to sleep. He went down the hall and showered and shaved, got dressed, and came back. But she was still sleeping so he quietly tiptoed past her room and went out on the porch and decided he would take a walk before she woke up.

It was nine-thirty and he went into the Rexall and had a cup of coffee at the counter, then walked along the main drag. When he came back she was still asleep so he sat in the living room and waited. About five minutes later he couldn't stand it any longer. He went into the bedroom and sat in a chair and stared at her, still astonished that it was really her, and that he was really here. She opened her eyes and looked over and saw him sitting there, all dressed.

"Hey . . . how long have you been up?"

He came over and sat on the bed. "For about an hour. I took a walk downtown."

"You did?"

"This is a great little town, you know that?" And while he went on and on about how great the town was, she kept looking at him and she said, "Do you know who you remind me of?"

"No, who?"

"I've been trying to figure it out ever since last night when you came in wearing those silly pajamas. Little Donald. You remind me of this doll I had, this great big boy doll."

"I don't know if that's a compliment or not."

"Oh, it's a compliment. I slept with him for years."

"Is there something about you and that doll I should know?"

"No, you goof. That was in the 1940s—besides, he was not anatomically correct."

"Whew, thank God for that. At least I don't have to compete with Little Donald."

"No," she said. "You've already won, hands down."

He leaned down and gave her a long, sweet, tender kiss and Dena, who never liked to be kissed in the morning, liked it.

Gerry came back the next weekend and although Dena didn't know how she felt about that, she was glad to see him. This time he stopped and brought groceries and cooked dinner for her. She was told to go in the living room and wait, and when called she came to the table. He had set the table, something she had not mastered—she could never remember what side what went on—but the thing that impressed her most was his salad. He had actually made a salad from scratch. The main course was baked chicken in a cream sauce, green beans, and new potatoes, and a cheesecake he had brought on the plane from New York. Between bites she said, "This is delicious; where did you learn to cook like this?"

"I hadn't wanted to tell you but I had an affair with Julia Child."

"Be serious."

"I don't know, I just picked it up here and there. It's not that hard. Just follow the recipe."

"I don't know how to cook. We always ate out."

"I don't know how you could cook in that kitchen, you don't have any utensils. We need to go out and get you a few things."

"Like what?"

"Oh, minor stuff—pots, pans, silverware, a can opener, mixing bowls, things like that."

"Oh."

"I worry about you not eating right. You need fresh food, not all that frozen stuff you have in the refrigerator."

"It says 'fresh frozen.' "

"Dena . . ."

"I eat at Norma's two or three times a week, so I figure—"

"No, you need to take the time to fix yourself something healthy every day. Do you eat fresh fruit?"

Dena made a face.

"Well, you need to eat some fruit and vegetables every day. You need to start building yourself back up."

"The next thing I know you'll pull down a chart of the basic food groups and give me a lecture with a pointer."

The next morning Gerry went down to the hardware store and walked in. Macky spotted him right away but waited for him to come over. Gerry walked over. "Mr. Warren?"

"Yes, sir."

"Mr. Warren, I'm Gerry O'Malley. I don't know if you remember me."

"Oh, yes. How are you?" As if he could forget a man wearing pink tights and a hat with a plume standing in his front yard.

Gerry adjusted his glasses. "I was kind of hoping you wouldn't remember, to tell you the truth."

Macky smiled. "Hey, don't worry about it, fella. All bets are off when it comes to love and war, right? What can I do for you?"

Then it dawned on Gerry. He had come in to buy pots and pans and mixing bowls and kitchen utensils and a meat thermometer. This man was going to think he was a fruitcake. But Macky made no comment and helped him pick out everything he needed and got a big kick out of watching Gerry trying so hard to be macho while choosing hot pads and just the right spatula and select a Mixmaster. They even had quite a long discussion about the pros and cons of Teflon versus an iron skillet. He bought both.

After Gerry had everything he needed and Macky rang it up, Gerry looked at the total. He was concerned. "Is this all I owe you? I've got a lot of stuff here."

"Yes, that's right, with your discount. And I'm throwing in a few things from Norma and me. We need to get her all outfitted."

"Well, thanks." While Macky was packing the bags, Gerry wandered around a little more. He came back to the counter. "I see you've got quite a collection of fishing lures and flies. Is there some good fly-fishing around here?"

You could see Macky's ears perk up. "You bet, some of the best in the country, no more than an hour from here. Last month I got a ten-pound walleye."

"Wow. What were you using?"

"A medium yellow spinner."

"You don't say?"

"Oh, yeah, he went for that thing like a duck on a June bug. Listen, if you get down here again sometime, I'd be happy to take you out."

"Great, I'd like to take you up on it."

That afternoon, Gerry started walking through the house again. He was in the den knocking on the walls when Dena came in. He said, "Look at this, this is Georgia pine. And these floors are oak. This house is as solid as a rock, you know that? They don't build them like this anymore. This is a *great* house. I was up in the attic and it is as dry as a bone."

Dena found herself pleased. He seemed to like the house as much as she did. "I wonder how old it is."

"I'd say by looking at the doorknobs and the windows, it was built some time in the early twenties." He pulled at the pocket doors in the den. "I think this used to be a parlor at one time. God, wouldn't you love to know who all lived here and what all went on in this house?"

"The woman I'm renting it from grew up here and her mother used to have a radio show in the living room."

"Is that so? Radio?"

"Yeah, and there used to be a big radio tower in the backyard."

"I'll be darned."

"I'm thinking about buying it."

"Really? Well, it's a great house."

The next weekend Gerry took everybody to the Pancake House for dinner. On the way over, Norma, in the backseat, remarked, "I just want you to know this is a first for me. I have never even met a psychiatrist, much less had a pancake dinner with one."

Gerry glanced in the rearview mirror. "Is that so?"

"Yes. We have never had a psychiatrist in Elmwood Springs. Not that we probably don't need one, but nobody would go if we did have one."

"Why is that?"

"Because everybody knows everybody else's car. Nobody would dare park in front."

Aunt Elner was sitting in the front seat holding her purse in her lap, happy to be going. She piped up in defense of Elmwood Springs. "We had a crazy person here once, Mabel Bassett, she was as crazy as anybody. Don't you remember, Norma, she kept batting at imaginary flies? They took her off to the loony bin but I don't think she was really crazy, I think she was just tired. She had seven children." Aunt Elner turned to Gerry. "I'll bet you have met a lot of crazy people in your line of work, haven't you?"

Dena had her eyes closed and was biting her lip.

Macky spoke up. "I think he's just met a couple of them."

"Oh, don't pay any attention to Macky," Norma said, "and if anybody is crazy, he drove me to it."

The day before Christmas Gerry flew down again and he and Dena decorated the house with all the old Christmas decorations they found up in the attic and in the cedar chest. Christmas Eve after they had a glass of eggnog, they walked over to the church for the midnight service.

Macky and Norma and Aunt Elner had saved them each a seat. Aunt Elner had on a Rudolph-the-red-nosed-reindeer pin that her friend Merle had given her. Later, as they walked home, they agreed it was a perfect cold Christmas Eve night. The stars looked as if they had been polished, they were so bright. When they turned the corner at 1st Avenue North, they could see the blue candles glowing in the windows from a block away, and to Dena the house looked exactly like a cheerful Disney cartoon.

Before they finally went to sleep, Dena walked back into the living room to turn off all the Christmas lights. But as she stood there and watched them, glowing and bubbling in the dark, they looked so beautiful she decided to leave them on all night.

After Gerry had gone back to New York on Monday, Norma called Dena. "Well, I'm not saying anything, it's none of my business, but if you were to ask me, he seems like a very nice person. And that's all I'm going to say on the subject. . . ."

But of course it wasn't.

Blue Skies Trailer Park

Arden, Missouri
June 22, 1979

Ralph Childress had walked over to the office to pick up the mail and was sitting in his living room going through it. It was, as usual, mostly bills, but he saw one handwritten letter addressed to him personally, written on Hotel Halekulani stationery from Waikiki Beach. He thought: Who in the hell do I know that could be all the way out in Hawaii?

Memo to State Trooper Ralph Childress

As promised, here is the update on the present status of the 15th-century troubadour you stopped on Missouri Interstate 34 on the morning of February 14th, 1976.

I am happy to report that the lady in question and I were married a week ago and are now enjoying a wonderful honeymoon.

As the man says, "All's well that ends well."

Best wishes,
Gerry O'Malley

Trooper Childress chuckled. "Well, I'll be damned. That old boy finally got her. There's a new fool born every minute."

Edna Childress walked into the living area carrying a Mexican Chihuahua in one hand and a *TV Guide* in the other. "Are you gonna fix that antenna for me or am I gonna have to hire me a handyman? You're gonna make me miss my soap." He put the letter back in the envelope.

"Oh, all right, hold your water, old woman. I'm going. Can't a man sit down and read his mail without being pecked to death?"

He opened the cabinet and pulled out a pair of needle-nose pliers and headed out the door. "If you'd do it when I asked you to instead of waiting so long, I wouldn't have to nag you. Did you ever think about that?"

He walked away, saying under his breath, "Yeah, I've thought of that."

She turned on the TV set and walked over to the window so she could holler up to him when the picture came in good. She hated to nag at poor old Ralph, he was a good soul. But she couldn't miss her soap opera today. Today Faren was going to come out of her amnesia and remember who she really was!

Gerry's Surprise

Elmwood Springs, Missouri
1984

Dear Dr. O'Malley,

I have discussed the matter with my brother, Robert, and we both agreed to sell at the price you named. Although it is always hard to give up your family home, we know that our parents would be pleased to know that you and your wife are, as you say, "in love" with it and feel the same way as our family did. I understand this purchase is to be a surprise for your wife on the occasion of your fifth anniversary and I will deal directly with Beverly as per your wishes. I wish you both as many years of happiness as my parents, when they lived there at 5348 1st Avenue North.

Sincerely,
Mrs. Anna Lee Horton
Tucson, Arizona

cc: Robert Smith
Beverly Cartwright

And So

Elmwood Springs, Missouri
June 1979

At the age of thirty-five, Dena Nordstrom, who had thought that she could never love anything, had fallen in love with a house, a town, and a psychiatrist. It turned out that she was more surprised than anyone. Except maybe for Sookie.

When she had told her the news Sookie screamed over the phone, "You're getting married! I knew it, I told you so. Didn't I tell you so? Hurray and hallelujah. I have my dress picked out and ready to go. It's peach. And we can get the girls little matching outfits; won't they be darling coming down the aisle? Of course, you know Mother will have to come. Buck will fly us up there. Oh, Dena—why don't you come do it here? At least let me give you a shower, you'll get the best presents . . . nothing silver plated. Wait a minute. Who are you marrying?"

"Gerry O'Malley."

"That New York psychiatrist! Oh, dear!"

Dena laughed. "Yes, he's the one. But the good news is that his mother is from Virginia."

"Virginia." Sookie sounded a little bit hopeful. "Well, that is a border state but . . . who was she before she married?"

"What do you mean?"

"What was her maiden name?"

"Hold on. Gerry, what was your mother's maiden name?"

"Longstreet, why?"

There was a gasp on the other end of the phone. "Dena, now, this is very important. Is he standing right there?"

"Yes."

"Can he hear you?"

"No, not really."

"Try not to embarrass him, but ask him if they were the cotton Longstreets or the lumber Longstreets."

"Gerry, were they the cotton Longstreets or the lumber Longstreets?"

"Cotton. Why?"

"He said cotton."

Sookie screamed, "Oh, my God!"

Dena said, "Is that good or bad?"

"You are marrying a direct descendant of General James P. Longstreet, that's all."

"Who's that?"

"*Who's that?* He's just one of the most famous Confederate generals that ever lived. Wait till I tell Mother; don't tell me I don't have a personal friendship with Jesus Christ!"

In the meantime, back in New York, just as Sandy had predicted, the network had gone on without her. They had hired another beautiful blonde. Just as Wall-Cap Productions had hired another beautiful blonde to anchor their first show, and they were off and running. The ratings shot through the ceiling. Evidently, the public was ready for a tabloid "news" show. And soon other copycat shows started popping up everywhere until the usual network news seemed as dull as Sidney Capello had predicted. Syndication was turning out to be a gold mine.

❧ ❧ ❧

Every once in a while, Dena would wonder where Capello was, and as it turned out, Capello wasn't anywhere at the moment.

That fall, it rained in New York City for five days straight. Con Ed was having a hell of a time making sure all the sewers under the city were kept clear of debris and any blockage. Mike Mecelli was exhausted. He and his crew had been up for three days and nights. By the time the truck pulled up at Forty-eighth and Ninth Avenue, it was four in the morning. Mike pulled on his yellow slicker and left the truck and located the round iron cover on the Forty-eighth Street sewer line and he lifted it up and pushed it aside. He got out his flashlight, switched it on, and saw down inside the sewer the water rushing by like a raging river. It seemed to be moving without any obstruction but the water was high and they needed to check it to make sure. He went back briefly to get the rest of the crew, who were sitting inside the big truck's cab, when Capello, who had been working late on a story involving a movie star's love child, came out the door, started to cross the street, fell in the hole, and landed in the icy-cold, raging water. Before he knew what hit him, he was shooting under Manhattan at sixty miles an hour. Capello screamed but the storm and the roar of the water was so loud he was not heard. He was swept under and did not stop until he was in the Hudson River, headed to Jersey, where his body would be found three days later.

His funeral was well attended for a man hated as much as he was. But as several said, including Ira Wallace, "They came just to make sure the bastard was really dead."

❀   ❀   ❀

In the end, Sidney Capello's paranoia and greed saved a lot of reputations. He had been so neurotic about someone in the office sneaking into his files, where future scandals were still cooking in the oven, ready to be brought out at the right time, he had taken them home and hidden them in between his old income tax files. After he was buried, a cleaning crew came into his apartment and threw out everything. Information and rumor, true and false, waiting to wreck careers, including Dena's file, would never be aired, including photos of his partner Ira Wallace's daughter, romping naked in a Chelsea hotel room with three members of the heavy metal group known as Pit Bull.

All the rest in the file were safe now. Barbara Zofko, the only other person who had known it existed, had left Sidney's employ and had gone on to make quite a name for herself writing unauthorized biographies of the famous. But two years earlier Barbara had nearly choked to death at Rumplemeyer's when the stem of a cherry sitting on top of the hot fudge sundae she was inhaling at the time got caught in her throat. As she lay on the white tile floor, with her large face turning blue and a woman in a pink and white uniform pounding away on her chest, her life passed before her eyes. She woke up in the hospital and discovered that she had suffered a heart attack brought on by the strain of choking. However, it was not the near-death experience that changed her. It was the fact that her doctor ordered her to lose one hundred pounds. And so several days after she was released from the hospital, she took her doctor's advice and joined Overeaters Anonymous. Six months later in Los Angeles, California, Frank Sinatra's secretary opened the mail:

Dear Mr. Sinatra,
    I am now in a Twelve Step recovery program and as part of my program I am making amends to all that I may have harmed in the past. I am sorry if my book harmed you or your family in any way.
    Please accept my apology.

Sincerely, one day at a time,
Barbara Zofko

P.S. I wonder if you would consider granting me an interview in the near future or if you could recommend me to some of your friends. Any help would be greatly appreciated.

Similar letters were sent to Elizabeth Taylor, Nancy Reagan, Robert Redford, Jackie Kennedy Onassis, Dolly Parton, Priscilla Presley, Cher, Marlon Brando, and Michael Jackson.
    But even with Sidney Capello and Barbara Zofko out of commission, hundreds of others like them popped up.
    And just as Howard Kingsley had predicted, network news anchors soon started to do stories that they would never have considered five years earlier. The business of news had gone into such a feeding frenzy that human beings began stalking other human

beings in packs. Talk shows were offering money to anybody to come on and discuss all the details of their sex lives, or to come on and have a family free-for-all. This end to privacy was clearly an idea whose time had come. Spotlighting the worst in human behavior became big business, and the more shows fought one another for ratings, the closer to the bottom of the barrel they scraped.

But life in Elmwood Springs went on pretty much the same. Every once in a while someone would come to town and inquire about Dena Nordstrom, ask where she lived, but the answer they always got was, "Gee, fella, I really don't know. Not sure she even lives here anymore." Or they would say, "I heard she moved back up to New York."

Years later, when Dena and Gerry went to New York to take Elizabeth Diggers to dinner and to see a few shows, Dena was walking down Fifty-eighth Street, where she used to live, when a woman stopped her and asked, "Hey, aren't you that girl that used to be on television?"

Dena had to grin. She answered, "No, I'm afraid that wasn't me."

As she continued down the street, Dena realized that she barely remembered that girl at all anymore.

And she smiled all the way back to the hotel.

Epilogue

In the early eighties, something wonderful happened, thanks to Norma Warren's "Elmwood Springs Is a Good Place to Live" campaign. *USA Today* ran a story naming it one of the ten best places in America to live. Suddenly, yuppies and others who were trying to get away from big-city crime and back to small-town America came pouring in. New schools were built, downtown was restored, the Elmwood Springs movie theater reopened and sometimes showed a foreign film. Nordstrom's bakery was taken over by a young couple from Boston and renamed Bread & Things, and Macky over at the hardware store had a cappuccino machine. A junior college sprang up and Gerry became head of the psychology department, and did not have to commute to Kansas City anymore. And Dena actually signed up for a cooking class and liked it.

Every day, of course, there were thousands of newspapers, and news shows screaming and shouting murder, scandal, conspiracy, doom and gloom. And every day between Malibu and Manhattan, millions of nice people, happy and good-natured, were quietly living their lives, and not paying much real attention to them. As a matter of fact, many had begun to turn off their television sets or to watch old movies. But perhaps the best news locally was that in 1986, a radio tower was put up in Neighbor Dorothy's backyard and a woman whose voice sounded familiar started to broadcast from her home. It wasn't much of a show, merely lots of different things—news, guests, interviews, even recipes. But even though WDOT was only a 700-watt station, because the land was flat, on cold, still days when the skies were crystal clear and it was really good radio weather, its signal could tear a hole straight through the midwest, all the way up into Canada, and on out to all the ships at sea. And the news was mostly good.

ABOUT THE AUTHOR

FANNIE FLAGG began writing and producing television specials at age nineteen and went on to distinguish herself as an actress and writer in television, films, and the theater. Her first novel, *Daisy Fay and the Miracle Man*, was a *New York Times* bestseller, as was *Fried Green Tomatoes at the Whistle Stop Cafe*, which was produced by Universal Pictures as *Fried Green Tomatoes*. Flagg's script was nominated for both the Academy and Writers Guild of America awards and won the highly regarded Scripters Award. Her acclaimed novel *Welcome to the World, Baby Girl!* is also a *New York Times* bestseller.